A retired cop falls victim to a staged suicide in the new police thriller in the #1 *New York Times* bestselling crime series.

After a trip to sunny Greece and a visit to Roarke's Irish relatives, homicide detective Eve Dallas is back in her element in gritty, crowded New York City. She has barely put her suitcase down before she is called on scene to examine the death of retired Internal Affairs Bureau captain Martin Greenleaf.

At first glance, all the evidence points to suicide, but after a more thorough investigation, Eve concludes the suicide was staged. Greenleaf had a long career taking down dirty cops—bribe takers, rule breakers, and other miscreants. Was there one disgraced officer out there bitter enough to plan an elaborate revenge? Dallas is as tough as anyone in law enforcement, but she's also by the book—and as long as she's on the job, anyone who kills an honorable cop needs to watch their back . . .

TITLES BY J. D. ROBB

ANTHOLOGIES

Silent Night
(with Susan Plunkett, Dee Holmes, and Claire Cross)

Out of This World
(with Laurell K. Hamilton, Susan Krinard, and Maggie Shayne)

Remember When
(with Nora Roberts)

Bump in the Night
(with Mary Blayney, Ruth Ryan Langan, and Mary Kay McComas)

Dead of Night
(with Mary Blayney, Ruth Ryan Langan, and Mary Kay McComas)

Three in Death

Suite 606
(with Mary Blayney, Ruth Ryan Langan, and Mary Kay McComas)

In Death

The Lost
(with Patricia Gaffney, Ruth Ryan Langan, and Mary Blaney)

The Other Side
(with Mary Blayney, Patricia Gaffney, Ruth Ryan Langan, and Mary Kay McComas)

Time of Death

The Unquiet
(with Mary Blayney, Patricia Gaffney, Ruth Ryan Langan, and Mary Kay McComas)

Mirror, Mirror
(with Mary Blayney, Elaine Fox, Mary Kay McComas, and R. C. Ryan)

Down the Rabbit Hole
(with Mary Blayney, Elaine Fox, Mary Kay McComas, and R. C. Ryan)

PAYBACK IN DEATH

J. D. Robb

St. Martin's Paperbacks

This is a work of fiction. All of the characters, organizations, and events portrayed in this novel are either products of the author's imagination or are used fictitiously.

Published in the United States by St. Martin's Paperbacks, an imprint of St. Martin's Publishing Group.

PAYBACK IN DEATH

For information, address St. Martin's Publishing Group, 120 Broadway, New York, NY 10271.

www.stmartins.com

Library of Congress Catalog Card Number: 2023015101

ISBN: 978-1-250-86612-7

Our books may be purchased in bulk for promotional, educational, or business use. Please contact your local bookseller or the Macmillan Corporate and Premium Sales Department at 1-800-221-7945, ext. 5442, or by email at MacmillanSpecialMarkets@macmillan.com.

Printed in the United States of America

St. Martin's hardcover edition published 2023
St. Martin's Paperbacks edition / January 2024

10 9 8 7 6 5 4 3 2 1

A man that studieth revenge
keeps his own wounds green.
—Francis Bacon

Love does not delight in evil
but rejoices with the truth.
—1 Corinthians 13:6

1

Someone had either kidnapped the sun or decided screw the ransom and killed it dead.

For two glorious weeks, before its abduction or demise, it had blasted heat and light so the sea below the villa in Greece sparkled, diamonds on sapphire. It had baked every ounce of stress away and left generous room for sleep, sex, wine, basking, and more sex.

No better way, to her mind, to spend a slice of summer in 2061.

Lieutenant Eve Dallas, murder cop, hadn't thought about murder and mayhem for days. That alone equaled vacation. Add a villa of sunbaked gold stone, views of sea and hill, of olive groves and vineyards out every window, top it all off with lazy, private time with the man she loved, and you had it all.

It was a hell of a perfect way to celebrate their third anniversary.

Sometimes it still amazed her. How the cop and the criminal (former), two lost souls who'd pushed, punched, and kicked their way out of misery, somehow found each other. How they'd managed to build a good, strong life together.

Whatever changed, shifted, evolved, that remained constant.

They built together.

Now, after two weeks of ridiculous indulgence—not that Roarke would think it at all ridiculous—they'd arrived in Ireland under a sky of stacked clouds and dripping rain.

Maybe the Irish were sun killers.

And yet, the green shined so vivid here as the fields spread, the hills rose, the stone walls glistened in the wet. The skinny road they traveled snaked, and hedgerows dripping with bloodred fuchsia closed in like living walls.

She checked herself. Maybe a touch of stress but only because the Irish, in addition to being suspected sun killers, opted to drive on the wrong side of snaking, skinny roads, and Roarke drove as if he powered down a straightaway.

He was so damn happy, and his happiness rolled right through her. She didn't consider it a Marriage Rule to share such a cheerful mood, but it did stand as an advantage.

She studied him awhile—a more pleasant view than the breaks in the hedgerows that displayed sheep, cows, occasionally horses, and various other four-legged animals.

He had that face. Those wild Irish blue eyes, that perfectly sculpted mouth, and all that black silk hair to frame it.

Those lips curved, those eyes smiled—just for her—when he glanced at her.

"Not much farther."

"I remember."

The last time they'd visited his family's farm in Clare—a family he hadn't known existed during his nightmare childhood, or his very successful career as a thief, a smuggler, a (fairly) legitimate businessman who'd built an empire—they'd pursued a contract killer.

Lorcan Cobbe, the vicious boy from Roarke's childhood, became a vicious man, and one who'd wanted Roarke dead.

Tables turned, she thought. And now Cobbe sat in an off-planet concrete cage, and would for the rest of his vicious life.

"There's a break in the clouds ahead."

She peered at the leaden sky. Maybe, if she squinted, there was a slightly less gray patch.

"You call that a break?"

"I do, yes." Ireland, like the green, wove through his voice as he reached over to lay a hand on hers. "It means much to them for us to come like this, spend time with the family. It means everything to me that you're willing to."

"I'm happy to go. I like them, the whole insane mob of them. And it's nice to spend some time here when we're not with a bunch of cops."

"It is. And yet, that was a satisfying visit after all."

"Because I stood back and let you kick Cobbe's ass."

He smiled again at the "let you." "My cop understands me, and loves me anyway. And there now, see, there's a bright spot."

She couldn't deny what he'd called a break now showed hints of blue.

"*Bright*'s a strong word."

He turned, turned again, and there she saw the field where she'd once landed in a jet-copter—with the damn cows—because he'd needed her. Where she'd first met Sinead Brody Lannigan, Roarke's mother's twin.

The stone-gray house, the barns and outbuildings, the thriving gardens.

Even as Roarke turned into the drive, the front door burst open. Sean, Sinead's freckle-faced grandson, ran out.

"You're here at last! We've been waiting forever, haven't we? And Nan and Ma made a welcome feast. I'm fair to starving, as they won't let me have so much as a nibble."

He stood, fair-haired and bright-eyed, in the dripping rain.

"I'll help with the bags."

"There's a good lad. And how's it all going, Sean?"

"Fine and well. Are you wearing your weapon then?" he asked Eve. "Can I see it?"

"No and no."

"Ah well." He shouldered a bag Roarke handed him. "Maybe later then. We've had no trouble, not even a bit, since last you came. But maybe now we'll have some."

"Bring that bag in," Sinead, honey-blond hair in a sleek tail, hands on narrow hips, called from the doorway. "And stop badgering your cousins. Welcome, welcome to you both. We've missed your faces. No, no, don't bother with the bags."

She embraced Roarke, held a moment, then turned to Eve to do the same. "We've enough able men to bring them in and up to your room."

Inside, all color and movement, voices raised in greeting, more hugs. Eve figured she hugged more in five minutes at the Brody farm than she did in a couple of years—or more— otherwise.

Someone handed her a glass of wine.

Food covered the counters in the farmhouse kitchen that smelled of fresh-baked bread and roasted chicken.

The chicken might've been clucking out in the coop that morning, but Eve wasn't going to think about it.

Someone handed her a plate piled with enough food for three starving people. A pair of dogs raced by, then a couple of kids.

Sinead drew her aside.

"I've the gift you had sent ahead tucked away. You'll just let me know when you want it."

"I guess after all this."

"We'll take it up to your room then?"

"Oh. No. He should have it here. Everyone's here. At least I think they are."

"Every mother's son and daughter. I didn't know if you'd want a private moment for it."

"No, it's . . . family. It's a family thing."

Green eyes soft, Sinead kissed her cheek. "I'm grateful for you, Eve. If I haven't said so, know I'm grateful for you. Now, let's get you a seat so you can eat. Make room there, Liam, our Eve has legs longer than yours."

So she sat, the long-legged cop with her choppy brown hair and whiskey-colored eyes, in the middle of noise and confusion that could rival a New York traffic jam.

She hadn't known family, only abuse and violence, and had forged a career founded on standing for the dead. She had family now—the family she'd made, often despite herself, in New York.

And family here, in an Irish farmhouse.

She caught Roarke's eye in the melee. When he raised his glass to her in a quick toast, she did the same.

She hadn't planned just how to give him his anniversary gift, hadn't been entirely sure she could pull it off since she'd come up with the idea.

But when she'd considered giving it to him in Greece, alone, it hadn't seemed the right way.

After the feast, with the family sprawled in the living room, dining room, and kitchen, with a dog snoring and a baby nursing, with Roarke's great-grandmother knitting something or other, seemed like the right way.

"Are you sure now?" Sinead asked when they went into a parlor, into a cupboard. "I haven't seen it or—at great cost, I'll add—given in to the temptation to take a peek, but I know the idea of it, and there'll be tears. Some will be my own, I expect."

"I think it'll mean more to him this way."

She hoped so.

She carried the brown-wrapped gift to where Roarke and his uncle held a conversation having to do with sheep.

"A few days late—in case you thought I forgot."

She knew she'd surprised him—a rare thing—when she handed him the long, wide package.

"Tear it open, would you?" Sean demanded. "Nan wouldn't so much as give us a hint what it was."

"Then we'd best find out."

More family crowded in as Roarke removed the paper, the stabilizers.

And inside, found family.

The painting held the farmhouse, the hills, the fields in the background. And everyone stood together—the whole insane mob of them, young, old, babes in arms, Eve and Roarke centered.

Sinead stood behind Roarke's right shoulder. Roarke's mother, lost so long before, at his left.

"It's the lot of us. Is that my aunt Siobhan, Nan?"

"It is, aye. Aye, that's our Siobhan. Ah, it's beautiful. It's brilliant." Turning, she pressed her face to her husband's shoulder. "And here I go, Robbie."

"This is . . . Eve." Roarke looked up at her, his heart in those wild blue eyes. "I have no words." He reached for her hand. "You've put Summerset in it."

"Well." She shrugged at that. "Yancy painted it."

"I see the signature. It couldn't be more precious to me. How did you manage this?"

"Sinead sent photos, and Yancy figured it out."

"Hand it over, lad." Robbie took it from him. "And stand up and kiss your wife."

"That I will. I love you, beyond reason."

When he kissed her, the family cheered. Then crowded around to get closer looks at the gift.

Young and old, the Irish partied well into the night. Music—which meant singing, dancing—plenty of beer, wine, whiskey, and yet more food. Since the patch of blue had spread its way over the sky, the revelers spilled outside to keep right at it under moon and starlight.

When Eve found a moment to sit—hopefully far away enough so no one would pull her into another dance—Sean settled beside her with a plate of the cookies they called biscuits.

"I liked the case about the girls taken, then locked into that terrible school place. Well now, I didn't like how they were shut up in there," he qualified, "but how you got them out again."

"How do you know about that?"

"Oh, from the Internet," he said easily, and bit into a cookie. "And there was talk of it all even in Tulla. I heard my own father saying how proud he was our own Eve freed those poor girls from a terrible fate, and saw those who harmed them got their comeuppance right enough."

"I had some help with that."

"Well now, of course. You're the boss of the police, and wasn't it fine meeting them when you came last? So, when you found the bad ones, did you stun any of them?"

What the hell, she thought, and took a cookie from the plate. "As a matter of fact."

"Brilliant, as they deserved it and more. And did you have a chance to—" He punched a fist in the air. "And get in a good one."

"Yeah, I got in some good ones."

"As did Roarke, I'm sure, as they all say he fights like a demon."

"He holds his own."

"The one who came here in the spring meant to hurt my nan, and any of us he could." Those bright eyes darkened with a hard fury she not only understood but respected. "He came to hurt Nan, as it would hurt Roarke."

"He'll never touch your nan, or any of you."

"And that's the truth of it because you locked him up. I think I'll not be a farmer, even as I love the farm. When I think on it, I think I'll lock people up—the bad ones, of course."

"There's more to it than that, kid."

"Oh sure and there's more. You have to train so you know how to protect people, and take an oath. It's why I like reading about your cases. And I watched the vid about you and Roarke and the clones."

He looked around at his family with those green Brody eyes.

"Tulla's a quiet place, but still people need protection, don't they then? I saw the dead girl last year, and she didn't get protection in time. Things can happen here as well. So I think I'll be a cop who loves to farm."

"A good way to have it all."

He gave her a quick nod as if that settled it. "That's my thinking on it."

When she mulled it over, she'd been his age, even younger, when she'd decided to be a cop. Different reasons, and thank Christ for that, but the same goal.

"Maybe when you come to New York for Thanksgiving, you can come into Central."

His face didn't light up. His whole being illuminated. "Do you mean it?"

"It'll depend on if I have an active case, and—"

"I won't be any trouble at all. I talked to the Captain Feeney when he was here, and maybe I can see the EDD as well? It all seemed so grand in the vid."

Too much wine, too much relaxation, she thought, and she'd backed herself right into a corner. "We'll try to work it out."

"I have to tell Da!"

When he barreled off, Roarke took his place.

"And what was all that? It looked like you brought his Christmas early."

"I somehow sort of offered to bring him into Central when they come for Thanksgiving."

When Roarke laughed, kissed her cheek, she shook her head.

"He's slippery. They're all slippery when you come down to it." She picked up her wine, again thought what the hell, and took another sip. "He reminded me of me—without the baggage. Anyway." This time she shrugged. "He's following my cases on the Internet."

"Ah, well of course. You're a hero to him."

"If he wants to be a cop, he'll have to learn the difference between a cop and a hero."

"From where I sit, they're one and the same." He took her hand. "The painting, Eve."

She smiled, smugly. "Nailed that one."

"You undid me. How did you think of such a thing?"

"You have to ask yourself what do you get for the man who if he doesn't have it already, it's because it hasn't been invented. Then he'll figure out how to invent it and have it anyway. Has to be personal. So, chronologically, Summerset found you, we found each other, you found all of them."

She tipped her head to his shoulder. "When you gave me my gift back at Central, magic vests for my bullpen? You undid me. We get each other. We get what's important to each other."

"You've time for mooning over each other later." Robbie strode up to pluck Eve off the wall. "I'm for another dance with my niece."

For a third time, Eve thought what the hell, and danced.

She woke alone, and in a stream of pearly sunlight. A memo cube sat on the stand by the bed. Once activated, Roarke's voice streamed out.

*It seems I'm off to the fields. There'll be coffee and
breakfast down in the kitchen whenever you're up
and ready.*

If coffee was involved, she could be up, and she could get
ready.

The shower didn't come close to the multi-jets and steam
at home, or the luxury of the villa in Greece, but it did the
job.

She dragged on pants, a shirt, and, with her mind still
blurry, automatically reached for her weapon harness. It took
her a second to remember she'd locked it away in her bag.

She walked out in the quiet—unless you counted the
occasional mooing cow or baaing sheep (which she did,
absolutely).

Down the creaky stairs and toward the kitchen. Already
the air smelled like glory—with coffee a happy top note.

"Good morning to you, Eve. I heard you stirring, so there's
coffee fresh and ready for you."

"Thanks." Eve grabbed a mug while Sinead, an apron
over her own shirt and pants, her red-gold hair bundled up,
heated a skillet on the stove.

"Roarke's own blend it is, so not to worry. He told me coffee was his first gift to you."

"Yeah. A sneaky way to get past my defenses."

"A cagey man is Roarke. And now, can you handle a full
Irish for breakfast?"

"After last night I figured I was good for a week. But
maybe."

"Danced it all off, as did I. Why don't you start with a bit
of the soda bread—it's full of currants and baked just this
morning."

"That's what I smelled. I remember it from when we were
here last year."

Now the smell of frying meat joined the chorus.

Eve sat at the kitchen table. It seemed odd to just sit there while somebody cooked. No AutoChef for Sinead. But it seemed the right thing.

"Roarke's in the field?"

"Aye, didn't they drag him off—and his own fault for being an early riser. A Brody trait."

"Is it? He's up before dawn pretty much every day. 'Link meetings, holo-meetings with somebody on the other side of the world."

"It is, yes. The farmer in us, I suppose."

"It's hard to see farmer in Roarke."

Sinead sent a smile over her shoulder. "But he plows and plants and tends and harvests right enough."

"You could say that." Eve drank more coffee. "Yeah, you could say that."

"And you, you guard the fields and those who work them, and keep the predators at bay. It's a fine match you've made."

In short order, she put a plate in front of Eve.

"I see his face still, the first time he knocked on my door. The grief in his eyes—my sister's eyes. Sure Siobhan's were as green as mine, but the look in them, the shape of them. My sister's child. And I see his face as so much lifted from him when he saw you land in the near field. And I knew, as he looked at you, he'd found the love she never did."

She set aside a dish towel. "I wonder if I could speak to you about things on my mind."

"Sure. Is there a problem?"

"It's not the now, but the before. I'll have some tea and sit while you eat."

Sinead took her time about it, and Eve realized she sensed nerves.

"Sure I thought this a good time, with just the two of

us, to say what so troubles me." She sat, sighed. "We didn't fight for him, you see, for our Roarke. Just a babe, and with that bastard Patrick Roarke. My sister's child, and we didn't fight for him."

Because she thought it helped those nerves, Eve ate. "That's not what I heard. Patrick Roarke nearly killed your brother when he went to Dublin to try to find out what happened to your sister."

"He did, oh sweet Jesus, he did, and would see us all in the ground, he warned, if any of us came back. In those times, those hard times, Patrick Roarke had cops and more in both his hands and his back pocket. Still, we knew of the baby and let him go. We let Siobhan's son go. And as time went on, we thought—on my life, we believed—Roarke himself knew of us, of his mother. And more time went on, and we heard—some time after it happened—that Patrick Roarke was dead. I thought of my children, not much younger than my sister's child."

"You thought he knew," Eve said as Sinead stared into her tea. "And if he'd wanted contact, he'd reach out to his mother's family, since Patrick Roarke couldn't stop him. You thought—why wouldn't you?—maybe he's his father's child, and I have my own to protect."

Tears swirled, but Sinead didn't shed them when she nodded. She sipped some tea as she gathered herself to say more.

"And that became a kind of comfort as more time passed. You'd hear of Roarke—the young man who made fortunes—you'd hear of deeds done in shadows—rumors of them. His life in New York City. A kind of empire, isn't it?"

"And not really 'kind of.'"

"I'd wonder, when I let myself wonder, what kind of man he was. Like his father? Ruthless, murderous, heartless? I might see a picture of him at some fancy place with some beautiful woman on his arm. I'd think: Where is Siobhan, where is my sister in this man? I couldn't find her in him, you see. I couldn't see her in him a'tall, so easier still to turn away, to let go."

She sighed again. "Then I saw a picture of him with you, this policewoman with serious eyes. Not so glamorous as others, but more memorable to my thinking. And when I looked at him standing with you, I thought: Ah, well now, oh aye, there she is, there's a bit of my sister after all. Who is this woman who brought Siobhan out in him?"

"She was always there, Sinead."

Those tears shimmered over the Brody green. "I know that now. I think I knew that the moment I opened the door to him. But—"

"You opened the door to him," Eve interrupted. "You let him in. You gave him family. Regrets aren't just useless in this case, they're just wrong."

"We let him go."

"You took him in," Eve corrected, "when he needed you, and opened a door he hadn't known existed. One he thought you'd shut in his face. His years in Dublin, with that fucker Patrick Roarke, and beyond that made him what he is. Who he is. Regret what you did or didn't? You regret who he made himself."

Blinking at the tears, Sinead sat back. "That's very Irish of you."

"Is it?" With a shrug, Eve polished off her breakfast. "Just strikes me as logic."

"You love him, very much."

"He's a complicated, irritating, arrogant, fascinating, generous man. I love him, very much, even when he pisses me off. Which is fairly regularly. And yet. Do you know what he gave me for our anniversary?"

Now Sinead smiled, dashed away a tear that got through.

"I was hoping you'd tell me, or show me. I imagine it's blindingly gorgeous."

"To me it is. He researched, developed, and is manufacturing what's called Thin Shield. It's a lightweight, flexible body armor that can be worn as a lining in a coat, jacket, vest, uniform. He gave them to my entire bullpen. He's giving the next round of them to the NYPSD."

For a moment, Sinead said nothing. "He loves you, very much."

"Yeah, how about that? I'll never figure out why, so I've learned to take it. You'll never figure out the what-ifs, the if-only, Sinead, so regrets are useless. And they disrespect the man he is. That's Siobhan's son."

"You've lifted a weight off my heart. That's pure truth."

"Good, because it didn't belong there."

"Hearing you say so makes a difference. You trusted us with him."

After a beat, Sinead's eyes widened. She grinned as she ticked a finger in the air. "Ah. I see. You looked into us."

"I'm a cop," Eve said simply. "And watch out, because Sean's heading in that direction."

"So it seems. You . . . investigated us?"

"You better believe I checked you out. Every one of you. And there are a hell of a lot of you." Eve nudged her plate aside. "You're an exceptional family."

"More exceptional now. I'll say again." Reaching out, she gripped one of Eve's hands. "I'm grateful to you, and for you, Eve."

"Roarke's out in some field, probably stepping in cow shit in his five-thousand-dollar boots."

"Oh Jaysus, not so dear as all that, surely."

"Conservative estimate." Rising, she helped herself to another mug of coffee. "And the idea of it really brightens up my day. So gratitude right back."

"I've a mind to go out, cut some flowers. I feel light and happy thanks to our talk here. Will you walk with me?"

"Are you going near any cows?"

"Ah, we'll keep a good distance there."

"Then I'm game."

Maybe it surprised her how much she enjoyed several days on a farm in the Irish countryside, not far from the wild Irish coast. But the people brought the pleasure. She considered the many dogs and cats normal, even acceptable.

Cows and sheep within a stone's throw of the house? Not so much. But she learned to sleep through the insistent call of the rooster, and kept her distance from the rest of the stock.

On the other hand, Roarke dived right in, tromping through fields in those five-thousand-dollar boots—they'd never be the same—riding on weird-looking machines.

She wondered, seriously, if he'd gone over the top when he milked a cow.

Machines did the real work, but you still had to get up close and personal. And because he wanted to see how it was done the old-fashioned way, his uncle obliged him.

So she stood, well back, in the doorway of the milking parlor, watching possibly the richest man in the known universe sit on a three-legged stool at the enormous back end of a cow who munched on a bunch of hay.

With his hair tied back in work mode, he used those clever and elegant hands to yank on a cow tit. A huge cow tit, the sort of tit she firmly believed had no place in a civilized world.

When milk squirted out of it and into a pail, she had to hold back a shudder. In contrast, Roarke grinned and kept on going.

"Will you have a go at it then, Eve? Our Gertie here's gentle as a lamb."

"Absolutely not. No. Never." Plus, she'd heard the sounds lambs could make, and didn't consider them gentle.

"It's satisfying," Roarke told her.

"Yeah, I bet. What man wouldn't want to get his hands on a tit that big?"

When Robbie roared with laughter, she stepped back. "I'll just leave the two of you to it."

And when the three weeks away ended, she figured they'd done it all—and more. From the quiet of sun-soaked Greece to the quiet of green-soaked Ireland.

And cows aside, she'd enjoyed every second of it.

2

Arriving in New York equaled noise, heat drenched in humidity, snarling, bad-tempered traffic, and sidewalks flooded with people.

A perfect welcome home. Eve loved every grimy or shiny, every rude or welcoming, every high-class or low-class square inch of it.

"It was good," she said. "Everything was as good as it gets. So's this."

"Home's always best."

Roarke drove through traffic, the stop and go of it, with the same ease he'd milked a damn cow. They'd sent their luggage ahead, so it was just the two of them for a little while longer.

"And home on a Sunday means neither of us have to get back at it until tomorrow. I vote for pizza, a whole lot of wine, then popcorn and a vid and a whole lot of sex."

"Do you now?"

"Gotta stretch the vacaying to the last minute."

"I couldn't agree more with any and all of that."

They drove through the gates, and she looked at the towers, the turrets, the spread of the house Roarke built, at the expanse of lawn, the summer green of the trees, the vibrant flowers and shrubs.

"Yeah, home's best."

Still best, she thought when they went in, to find Summerset, in his habitual funeral black, waiting in the foyer. Galahad sat beside him, but instead of padding over to greet them, he just gave them the hard eye.

Eve crouched down. "Come on, you know you missed me."

He looked deliberately away, then back, then sort of sashayed over as if granting a favor.

But when she gave him that first long stroke, he purred, then rubbed his pudgy body against her knees.

"Welcome home," Summerset said. "You both look as if the time away did you more than good."

"It did. And all's well here?"

"Yes, it is. Your family's well, I hope, one and all."

"They are, and send you their best."

"The bags you marked for me are unpacked, and the others upstairs. Except for the lieutenant's gift to you." Summerset gestured toward the main parlor. "As you requested."

Taking Eve's hand, Roarke walked into the parlor.

The painting hung in a place of prominence over the mantel.

Surprised, Eve turned to him. She'd expected him to hang it in his office, maybe the library. "Here? You're sure about that?"

"It's personal, but not private. It's family, so I'm sure, yes."

"It's a precious gift. I'm honored to be included in it," Summerset added.

Eve just shrugged. "You're his real father, so . . ." She scooped up the cat. "See? We didn't leave you out, either."

The painted Galahad sat between Eve and Roarke, looking pudgy yet dignified.

"I'm going to head up and unpack." But she lingered another moment. "It looks good there."

She set down the cat so he jogged up the steps beside her.

The minute she walked into the bedroom, he made a beeline for the bed, leaped up, sprawled out.

Obviously, all was forgiven.

She sat beside him, gave him a belly rub. "I missed you, too. You'd probably have gone for the villa in Greece—luxury's your speed. But you wouldn't have gone for the farm, trust me. Too much competition, to start—dogs and cats swarming. Too much outside for you, with big-ass cows and weird-eyed sheep. You're an urbanite, pal. It takes one to know one."

"So are we all," Roarke agreed. "I can't imagine what it's like to do what the family does every bloody day. A bit of a lark for me to have a hand at it for a very short time, but the farmer's life? It's a hard one. And one they love."

When he sat, Galahad shifted his affections.

They unpacked and, by tacit agreement, both stayed out of their offices and had pizza on the patio as the sun set.

"Maybe we scratch the popcorn and vid." She sat back, sipped a little more wine. "It's barely nine, but it doesn't feel like it."

"There's the earth on its axis moving around the sun again."

"Yeah, you ought to find a way to fix that. We can skip straight to the sex."

"How could I argue with that?"

"I figured that would get your vote." She closed her eyes, lifted her face to the night. "I'm going to have a shitload to catch up on tomorrow. You, too."

"The price we pay."

"Worth it. I did miss the cat, and New York pizza, but worth it. What time's your first meeting?"

He smiled at her. "You'll still be sleeping."

"Figured. Then let's go get this vacation capped off."

They walked inside, then up to the bedroom, where the cat already stretched across the bed.

"Some things don't change," she commented.

And as they turned to each other, the communicator on her dresser signaled.

"No, they bloody don't."

"What the serious fuck? I'm not on the roll until oh-eight hundred."

She snatched it up. "Dallas."

Dispatch, Dallas, Lieutenant Eve. Official request
for your assistance from Webster, Lieutenant Donald.
Unattended death, 14 Leonard Street, apartment 321.
Will you respond as primary?

"Crap. Affirmative. Responding now. Dallas out."

She looked over at Roarke. "I don't know why, but he wouldn't ask if it wasn't important."

"Understood. I'll drive—and don't wonder if I'm going with you because he once tried putting moves on you, and in our house. That's all done. We'll consider it our alternate way of capping off our vacation."

"Fine." She strapped on the weapon she'd put on the dresser for the morning. "What the hell is IAB doing at an unattended death?"

"I suppose we'll find out."

She grabbed her badge, her 'link, the rest of her pocket paraphernalia. "I'm going to see who lives—and possibly died—there while you drive."

They left the cat on the bed and went out to the car Roarke had remoted from the garage to the front of the house. She pulled out her PPC, started the search while he sped down the drive, through the gates.

"Shit. Shit. Martin and Elizabeth Greenleaf have that unit. Captain Martin Greenleaf, IAB—retired. I know—or maybe knew—him some. He's Webster's guru or mentor, father figure. I know they're tight. He was tight with Greenleaf and his wife."

"He requested you because, as you said, it's important. I assume he didn't just tag you so as to keep it official?"

"Yeah, yeah. Still stretching it some. And he wouldn't have stretched it if it's, or looks like, natural causes, or an accident. Or maybe he would," she considered. "Because they were tight, and he just reacted."

"You'll sort it out."

"Yeah." She looked at him again. "Welcome the hell home."

"Well then, it is our home and our life here, isn't it then? It's what we do, who we are. I wouldn't change it. Would you?"

"No." That part came easy. "But I didn't expect to dive right back into murder. And he wouldn't have asked for me, especially this way, if he didn't think murder. And I can't go into whatever this is influenced by what he thinks or feels."

"He'd know that, wouldn't he?"

"He should. Crap, crap, Captain Greenleaf, or his wife. Or somebody else in their apartment. But odds of somebody else don't fly."

"Because?"

"What I know of Greenleaf is by the book, and the book is sacred. No deviation. And I have to wipe that out, go in blank. That's how it has to be.

"Webster's been taking a lot of time off-planet."

"I wouldn't know."

"Bollocks to that. He's spending that time at the Olympus Resort, and with Darcia Angelo. Olympus is basically yours, and she's your top cop there. You know."

"She does her job, and well. Her off time is her own. And yes, he visits often enough. They made a connection—we saw it for ourselves."

"Pretty damn quick connection."

Amused, he shot her a look. "And didn't we?"

She lifted a shoulder. "Maybe. Yeah, okay. Listen, I'm going to need you to be Peabody," she said, referring to her partner. "Either assisting me if I need you to, or keeping Webster out of my way. Can you do the second part without punching him in the face?"

"It's been a bit of time since I punched him in the face, or elsewhere," Roarke said easily. "We came to an understanding."

"Great." When he turned onto Leonard, she felt a wave of relief. "He called in uniforms. That's a good step. Follow procedure, secure the scene."

"I'll get your field kit from the trunk and put on my Peabody."

A good, solid building, she noted, brick, pre-Urbans. A decent neighborhood, good security on the entrance. And a uniform standing there now.

She badged him as they walked up the short steps to the doors.

"Lieutenant."

"What do you know, Officer?"

"My partner and I responded to a nine-one-one by Lieutenant Webster. Ambulance also requested, but the victim was DOS. Lieutenant Webster ordered me to take the entrance door, and my partner to remain on scene with him to ensure it remained secure. DB is male, mid-seventies, at a desk in what appears to be a home office. No visible signs of forced entry."

"Stand by."

She went in, barely glanced at the pair of elevators before taking the stairs.

"He was smart to have the uniform stay with him on scene," she commented. "Smarter maybe if he'd just called it in, then stepped back, but smart enough."

"And smart enough to ask for you if he suspects foul play."

"We'll see about that."

On three, she walked to the apartment. It had a door cam—but Greenleaf was a cop, after all—and a solid set of locks. She pressed the buzzer.

Webster answered, and she thought: Fuck. He's a mess.

His light blue eyes held nothing but grief and despair, and his body language told her he was using every ounce of self-control to hold it in. Rather than crowning his narrow face, his brown hair looked as if he'd dragged a garden rake through it.

Casual dress, she noted—so he'd changed from work before he'd come here.

"Dallas. I'm sorry, but I needed the best. Martin deserves the best."

"Okay. Step back, Webster."

"Sorry," he said again. "Roarke, I appreciate you coming. I know you weren't on the roll, Dallas, but . . . It looks like suicide, but not in a million years. Not in two million. I need to tell you—"

"Nothing yet." His grief aside, she cut him off. She had to. "Nothing. I want you to stay out of my way. I'll talk to you after I look at the scene and the body."

"Just let me—"

"No. Officer, stay with the witness. Where's the body?"

The uniform stepped forward, gestured. "In there, Lieutenant. The MTs examined the body, but didn't disturb the scene. My partner and I arrived approximately four minutes after the nine-one-one."

The apartment opened into a living area, with a short foyer holding a catchall table. She noted a bag on it, a six-pack of upscale brew inside.

"I—"

"Not now," she told Webster, and moved into the living

area with its sofa and plumped pillows, a recliner, a wall screen, some floral prints on the wall, a pair of shoes by a chair.

Neat enough, not obsessive. Lived-in, and lived long.

A kitchen area tucked behind a half wall to the left with a small dining area. It sparkled clean, no question, but still more lived-in and lived long to her eye. A bowl of summer fruit on the counter. Mugs on an open shelf above an old-model AC, a cooktop over a stove beside it.

Someone probably cooked on it.

And to her right, as she stepped forward, what might have been a small bedroom at one point and now served as a den/office.

There, at a desk painted black, Captain Greenleaf slumped.

"I—"

"Later, Webster. I need to examine the body and the scene, and you need to step back."

Roarke handed Eve her field kit. "Why don't we take a walk," he said to Webster, "and you can tell me. We'll let the lieutenant do what's best for your friend."

"I haven't contacted Beth yet—his wife. I didn't want—"

Eve turned at that. "Where is she?"

"A ladies' night, a regular thing. She would've left about eight-thirty, I guess."

"Okay, let's leave that for now. Take a walk."

"Dallas—just let me say this, damn it. I know what it looks like, but it's not." Grief soaked him. Face, body, voice. "It's just not."

"Let me see what it looks like, then we'll talk. For now, stay out of the way. You want me to stand for him? Let me stand for him."

She walked into the crime scene and, to discourage any more conversation, shut the door behind her.

Greenleaf slumped in his desk chair like a man taking a

quick nap—though he wouldn't wake from this one. On the floor by the chair lay a police-issue stunner, and she could see the marks from it on the side of his neck.

Deep marks, she noted. Deep enough to break and burn the skin.

On the wall screen, the Mets and the Pirates battled it out. Bottom of the seventh, 0–1, and the Pirates with a man on first. Since his chair faced the screen, logically he'd watched at least some of the game, or had intended to.

He had a data and communication unit on the desk, still running. The message on the screen read:

> Beth, I'm sorry, but I just can't go on this way.
> Too many good cops' lives ruined, their families
> broken. My fault. Forgive me because I can't
> forgive myself.

"Yeah, Webster, I see what it looks like."

She opened her field kit to formally identify the body, and pressed Greenleaf's left thumb to her Identi-pad.

"Victim is identified as Greenleaf, Martin, retired captain, Internal Affairs Bureau, NYPSD. Age seventy-six, resident of this address."

She took out her gauges. "Time of death, twenty-one-eighteen."

She crouched down, recorded the weapon. "A police-issue stunner recovered on scene on the floor, right side of the chair. Identifying code has been removed."

She checked it—on full—then set her first marker for the sweepers.

"The victim sat with his back to the doorway leading from the living area of the apartment and facing the wall screen. Both the wall screen and the computer activated. No visible signs of struggle, no visible signs of violence to the body but the stunner burns, which indicate direct contact with same at the throat. The stunner is set on high."

She shifted to change the angle of the recording.

"Victim has a wrist unit, left wrist, and a band style ring on the third finger of his left hand."

Carefully, she checked Greenleaf's pockets. "Wallet, right front pocket of his trousers, containing . . ." She flipped through.

"ID, license to drive, credit card, four photos, and . . . thirty-six dollars in cash. A 'link, passcoded," she said after trying to access, "and a glass of unidentified liquid, with ice . . ." She bent close, sniffed. "Smells like tea, lab to confirm contents, on the right side of the computer screen. The glass is about half-full, on a coaster."

Maybe he added some courage to the tea, she thought. But.

Why does a retired cop intending to self-terminate get himself some iced tea, turn on the ball game, and use the comp to write his last words when there's an actual pen and a pad of paper on the desk?

"What appears to be a suicide note on the monitor of the D and C on the desk. Current information indicates the victim was alone in the apartment at TOD."

Wouldn't be the first cop to end his watch by pressing a stunner to his throat, and wouldn't be the last, she thought.

And yet, it was all pretty damn tidy, wasn't it? A note that says basically nothing before he offs himself while his wife's out. Married a long time, she considered. Would he want her to come home and find him like this?

Depends on the marriage, she decided, so she'd go down that road.

Closed window—closed and locked—and the aging temperature regulator pumped and buzzed some. Made some noise along with the color commentary on the game.

His back to the door. And the ball game on-screen. Ice melting in a glass that was likely tea.

She went through the desk, found his memo book. Appointments listed for the next several weeks, a note to remind him to buy flowers for his wife—anniversary in ten days, dinner booked at a swank place nearby.

He had *47 years!* inside a big heart.

She stepped out, walked through the apartment, into the bedroom. Seriously clean but a little less tidy, with signs of someone hurriedly dressing—or someone who'd changed their mind about wardrobe a couple of times.

Some facial enhancements and grooming tools on the bathroom counter, another discarded pair of shoes—female, this time—right next to the closet door.

And two windows leading to a fire escape. One locked, one not. Curious, she walked through, checked all the other windows. All locked. Just that one, in the bedroom.

She went back, opened it, peered up, peered down.

In the closet, a shared one, she found Greenleaf's clothes, very organized. His wife's—she assumed—not as much.

Ladies' night, she thought. Choosing and rejecting outfits.

In the bedroom drawers, the same deal and, in the nightstands, some electronics, some night creams, a bottle of meds for helping with an erection, and some lube.

Since both were about half-full, she assumed the couple had remained sexually active.

In the kitchen a note stuck to the friggie.

SNACKS INSIDE FOR YOU AND DON, SWEETIE. SEE YOU BOTH IN A COUPLE HOURS. DON'T DRINK TOO MUCH BREW!

She'd drawn hearts at the start and finish of the note.

She walked back to the body.

"Okay, Captain. Okay."

She contacted the sweepers, the morgue—requested Chief Medical Examiner Morris. No need to bring Peabody in yet, she decided. The morning was soon enough for that.

She texted Roarke instead.

Bring him back.

While she waited, she checked the time stamp on the suicide note. Within a minute of TOD, so that could go either way.

Back in the kitchen, she checked the AutoChef. It looked like the couple had shared a meal of linguine with cream sauce and a salad. In the friggie—well stocked—she noted the snack tray. Cheese, pickles, carefully sliced disks of a meat-like product, some sort of dip, some salsa.

A tray of crackers sat on the counter beside a bowl of chips and a pile of cocktail napkins.

Expecting Webster, no question, and that could go either way.

Let Webster find me, deal with it while Beth's gone.

Or somebody didn't expect a cop on scene minutes after TOD.

For now, she'd keep both possibilities wide open.

When she heard the door, she stepped out again.

"Have a seat, Webster." She gestured to a chair out of eyeline with the body. "Run it through for me."

"I'm going to start at the beginning, all right?"

Calmer now, she noted, and knew she had Roarke to thank for it.

"Go."

"Martin came by to see me this afternoon. I've been off-planet for a week, so doing weekend work, flexing time.

He thought we could have some lunch, catch up, but I was swamped. We just had some coffee at my desk."

"What was his mood?"

"Good. Up. Fine. He talked some about his granddaughter's Little League game, and just wanted to know how things were going with me. I had some things I wanted to talk to him about, and we didn't have time then, so he said I should come over about nine or so because Beth had her girls' night, and we could drink some brew—if I brought it— bullshit awhile."

"He expected you."

"That's right. I didn't get here until about nine-thirty. Had a lot to clear at Central, wanted to change, buy the brew."

"How'd you get in?"

"I have a swipe and their passcode. I didn't bother buzzing in downstairs, but he didn't answer when I knocked. I just let myself in, figuring he didn't hear me. He's had some hearing issues off and on for the last year or so, and I heard the game on in his den. I called out."

He took a moment, gathered himself.

"I set the brew down and, when I looked in his den, I saw him."

"Did you touch anything?"

"His shoulder. His left shoulder. I didn't touch the weapon, the monitor, anything else. I just put my hand on his shoulder because I couldn't believe . . . Jesus."

Webster covered his face with his hands as the words shook out of him. "I need a second."

"You read the monitor."

Face still covered, Wester nodded. Then he dropped his hands, and his eyes burned hot. "And it's bullshit. It's bullshit, Dallas. He'd never do this to Beth, to his kids, his grandkids. He wouldn't do this to me. And he'd never take this way out."

"Do you know if he had any medical issues other than his hearing?"

Now, as he shook his head, Webster dragged his hands through his hair.

"Nothing, not that he ever told me, or Beth told me—and she would if he didn't. Slowing down, he'd say, and it pissed him off some. That's bullshit about good cops, his fault. He honored the badge, do you get me?"

Webster's voice hitched, then hardened.

"Yeah, he was a hard-ass, and straight down the line. If a cop smelled bad, he'd go after them all the way, and he taught me to do the same. It doesn't make you popular, but it's the job.

"It's a setup, Dallas," he insisted. "Martin wouldn't do this. I know that without a fucking doubt."

Right now, she thought, they needed facts. Not feelings.

"You say you knocked. How many times? How long did you wait before you came in?"

"I knocked twice. Slowing down, right? So I wanted to give him a minute. A minute, maybe a little less, and I swiped in. No more than about a minute."

"Did you hear anything from inside?"

"No. Well, the game. I heard the game coming from his den, so figured he didn't hear me knock over it."

"Did anyone else know he expected you tonight?"

"I don't know. Beth—he'd have told her, the way you do."

He lifted his hands, dropped them again. Then linked them together as if he didn't know what to do with them.

"I don't know if he told anyone else, or why he would."

"Describe your relationship with him."

"He was my captain when I joined IAB, and until he retired. And he was the next thing to a father to me. My parents split when I was a kid, and my father didn't have much interest. My mother remarried, and they didn't have a lot of interest. Martin and Beth did. I have Christmas with them every year. I loved him, and I want whoever did this to him."

"As of now I haven't determined homicide. I've requested Morris, and the sweepers are on the way. You are not part of the investigation. You can't be. You know that."

She held up a hand before he could speak. "I'll keep you in the loop. I can do that, but that's all. Don't get in my way."

"I know you didn't especially like him."

Eyes flat, she spoke coolly. "Do you think that applies to my ability to investigate his death?"

"No. Absolutely no. That's why I asked for you. Dallas, I need to be here for Beth. This is going to— They really loved each other. She needs somebody who loved him here. I don't want to contact her, bring her home like this. I don't want her to see him like this, or watch them carry him out in a body bag."

"I need her statement. I need to interview her. She's most likely the last person to see him alive."

"He said she'd be home before midnight, earlier, probably. She just meets some friends once a month, and they drink wine and hang out for a couple hours."

"Did you tell anyone you were coming here tonight?"

"I messaged Darcia. My door was open when Martin came by. Sure, somebody could've heard us set it up, but I didn't say anything specifically to anyone."

"Roarke, would you see about getting the security feed for the building, and the feed for this front door cam on this unit?"

She waited until he'd walked out.

"If there's anything, any detail, any single thing you're leaving out, softening up, shifting on me, spill it now, Webster, or I swear to God when I find out—and I will—I'll slice you to pieces."

Closing his eyes, he nodded. Then looked at her straight on.

"That's why I wanted you on this. Exactly why. No. There's nothing. I swear to God right back at you. What's the TOD? In the loop, you said."

"Twenty-one-eighteen."

"Christ, Christ, I was probably walking in the door of the building, or on my way up five or ten minutes later. If I'd gotten here just a few minutes earlier—"

And she could see, literally see, his control crack. And so spoke briskly.

"Ifs don't solve anything. Put it away. Did he say anything to you, even just shooting-the-shit cop stories about a threat?"

"No—" Backtracking, Webster waved a hand in the air. "I mean sure, before he retired. IAB cops get threats all the time, it's part of the package. You get verbal bullshit, you get physical altercations. Mostly, it's just blowing air, so you document and let it go. Same as you, Dallas, or any cop, but the difference is the threats and altercations are usually from other cops.

"We're not popular," he added with a shrug. "That's how it goes."

"Anything recent, anything specific?"

"No. Listen, he didn't have to retire. He chose to. He told me it was time to, like, pass the torch. And he wanted time, more time to just be a husband, a dad, a grandfather.

"He liked being retired. Beth retired a few years after he did, and they did some traveling. They made noises about moving south, getting a place on the shore, buying a boat, but their family's here, so they never followed through. The only time anything like threats came up is when we talked shop and it was: 'Remember that asshole who said he'd cut out your rat heart with a dull knife and feed it to the other rats?'

"It was yesterday for him, Dallas, and he'd put in his time."

At the knock, Eve rose, let in the sweepers. While she read them in, gave them her priorities, the morgue team arrived.

"Why don't you wait in the kitchen?"

Webster shook his head. "He deserves someone who knew him, cared about him, to stand by." Then he turned to her. "You're calling it homicide."

"Right now, it's suspicious death. Where's his service weapon?"

"He turned it in when he retired. I know he did because I was there."

"How about his clutch piece, his backup, a drop weapon?"

"Dallas, Martin rode a desk the last fifteen years of his tour. He didn't have a clutch piece, he'd never use a drop weapon, and he didn't have a backup. That stunner's not his."

"And if it is?"

"Then someone found a way to make it look like that."

He stood silently as the morgue team rolled the bagged body away. "I want a drink—a real drink. He keeps a bottle of whiskey in the kitchen."

"No. I'll get it," Eve told him when he stepped that way. "I'm sealed up, you aren't."

Roarke came back in, nodded at Eve.

"Where's the bottle?"

"Cabinet by the window. Glasses in the cabinet to the right of the sink."

"I'm sorry, Webster," Roarke said when Eve went into the kitchen. "Truly sorry for your loss."

"I get that. I appreciate that." He sat again, pressed his fingers to his eyes. "She'll find who did this. You'll help her."

"However I can. But she'll find the one who did this. Will it be enough?"

"It's never enough, but it has to do."

He took the two fingers of whiskey Eve brought back.

"When's the last time you were in this apartment?"

"Three—no, four weeks ago. Four weeks ago. His daughter's birthday dinner."

"So I'm not going to find your prints anywhere on scene?"

"The way Beth cleans? Not a chance." He downed the whiskey. "You got the security feeds. I'd like to see them."

"Tomorrow," Eve told him. "I want you at Central at noon."

"But—"

"I need to report to Whitney, meet with Morris, do what I have to do. Then we'll go over everything again. If I'm satisfied, I'll let you view the footage. I'm letting you stay on scene," she added before he could object, "to be here for the captain's widow. Don't fuck with me when I'm questioning her, Webster. Don't make it harder."

"She loved him. They loved each other, and family was their world."

"Then she'll want me to do my job."

"She will." He glanced at his wrist unit. "She'll be home soon. Let me tell her. Please. Let me be the one to tell her he's gone. I won't get in your way."

The hardest part, always, Eve thought, was telling someone their world had shattered.

"Do it fast," Eve advised.

3

After signaling Roarke to stay with Webster, Eve went into the crime scene to consult with the sweepers.

"No prints on the bedroom window lock," the head sweeper told her. "None on the window, or any window in that room, inside or out. Clean as they come. We bagged the glass and contents. Victim's and his spouse's prints there."

"She brought him the drink."

"Logically, yeah. The only prints on the victim's workstation, the D and C, his 'link are his own. Same with the weapon recovered on scene. But I want a closer look at the prints on the weapon in the lab."

"Because?"

"They're perfect. Right thumb, right index finger." The sweeper cocked her fingers as if on a trigger. "One print each, one print only. Otherwise, it's clean."

"Okay." Eve nodded. "A guy's going to self-terminate this way, he's likely to handle the weapon more than once. He's going to check, make sure it's on full. He's probably going to hesitate, no matter how committed."

"That's my but."

"It's a good but, Frowicki."

"Pilates," she said, patting her own ass. "Three times a week."

"Funny. Other prints, bedroom, crime scene."

"Elizabeth Greenleaf. Several of hers on the bedroom closet, the dressers, nightstands, the bedroom lamp to the right of the bed. A few on the doorjamb to the crime scene. Some hair on the bedroom floor, a few strays that match the strays in the brush on the dresser."

The sweeper looked around. "Not much to sweep, Dallas. The place is seriously clean. We're picking up traces of what's going to be furniture polish and over-the-counter cleaners, so somebody did the job recently. But we'll keep at it."

"You're going to find Webster's prints on the front door. Let me know if you find them anywhere else."

"Will do."

"Did you know the victim?"

"Only by rep. A hard case is what you hear."

"Yeah."

As she stepped back into the living area, she heard a trill of female laughter outside the door, and the slide of the lock. Webster surged to his feet.

"Please, let me."

At her nod, he moved to the door. More laughter spilled in when it opened. "I'd've paid twice as much, she says. I can't get over it. Don! You're still here."

Beth Greenleaf, a small, trim woman, had ashy blond hair that curved toward both cheeks. Laughter still lit her bright blue eyes as she threw her arms around Webster.

"I've missed your face!"

"Beth."

"I don't think you've met my friend Elva Arnez. Elva and Denzel live upstairs. She's seeing the old lady to her door."

"I don't see any old lady." Elva, a beauty in her late twenties, stood back, just a step.

Mixed race, curvy in black skin pants and a hip-swinging white tank, she smiled with the statement. Then her gaze shifted over Webster's shoulder, skimmed over Eve to Roarke.

"You've got company," she began. "I'll get going."

"Don's not company. He's family." As Beth pulled back, she spotted Eve, and those bright blue eyes reflected recognition and confusion.

Then fear as one of the sweepers moved into view.

"What—Don? What is this? Where's Martin?"

"We need to sit down."

"What are they doing here? What happened? Martin." As she called her husband's name, she tried to pull away from Webster. He held her fast.

"Beth, I'm sorry. I'm sick and I'm sorry. He's dead."

"Don't you say that! Don't you say that! He's fine, he's fine. I've only been out a couple hours. He's fine."

She struggled against him when he wrapped around her. "I found him when I got here." He rocked her as he spoke. "He was gone. He was already gone."

The struggle stopped. Eve saw her sag as the hard truth hit, as it had to hit—mind, body, heart, soul. She let out one long wail as Webster picked her up like a child, carried her to a chair, and cradled her while she wept.

"What should I do?" Elva stood in the doorway, hands clasped tight between her breasts. "Can I help? Should I go? Oh God."

"Close the door," Eve told her. "Take a seat." Eve took out her badge. "Lieutenant Dallas, NYPSD. You're Elva Arnez. You live upstairs?"

"I—yes—I—my cohab and I live two floors up. He was fine. Absolutely fine. He—Martin—he let me in when I came to get Beth."

"You were in the apartment tonight?"

"Yes. I mean, just to get Beth to go out with some friends."

"What time did you get here? What time did you leave?"

"Um, God. About eight-thirty. A little after, I guess. We were supposed to leave at eight-thirty, but Beth tends to run late. I was actually a little behind anyway, so maybe eight-thirty-five or so. Martin let in, and he was fine. He joked how Beth was still putting her game face on, something like that. And she called me back."

"To the bedroom?"

"Yes. She couldn't decide on what earrings she wanted to wear. Or shoes. It's her way." Tears started to leak. "And—and—and—" Elva stopped, closed her eyes, held up a hand while she drew a couple breaths. "I'm sorry. This is so horrible. I helped her decide. Ten minutes? I don't know, really. Then she went in to say goodbye to Martin."

"In where?"

"Oh, in the little office he has. He called out 'Bye' to me, and 'Have a good time.' I don't understand what happened. Did he have an accident? Did somebody break in and hurt him?"

"We need to determine that. Where'd you go?"

"Bistro. It's a fancy little bar about three blocks from here. Can I do something for her? For Beth?"

"You are," Eve said. "Right now. Who did you meet there?"

"Okay. Okay." She closed her eyes again and gave Eve a list of three names.

"Did anyone leave between nine and nine-thirty?"

"No, we all stayed until about eleven, I guess."

"No one left the table?"

"Well, to go to the restroom. We were all having fun. Having some drinks, some bar munchies, that's all. Did he have an accident? But there are so many police so I don't—"

"We're investigating. I appreciate your cooperation, Ms.

Arnez. Please stay available, as I may have follow-up questions."

"I— Yes. Of course. We live upstairs."

"You're free to go."

"All right, but . . ." As she rose, she looked over at Beth. "Please, please, tell her I'm here for her, for whatever she needs. I'm so sorry."

When she left, Eve turned to Webster.

"Beth." He murmured it, pressed his lips to her temple. "Lieutenant Dallas needs to ask some questions."

"I know it." She patted his arm as she got to her feet. "Would you get me some water?" As he rose, she took the chair, then opened the little purse she wore cross-strapped, took out tissues. She mopped her face, lifted the purse off to set it on the table beside her.

"I know who you are, both of you, and you're here because someone murdered my husband."

"I can't, at this time, verify homicide, Mrs. Greenleaf."

"You sure as hell wouldn't be here if Martin had slipped in the shower. Which he wouldn't. Martin's rock steady. You've got questions. I'm a cop's wife, and I know how this works. But I have one first. How was my husband killed?"

Those blue eyes weren't bright now, but piercing, and rage was slowly smothering the grief in them.

"Lieutenant Webster let himself in when Captain Greenleaf failed to answer his knock. He found Captain Greenleaf at his workstation, deceased. There was a stunner on the floor by his chair, burn marks of a contact stun, on full, on his throat, and a note on his comp screen. 'Beth, I'm sorry but I just can't go on this way. Too many good cops' lives ruined, their families broken. My fault. Forgive me because I can't forgive myself.'"

She waved the water away when Webster brought it and

kept her eyes on Eve. "You're looking at suicide? That's nonsense, complete nonsense. Every bit of it. And if you believe that for one hot minute, you're not as good as everybody thinks you are."

"You asked the question, Ms. Greenleaf. That's the answer I can give you at this time."

Beth looked up at Webster. "Do you think Martin killed himself?"

"No." He pressed the water on her, then sat on the arm of her chair. "Beth, I contacted Dallas, asked her to lead the investigation because she's not just as good as everyone thinks, she's probably better. Martin deserves the best."

"He wouldn't do this, not to himself, never, never to me or the children. And he believed in the work he did for the NYPSD. You know that, Don."

"I do know that."

"He weeded out bad cops, wrong cops, dirty cops. He had no regrets. I'd know. I was his sounding board. Aren't you that to her?" she asked Roarke.

"I am, yes. When she needs it. It's part of the promise we make, isn't it? Or it should be."

"Do you love her?"

"Madly," Roarke said before Eve could object to the question.

"If it's real and true and deep, it only grows with time. We loved each other. He'd never leave me this way. He loved Don like a son. He'd never have left Don to find him this way."

She laid her head back a moment. "I don't understand how he died in his chair. If he'd opened the door to anyone and there was a threat, he'd have fought. There'd be signs of that."

Slowly sipping the water, she glanced around. "Everything's exactly as I left it."

"I need you to verify the timing and activities from your

neighbor's statement, Mrs. Greenleaf. What time did she arrive tonight?"

"I can't tell you exactly. I knew I was running late—and that's when I refuse to look at the time, as stressing over that will only make me later. It was probably about eight-thirty, or a few minutes later." On a sigh, she said, "Probably a few minutes later, because Elva knows I'm always late. I called her back to the bedroom when I heard her and Martin talking, so she could help me decide what to wear. We were meeting friends at Bistro—it's just a few blocks away. I knew I was running late because after dinner, after the dishes, I put together some snacks. I made some salsa. Don's fond of my salsa."

"Best there is."

"Did you mention to anyone that Webster was expected tonight?"

"I don't think so. Martin told me at dinner. I'd been out shopping. Bought the new shoes I decided not to wear tonight after all. He was looking forward to spending some time with you, Don. He'd never have done this. Never."

"Did anyone in your party leave the table for any length of time?"

"No. A couple of bathroom breaks. We had fancy drinks and fancy bar snacks and lots of laughs." Her eyes welled again; she shut them tight, willed the tears back. "We all left at the same time. Anja caught a cab, the rest of us walked. Elva always walks me to the door after a girls' night. It's sweet of her."

"Was she ever alone in your bedroom?"

"What? No. Fashion consult, that's all. Why?"

"When's the last time you had the apartment cleaned?"

"This morning, when I cleaned it. I clean my own home."

"Like nobody's business." Webster lifted her hand, kissed it.

"I may be a little obsessive about it, but I need a clean home."

"Does that include the windows?"

"Of course."

"Did you clean them this morning?"

"No. That's a once-every-four-to-six-weeks job. And I do it when Martin's out of the house because he frets about me washing the outside. As if I'd fall out."

"You keep the windows locked."

"Yes. Martin's obsessive there. When I do the windows, and he always knows when I do, he checks every blessed one."

"Have you had any visitors recently, any repair or maintenance people in the apartment?"

"Our children, grandchildren visit regularly. We haven't had any repair people in since . . . early April. The dishwasher went out. He tried to fix it," she said to Don.

He smiled. "Naturally."

"He failed."

"Naturally."

"You've washed the windows since early April."

"Yes. The middle of May, toward the end of June."

She set the water aside, gripped Webster's hand.

"An unlocked window's how someone got in and did this to Martin. Someone got in and unlocked a window. We wouldn't notice. I don't think we'd have noticed."

"Did you check them nightly?"

"No. No, after I'd wash them, he'd check. They stayed locked because he wanted them locked. Which window was unlocked? You can tell me that. It'll come out anyway."

"The bedroom window, facing east. It has a privacy screen engaged."

"Yes, always. It's our bedroom. We have a door cam, you need . . ." She broke off. "You'll have that by now. But if someone got in a week ago, two weeks ago, it wouldn't be on there. It overwrites every seventy-two hours."

"Mrs. Greenleaf, did your husband keep a weapon, a stunner?"

"No. He turned in his service weapon when he retired. And he gave me that. No weapons in our home for the first time since we married. I didn't have to ask for him to give me that. The stunner you found wasn't his. Martin wasn't suicidal."

At the head sweeper's signal, Eve rose. "Excuse me."

When she came back, she remained standing. "The Crime Scene Unit's finished for now. We will have to keep this apartment sealed for the time being. Is there somewhere you can stay, ma'am? Someone we can contact for you?"

"I'll take you to Carlie's." Webster pressed her fingers to his lips again. "We'll tell her together. I'll contact Ben and Luke."

"Yes, yes, that would be best. God, oh God, our poor babies." A tear escaped this time, and she swiped it away. "I need to pack a few things."

"I'll help you."

"No. Webster." Eve shook her head. "It would be best if I went with you, Ms. Greenleaf."

"To make sure I don't try to sneak any evidence away."

"To go by the book," Eve countered. "Something I believe the captain would value."

"You're right about that."

"Mrs. Greenleaf." Roarke rose as she did. "I'm very sorry for your loss."

"I believe you are, and thank you. We're a different breed, aren't we? Cops' spouses. Nobody else quite fully understands."

"No, I don't suppose they do."

Eve followed her to the bedroom, waited in the doorway to be as unintrusive as possible.

"Oh, come in. Don't hover. I need some clothes, and I'll need some things out of the bathroom."

She wrenched open the closet, then just froze.

"Just look at us," she murmured. "I'm the one who can't stand dirt or clutter, but in here? My clothes are jumbled, and his lined up straight as an arrow. What a pair we are—were—always will be. I can't reach the damn shelf for my bag. Martin always got it down for me."

"Let me help you."

Eve got the bag, set it on the bed while Beth pulled out some clothes.

"I loved him with every fiber of my being. Can you understand that?"

"Yes, I can."

She looked back as she pulled some things out of a dresser. "I believe you can." She lifted a framed photo from the dresser top, one of the two of them grinning at the camera. "Hold on to that. Hold on tight."

She laid the photo in the bag. "He admired you."

"I'm sorry?"

"Martin admired you. You had some trouble several years back, had to turn in your badge and weapon until it cleared up."

"Yes." It still stung. A wasp bite in the gut.

"He knew about that and, though he was retired, followed the investigation. And he told me—his sounding board—that you were an exceptional police officer, one of honor, of duty and integrity. I hope you'll remember that, because you hold him in your hands now."

"Mrs. Greenleaf, I promise you I'll do everything I can, as will the whole of my department as needed, to find out the truth of what happened here tonight."

"I believe you because he would. Will you let Don help?"

"I'll keep Lieutenant Webster apprised of the progress on the investigation. I can't let him in more than that."

She opened a drawer Eve had identified as the victim's, took out a precisely folded white handkerchief. Pressed it to her cheek before she packed it.

"Don loved Martin, so he'll push some. He was in love with you once."

"No, he wasn't."

Now she smiled. "No, he wasn't, but he thought he was, and that's nearly the same. What he's found with Darcia, that has a good chance. I hate that I'm glad Don found him before I did. I think it would've broken me. Shattered me so I'd never find all the pieces again."

"No, it wouldn't." Eve said it almost casually, because she knew it for truth. "You're a cop's wife."

"That's right. That's right." She pressed her fingers to her eyes as if pushing tears back, then let them fall. "I need a few things from the bathroom, then I'll get out of your way. I need to see Martin tomorrow. All of us do."

"I'll contact you as soon as possible."

Nodding, Beth walked around the bed, laid a hand for a moment on the pillow on the left, then carried her bag from the room.

When Webster led her out the front door, she didn't look back.

And when the door closed behind them, Eve breathed out, shoved both hands through her hair. "All right. Okay."

"A hard night all around."

"Yeah. Listen, I appreciate you."

His eyebrows lifted. "I know it."

"I appreciate you keeping Webster contained while I dealt with this."

"Is that what I did? Contain him?"

"You gave him someone to unload on, someone to listen—and you kept him out of my way. He did it right, he gets that, and it couldn't've been easy. Greenleaf was a father to him, and he walks in, finds him dead."

Eve circled the room as she spoke. "Finds what looks like self-termination. He could've tried to cover it up, not that hard to do. Stage a break-in, a struggle, get rid of the message on the comp."

"You'd have seen through that like polished glass."

"Yeah, but he could've tried; he didn't. He called it in, got uniforms and the MTs on scene. He requested me through channels. He kept his head, and it couldn't have been easy."

"And still, as he discovered the body, had a connection to the victim and a key to get in, you have to eliminate him as a suspect."

"His statement holds up, and the security feed's going to cover the rest. They came in through the window in the bedroom, which means someone got in and unlocked it between the last time Ms. Greenleaf washed it and tonight. And since the upstairs neighbor was in there tonight, she's on the list."

"You're ruling out suicide."

"Officially, not yet. Can't. But this was staged, planned out, timed to hit when he was alone in the apartment. Do it quick so he doesn't have time to react or fight, press his fingers to the stunner, drop it, get the message up. Time stamp on the message is less than a minute after TOD, but you can't hang a case on that. Time stamp could be off, gauges aren't a hundred percent to-the-minute accurate. It's close enough to hold."

She walked back to the bedroom. "You have to know he'll be alone for two or three hours, so you time it for well after the wife's out. Don't want her doing a: Shit, forgot my whatever, and running back. Then it's up or down the fire escape, depending. Do you know he's a little hard of hearing? Bet you do. You know how he lives, his habits, his basic schedule.

"He's got the game on-screen," Eve added as she envisioned it. "Not too loud, but loud enough. Still, you're quiet as you cross the room, look out, listen."

She went back to the door, walked out. "Stop, check the stunner, make sure his back's to the office door. Step behind him." Eve stopped behind the chair. "Jab the stunner to his throat, deploy. Done. He convulses for a few seconds, then slumps.

"Now, first mistake. You press his thumb and index finger on the stunner, firm, clear, perfect prints. But they wouldn't be if Greenleaf had deployed it. Why weren't his prints on any other part of the weapon? Am I going to buy he wiped it clean before he picked it up to kill himself? No, I'm not. Am I going to buy his fingers wouldn't shake a little when he held it to his own throat? And especially after, when his nervous system went wild? Negative on that, too. His hand didn't sweat or shake, even a little?"

"And there's something else."

She glanced back at Roarke. "Is there?"

"The note, it's too impersonal, too brief and cold, really, when you understand what they were together, meant to each other, how long they'd been together. It speaks of guilt and regret, asks for forgiveness, but says nothing of love, nothing of the children they made or the children who come from that."

"Exactly." Eve fisted her hands on her hips as she paced. "You know, if you don't like being told you think like a cop, you shouldn't analyze evidence like one."

"So noted."

"Whoever left that message had a priority. The guilt—the job Greenleaf did. A cop who took down cops. That's the motive, or the one I see with what I have so far."

"There's little more for you to see tonight—though your body clock's likely telling you it's morning."

"May be why I've got a second wind." And was revved up with it, she realized. "But no, nothing much more to do here tonight but seal it up."

She retrieved her field kit.

"If you drive home, I can write up a brief report for Whitney to see when it actually is morning. I'll send a text to Peabody, have her meet me here. We'll go over the scene again, then I want another round with the neighbor, one with her cohab, after I run them both."

She picked up her field kit. "I want to take a look at the security feed—apartment door, main door."

"You'll use your second wind for all that, then get some sleep."

"That's the plan," she said as they stepped out of the apartment. "I didn't really know him. Didn't much like him, but didn't really know him."

"You'll know him now." In a gesture of understanding and support, he pressed a hand to the small of her back. "Few will know him better than you when you're done. Whatever you learn, you'll stand for him. Webster reached out to you because he knows that."

"The captain did his job as he saw it. I'll do mine."

She sealed the door.

4

She woke before first light, and with only the cat curled against the base of her spine.

"Time," she muttered, then stared at the display that popped on the ceiling.

5:04.

She lay there sincerely wishing the five had been a six, because she was damn well awake. Roarke, she imagined, was fully dressed in one of his gazillionaire suits and heading a meeting with someone somewhere on the other side of the planet, or beyond it.

On the off chance she could think herself back to sleep for an hour, she went over what she had.

Plenty of people going in or out—or out and in—Greenleaf's building in the twelve hours prior to his death. She spotted the neighbor/friend—black, sleeveless dress, sky-high black sandals—heading in just after eighteen hundred. And she'd come out, with Beth Greenleaf, talking, laughing, at twenty-forty-eight.

Webster, carrying the brew, walked to the building entrance at twenty-one-twenty-three. Eight minutes later, MTs rushed to the door. The two uniform cops followed a scant minute after.

That had Webster approaching the main doors five minutes after TOD. The apartment door cam feed showed him arriving, knocking, then finally entering the apartment a full seven—close to eight—minutes after TOD.

Gauges and operator might be off a minute or two—three tops. Not seven.

She could, with absolute objectivity, take Webster off the suspect list.

She'd run the apartment door feed back twenty-four hours from TOD. No activity until Greenleaf left shortly before noon. Then his wife went out around fourteen hundred. He came back about an hour after she left, and she returned about an hour later.

No one came to or out of the apartment door until Elva Arnez arrived at twenty-thirty-seven.

Bedroom window, she thought again. The point of entry, the point of egress.

Since thinking only kept her awake, she rolled out of bed, calling for lights. Galahad rolled, too, but only onto his other side while she went directly for coffee.

She'd had plans for her first morning back, she considered as she drank that first sip of heaven. Catching up on paperwork, reviewing cases opened in her absence, closed in her absence. She'd had a nice vision of easing her way back into work, maybe even pulling out a cold case to dig into if nothing came in hot.

No chance of that now.

After downing the coffee, she headed into the shower.

She ordered the jets on hot and full, and just basked in them while she went over her morning schedule.

Crime scene, re-interview Arnez, interview Robards, her partner. Her run on them the night before hadn't given her any prior connection to Greenleaf, no relations who'd been cops.

Robards had a couple of minor bumps in his teens. Shoplifting, defacing public property (graffiti), assault— charges dropped when witnesses corroborated he'd punched a guy who'd gotten his jollies grabbing a female by the tits and dry-humping her without consent.

Otherwise, their records looked clean. Both were gainfully employed, she as the manager of a downtown boutique, he as a vehicle mechanic.

Still, other than his wife, Elva Arnez was the last person known to see Greenleaf alive.

Except his killer.

Eve stepped out of the shower and into the drying tube. She closed her eyes, let the warm air swirl.

Ready for more coffee, she grabbed a robe. When she stepped out, Roarke stood at the AutoChef—yeah, a gazillionaire's suit—with the cat circling his feet.

"You'll get yours, mate." He glanced over his shoulder.

That face, Eve thought. They'd passed the three-year mark, and that face could still deliver a short-armed jab straight to her heart.

"As will you. I'm thinking waffles would strike a note with you this morning."

"They strike one with me every morning. I woke up at five."

"I wasn't far ahead of you. Here you are now, as it's our first day back." He set a plate of salmon on the floor. "Don't bolt it. I've breakfast, so why don't you see to a pot of coffee."

"Got it."

The cat bolted the first couple bites, then slowed down to savor—if cats savored—when no one snuck up to steal the rest of the salmon.

Eve programmed the coffee while Roarke set the domed plates on the table in the sitting area. Her 'link signaled.

She grabbed it from the table by the bed. "It's Whitney."

"Go on then. I have the coffee."

"Sir," she said as Whitney's wide, dark face filled the 'link screen.

"Lieutenant. This is difficult news."

"Yes, sir."

"I knew Martin Greenleaf thirty years, I suppose. We didn't always agree, but I never doubted his integrity or his dedication. Suicide is sometimes a brutal by-product of the job. From your report, I sense you don't see this as the case."

"I want to reexamine the scene this morning and consult with Morris before making that determination, Commander. But no, sir, I don't see it as the case."

"Lieutenant Webster finding him adds a complication."

"Actually, Commander, I feel that's an advantage. I can clear Webster, as I reviewed the security feed for the main building and the captain's apartment. Webster arrived after TOD, and entered the scene minutes after that. The logs show he made the nine-one-one for the MTs and uniforms barely two minutes after the time stamp shows him entering the apartment. The captain had been dead nearly eight minutes before Webster entered the apartment."

"From the detective's and the department's vantage point, that's a relief. How is it an advantage?"

She'd thought that through as well. Point by point.

"If this is homicide, the killer didn't expect anyone, and assumed the body would go undiscovered for another two or three hours. Webster gave us a jump. Added, the spouse may have compromised the scene if she'd discovered the body. Even a cop's wife would react, might touch or move the body, the weapon. Webster secured it, followed procedure. He didn't contact me personally, but went through Dispatch with a request."

Never taking his eyes off hers, Whitney nodded. "He can't be part of the investigative team."

"No, sir, understood. I've agreed to keep him apprised of developments and would like to use him, as needed, for insight. He's very close to the family, Commander."

"I'll leave that to your judgment. I need to know when you've determined homicide. As I believe you will. We weren't friends, but I knew the man for three decades, and I know he had pride in his record on the job. I don't believe he'd mark that record with suicide."

"I appreciate your insight there, sir. I'll contact you after I've consulted with Morris."

"Good. Welcome back, Lieutenant. Whitney out."

"So the day starts early," Roarke commented.

"Yeah." She set the 'link back down. "At least it starts with waffles."

And bacon, she saw when he removed the domes. And plump berries.

Eve drowned the waffles in butter and syrup.

"I can't say it's murder yet, not even to Whitney. Not until I get Morris's report."

"But it's murder."

"It sure as hell is. A decent plan to set it up as suicide. Decent," she repeated. "Not close to foolproof. But say Webster doesn't find him. The spouse does and, in her understandable shock, she grabs the body, so that's compromised. She kicks the weapon in her rush to get to her husband, or she picks it up. That's compromised."

She could see it, she thought as she ate waffles. She could see just how it had been meant to go down.

"Maybe whoever catches the case doesn't notice the single unlocked window. I'd kick their stupid ass, but maybe. Or maybe Webster arrived before the killer locked it again. Could you lock a window from the outside?"

"Me personally, or anyone?"

Walked into that one, she thought.

"Start with you personally."

"Yes, and I have."

She considered that over a bite of waffle. "How?"

"Depends on the lock and the window, of course. No alarms wired on these, and simple—but sturdy—thumb-style locks. The simplest way, if you want to ghost it, would be a high-powered magnet pressed to the glass at the point of the lock. With finesse you could unlock and relock.

"Unless you're well practiced, it would take some time, some patience, and that considerable finesse."

"Maybe. Maybe." As she ate, she tried to picture it. "More time on the fire escape adds more risk somebody spots you on there. It's dark, but it's barely after nine, and people are out and about. It's a nice night. That's a maybe."

"Another maybe is the widow left it unlocked, simply forgot. You take her at her word she didn't. And I agree. Another investigator might not."

"One or two windows unlocked, that's careless, most likely on the victim or widow's part. A single one unlocked that leads to the fire escape?"

Shaking her head, she ate some bacon.

"That's a rookie mistake. Whoever did this had a decent plan, but isn't a pro. And I don't think a cop."

"You worry about that."

"Sure."

Had to, she knew, when the victim was an IAB captain. Retired or not.

"But a cop would know better than to put just two clear prints on the weapon. And if it's me doing it? I find a way to lock that window from the outside, or I unlock a few more before I leave the scene. An investigator could wonder, justifiably, if the widow's just confused about the locked windows, or if one of them opened a couple to get a breeze, then forgot to lock them up again.

"It's the one that sticks out, the one that wants to say: I'm just a coincidence. And bollocks to that."

Roarke pointed a warning finger at the cat, who'd finished the salmon and hoped for a bacon chaser.

Galahad sat and furiously began to wash.

"Then there's the note," Roarke said.

"And you had that right. It's the wrong tone. And she'd have known—he couldn't have hidden it from her—if he'd been planning to self-terminate. Add now I trust Whitney's judgment, and he says Greenleaf had too much pride in the work he did to end it with a scar like this."

She drank some coffee. "Why does a man who's about to kill himself have the game on-screen? Maybe, you could say maybe, for the comfort, the normality. But I don't buy it.

"Webster tips the scales," she added. "Greenleaf's not going to tell him to come over, shoot the bull awhile if he's going to shove a stunner under his jaw. If you want to try the theory he wanted Webster to find him, then why did he wait until nearly twenty after nine when Webster was coming by about nine? He didn't do it until nearly twenty after nine—that's a half hour after she and the neighbor left."

She shrugged. "Timing's off, and that's a fact. Timing's off because the killer didn't know anyone was coming over."

She got up, walked into her closet, and realized all at once she had to actually think about clothes for the first time in weeks. And to think about it inside a deep, thick forest of clothes.

"Shit. Shit. I'm out of practice."

"It's midsummer." From behind her—quiet as a cat—Roarke laid his hands on her shoulders. "Go for the cool and light. Here, I'll steer you through it until you get back into the swing of it."

He took down pants nearly the same shade of pearly gray as his suit. "A splash of pink in the top would set this off, but I know you better."

"Damn right."

"So white it is, and the linen jacket with the thin line of darker gray leather at the lapels and cuffs. You'll want dark gray boots and belt to pick that up."

"Okay." She took the jacket, noted it already had the magic lining inside. "Is this new?"

He just smiled. "Possibly."

Now she glanced at the label. "Leonardo."

"He does know what you like as well as what suits you. We'll have to go by, see the progress on the house. In three weeks it'll be considerable."

"Okay. We'll make time. I'm going to get an earful on it from Peabody anyway."

They both heard the domes he'd set back on the breakfast plates clang to the floor.

"Bloody hell."

As he marched out to scold the cat, Eve dressed.

When she came out to get her badge and weapon, he'd set the domes back in place. And the cat was nowhere to be seen.

"He tried to play the innocent bystander."

Amused, Eve strapped on her harness. "Okay."

"When I made it clear I knew better, he stalked out, as if insulted by the lack of trust."

"I wonder what your business rivals would think if they knew you argue with your cat."

"I wouldn't call it an argument."

After shrugging into her jacket, she stepped to him, took his gorgeous face in her hands, kissed him. "I've got enough time to set up my murder board. Case board," she corrected, "before I head out."

"Want help with that?" he asked as he walked out with her.

"I've got it, and you must have a solar system to buy."

"That's not scheduled for another twenty minutes."

"In that case, you could generate the ID shots—that includes Webster. I'll take care of the crime scene images."

When they got to her office, he did just that, then got them another round of coffee as she arranged everything to her liking on her board.

"A high-powered magnet," she mused as she worked. "To handle the window lock from the outside."

"It's one way. Low-tech lock," he pointed out. "Low-tech tool."

"Maybe, and if I'm wrong about this being a pro job, or at least someone with solid B and E experience who doesn't mind killing a retired cop."

She stepped back, studied the board. "It sure isn't much for now."

"You'll get more."

"Yeah, I will. And I'm going to go do that."

"My best to Peabody." He drew her in, kissed her forehead, then her lips. "Take care of my cop."

"Affirmative."

He thought of Elizabeth Greenleaf, facing the first day of her life without the love of it. And slipped his hand in his pocket, rubbed the gray button he kept there as he watched the love of his leave.

She drove downtown knowing she'd arrive on scene well ahead of Peabody, but she wanted that solo walk-through. In the quiet, in the light of day.

It felt good to sit behind the wheel, driving on familiar streets, bombarded by familiar sounds. Too early yet for the ad blimps to paste the air with their hype for bargains. But maxibuses farted along on their stops and starts to pick up early shifters, disgorge the night shifters.

Most street LCs would've called it around dawn, but she caught sight of a couple of them, likely aiming for a bagel and schmear and some shoptalk after a long night's work.

Dog walkers herded their charges—all sizes and shapes—and day nannies headed in to herd theirs.

With the windows down she caught the scent of cart coffee and breakfast burritos. Then a block later, the unfortunate stench of a broken recycler.

She heard the metallic clang as shopkeepers rolled open their security doors for the day, and the bouncing beat of bass from another open window.

Rather than hunt for parking, she pulled straight into a loading zone and flipped on her On Duty light.

She studied the building from the sidewalk. The bedroom of the apartment faced the side street and the apartment building across it. No shops or restaurants street level on either building.

She'd send some uniforms to knock on doors on the off chance somebody looked up or over and saw activity on the fire escape.

She walked around to it, looked up.

Easy enough to bring the ladder down to street level, just needed a hook. Since she'd brought one with her for that purpose, she crooked it around the bottom rung.

It rattled down.

Would anyone have noticed the sound? Why would they? She studied the rungs, noted the dust on the handles confirming the sweepers had worked there, too, as requested.

She climbed up.

She'd reached the second floor before someone stuck a head out of a window. The woman of about fifty had angry eyes and a really large kitchen fork.

"What the hell you think you're doing?"

Eve took out her badge.

"Fine. What the hell you think you're doing, Officer?"

"Lieutenant. My job, ma'am. Did you see anyone on this fire escape last night, between eight-thirty and nine-thirty?"

"No. We didn't have a fire, and this is a decent neighborhood. If I'd seen someone sneaking around out here, I'd've given 'em what for and called the cops."

The woman lowered the kitchen fork, but didn't put it down. "Did somebody break in the building?"

"We're working on establishing that. You're directly below apartment 321. Did you hear anything from overhead last night—again, between eight-thirty and nine-thirty?"

"No. That's the Greenleafs. They're quiet, respectful people. And we got a solid building here. You don't hear your neighbors unless they're stomping around or playing music or screen too loud."

Now she put down the fork, leaned out a bit to look up. "They got trouble up there?"

"Yes, ma'am, they do."

"That's too bad."

Eve crouched, saw a bedroom inside, the bed already tidily made. "How did you see me out here?"

"I heard the ladder go down, so I got this." She tapped a finger on the fork. "And I came for a look-see."

"You've got your windows open."

"Getting some air in here."

"Were they open last night?"

"Close them up before we head out to work. I open them when we get up, get some air. Wouldn't have them open at night. It's a good neighborhood, but you don't wanna be stupid, do you? Probably wouldn't've heard the ladder when you say anyhow. We'd've been watching some screen in the living room."

"Okay. Appreciate it."

"Hope it's not bad trouble."

So saying, the woman shut the window, turned the lock.

Eve continued up and now crouched at the Greenleafs' bedroom window, tried to imagine finessing that little thumb lock with a magnet.

Maybe not impossible—certainly not for Roarke—but tricky and tedious. Worth it, would be worth it, if you wanted to stage a murder as a suicide.

She straightened, looked up.

But easier ways.

Find a way to get in a few days before, and bank on no one noticing the unlocked window.

She ran it through as she climbed back down.

Middle of the day, most of the tenants at work. Repair person, delivery person—nobody notices.

A lot of trouble, a lot of damn trouble, which meant the appearance of suicide ranked as important, or nearly, as the killing.

After shoving the ladder back up, she took the hook back to her car.

She mastered in, took the stairs.

Decent soundproofing, she noted when she came out on three. She could hear some muffled voices—a screen turned up too loud—and what struck her as the inevitable wail of a baby, but it sounded as if the baby suffered in some far distant tunnel.

Working-class building, a solid one, people up and getting ready to start their day, or those night shifters grabbing a meal before turning in.

She engaged her recorder, sealed up, then unsealed the door. Inside still smelled of sweepers' dust. The streaming sunlight highlighted thin layers of it, had motes dancing in beams.

Eve went to the bedroom first, set her field kit on the bed before moving to the window.

She'd locked the window to secure it the night before, and unlocked it now. As she remembered, the lock moved smooth, easy, silent.

She looked toward the closet. Beth Greenleaf fussing about shoes and earrings. She hadn't put the rejected pair away, but set them by the closet.

Moving to it, Eve looked at the two-level shoe rack—mostly her shoes—and crouching, picked up what she assumed were the new pair.

No marks on the soles.

Still crouched, holding them, she looked back at the window.

Chat, chat, chat, she imagined.

I don't know why I bought these. Blah blah blah.

Back turned to the window, putting the new shoes down, picking out another pair from the rack.

Eve replaced them, walked back to the window, once again slid her hand under the privacy screen, flipped the lock.

Three seconds, no problem.

Elva Arnez could've done it.

No connection, no motive—so far—but the means. And the means required a partner to do murder.

Yeah, yeah, they'd have a follow-up conversation, and she'd have one with the cohab.

She unlocked the window again, and this time opened it. Silent and smooth like the lock. She climbed out, eased the window down.

Now counting off in her head, she opened it, climbed in, closed it behind her.

Seven seconds. Up to ten if you're slow and careful.

"Then he takes out the stunner, crosses to the door. He

stops, listens." She followed the route herself. "A careful look out. Slip out of the room and you'd see him from here, back to the door, in his chair. Game on-screen, the sound masks any you make. Step up behind him, jab the stunner to his throat, fire. Fast. He convulses, slumps. Get that message on the screen, as close to TOD as possible. Press his fingers to the weapon, drop it.

"Do you check, make sure he's dead? Maybe. Then you go back the way you came. You'd have to linger a few minutes to hear Webster at the door, but if you did—and why would you?—you'd bolt. No time for the magnet trick if you used it to get in. Just get out, get gone."

Still running it in her head, she went out to open the door at Peabody's knock.

"Hey, welcome home—hell of a welcome."

"Yeah."

"First, before we get down to work, was it wonderful?"

"It was wonderful."

And she was pretty sure Peabody had more red streaks in her hair. How did that happen? Why did it happen? But it was nothing to the bright pink jacket.

Eve didn't know whether to be relieved or just tired that her partner had switched her usual pink cowboy boots (her own fault) for pink skids.

"Sorry you didn't get any time to ease into things."

"It's how it goes. A lot harder on Captain Greenleaf."

"Yeah." Peabody's brown eyes shifted to cop mode. "A nice place. Homey, clean, but lived-in. Webster found him?"

"In here." Though she'd put it in her report, Eve ran it through briefly. "It's not going to be suicide. We're not calling it until we talk to Morris, but it's not self-termination."

"He'd have made a lot of enemies."

"Look around. What do you see?"

"A nice place," Peabody repeated as she walked through it. "Really clean. There's sweeper dust and all that, but under it, clean. Seriously tidy. Some pretty things, but no jumble. The office is his space. From the living room setup, I'd say they hang together here, watch the screen. Lots of family photos. Some kids' drawings on the friggie."

She moved into the bedroom, opened the closet. "His clothes are all organized. Hers not as much. It looks like she was shoving through them trying to find something or make up her mind what to wear."

"Did you hear that?"

"What? I didn't hear anything."

"Exactly. I just unlocked the window, but you didn't hear it. Point of entry."

"You think the friend—upstairs neighbor, right—who was here unlocked the window for the killer?"

"She was here. It's worth another look. I ran her and the cohab, and I got nothing. But it's worth another look." She locked the window again. "Roarke says you could use a magnet to finesse the lock from outside the glass."

"Seriously?" Peabody walked over. "Yeah, I can see that now that I think about it. Easy access to the fire escape, from the street, or from above. But why go to all this trouble to make it look like suicide?"

"Another question."

A good question, Eve thought. A cop question.

"I don't have the answer yet, but it's going to matter. You just want him dead? Lots of less complicated ways. But you want it to look like suicide, in his own home, with him taking himself out because of guilt and regret for working in IAB."

She looked back toward the office. "You have to know the wife's going to find him, so maybe you want that, too. It's personal, Peabody. It matters. Still . . . he didn't suffer, died unaware. It's the family left behind who'll suffer. Maybe that matters, too."

She stepped back. "Let's go have a talk with the neighbors. Contact EDD, have them come in for the electronics. We'll come back, go through the scene one more time, but I want to make sure we don't miss the neighbors."

5

Eve resealed the door before they started upstairs.

"I'm just going to say—really fast—we've had a lot of progress on the house while you were gone."

"Yeah, we figured. We're going to get by."

"You've just got to! I finished the water feature. It's wild mag, I mean mag-o-rama. And I won't say any more because I just want you to see."

"We'll get there. Arnez and Robards, two floors up, directly above the Greenleafs. Convenient."

"Yeah, it is. How long have they lived here?"

"Coming up on a year." Eve paused outside the door. No door cam, but solid locks. "And that pushes on the other side. A long time, and they're friendly. But."

She knocked, waited.

Denzel Robards answered. He wore a gray work shirt with his name in a white oval and gray baggies over a slight frame. A mixed-race male just shy of thirty, he limited his facial hair to a precise line of stubble running along his jawline up to the lobes of his ears. His eyes, a pale green, looked tired.

Eve held up her badge. "Mr. Robards, Lieutenant Dallas and Detective Peabody, NYPSD. We'd like to come in and speak to you and Ms. Arnez."

"She's, ah, getting dressed. We didn't sleep much last night. You're here about Martin. God." He rubbed his tired eyes. "Yeah, come in. I'll get her. Ah, you can sit down if you want."

He shut the door, walked back to the bedroom.

Same floor plan, Eve noted, as the one below.

Not as neat and clean and lacking, from what she could see, the personal touches of family photos. More contemporary furnishings, more neutral colors.

A jumbo wall screen, a quiet gray gel sofa placed to enjoy it, a couple of scoop chairs. A table—darker gray—near the kitchen with a shiny white vase of fresh flowers centered on it.

She'd just angled herself to get an eyeline on the second bedroom—an office setup, workstation facing the door—when the bedroom door opened.

Arnez's eyes looked tired, too, and a little damp with it, though she'd done her best to disguise the fatigue with facial enhancements.

She wore a navy dress today, belted, slit pockets, and navy heels with a white toe cap. She'd twisted her hair up to show off silver triangles that dangled from her ears.

Work mode, Eve concluded. High-end boutique manager mode.

"Lieutenant Dallas."

"I'm sorry to disturb you so early. This is my partner, Detective Peabody."

"I'm going to make you some tea, baby." Robards ran a hand up and down her back. "You sit down now, and I'll bring you some tea. We've got coffee if you want it. Elva doesn't drink it." He tried for a smile that didn't quite make it. "I don't know how she gets out of bed in the mornings."

"We're fine, thanks."

"You sit down now," he repeated, and nudged Elva onto the sofa, stroked her cheek. "Be right back."

She gave his hand a squeeze, nodded. "Please sit down. I can't stop thinking about Martin, about Beth, their family. I've gone over and over that few minutes I saw him before we left, and it was all so . . . ordinary. So usual. I can't believe this happened."

"You'd become very friendly with the Greenleafs?"

"Yes. Well, with Beth especially. She's so funny, and she's so sweet. She and Darlie came into the shop I manage right before Denzel and I moved into the building. We just hit it off, then I realized we were moving in right upstairs.

"She brought us cookies when we did." She blinked as tears swirled. "And we'd see each other in the lobby sometimes, or around the neighborhood. Then she invited us down for a Sunday brunch."

She smiled as Robards came back with her tea. "Denzel wanted to make an excuse."

"I didn't want to get all friendly, you know?" He shrugged, sat beside Arnez. "Didn't see getting all tight with a couple of old people." Now he winced. "Sorry, that sounds wrong."

"He went for me." She patted his hand. "And it was nice, wasn't it?"

"Yeah, it was. They're nice. I found out he'd been a cop. I never figured on getting friendly with a cop, even a retired one. Um, no offense."

"None taken," Eve assured him.

"But Martin, he was okay. And he did some gaming. I like gaming to relax, and he was up on all that because of his grandkids."

Elva dabbed at her eyes. "He beat you sometimes."

"Well, not often. But yeah, sometimes."

"You were home last night when Ms. Arnez and Ms. Greenleaf went out?"

"Yeah, I kicked back, watched some screen. A bang-and-boom vid—Elva's not big on those, so I had my chance.

Popped some corn, had a brew. And when she comes back, she's crying and telling me Martin's dead, and there's police, and she doesn't know what to do."

He put an arm around her, pressed a kiss to her hair.

"Did you see or talk to anyone while she was out?"

"No, just a solo hang for me. Put in a long one at the shop." He lifted Arnez's hand, pressed his lips to it. "Just wanted to stretch out and wind it down with a vid. Why?"

"It's just routine."

"Yeah, but . . . Elva said you never said what happened. How Martin died, and with all the cops, and the questions . . . We thought maybe he had like a stroke or a heart attack or something and couldn't get help, but . . ."

"An unattended death requires procedures." Eve decided to push the next button and see. "At this time we need to determine if his death was a result of foul play or self-termination."

"You think someone . . ." Arnez groped for Robards's hand. "Or he—he *killed* himself? Why? Why would he— Oh, this just makes it worse somehow, worse for Beth."

Peabody picked up the ball. "Do either of you have any reason to believe he would take his own life? Did you notice any change of mood, any signs of depression?"

"No." After the briefest hesitation, Arnez repeated, "No. I didn't really pay much attention last night, then I went in with Beth, and we left. But he seemed fine. He seemed like himself to me. Denzel?"

Robards shifted, drew Arnez closer. "Well, I mean, he'd go nostalgia time some on the old days. Sometimes when we were gaming he'd talk about going after the bad guys. And he said like it wore you down some when the bad guys you went after were other cops. But he was retired and everything."

"If someone broke in—but they have a door cam," Arnez

said. "And Martin always said the building had good security. And he *was* a cop. He knew how to defend himself. Are you sure it wasn't just—what do you call it—natural causes? I know he wasn't that old, but it happens."

"It wasn't natural causes." Eve changed tack. "Did you notice anything unusual when you were in the bedroom with Ms. Greenleaf?"

"In the bedroom? No. Beth had some things scattered around like she does when she's making up her mind, which means she has to put it all away again. She's a little obsessive about that. Everything looked just the way it does."

"Okay, thank you for your time."

As Eve rose, Arnez and Robards got to their feet.

"Can you tell me if I can—or should—contact Beth? I know she has family," Arnez added. "A close family. Martin was head of a lovely family, and we've gotten to know them. I don't want to intrude or anything, but I want her to know we're thinking of her. And if there's anything we can do."

"I'm sure she'd appreciate a text," Peabody told her. "That way she can answer it when she feels able to."

"Okay. I'll do that. I hope . . . Honestly, I don't know what I hope."

"If you think of anything, any small detail, contact me." Eve walked to the door, stopped. "I notice you have some windows open."

"When we're home, yeah." Robards moved to the door to open it. "Utilities aren't included in the rent, so we save where we can."

"Thanks again." Eve walked out, heading to the stairs with Peabody. "Just wanted to put the window deal in their heads. Impressions?"

"First, they seem good together. A good rhythm between them. And their reactions, questions, statements seemed genuine."

"They seem good together," Eve agreed as she unsealed the door on three. "Add he takes care of her—he's a protector. Their reactions, questions, statements seemed genuine. Right down the line," she added, and went inside. "Almost like they'd practiced."

"You're really looking at them? The window—I get that. She had the means and opportunity to unlock it. But why? What's the motive?"

"I'm looking at them because right now and, until we dig deeper, they're the only ones to look at. The motive, when we find it, and whoever we find, is going to be personal. So." She picked up her field kit. "Let's start digging."

They found keys to a safe-deposit box from a local bank and arranged for a warrant to access. Memo books for each of them containing the names and contacts for various doctors, dentists, lawyers, a financial planner, the building landlord, and others.

Greenleaf had an appointment for a hearing check the following week. She had an eye check the day after.

They'd both noted down their upcoming anniversary.

Eve found three herbal cigarettes carefully tucked away in a case inside one of Beth's handbags.

OTC meds, vitamins, two first aid kits—one in the kitchen, one in the bathroom. Heating pads, ice bags, a small, curated coin collection.

Plenty of the bits and pieces of daily life, of long lives in one place, and nothing relevant to murder.

"If he kept a threat file here, past or present, it'll be somewhere on his comp. EDD will find it. Let's leave that to them. I want to talk to Morris, and we need to get into that box when the bank opens."

"It'll be open now."

Eve glanced at her wrist unit as they packed it up. "Shit. I have Webster coming in. You take the bank, I'll take

Morris. Meet me at Central. Book a conference room. Better than my office for Webster's interview, and I don't want to put him in a box."

"It really is a nice place." Peabody took another look around. "And you can feel as much as see a lot of nice memories. You know what you don't feel?"

"What's that?"

"Much cop. Maybe it's just some Free-Ager vibe, but I don't feel much cop. More like he really left the job behind when he turned in his papers."

"I'm no Free-Ager, and I got the same sense—refusing to call it vibe. It jibes with Webster's statement." Eve resealed the door. "He said Greenleaf would come by, kept in touch with him and other cops he'd worked with, but he wasn't one of those can't-let-it-go types."

"How many years did he have on the job?"

"Forty-five," Eve said as they started down. "All but the first twenty in IAB."

"You'd make a lot of enemies, cop enemies, in a quarter of a century on the rat squad. Cops who'd know how to set up murder to look like suicide."

"Yeah, you would. And if that's the case, they should've done a better job of it."

They parted ways on the street, and Eve drove to the morgue.

Her bootsteps echoed in the white tunnel, and the air smelled of chemical lemons with a death undertone.

She could never decide if the fake lemon made it worse.

When she pushed through Morris's doors, he stood, his clear protective cape over a somber black suit paired with a black shirt and tie.

He'd coiled a long braid into a tight circle at the base of his neck.

At first she worried the grief over the woman he'd loved

had rolled back on him, then she realized he wore the black out of respect for Greenleaf.

Music played low, something that struck her as between tribal and military, as he closed the Y-cut with precise stitches.

"Closing him up?"

"Yes. I came in early. I didn't want him to wait too long."

"Did you know him?"

"We only met once, in here. One of the officers he'd investigated and was subsequently dismissed, as well as facing charges of felony assault—multiple counts—extortion, witness intimidation, opted for self-termination rather than prison."

"When was this?"

"Six, maybe seven years ago as I recall. I believe the captain retired a couple years thereafter."

"Do you remember the dead cop's name?"

"I don't, but I can find it for you."

"I'll find it. Tell me about Greenleaf."

"He took care of himself, and would likely have enjoyed a few more decades. Good muscle tone for a man in his seventies. A strong heart and lungs, no disease in his organs. No sign of deterioration in the brain, none of drug or alcohol abuse."

Stitching complete, Morris stepped over, washed his hands, then pulled tubes of Pepsi for both of them out of his cold box.

"A recent dental implant replacement, lower left molar—I'd say within the last four weeks. He's had four. A bit of arthritis in the left hip and the left knee that may have troubled him on occasion, but nowhere near the time for replacements. Normal wear and tear, Dallas. A healthy man."

"No marks but the stunner's?"

"A slight, healing bruise on the left buttocks." Morris

called the view up on-screen. "It's neither an offensive or defensive wound. He bumped his ass a couple of days ago. Older skin, thinner skin. And you bruise more easily."

"Okay. Tell me about the stunner marks."

He got them both microgoggles.

"Direct contact, on highest level. You can see it's not directly on the carotid, but close enough to do the job."

"Yeah, I noticed that when I examined the body on scene."

"And I assume you also noticed the force of the contact lacerated the skin slightly. Thin skin, as I said, but to actually scrape as well as burn?"

"Jammed it there. Hard. Unnecessary, as the direct contact alone would send the nervous system into overdrive, then shut it all down. He'd know that."

"He would, of course. It's possible the forceful contact came from emotion. However."

"I've been waiting for the however."

"Which I assume you also concluded, on scene."

"Not concluded. Wondered."

"If you wondered how the burn marks are so deep and distinct, you wondered well."

He brought the marks on-screen, zoomed in close.

"If the captain had held the stunner to his own throat, they wouldn't be so distinct. Couldn't. The instant the stunner is fired, the body would convulse—most particularly with direct contact. His hand simply couldn't hold anything, much less continue to press a weapon to the point of contact and firmly, for, by my calculations, between five and six seconds."

"It's homicide."

"As you already concluded, but I can confirm. It's unquestionably homicide. Captain Greenleaf didn't take his own life. Someone ended it."

"He had a glass of something on his desk."

"Tea, herbal."

"The lab's running tox?"

"Yes."

"Good. I want everything covered, right down the line." She cracked the tube as she paced. "The stunner was police issue, but not one of the newer models. There are ways to get them. I want the lab to date it, get me as much on it as possible. It wasn't Greenleaf's. He turned his in when he retired. That's confirmed. No serial number on it, filed off. The serial number would be recorded, when and if it was issued, and to whom, when it was turned in, reassigned.

"Fucking window."

"Sorry?"

"He kept the windows locked. It was a thing. One window unlocked last night, bedroom window. Direct access to a fire escape."

"Ah." Morris's lips curved. "A clue."

"Yeah, a freaking clue." She turned back. "He only came into the morgue that one time?"

"Actually, no. I only met him that once, but I was curious enough to check at the time. He'd been logged in three or four times before, as I recall. It could be more."

"Okay, I'll check on that. Appreciate the fast work."

"For him." Morris looked down at the body again. "I remember him coming in, specifically, because there was grief in his eyes. The man on the slab had disgraced the badge, but there was grief in Greenleaf's eyes."

She filed that away. She needed to get into Central, deal with Webster, report to Whitney.

And maybe something in the bank box would reveal another freaking clue.

Ad blimps blasted now, so Eve tuned them out. She went over everything she had as she drove to Central. She wanted to write it down, get her murder book started, her murder board up.

But Webster came first.

She pulled into the garage and managed to take the elevator all the way up. She'd missed change of shift—always a plus—and the cops and techs and perps and vics who piled on mostly piled off again quickly enough to leave her air.

She walked into Homicide, and was immediately assaulted by Jenkinson's tie.

Though she'd suffer the torture of the damned before she admitted it, it felt like home.

A home for the terminally insane, maybe, with pink elephants cavorting over a grass-green field, but home nonetheless.

"Hey, boss, welcome back."

She took the sunglasses she'd somehow hung on to and put them on for form.

Jenkinson just showed his teeth in a mile-wide grin.

"Hey, LT."

Since Santiago wore his cowboy hat, he'd obviously lost another bet with Carmichael.

She let the welcomes run their course.

"Baxter, Trueheart?"

"Caught one," Jenkinson told her. "Window diver on Avenue C." He slapped his hands together to indicate *splat*.

"Detective Webster's due in. Send him to—crap—Peabody booked a conference room."

"You got One."

"Send him there, and let me know."

"Heard about Greenleaf. Didn't strike as the kind to take himself out."

"He didn't," Eve said as she walked to her office.

Coffee first, she thought, then stepped in.

A big black balloon floated over her desk. Instead of a

smiley face, this one had exes for eyes and what looked like a dribble of blood out of the corner of the down-turned line for its mouth.

It read:

BAD GUYS BEWARE!

DALLAS IS BACK IN TOWN.

She shook her head and let the balloon float while she programmed coffee.

"Yeah, be-fucking-ware."

She sat to write up a brief update for Whitney, confirming homicide. As she sent it, she heard Peabody's familiar clump. Wearing skids, she thought, and still manages to clump.

She stepped in carrying a small evidence box.

"Contents of the bank box." And she grinned up at the balloon.

"Whose idea?" Eve asked.

"I guess the general idea was sort of mine, but it was a group effort, which included debate on the image and the wording."

"I like it."

She bounced on her toes. "I *knew* you would."

"Contents."

"Hard and disc copies of both their wills to start." She set the box down. "I skimmed through, and it's pretty standard. A few specifics left to kids and grandkids—more like mementos—and the rest to surviving spouse. In the event they go together, split in equal shares among the kids."

She took them out, laid them on Eve's desk.

"There's two thousand in cash, a wedding ring set—I think her mother's, because in the will the maternal grandmother's wedding ring set is bequeathed to their daughter.

Insurance policies. They each had a quarter-million life insurance policy, money goes to surviving spouse or divided among the kids.

"A really cool old pocket watch—that would be his great-great-grandfather's—goes to oldest son. Their passports, his badge. He kept his badge in here with important papers. And that's it."

"Okay, put everything back in, seal it before we go to the conference room."

"Webster walked in with me. I sent him down there."

"Good. Let's get going on this. I want to give Whitney a full oral report once we're through with Webster. Morris confirmed homicide."

"Not surprised."

"When I'm with Whitney, access the victim's files. We want a list of cops he investigated. Separated into resulting in discipline, in demotion, in dismissal. Any who were charged, any prosecuted, any incarcerated as a result. And from those, any who self-terminated thereafter, were killed or died under any circumstances."

"Let me lead with holy shit. That's going to take awhile."

"Ask Feeney for e-geek assistance. Pull in a tech-savvy uniform if needed."

She paused outside the conference room door. "The investigation may lead us to motives outside Greenleaf's work in IAB. If so, we follow that. Right now, we follow this."

Inside, Webster sat at the conference table, staring into a cup of coffee.

He'd changed into a suit, but it didn't disguise the fatigue or pallor that comes from a sleepless night.

"I'm sorry about Captain Greenleaf, Webster," Peabody began.

"Yeah. His family's just shattered. We finally convinced Beth to take a sleeping pill about four this morning."

Eve took a seat. "You stayed there last night? At the daughter's?"

He nodded. "Until a couple hours ago. I'll go back today. I want to be able to tell them whatever I can."

"You can start by informing them the captain's death has been officially designated as homicide."

He nodded again. "It had to be. There was no other way. I've gone over it and over it. I had to just miss whoever did this. Just miss them. It had to be that bedroom window. Unless you found something on the door cam. Did—"

"Detective Peabody's going to take your statement," Eve interrupted.

"I am?"

"Yes. Record on. Dallas, Lieutenant Eve; Peabody, Detective Delia, conducting witness interview with Webster, Lieutenant Donald, in the matter of Captain Martin Greenleaf's homicide. Detective Peabody will lead the interview."

"Ah. Lieutenant, you worked under Captain Greenleaf in the Internal Affairs Bureau."

"Yes, he was my captain when I transferred into IAB. I served under him for nearly six years until his retirement."

"You also had a personal relationship with him."

"I did. You could say he took me under his wing, personally and professionally. The Greenleaf family became my surrogate family. Martin was a father to me."

"In your statement to Lieutenant Dallas last night, you said you saw Captain Greenleaf yesterday, early afternoon, in your office in IAB."

"Yes."

"And at that time, you and he made arrangements for you to go to his residence that evening. At nine."

"That's correct."

"Would you detail your movements and actions from the

time you saw Captain Greenleaf in IAB until you discovered his body in his residence?"

Again, Webster stared into his coffee. Then he pushed it aside.

"I had a backlog of paperwork and some case reviews to handle," he began.

Eve listened as he went step-by-step. He'd had time to think, time to calm, she noted. And he had a few more details today, but his basic story remained the same.

And solid.

"What did you do when you found Captain Greenleaf deceased at his workstation in his residence?"

"I put my hand on his shoulder. He was still warm. I saw the stunner on the floor, read the message on the screen."

"Did you attempt to move him, to resuscitate him?"

"He was gone. I knew it was a setup. I knew him and I knew that instantly. I stepped back to preserve the integrity of the scene, and called it in. I requested medical assistance and uniforms. Then I sent a request to Lieutenant Dallas, through Dispatch, to come to the scene because I wanted Martin to have the best I knew.

"When the MTs arrived, I showed them my ID, informed them Martin was deceased. I told them to confirm same without disturbing the scene or the body, which they did. The uniforms arrived while the MTs did so. I identified myself again, ordered one to secure the apartment, wait outside the door for Lieutenant Dallas, and the other to remain with me and the captain to keep the scene secure."

After rubbing a hand over his narrow face, he took a long breath. "I disturbed nothing. After I found him, I touched nothing but the doorknob to admit the MTs, the uniforms. When I entered prior, I touched the door, both sides. I set the beer I'd brought on the table just inside, and may have touched that. I honestly don't know. I may have touched the doorjamb to his office, but I don't believe so. I touched his shoulder. Nothing else."

He paused, looked at Eve.

"It was as important as it's ever been since I picked up the badge to maintain the integrity of a crime scene."

It would have been, she thought. She didn't question that.

"Between the time you saw Captain Greenleaf at IAB and found him in his residence," Peabody continued, "did you speak to anyone about your plans to go to his apartment that night?"

"Detective Dennison also worked Sunday and worked late, and he asked if I wanted to go grab some dinner. I told him I was going to hang with the captain, and that's when I noticed the time. I closed down, and Dennison and I walked out together. About eight-thirty."

"Did you mention Captain Greenleaf would be alone in his apartment?"

"No, just that I was going over there. Dennison and I walked down the block, then I walked the rest of the way to my apartment to change. I ran late because I got lost in the work, then wanted to change out of the suit. I picked up some beer on my way to the captain's place. Dallas established TOD about the time I was walking in."

"Actually, TOD was five minutes prior to you entering the apartment building," Eve put in.

He gave her a look drenched in sorrow. "Either way, I was late."

"Lieutenant." Peabody pulled his attention back. "At any time that day at IAB, or previously, did Captain Greenleaf express any concerns to you regarding threats?"

"Not yesterday, no. He gave no indication whatsoever he had any concerns. And not since his retirement. He discussed threats with me and others in IAB when threats were made."

"Are threats documented?"

"If reported, any and all threats are documented and filed. I informed Captain Skylar this morning of Captain Greenleaf's death and requested he share those records with Lieutenant Dallas."

"Again, we're sorry for your loss. Your cooperation and information are very helpful."

"One more thing, for the record," Eve said. "You've had opportunities to observe, in a very personal way, the relationship between Captain Greenleaf and his spouse, Elizabeth. How would you describe it?"

"Rock solid. A marriage built on love and the love of family. Mutual respect."

He let out another breath. "They laughed at each other's jokes. Enjoyed each other, took care of each other. Anyone thinking about marriage would look at theirs and hope to build something as solid and lasting."

"Okay. Interview end. Record off. That's all we need for now," Eve told him.

"What did Morris find?"

"I need to write a detailed report."

"Dallas. Please."

She'd hoped to give it to him in writing. Have that small distance.

But he deserved to know.

"What I found, what the head sweeper found, but now confirmed by the chief medical examiner. First, Greenleaf's prints on the weapon are too firm and distinct. And there are only the two, which would mean a seasoned cop about to self-terminate only picked up the weapon once, and didn't check the power level—his prints weren't on the power mechanism, which didn't hold for me. More telling, the stunner marks on his neck. These are also too deep, too clear, and the ME determined for that level of burn, the slight laceration from the probes, the stunner would need to be jammed firmly in the area of the carotid, and held there for several seconds."

"Not possible."

"No, not possible. The position of the weapon on the floor struck me wrong. You get stunned, you flail. It's more likely the weapon would have landed farther away. If his fingers simply gave way, more likely it would have landed in his lap, or maybe bounced off the arm of the chair. But if his fingers just gave way, he couldn't hold the stunner to the killing point for several seconds."

"This is why I wanted you. Why I reached out for you. I didn't consider the position of the weapon."

"Roarke noticed something else. The note. It didn't read like the last words from a man to a woman he'd loved, lived with for decades. He didn't say he loved her, didn't mention the family they'd made."

"I missed that, too," Webster murmured. "I missed that."

"Because you're too close, and that's why you're not part of the investigation. We'll keep you in the loop."

6

He rose when Eve did.

"Can you give me something? Just drone work, just grunt shit. Anything."

"If your captain hasn't sent those copies, you could give him a push on it."

"I will." He walked out with Eve and Peabody.

"We're going to have to interview the family. They're among those who'd know about the windows, who'd have easy access to the bedroom."

"Ah Jesus." He shoved at his hair. "You'll clear them, but you need to talk to them. I'll smooth the ground there."

"Do you know the women Ms. Greenleaf was out with last night?"

"I've met two of them—three now, counting the one from last night. Yeah, I can smooth that ground, too."

"You hadn't met either of the upstairs neighbors before last night?"

She held up a hand before he answered, as she heard shouting from her bullpen.

She quickened her pace, turned inside.

Jenkinson stood, feet planted, arms folded, while a

man—another cop, Eve thought, with the cheap suit, hard-shined shoes—shouted in his face.

Still another cop had a hand on the shouter's arm, trying to pull him back.

Reineke stood on one side of his partner, Santiago and Carmichael on the other. Half the uniforms stood outside their cubes in the back, and the rest watched.

"You think I'm going to take any bullshit from you?"

Jenkinson, way too calm to Eve's mind, edged just an inch closer. "I think you're going to fucking stand down before I stand you down."

"You threatening me?" Now the shouter poked a finger in Jenkinson's chest.

"There it fucking is."

Eve caught the grin on Jenkinson's face before she pushed in.

"Hold it." She held a hand up toward Jenkinson. "You hold it. What the hell's going on?"

"Jesus, Lansing, what the fuck?"

When Webster spoke, Eve shot him a look. "You know this asshole?"

Lansing spun to her. "We're going to have a talk, you and me, right here, right now. I know who you think you are and, I'm telling you, if you think you're going to cover up the death of a good man with some bullshit excuse for an investigation, I'll bury you."

"Lansing, back off. For God's sake, back off." His companion pulled at his arm again, and this time got an elbow in the gut.

"You think being Whitney's pet poodle and some rich man's toy makes you invulnerable? I'm going to dig up everything there is to dig up on you, you bitch, then shove you in the hole and smother you with it."

She sized him up as he ranted.

Dark blond hair, heavy-lidded brown eyes, compact build. And out of control.

"What's his rank, Webster?"

"Goddamn it." Webster shoved at his hair. "Detective."

"Just want to get that straight. It sounds like you're going to be busy, Detective, so you'd better get started. Right now, you're going to cease any and all physical contact with my detective, and get the hell out of my bullpen."

"I don't take orders from you." And shoved her.

Eve had to slap her own hand against Jenkinson's chest to stop him—and nearly didn't.

"He fucking laid his fucking hands on you, LT. That fucker fucking laid fucking hands on you in front of my fucking face."

Lansing rolled his shoulders and sneered. "You think you can do something about it, old man?"

"Other than break you into pieces and pick his teeth with your bones after?" Eve kept her hand firm on Jenkinson's chest. "Not much. Me? I'm meaner, and while beating the crap out of you to the entertainment of my bullpen would be a highlight of my day—"

"Let's try it, bitch."

"Jesus Christ, Lansing. Webster, I couldn't stop him."

Webster shook his head at the second cop. "Let her handle it."

"Oh, so satisfying," Eve said, and smiled into Lansing's furious, red-streaked face. "But meaner. As you've shown you have no respect for a superior officer, for your badge, and have chosen to defile Captain Greenleaf's name by your stunningly stupid behavior—"

"Don't you say his name. Don't you let his name come out of your fucking mouth or I'll put your teeth down your throat."

"As my recorder's been engaged since I walked in, I've

documented your stunningly stupid behavior, your assault on a fellow officer, and another on a superior officer, I will make it a mission to see appropriate disciplinary action's taken. If you want to keep your badge after that disciplinary action's taken, you'll get the hell out now."

"Fuck you."

"Your choice."

He put a hand on the butt of his weapon. Eve actually felt the dozen cops behind her do the same.

Jesus Christ.

"Stand down, Detective." Eve said it quietly. "You need to stand down now."

"I said fuck you. You think you're going to screw over Captain Greenleaf, you're the one who's going to get screwed over. You and every half-assed excuse for a cop in your division. You're all going down because I'm taking you down.

"What the fuck are you going to do about it?"

When he fisted his free hand, Eve thought:

Yeah, shit. There it fucking is.

"Stand down, Detective!"

Whitney surged in. Eve wasn't sure she'd ever seen that much cold fury on his face before.

"Commander, I'm going to file formal charges for corruption and dereliction of duty against Lieutenant Dallas for her negligence in Captain Greenleaf's death. As well as—"

"My office, Detective Lansing. Wait in chairs in my admin area until I come."

"Commander—"

"I gave you an order, Detective. I won't repeat it."

"She's a disgrace to the department, and you know it. You've always known it." Lansing stormed out.

"I apologize, Commander," Dennison began. "Lieutenant, everyone. He just lost it when the captain informed us about Captain Greenleaf's death, and that Lieutenant Dallas was primary and had yet to determine if it was self-termination or homicide. I tried to calm him down, came after him, tried to stop him."

"Lieutenant?"

"This detective attempted to stop Lansing, and got an elbow in the gut for his efforts. This detective made no threats or accusations, sir."

"Dennison, go back to IAB and tell your captain to report to my office."

"Yes, sir. Webster . . ." Shaking his head, Dennison walked out.

"Lieutenant, sum it up briefly."

"I have it on record, Commander. I engaged my recorder when I heard the raised voices and stepped into the bullpen."

"Good. Your office."

"Party's over," Eve said as she turned. "Go be cops."

"I assume I'm going to need coffee."

"Take the desk chair, sir. I'll get the coffee and set the recording on-screen."

He settled into the chair, let out a long, long sigh. "Did he threaten you physically?"

"Yes, sir, he did."

Whitney nodded, took the coffee she offered. "One question before I review the record. How did you stop Jenkinson from laying him out?"

"It wasn't easy. On-screen."

Whitney watched without comment, and Eve drank coffee. It didn't do a thing for the banging in her head or the burn in her gut.

"'Pet poodle,'" Whitney murmured. "*Rottweiler* might work better. Hit me again," he said, and passed her his empty mug. "He assaulted Dennison, Jenkinson, and you, on record. He made threats to physically harm fellow officers, made baseless accusations, and threatened to use his position in

IAB to go after you for personal reasons, was insubordinate, violent, abusive, and out of control.

"He's done."

"Sir—"

Whitney waved that away. "He's been disciplined before, Dallas, for insubordination. He's been involved in altercations that weren't on record and got mired in he said / he or she or they said. There are often complaints about IAB, but he has more than his share. He's done."

Whitney rose. "Send me a copy of the recording and file a detailed report on same."

"Yes, sir."

"Would you have done so if I hadn't walked in on it?"

"Yes, sir. He's out of control."

"Agreed. One more question. How did you manage to keep your own control?"

Now she sighed. "It was harder not to take a shot at him than stopping Jenkinson from taking one. But if I had, the entire bullpen might have taken one. They don't deserve that on their record."

"Agreed again. Now, before I go deal with this, the reason I happened to walk in at that particular moment. Jenkinson's results from his DS exam. I wanted to inform his lieutenant in person."

"Yes, sir. He passed. No way he wouldn't."

"And yet another agreement. Will you call him in to tell him privately?"

"Permission to speak frankly, Commander."

"Granted."

"No fucking way. This division's a team."

They proved it every day. Hell, she thought, they just had.

"Would you like to inform him, sir?"

"This is for you. But I'd like to be there. By the way," he said as they walked out, "interesting balloon."

"Bullpen humor."

"Yours doesn't lack for it."

She approached Jenkinson's desk, looked at his mutinous face, his insane tie. "Jenkinson."

"I said what I said to that fucker, and I'd say it again if I get the chance. We stand up for each other in here, and we stand for our lieutenant."

"Do you think I couldn't take that fucker?"

"I think you'd have kicked his ass, then wiped the floor with what was left of it. That doesn't mean I don't regret some you didn't let me do it first." He shrugged. "I've gotta stand by that, Commander."

"So noted and understood."

"I appreciate the backup," Eve said to the room at large. Then she held out a hand to Jenkinson. "I appreciate the sentiment and the backup, Detective Sergeant Jenkinson."

At his desk, Reineke, the only one Jenkinson had told about the possible promotion, shot both fists in the air, and shouted, "Yes!"

"No shit?" Jenkinson murmured. "Son of a gun."

He got backslaps, arm punches, congratulations as Whitney held out a hand. "Congratulations, Detective Sergeant. Well earned."

"Thank you, sir. Jesus, guys, give a DS some room. I wouldn't've taken the exam if you hadn't talked me into it, boss. I appreciate the backup."

"Anytime, anywhere. Five minutes to act like lunatics." She raised her voice over the din. "Five. Then back to the work the city pays you to do. Peabody, get me those names."

In her office, she created her board and book.

It was irritating to have to take out time to write up the report on Lansing, but it had to be done.

She opened the evidence box, took a careful look at

Greenleaf's will, the insurance papers. She wondered if Webster knew Greenleaf had left him his badge.

She resealed the box before getting more coffee, then dug into the Greenleafs' financials.

If a motive connected to money, she knew well people killed for a cheap wrist unit and pocket change. The Greenleafs had more than that. They'd lived within their means, saved, invested a little. She found they'd had college funds for their children, and had started the same for their grandchildren.

No gambling, no out-of-line expenses. The biggest hit in twelve months, a beach house one-week rental on the Jersey Shore slated for mid-August.

Family, she thought again. The foundation of their lives, and the core.

When her 'link signaled, she read a text from Webster.

> I'm sorry about Lansing. He's always had a hair
> trigger, but it's worse since his wife left him a
> couple years ago. No excuse. Wanted you
> to know we're going in to see Martin in a few
> minutes. If I can tag you when we have, that
> would be a good time for you to talk to the family.

She answered with a simple:

> Tag me when they're ready.

Then, because she could neither eliminate them as suspects nor upgrade them, she started deeper dives on Arnez and Robards.

Denzel Robards, born in Queens, single mother, two younger siblings—both female. Minor bumps, juvenile, then the dropped assault charges. Graduated from high school and did two years in a trade school to receive certification in vehicle mechanics.

Employed at Kenner's Auto Repair and Body Shop, Queens, nearly thirteen years. Part-time through high school. Last five years as head mechanic, solid salary.

And still, Eve thought, a long daily commute since he moved to Lower West Manhattan. He'd boosted his certifications every two or three years. He carried them for commercial vehicles, heavy equipment, motorcycles.

With that experience and training, she imagined he could land a job as head mechanic pretty much anywhere.

She made a note. *Loyalty.* And circled it.

As she dug she found he used part of that solid salary to buy what they termed classic cars, then rebuilt and restored them, sold them.

He pulled in an impressive income there.

And it appeared he used part of that to add to his mother's income as shift manager and head server at an eatery in Queens. He'd also contributed to the cost of tuition for both his sisters, and helped pay for the elder sister's wedding two years prior.

She made a second note. *Family.*

His finances looked clear—biggest expenses, the old cars and the parts needed to restore them. But he made a good profit on those investments, at least to her eye.

She didn't have to make a note to remember to have Roarke dig yet deeper into those finances and transactions.

No marriages, one cohab when he was twenty-four—with Diane Zed. Lasted eleven months.

No criminal bumps since the dropped assault charges.

More, she had to admit, no connection to be found with Greenleaf. No indication they'd met before Robards and Arnez moved into the building.

And no choice but to bump him down on the suspect list.

But she gave Arnez another push.

Born in Brooklyn Heights, only child, parents divorced when she was nine. Father relocated to Colorado, where he remarried, had one offspring, divorced, then relocated to Alaska.

Mother relocated, taking Arnez, to the Lower West, got a job as a secretary in a law firm—tax and estate law primarily. Went back to school—night school—worked her way to paralegal.

No second marriage there, but a ten-year cohab. Relocated with same to Atlanta.

Arnez graduated NYU business college—primarily remote option. Employed as sales clerk—part-time at Fashionista, eighteen months, high school years. Part-time at Gloria's—later high school years. Part-time at In Style, college years. Part-time at Be Bougie, assistant manager, twenty months, more college years. Full-time at La La, assistant manager, twenty-three months. Full-time, co-manager, Opulence, sixteen months. And since, manager, Très Belle.

Stepping stones, Eve judged, moving up, steady salary increases with every step, and classier, higher-end shops along with it.

So ambitious, smart, practical. Couldn't fault any of that.

No marriages for Arnez, no cohabs on record until Robards.

No criminal.

Her biggest expenses, by far, wardrobe.

Add a trip to Paris shortly after college. Not a great deal of travel since. Jersey Shore, the Hamptons, what she took to be a winter vacation in Mexico.

Nothing out of line with her income and lifestyle.

No connection that showed to Greenleaf prior to moving into the building with Robards.

That left, again, means and opportunity, but no motive.

She'd have Roarke check the finances, but Arnez bumped down on the list.

Time to change her focus.

She hit the interoffice. "Peabody, send me whatever you have so far on the dead/incarcerated cop list connected to Greenleaf."

"Can do. I haven't gotten very far, but I'll tag up McNab, have him send you his. I'm working on altogether dead. He's on incarcerated."

"That'll do."

While she waited, she got more coffee, sat to study her board.

She had to clear the other women Beth Greenleaf met with. She didn't see it, but they'd known—or rather, expected—Greenleaf would be alone. They likely knew about the windows, and any one of them could have dropped in at some point, unlocked the bedroom window.

She'd run them already, and they'd come up clean. Unless counted Darlie Tanaka's numerous arrests in protests ut a half century earlier.

Tanaka and Beth Greenleaf were the closest in age.

Anja Abbott came in at age sixty-three and Cassidy Bryer at thirty-six. That put Arnez at the youngest of the group at twenty-eight.

Just what, Eve wondered, did the under-thirty, ambitious manager of a high-dollar fashion boutique have in common with the over-seventy, recently retired teacher and wife of a retired cop? Or the former (maybe) protestor now owner/operator of Another Chance, a nonprofit that assisted the displaced and disenfranchised in finding housing and employment, while providing clothing, food, legal aid, and education opportunities?

Or the pediatrician, who, Eve learned on the background check, volunteered twelve hours a month in Louise Dimatto's free clinic.

Or the photographer, currently professional parent, with two kids—ages four and two.

Then again, look who she ended up with in the friendship pool. Mavis, former grifter now singing sensation, mother of one and one in the oven. The aforementioned Louise, doctor, rich girl, free clinic founder married to a former LC—now sex therapist.

Nadine, of course, crime reporter with her own screen show, author, Oscar winner.

Peabody, Free-Ager, smart-ass, solid cop with it. But it made sense to form friendships with a partner. As she had with Feeney.

McNab had snuck his way into the pool. Not just because he clearly loved her partner. Maybe she didn't understand his e-speak even half the time, and never understood his wardrobe. But he stood up, never bitched about extra work she often tossed his way in EDD.

Cher Reo, but that made sense, too. Under the Southern drawl and soft looks lived an ass-kicking APA.

Add Mira, though she'd never anticipated having a close, personal relationship with a shrink—especially the top shrink in the NYPSD. Then Mr. Mira, so much sharper than those dreamy green eyes indicated. And he could make her go butter soft inside.

Morris, but that made sense, too.

You didn't have to be friends with associates, and sometimes it complicated things. But she had what she had.

Would she count her bullpen? Yeah. Not that she wouldn't kick any one of their asses when needed.

And Roarke because beyond the insanity of love, they had a genuine friendship.

So okay, people could and did form relationships, attachments, friendships with others that on the surface showed no special common ground. But there had to be something under the surface to cement the bond.

A strongly fused bond could, and often did, convince someone to act well outside of their comfort zone. Or cover the act of another. To find ways to justify misdeeds.

Even murder.

Something to factor in.

But now, as her comp signaled incomings, she set it aside to look at cops.

She started with what Peabody called her altogether dead list. Given the span of Greenleaf's career, it made a long list.

Cops investigated—some cited, disciplined, others charged with crimes. Still others cleared.

For now, she set aside the natural causes and ruled accidentals. They'd need a look, but down the road.

She started on the generous handful who'd died in prison.

Bad cops, dirty cops. Cops who'd killed, maimed, destroyed lives, betrayed other cops.

And paid for it.

She picked through, one by one, looking for any current or recent connection to the Greenleafs. A spouse or partner, a relative, a lover, another cop.

And started her own list with possibles.

From there she looked at cops who'd done time or were still doing time. A few more possibles.

She took a closer look at the former Detective Serene Brenner. Brenner had climbed the ranks to detective, worked Illegals out of the three-eight in the Lower West.

And according to the file had helped herself to some of the product, cashing in, accepting bribes—cash or product—from dealers. To feed a gambling addiction.

In the end, to try to cover her tracks, she cornered the

weasel who'd given her up, broke his fingers, and threatened to do worse to his mother.

Though he recanted, or tried to, Greenleaf convinced him to testify. Brenner took a plea, got eight to ten, and served six.

She'd been out for two, and now worked as a live-in counselor for a center for former female inmates.

"Just a few blocks from the captain's apartment," Eve mumbled. "Let's put you top of today's list."

She'd moved on to the next when her 'link signaled.

Webster.

> We're back, at Carlie's place—Beth's daughter.
> The whole family's here, so it would be a good
> time.

> On our way.

She gathered what she needed, shot the work she'd done to her home office in case she didn't get back.

In the bullpen she noted the newly minted detective sergeant and his partner had caught one, and Baxter and his were back.

"Splat?" Eve said.

"Yeah." Baxter kicked back at his desk. "Guy got caught cheating on his wife—and not for the first time. They got into it—and not for the first time. He busted her nose, blackened her eye."

"And not for the first time."

"Got the medical history to back that up. She cops to giving him a good shove, states he went backward over a chest under the window and just kept going. The window was open, screen broken already. We've got that at the lab to confirm, but it looked like it.

"After he went splat, she called it in. She's claiming self-defense. We could push for Man Three, but hell, Dallas, we wouldn't get it."

"I believed her," the earnest Trueheart said from his desk. "And the neighbors confirmed he'd tuned her up before."

"Might've left the window open for this eventuality," Eve considered. "Hard to make that stick."

"Yeah. I'm not going to say she's grieving for the cheating bastard," Baxter added, "but she was shook. And maybe she got him to throw those punches first, for this eventuality. But he threw them. She came home—works the night shift—and the guy's side piece is just leaving the apartment. We confirmed that, too. They got into it first, and the side piece ran off. Doesn't read premeditated."

"Write it up. Peabody, with me."

"Hey, we heard about Jenkinson's promotion. We got us a detective sergeant."

"And where is he?"

"A couple of out-of-work bad boys playing pool in a bar. Knocked more than a few back, then got into it over the game. Got into it so the one bashed the other to death with his cue."

"That's one way to spend your afternoon. Let's go, Peabody."

7

"It's fabutastic about Jenkinson." Peabody scrambled to catch up with Eve before she hit the glides.

"He earned it."

"Oh yeah. He never let on about going for the promotion. You, either."

"That's how he wanted it."

"Not surprised. It's pretty frosty having a DS in the bullpen. And you can dump some admin stuff on him."

"A handy side benefit."

"So, are we going to interview Captain Greenleaf's family?"

"That's the plan. We'll see where it takes us. I'll be sending you a list of possibles from what you sent me."

"Really? Already?"

"For now, one stands out. Former Detective Serene Brenner, did six years of an eight-to-ten for corruption, assault, witness intimidation. Worked in Illegals and helped herself to product to pay off gambling debts. Beat up the CI who rolled on her. She's out and works-slash-lives a handful of blocks from Greenleaf's apartment."

Eve switched to the stairwell to jog down the stairs to her garage level.

"A couple of others give off a whiff, but she's first."

"You wouldn't think somebody who'd been a cop, and did six years in for being a wrong cop, would want to live and work that close to Central."

Peabody got in, strapped in while Eve plugged the address Webster had given her into the dash unit.

"Speaking of wrong cops," Peabody continued. "Not in the same way, but wrong. Lansing, wow. Not just out of line, out of control. Swear to the goddess, Dallas, I thought he might draw down on you."

"He wanted to," Eve said coolly, "and he's paying for it."

"Damn well should. He came right at me."

"What?" Eve whipped her head around. "In the bullpen?"

"Yeah, he comes busting in, the other one—Dennison— he's trying to hold Lansing back. He must've known we were partners, because he came right at me."

"Did he put hands on you?"

"No. No, he just started going off—at first I thought he was a civilian—just going off on me, asking where you—my bitch partner—was. By the time I realized he was another cop and he started going off about Greenleaf and how we were covering up murder and he was threatening to kick my fat ass, Jenkinson blocked him."

When Eve said nothing, Peabody hunched up her shoulders, let them fall. "He threw me off at first, just the way he bulled in there, went for me. I'd've handled it. I would have, but Jenkinson got between us, then everybody's up and Lansing went after Jenkinson. Then you came in."

As if to shake it away, Peabody gave a full body shudder. "Good thinking, fast thinking, to switch on your recorder."

"I hear the next thing to a brawl in my bullpen, I want it on record. Jenkinson wouldn't throw the first punch; he's too smart for that. I want that on record. Goddamn it. You should've told me."

"Well, I didn't exactly have a moment for that, considering."

"Okay, okay." Eve ordered herself to simmer it down. "That's valid."

"And, the truth is, I was—am—kind of pissed at myself for not handling it myself. Jenkinson shouldn't've had to intervene."

"Yes, he should have. He did exactly what he should've done, and so did everyone else. Including you. You were on that line. When we're done with this fieldwork, I need you to write it up."

"Ah, Dallas."

"It needs to be done. Whitney's going to take Lansing's badge, no way around it. This wasn't his first out-of-line, out-of-control incident. Lansing will fight it. We give the commander everything, including what you just told me. As your lieutenant, I'm ordering you to write this incident up, in detail, with accuracy, send it to me, to Whitney, and to Lansing's captain."

Hissing, Eve smacked her fist on the steering wheel. "Goddamn it."

"I'm sorry, I—"

"Don't you apologize," Eve snapped. "You do not apologize."

She pulled over a block from the address, not because she lucked into a street-level spot, but because she'd need the walk.

"He threatened you, me, Jenkinson with physical harm. And by Christ, he'd have followed through on swinging away, worse, he very well might've drawn his weapon, if Whitney hadn't shown up when he did. He leapt to conclusions without evidence, and had no intention of attempting to gather evidence to support that leap before committing violence against you, me, and anyone who got in his way.

"Now think about this," Eve demanded. "If he behaved in this manner to and with other cops, armed, trained individuals, how might he have acted with civilians, suspects, a neighbor who pissed him off?"

"You're right. You're right. I didn't think about that. The whole thing twisted me up. I'll write the report, in detail, when we're done in the field."

"Damn right." She started to get out of the vehicle, paused. "And because I know this single point will stick in your craw, let me dispute it, factually. You don't have a fat ass."

Peabody let out a half laugh. "Thanks. It's been more stuck in my brain."

"Well, pluck it out, and put the rest away while we do the job. Whitney's right to take Lansing's badge, but we still have ours."

The walk helped. A busy New York sidewalk, the quick flick of sweet from an open-air flower cart, the lazy rumble-fart-rumble of a maxibus pulling up at a stop. The color and unrelenting hope from street artists displaying their work on this southern edge of SoHo.

She caught Peabody's eye wandering in that direction.

"No. No stops."

"Not stopping, just considering. We're thinking of hanging street art in the living room. Sort of a theme. I wouldn't buy anything without McNab unless I was abso-pos he'd like it. You've gotta agree on art for your shared walls."

"Is that a rule?" She didn't have that one in her Marriage Rules. "There's all kinds of art everywhere at the house."

"Roarke already had it before, right?"

"Yeah. Mostly. Probably. I don't know."

"And you're fine with it. But we're doing this from scratch, so you have to consult."

A situational rule then, Eve concluded.

Greenleaf's daughter, Carlie, lived with her husband, Jed,

and their three children in a three-story townhome in the middle of the next block.

They'd trimmed out the whitewashed brick in a deep, dark navy, added window boxes to the base of a trio of tall windows, filled them with a lot of pink flowers and spilling greenery.

Solid security—she'd expect same from a cop's kid—cams, palm plate, intercom, and good—if fancy—lock sets.

And still, when she buzzed, the door opened quickly and without inquiry.

"I kept an eye out for you," Webster told her. "They're all back in the family room. It's been a hard day, so—"

"I left my sap and bamboo shoots at the office. Give over, Webster."

"Sorry. Sorry. It's been a hard day," he repeated. "Lansing didn't make it easier."

"He has nothing to do with this. Give that over, too."

"Trying."

He led them back—a good-sized living room, a glass-doored home office, powder room—into a space where the kitchen, dining, and lounge areas spread open to each other.

Reinforced glass doors opened to a tiny paved patio now occupied by several kids—a teenage spread for the most part.

Inside, younger ones sprawled on the floor, playing with toy cars, while the adults sat or stood. Spread out again, Eve thought, but unquestionably united.

"Lieutenant Dallas, Detective Peabody. Ah, Ben Green-leaf, and his wife, Mina; Carlie and her husband, Jed Met-calf; Luke Greenleaf and his husband, Shawn Bee.

Carlie stepped forward first. Tall and lanky like her father, she'd opted for bold red hair, had tamed it back into a sedate roll at her nape. She wore a severe black dress and signs of recent weeping.

"Thank you for coming to us. I'm going to get everyone coffee. Jack, take the little guys outside."

The older kid on the floor looked up, mutiny in his eyes. "I don't want to."

"Out," she repeated. "Take the cars, too. I'm going to send for some lemonade."

"Fine." He rolled those mutinous eyes so hard, Eve found herself surprised they didn't pop and fly out of the room. "Grandpa died," he told Eve.

"I know. I'm very sorry."

"He played catch with me and came to watch me play in the park. Now he won't. Come on, Henry, and you, too, Kaylee. We're going to play outside."

"I'll give you a hand with the cars." Shawn, gym fit, mixed race, red-rimmed brown eyes, scooped up the youngest—Kaylee—along with a handful of cars.

He led the kids out to the patio.

"Have a seat." Jed Metcalf gestured to two chairs, obviously left unoccupied for this purpose.

Mid-forties, mixed race, he had smooth good looks and the faintest accent. From his background check, Eve knew he'd come to New York from London twenty years before.

"I apologize for the need to intrude at such a difficult time," Eve began.

"My father did his duty." This from Luke, the youngest sibling. "He'd want you to do yours."

Beth reached over, laid a hand over her son's.

He had his mother's eyes, and a more compact build than his siblings.

Mina, Asian, model slim with ink-black hair, porcelain skin, rose. "I'm going to give Carlie a hand with the coffee. I'll make you the tea, Beth."

"Yes, yes, I'd like that."

"Don said he asked for you because you're the best." On the other side of their mother, Ben Greenleaf studied Eve, then Peabody, then Eve again with cool, assessing eyes. "I've seen you address the media on investigations. You seem very confident."

So did he, she thought, and noted that the resemblance to his father went beyond the physical.

"If you're not confident when addressing the media, they'll eat you alive. Webster asked for me because, from experience, he knows my partner and I will do everything that can be done to identify and apprehend your father's killer."

"They tried to make it look like suicide." Luke turned his hand over under his mother's, linked their fingers. "They didn't know him. You weren't fooled by that."

"There were indications on scene that the suicide was staged. The chief medical examiner confirmed my findings, added his own. We're sorry for your loss, we regret, deeply, that Captain Greenleaf's life was cut short, particularly when he devoted so much of it to public service."

"IAB cops aren't popular cops," Ben put in.

"No, they're not. Do you know of any cops who wished your father harm?"

"I might've said you a couple years ago."

"Ben."

The single word came from Webster as his wife and sister in the kitchen both sent him long, disappointed looks.

"I'm sorry. I'm sorry." He shut his eyes a moment. "That was rude and wrong and stupid."

"It would be all of that, seeing as the captain had retired for some time when I was, briefly, suspended."

"And he backed you all the way on that, rightfully so as it turned out. I apologize," Ben said again. "And to you, too, Mom, for embarrassing you."

"None of us are at our best right now." Beth patted his thigh in support.

"Coffee, Lieutenant, Detective." Carlie set up a coffee tray on the wide kitchen island and brought two cups into the family area. "Black and coffee regular. I read the books, saw the first vid. I've also had a few brushes with Roarke, so to speak."

"So to speak?" Eve repeated.

"Independent Design, the company I work for, has done some business with and for him. He wouldn't know me. I'm a cog in the wheel."

"A big cog," her younger brother said. "High on that wheel."

"Maybe, but not big or high enough to connect directly with Roarke."

Change the subject, Eve thought, give the room time to settle again. And her big brother time to compose himself.

A peacemaker.

"I'd also like to answer the question you asked Ben. I know our father received threats. He didn't talk about them at home, or not in our hearing."

"Kids hear things," Peabody began, "adults, parents don't think they hear."

"Oh, so true," Carlie agreed with a glance toward the patio. "I imagine that's only one of the reasons Dad was so careful about it."

Shawn came back in. "Settled down. Hal and Flynn took charge."

"Thanks."

As Mina came in, served the tea to her mother-in-law, Carlie poured coffee for herself, then sat.

"But twice before he retired, he did speak about it, to all of us. The first time, I was pregnant with Flynn, our oldest, so it was about seventeen years ago."

"Who was he worried about?"

"Well, us, but yes, a specific cop who made threats he took seriously enough to ask us, all of us—well, not Shawn, as Luke hadn't even met him back that far—to take precautions."

"Do you have a name?"

"Adam Carson," Ben said. "I remember and, yes, about seventeen years. Hal was just a baby—just a couple months old. Mina and I were still trying to rehab the brownstone. He insisted I put in better security even though we wouldn't officially move in for another six months. We were there a lot. Mina and Hal were there a lot alone or with workers handling what we couldn't."

"I was in grad school," Luke recalled. "But I'd zip home on weekends sometimes, and for holidays. He gave us the name, showed us an ID shot, and told us if we saw this person, to tag him immediately, and to get off the street, if that's where we were. To keep the doors locked if we were at home."

"It scared me," Carlie said. "He'd never come to us that way before, so I knew he was scared, too. He said this Adam Carson had been a street cop—a dirty cop, a violent cop he'd investigated. He'd built a case that had Carson fired, and he—Carson—had been charged with taking bribes, and for causing the death of a suspect in his custody. My father firmly believed he'd go to prison—and he did—but before, he made bail. And Dad said he'd promised him—Carson had promised Dad—that he'd take retribution on him through his family."

"Did he attempt to harm any of you?"

"Jed and I were living in a foursquare just a few blocks from here. Downtown people," Carlie added. "Dad had a couple of plainclothes cops sitting on the place—something he didn't tell us—and they caught Carson trying to break in. He had a drop piece and a knife on him, some restraints. He'd had to turn in his service weapon, but he had the drop piece, the knife. I'm sure he'd have used them."

"They rescinded his bail," Jed went on. "He got life, no possibility of parole. More came out in the trial, because I paid attention. Raping suspects, running a protection racket. More. What I know is even though we had good security, because Martin insisted, if Carson had gotten through it . . . Those cops saved our lives. They saved our lives because Martin asked them to watch out for us."

"Has he made more threats?"

"He's on the list, Dallas," Peabody told her. "You haven't gotten that far into it yet, but I remember putting this one on the list. He got shanked in prison, ten or twelve years ago."

"Okay. We'll look at any connection there. Relatives, cell mates he might've gotten friendly with, other cops who ran with him back then. You said twice."

"Yes. It was—Jack was just starting to walk, wasn't he, Jed? If I'm right, that would be about eight years ago. A detective. Serene Brenner."

Though the name popped, Eve only nodded. "She also threatened to harm your father by harming his family?"

"Dad said she was desperate. I remember this," Luke said. "Shawn and I had just gotten married."

"We had that crazy little place in the Village," Shawn added, "over Tarot Tattoo."

"Get your cards read while you get your tat. Those were the days. Anyway," Luke continued, "Dad came to the door with a tech and a security system. One of Roarke's, if that says anything."

"I'd say he wanted the best for you."

Luke nodded at Eve. "I was all, 'Come on, Dad, lighten it up,' but he sat us down, and said this woman he'd investigated was desperate, a gambling addict in deep. He hadn't proven it, but suspected she might also use some of the illegals she lifted before they went into Evidence."

"She said he'd taken everything from her, so she'd make damn sure to take everything from him. Isn't that right?" Ben asked his siblings.

"That's what I remember. And she'd put the guy who turned her in in the hospital. She'd made bail because her mother was sick," Carlie added.

"She went to prison, too. Not for life," Shawn recalled. "She hadn't killed anybody."

"Has she made any threats since?"

"No." Carlie looked at her mother, her brothers, then repeated, "No. I wouldn't have given her another thought except for this."

"All right. That's helpful. Is there anyone else?"

"Not that he told us about." Ben took his mother's hand. "Mom?"

"There were threats. Most of them he considered hot air, the heat of the moment, the anger of being investigated even if cleared. IAB cops aren't popular cops," she repeated. "But the unlocked window . . ."

"Yes, ma'am. We believe the killer entered through that window. We believe the killer had knowledge of your apartment layout and your household routine. Believed that Captain Greenleaf would be alone from the time you left until you returned. Is there anyone you can think of who would have this knowledge, hold these beliefs, and who wished the captain harm?"

"No. I've hardly thought of anything else, but no."

"It had to be a cop."

Eve shifted her attention to Ben. "No, in fact, at this time I don't believe that to be the case, or at least not a cop with good training, or fresh training."

"You'll always cover for each other," he said in disgust.

"That's bullshit, Ben." Webster shoved away from the island he'd leaned on during the interview. "That's bullshit. These two took on a ring of dirty cops IAB didn't have a whiff of. They took them on, took them down, and put themselves in harm's way to do just that."

"Leave it, Webster."

He rounded on Eve. "I won't. I pulled you into this. Do you think I'd have pulled her in if I'd had a single doubt she and Peabody would put Martin first? They're murder cops, Ben, the best I know. Dallas runs a division of murder cops, the best I know. If I ended up on a slab, I'd damn well want them standing for me."

"Don't say that, Don," Beth murmured. "Don't say that."

"We're all struggling," Mina began. "We—"

"No excuses." Ben shook his head at his wife. "I have to apologize again. Jesus, Don, he'd have come down on me just like you did, and he'd have been right, just like you are. I need a minute. I'm not handling this well. I'm just going to go outside with the kids for a minute, get some air."

Shawn waited until Ben went outside. "Why don't you think it was a cop? I'm not questioning, just asking. There's a difference."

"There were mistakes," Eve told him. "Mistakes a trained cop might make acting on impulse, but we see this as well planned. A cop who's no longer a cop, rusty? Maybe."

"But then . . . Why would anyone else do this?"

"You're all in this room now because you lost someone you loved. You have grief, anger, you look to blame someone, hold someone responsible."

"Of course we do." Carlie spread her hands. "Of course."

"Of course. Due to your father's work, his diligence, his duty, law enforcement officers lost their badges, their livelihood, in some cases their freedom, in some cases their lives."

"That's just what we're saying," Carlie insisted.

"Wrong cops have people who love them, too."

"Oh," Carlie slumped back in her chair. "Oh God."

"We'll look at the cops your father investigated, and at the people connected to them. We'll keep looking, following the facts and the evidence. If you remember anything, if you think maybe this is something, just maybe, you contact me or Detective Peabody. We'll follow it up."

She rose. "I'm sorry for your loss. Captain Greenleaf was retired, but as far as I'm concerned, he died in the line of duty."

"Thank you for saying that." Carlie rose, held out a hand as she stepped to Eve. "Thank you for meaning it."

"I'll show them out, Carlie."

Webster led the way back. "Ben—"

"There's no need, Webster. No need at all."

"He told me today . . . Mina had a late class last night. She teaches pottery, and scheduled this extra class for a couple of promising students. He remembered it was his mom's night out and was going to drop by, see his dad, talk him into going out for a brew at this sports bar they liked.

"Then when he got home, his neighbor was out grilling— they have a great place on the Lower East—and said come on over, bring the kids. So he ended up hanging with the neighbors and the kids and didn't go over to see his dad. He can't shake it yet."

"Help him shake it. It'll take awhile, but you'll help him shake it."

"Look, if I can help you follow up on either of those leads Carlie gave you—"

"You can't. We've got it. You can't push into it."

Misery in his eyes, he shoved his hands in his pockets. "I feel useless."

"You're not. You're helping hold the captain's family together. Keep doing that. We've got to move."

He stood at the door, watching them as they walked up the block.

"Serene Brenner," Peabody said. "She might just ring the bell."

"We're sure as hell going to find out."

8

While the building housing Open Doors sat only blocks from Greenleaf's apartment, the neighborhood crossed the line into the edge of shabby. Low-rent tat parlors and bars dominated street level with, for the most part, flops overhead.

A dingy twenty-four/seven squatted on the corner. Eve watched a pack of teenage boys stroll out, slurping on fizzies and looking for something to do. Eve predicted what they looked for began and ended with trouble.

But at the moment, that wasn't her problem.

Open Doors stood mid-block, squeezed between one of those tat parlors and a bar named, accurately Eve assumed, the Dirty Glass.

The building, one tossed up on the cheap post-Urbans, hadn't been built to last. Somehow it had, and she could see patches of repair on the exterior. It bore no sign to indicate what went on inside.

Probably smart, she thought, to keep it low-key.

"They've tried to make it pretty," Peabody observed, then shrugged at Eve's raised brows. "They painted the door that nice blue, even painted the riot bars the blue. They've got those window boxes on the windows of a couple of upper floors—where nobody can steal them. Those look like fresh patches on the prefab, so somebody's trying to maintain the building."

Peabody scanned up. "I didn't see how much of it Open Doors has."

"All of it."

"Seriously? It's . . . eight floors."

"Let's see what they're doing inside that. High-end security—one of Roarke's systems. Smart—and pricey."

She pressed the buzzer.

A human voice—female, not computerized—answered.

"Good afternoon. How can we help?"

Eve held her badge up for the cam. "NYPSD, Lieutenant Dallas and Detective Peabody. We need to speak with Serene Brenner."

"Um. I'm supposed to scan your ID, but—I can't remember how. Bibi! Sorry! I need some help! It's cops, and I can't remember how to do the scan thing."

Eve heard another female voice—older, patient. "Okay. You see how the officer is holding up her badge? You capture that—that's right. Now click for scan and verify. That's the way! See how it verified her badge number, her name and rank?"

"Yeah, yeah. So she's all good. There are two of them."

"I see that. And now see the second officer holding up her badge? Do the same thing."

"I got it. I'm sorry."

"Don't be sorry. You did good. Now you can buzz them in."

"I remember that!"

The buzzer sounded; locks clicked and thumped.

Inside, a kind of lobby—buffed clean and smelling lightly of whatever little flowers stood in a jar-type vase on the counter—had fake wood floors and bright white walls.

On the walls hung paintings—street scenes, still lifes—some showing genuine talent. A dark-skinned woman, early twenties with perfect rows of braids, sat behind a waist-high counter biting her full bottom lip.

The older woman, one looking behind her at sixty, stood next to the younger, had one narrow hand on the girl's shoulder. The girl wore a white collared shirt, the woman a round-necked floral one.

"Greet our guests, Shonda."

"Um. Welcome to Open Doors. How can we help?"

"Lieutenant Dallas, Detective Peabody to speak with Serene Brenner."

"Don't say *um*," Bibi murmured. "Take a breath instead."

Full of obvious nerves, Shonda did so. "Ms. Brenner's in a session." She glanced at Bibi for approval.

"That's right. You can check the schedule on-screen, see when she'll be finished so you can tell our guests."

Eve could see the next *um* forming before Shonda caught herself, took a breath. "Ms. Brenner should be available shortly. Would you like to wait?"

"Yeah, we can wait."

"Excuse me a minute." Shonda gestured Bibi down so she could whisper in her ear.

"That's okay. That's fine. Now, do you remember how to give Serene a tap so she knows she has visitors waiting?"

"I got that. I got that."

As she worked, the door buzzed. A woman came in, sliding her swipe back in her pocket. Mid-thirties, very thin, and tired eyes that made Eve and Peabody as cops instantly.

"Welcome back, Tonya. How'd it go today?"

Tonya flicked those tired eyes toward Bibi. "Good enough." She held up a takeaway bag. "Boss let me bring home some potato salad. I'm going to put it back in the kitchen."

"Did you make it?"

The woman flushed a little, nodded.

"You label that, 'cause I want a sample. Now, Shonda,

since Serene's nearly finished, I'm going to take our guests up to her office. You know how to give me a tap if you need help?"

"Sure. I'm supposed to log Tonya in, right?"

"That's exactly right."

"How long have you been training on the desk?" Peabody asked Shonda.

"It's my second day. I'm sorry I—"

"You're doing really well," Peabody interrupted.

"Yeah?" Shonda beamed like a spotlight. "Thanks. If I learn everything and get good at it, I can get a job on the outside." She bit her lip again, sent Bibi a sidelong look. "I mean in the city."

"Good luck."

"Do you mind if we take the stairs?" Bibi asked. "Both elevators are acting up. We have someone working on them right now, but I don't trust them."

"Stairs are fine," Eve told her, and followed her into the stairwell.

"That was kind of you," Bibi said to Peabody. "Shonda needs to build her confidence."

"I remember what it was like to start training, and be terrified you'd screw everything up."

"I think the trainer bears some responsibility if that happens. She was extra nervous because you're police. So was Tonya. I'm sure you know that."

"We're not here to hassle your . . ."

"We call them clients, Lieutenant. It lets them know we're providing them with a service. It takes awhile to lose the instinct to run at the sight of a cop."

"How long did it take you?"

Now Bibi let out a laugh. "Oh, there are still times."

They came out on the second floor.

"We have counseling rooms, some classrooms, some

offices on this level. Downstairs, as you saw, the reception/ check-in, a common area for gathering, the kitchen and communal dining hall. We have a sorting area on the second floor. For donations. Clothes, shoes, toiletries. In any case, I'm sure Serene will give you a tour if you want one.

"She should be finishing up." Bibi gestured to a closed door on three. "A group session. Her office is at the end of the hall."

Before they started down the hall, Eve glanced up. "Do I hear singing?"

"Old building, no soundproofing. But it's nice, actually. More classrooms on the next level. That's our Songbirds. We have some good, strong voices, and some with hopes of making a living using theirs. We put on shows, here at Open Doors, at homeless shelters, rehab centers, convalescent centers, and so on.

"The fourth floor centers on the arts, vocal and instrumental music—we have some donated instruments—arts and crafts, while here, it's counseling and some staff rooms. Rudimentary education on five. A lot of clients come to us barely literate, and many without enough English to get a decent-paying job. So reading, language, math skills."

"How long have you worked here?"

Bibi paused outside another closed door. "I did twelve years inside—two stretches. They took my boy away, and were right to. I was an addict, doing more product than selling, selling my body to make up the difference, putting my boy through that. Stealing when I could. When I got out the first time, I went right back to it. Just one hit to smooth things over, right? I went back inside and, when I got out again, I knew I couldn't go back in. I knew I'd die if I went back."

She opened the door to an office smaller than Eve's at Central, one with an old metal desk covered with disc files, a

comp system that looked like somebody had cobbled it together the previous century, a single plastic visitor's chair.

A narrow counter held an old coffee maker—no
AutoChef—and a small water bubbler.

"My parole officer told me about Open Doors. They were
just really getting off the ground, but she thought it might
work for me. I came here. I'd hit bottom, had nowhere else to
go. I figured I'd put in a little time, just get my feet back under
me again. That was twenty-six years ago. Open Doors saved
my life, I absolutely know that as fact. I was twenty-two the
first time I went in, and thirty-six when I buzzed in the first
time downstairs. My son was just three when they took him
from the woman I was. Took awhile for him to forgive me,
and awhile for me to deserve that forgiveness. He's a good
man despite what I did to and didn't do for him. I've got two
grandbabies, a family, a life, and a purpose. I wouldn't have
any of that without Open Doors."

Bibi glanced back at the sound of a door opening, of voices,
footsteps. "Looks like Serene's finished. If you'd wait a minute, I'll go tell her you're at her office."

She took a step away, hesitated. "Back in the bad old days,
one of my best customers was a cop."

"Got a name?"

Bibi's eyebrows winged up. "It was over forty years ago."

"Got a name?" Eve repeated.

"Well. Well. Let me think about that. I'll get Serene."

"I wonder what their success rate is."

"There's one." Eve's chin pointed after Bibi. "I'd say the
one on the desk downstairs has a better than decent shot."

She watched the woman walking toward them. She recognized Brenner from her mug shot, her ID shots. Mixed
raced, dark brown hair pulled back in a tail, a thin face with
wide, hooded hazel eyes and a blank expression as she approached.

"Lieutenant, Detective, I'm Serene Brenner. What can I do for you?"

"Why don't we take it in your office?"

"All right. I've got a one-on-one session in twenty minutes."

"We'll try to keep it brief."

"I can offer you terrible coffee or water," she said, then gave Eve a long look as Eve closed the door behind them.

"We're good, thanks."

"I'm having terrible coffee. Our budget doesn't stretch to what you're used to anyway. I know who you are. You were already Captain Feeney's pet when I went inside."

Eve thought that made the second time in one day someone called her a pet. "Pet?"

"No offense. I think you'd already made detective before the cage door locked behind me. Come on, you bastard," she said to the coffee machine. "One more time. I've been out for two years, so I know your rep. There it is, one more cup of sludge."

She took it, leaned back against her desk. "And since I do, I have to figure you're here to talk to me about Captain Greenleaf."

"Then we can cut through it. Your whereabouts last night?"

"Media didn't give a TOD."

Eve didn't hesitate. "Twenty hundred hours."

"Well, shit." Fear snapped into her eyes before she closed them. "I was out about that time. I live and work in the building. Sometimes you need to get out. I took a walk."

"Alone?"

"That was the point of the walk. Alone. Finished my last session, did some paperwork, had some dinner downstairs. We've got clients in training for food services. The food's hit-and-miss, but we get plenty of hits. It had to be about seven-thirty when I went out. We have cams on the doors, so you can review that."

Brenner took a long hit of coffee. "It had to be about that time. I'm going to tell you, without expecting you to believe me, I don't know where the captain lived."

"About three and a half blocks from here. Easy walk."

"I repeat, well, shit. Of course, close to Central. Makes sense."

It came into her eyes, first the fear again, then a kind of resignation.

"Hell of a time for me to take a walk. There's a park a few blocks south. More of a playground, really, with benches for parents or nannies if you've got one. I headed there, bought what's actually pretty decent lemonade from a cart, sat on a bench, let the day fall away. I do that a couple nights a week in good weather. Especially on a hard day."

She swallowed some coffee. "It was a hard day. One of our clients got busted. Shoplifting, for fuck's sake, and she had illegals on her. Stupid, stupid. I'd worked hard with her, and thought we'd made good progress. I was wrong, and I needed to let the day fall away."

"What time did you get back?"

"Before dark. Maybe about eight-thirty, I guess. I'd had enough alone. Bibi lives here, so does Kit. We've got an excuse for a staff room on three, separate from the common areas."

She shrugged, but kept staring into her coffee.

"Sometimes the clients don't want you around, sometimes we don't want to be around the clients. The three of us sat in there, bitching to each other about Aster—the busted client—then Kit said fuck this, went down, made popcorn, got tubes of Coke from our stash—we have a stash—and we watched some screen. A comedy. We needed to laugh.

I'd say we all turned in about ten-thirty. I felt better. Then this morning, I heard about Greenleaf, and knew you'd work your way to me.

"Dirty deeds leave a stain no matter how much you wash it out. And I did dirty deeds. No excuse."

Could be bullshitting me, Eve thought, just like I bullshitted her on the time.

"You threatened him, and his family."

"Did I?" Brenner shook her head, looked up to the ceiling. "Yeah, I probably did. Probably meant it at the time. I was scared, and I was pissed. A lot easier to be pissed than scared. Not my fault, right? Never my fault, because circumstances. So, obviously, his fault. I'm sure I threatened him. Probably offered to blow him, too, if he looked the other way. And I would have."

Now she set the coffee aside. "I fucked up, Lieutenant, Detective. I fucked up and I found out. I wanted to be a cop. I really wanted to be a cop, and I threw it away because I couldn't stop gambling—and losing—and finding ways to justify what I did to pay off the losses and gambling some more."

She shook her head. "I fucked it all up. One of the things I found out inside? Mine wasn't the toughest. Women lost kids—I didn't have kids. Or they ended up inside because they'd done desperate things just to survive. I had a job I wanted and worked and trained to get. A decent place to live. And I tossed it all aside, and I hurt people, stained the badge I'd wanted so much."

She looked up again as thumping sounded above. "Dance class," she murmured.

She walked over for a tube of water as the thumping—reasonably rhythmic—continued.

"I heard about this place inside, from my counselor, my rehab counselor. When I got out, I came here because I was afraid I'd start gambling again. I wanted to. Still want to, but I didn't. And I haven't. I trained to counsel others, and I'm good at it. Better at it than I was on the job. You can look at my record here, talk to Della—Della McRoy, the founder. This is hers. She's the reason for Open Doors."

She scrubbed her hands over her face. "I didn't go after Greenleaf. I can't say I wouldn't have years ago if I'd had the chance, because I convinced myself it was his fault. It had to be. I've long since accepted and acknowledged it was my fault. All of it. My choices, my actions. And I paid for those choices, those actions. I did my time."

"We'll need to see the security feed for last night."

"Sure. I can't remember who's on the desk right now."

"The trainee."

"Right, right, Shonda. She won't know how to do that yet, and you won't want me doing it. Bibi can get that for you."

"All right. And will she and this Kit verify your where-abouts and actions from twenty-one hundred until twenty-one-thirty?"

"Yeah, but—"

"Captain Greenleaf's TOD was between twenty-one and twenty-one-thirty hours."

Eve saw the shock that widened Brenner's eyes, then the relief that filled them. "You bullshitted me. Smart."

"Maybe. But we need to see the feed, and speak with the two people you were with at the time in question."

"I'll set it up." She pressed her fingers to her eyes. "Okay, okay. I'll go set it up. Bibi can bring a copy of the feed in here, and you can use the office to interview her. I'll find Kit."

When she went out, Peabody looked at Eve. "You believe her."

"Do you?"

"Yes, and so do you."

"Why?"

"For one thing, she went pale—just lost her color when you gave her the earlier TOD, and her walk to the park rings true."

"We'll check on this Aster, make sure of that."

"Right, but that's going to check, and so is the hang out with her two coworkers, the vid, the whole thing. She didn't get pissy or try to evade, didn't say: Lawyer."

"And all of that could just be strategy."

"Could—and she'd have to have doctored the feed and convinced her two coworkers to cover for her—for murder. You don't believe any of that."

"I don't believe any of that. But we check, and we verify."

And when they had, they moved on.

Another Chance and Darlie Tanaka didn't have an eight-story building. She ran her organization out of an old—post-Urban again—warehouse. It didn't have a cheerful blue door, but it boasted exterior walls covered in graffiti and street art oddly lacking in obscenities and sexual content.

Decent security, Eve noted. Not high-end, just decent. No palm plates, no cams, but good, solid locks—currently disengaged.

They walked into what struck Eve as a mash-up between a casual living room and friendly medical waiting area.

Tables, chairs, a small sofa—all on the shabby side—a kids' play area with cubbies holding various toys.

People sat around talking, sipping from short, clear glasses.

A long, scarred table served as a reception desk, currently manned by a male too young to buy a legal brew. His orange hair flopped down over one eye as he pecked carefully at the keyboard of an ancient comp, and with the focus of someone defusing a bomb.

When she stepped up, he studied her with one vividly green eye.

"Darlie Tanaka."

"Okay." He slid his rolly chair to the end of the table, shouted down a hallway. "Hey, Darlie. I'm sending a couple cops back to see you. Intercom's busted," he added to Eve.

"We didn't identify ourselves as police."

He snorted. "Come on, man."

"How long have you worked here?"

"On staff? Like six months."

"How old are you?"

"I'll be nineteen in November. I'm legal. What're you hassling me for?"

"Not. Just curious."

"Darlie's three down, on the left."

With Peabody she walked down the hall. She judged it had once been an open area. To separate it into offices, storage, what looked like a small break room, they'd thrown up partitions, more or less like cube walls.

They found Darlie Tanaka in one of the makeshift offices, sitting at a desk that might just have come over on the ark. Notices, flyers, uplifting sayings, old posters of rockers (Avenue A featured) plastered the walls.

She held up a finger as she continued a conversation on her 'link.

"Just two large, Nicko. It'd make a huge difference right now. Everybody poops, right? If we don't get the plumbing fixed, and fixed right this time, we're going to be swimming in it."

She sat, swiveling in her chair as she talked. Her streaky hair—white and gray—fell in wildly careless waves past the shoulders of a T-shirt that read: ALWAYS ONE MORE FUCK TO GIVE.

She'd dyed her lips a bold red, had sharp dark eyes, and wore hoop earrings Eve thought she could put a fist through.

Those bold lips spread in a smile. "I knew you'd come through, Nicko. I dedicate my next poop to you. Cha."

She clicked off, set down the 'link on a pile of folders.

"So, Dallas and Peabody. Have a seat. It's begging day, which means I leave my pride at home. But you're here about Martin. I spoke with Beth right before she and the family left to see him. My wife and I are going by Carlie's when I can break away from here."

"You were with Ms. Greenleaf and others on the night Captain Greenleaf was killed."

"Yeah, our monthly meetup. We started as a book club. Jesus, has to be twenty, twenty-five years back. Then we admitted that was just an excuse to sit around, talk, drink a lot of wine. So we cut out the book club portion. Beth and I, original members. We go back. We've known each other longer than she knew Martin."

"And you and the captain were friends?"

"We had our differences." She smiled as she said it, even when grief showed in her eyes. "I'm an old activist and he was a cop down to the marrow, so we sure as hell didn't always see eye-to-eye.

"And still . . . still. He supported what we do here. This desk?" She knocked a fist on it. "Was his father's. His old man gave it to him when Martin got out of the Academy, and Martin gave it to me when I started up here. He helped us set up. Since he retired, he'd come in now and then, do some little repairs.

"I loved the son of a bitch."

"How did you meet Ms. Greenleaf?"

"Gun ban rally. Back then, there wasn't a rally, protest, march I'd walk away from. But this was a particular mission of mine. And hers. She was a teacher. Young, Jesus, we were both so young. She'd survived a school shooting. One of her coworkers and two of her students—twelve years old—didn't. So it was a particular mission of hers, too. She spoke—passionate, eloquent. And I admit I found her very attractive."

"Did you have an intimate relationship?"

"Honey, I don't hit on the straight, and she clearly was. But we hit it off, ended up going out for a drink after the rally. And that, as the line goes, was the beginning of a beautiful friendship. I stood up for her when she married Martin. She stood up for me when Flora and I got married."

"You said you and Ms. Greenleaf were the original members of this group. How did the others come into it?"

"Oh, well, some have come and gone. Moved away, lost interest, got too busy. There's Pru, for instance. Pru wasn't there. She and her family spend the summer in Maine. I went to college with Pru. She married rich—nice guy, too. And it's a benefit for me, as she and her guy helped us buy this building. She swings in, mostly when we get together in the spring and fall. They spend most of the winter in Belize. Anyway, I brought Pru in, and Beth brought Anja in. Anja's a hoot and a holler. A pediatrician who ought to be a comic. Beth met her when Anja came in to give a presentation at Beth's school. Then I brought Cass in. Cass is the daughter of the gallery owner where my wife shows her work. And of our current gang of girls, there's Elva. Beth brought her in. She lives in Beth's building."

"You know all of them well then."

"I'd say. Well, Anja, we've been friends for about thirty years. She makes me laugh, and our politics mesh. Not a requirement, but it doesn't hurt. I know if there's a protest or march I want to support, I can count on Anja. Cass? I've known her since she was a kid, and I love every inch of her. She's here today, volunteering. She's got two kids, and she's doing the pro parent thing. This gives her a chance to work, and we have a small day care set up for kids. It's good for everyone."

"Is she available to speak with?"

"Sure. She'd be next floor up, working with some of the

Chancers on interview skills. One of our purposes is to help people find work, and stick."

"'Chancers.'"

Darlie smiled. "It became a thing."

"Peabody, why don't you go talk to Ms. Bryer."

Peabody rose. "I really like your shirt, Ms. Tanaka."

"Thanks. Somebody's got to give a fuck."

When Peabody went out, Darlie's 'link signaled. "I really need to take this. I'll be quick. Pru! I was just thinking about you. Yeah, yeah. I wasn't sure you'd heard."

Tears swam into her eyes again. She snatched up some tissues to wipe at them.

"As bad as it gets. Flora and I are going over tonight. I will," she said after a minute. "I'm talking to the police now."

She let out a watery laugh, swiped at her damp eyes. "Yes, voluntarily. I will let you know, of course. It'll mean a lot to her. No, babe, I really don't, but— What?"

She sat back in her chair as if her limbs had gone weak. "I— Are you serious? Pru— Oh my God, oh my God. You're my goddess. Jesus, I can't tell you . . . Tell Sam . . . I don't have the words right now. Yes. Jesus, yes. Can I tag you back when I'm done here and can be more coherent? I love you. I love you both. Give me an hour, okay? I'll tag you back. I love you," she said again.

When she clicked off, she pressed her fingers to her eyes. "Sorry, sorry," she said as they streamed. "I need a minute. I just . . . this strange, wonderful, smack-talking girl I met in college just told me she and her amazing husband, with the full support of their stupendous family, is giving us a quarter million dollars."

"That's very generous."

"She saved us. They saved us. Shit, shit." She opened a drawer, pulled out more tissues. "This place is everything to me. This old building, in the last year, it's just . . . Get old, fall apart, you know. If you can't offer a safe place, you can't help. You must know, with Dochas, with An Didean, what it takes financially."

"I don't. Roarke does."

"And I praise him for his combination of deep pockets, his glorious generosity, and his vision. I meant to tell you, you can check my bona fides with any of the staff at Dochas. We often work with them. I'm sorry for losing it. The combination of knowing she and Sam are going to come back for the memorial—whenever it happens—then this gift, it wiped me out."

She dried her eyes, breathed out. "So, I don't know what else I can tell you."

"We hadn't gotten to Elva Arnez. She'd be the most recent addition to your group, right?"

"Yeah, just a year, if that. Gotta bring in that young, fresh blood, keeps us on our toes. Certainly I don't know Elva as well as the others, but we've gotten to know one another. I give her grief for being a fashion plate and selling ridiculously expensive clothes to women who don't need more of them. She doesn't mind it. And she's donated clothes— damn good clothes the Chancers can use at interviews, at work. She even hired one of the women as a clerk about six months ago. Tawny's still there, and doing very well."

"I suppose it would be natural for Ms. Arnez and Ms. Greenleaf to be closer, living in the same building."

"Beth jokes that Elva looks after her—or tries. Checks when she's doing any marketing to see if Beth needs something. Always walks with her to and from our get-togethers, that sort of thing. It's sweet, but Beth's as self-sufficient as they come. Or was," she said. "Martin's death will shake that. She'll be strong, but he was her true and abiding love. They were each other's."

"When's the last time you were in Ms. Greenleaf's bed-room?"

"Her bedroom?" Darlie looked blank. "That's a strange one. I'm not sure about that, but— No, wait. Yes, I am, now that I think. Though I can't think why it matters. It had to be April, because Beth goes on a spring cleaning war. I mean war. As if her place isn't always spotless. But she goes to war, and part of the combat is cleaning out closets. She had clothes, shoes—hers and Martin's. I went over to get them. Helped her box them up. It would've been April. Why?"

"Just details. Do you also work with Open Doors?"

"Yes, we do. It's a wonderful and much-needed organiza-tion."

"So you know Serene Brenner?"

"Ah . . . I don't think I do, but I work most directly with Della. Della and I also go back a few decades. Old activists. She founded Open Doors."

When she heard Peabody's clomp, Eve rose. "I appreciate your time, your cooperation."

"I've learned to cooperate with the cops when I have to. In this case, absolutely anything I can do. I loved Martin, truly loved him."

"Do you know of anyone who'd want to harm him?"

"I imagine there were scores, and many of them once held badges. But you know that. I don't know specifics. Mar-tin didn't talk about his work with me, not in detail. But I'm glad it's you, and your partner," she added as Peabody stepped into the doorway, "who're looking for who did this. I've enjoyed Nadine Furst's books, very much."

"Right." Eve turned to go, turned back. "Do you also work with Sebastian?"

As her lips curved, Darlie tapped a crooked finger on them. "I believe I'm about to take the Fifth."

"Figured. Thanks again."

Peabody waited until they'd walked outside. "She couldn't really add anything, Dallas. She cried a little—tried not to. She went over the night in question and all that. It all jibes. I asked her when she was last in the bedroom, and she said the week before Christmas. The Greenleafs had a party, and everybody put their coats on the bed in there."

"They're not in this. See if you can reach the last one— Anja Abbott—by 'link. Run her through it. If you get any buzz, we'll follow up in person."

"You got it."

"Shit," she said when she checked the time. "Look, what I'm going to do is drop you home—we're close enough. Then I'll go home and finally update Whitney by holo, start digging more on the dead and disgraced cop list."

"Okay, but . . . We're really close to the house, too. Maybe you could drop me there instead, and just take a quick look? Like, fifteen minutes? I'll tag McNab and we'll put in more time on the list, get you more names."

Since Eve considered it a pretty good deal, she pulled out her 'link. "Let me tell Roarke what I'm doing. We're already past end of shift."

9

When Roarke came on-screen, he smiled. "Great minds," he said. "I was about to check and see where you were and what you were doing."

"I'm in the city of New York, hunting bad guys."

"So, the usual. And literal, as I see you're on the street. Find any bad guys?"

"Not yet, but the day's not over. Shift is, work's not. I'm going to drop Peabody off at the Great House Project. Deal is, she and McNab will put in more time tonight on the Greenleaf investigation if I take a look at the progress. Do you want in on the deal?"

"As it happens, I'm already downtown and intended to make the same deal with you."

"Then I'll meet you there. Soon."

"This is mag!" Peabody climbed in the car, then bounced in her seat.

"Joyful bouncing is forbidden on the job."

"We're off shift."

"Off shift doesn't mean off duty. It's got to connect with somebody on that list."

She asked herself if she'd stuck the investigation on that point, just bogged it down looking for that connection.

No. The connection *was* the point.

"Nothing else plays through," she concluded. "And no one we've talked with so far connects there. Or we haven't found that connection."

"At the same time," Peabody continued, "the killer had to be able, or work with someone who was able, to gain access to that window, from the inside most likely. And they had to know Greenleaf—or his wife—well enough to know their routine, to know the layout of the apartment."

At the light, Eve watched some kid execute a tight back-flip on his airboard.

Good form.

"Arnez and Robards's apartment has the same footprint," Eve pointed out. "It's likely others in the building do, too. So we could have someone who lives there, or did. Or knows someone in the building."

"Or who knows the security feed overwrites every couple of days. So find a way in outside that time frame. A week ago, say. Two weeks. I don't see longer than that, Dallas. Too chancy that one of the Greenleafs would notice the window's unlocked."

"Agreed. It's too well planned for leaving that to chance. Arnez was the last outsider in there, and roughly thirty minutes before the murder."

"Yeah, and if it wasn't for that pesky motive she'd look good."

"She had a . . . look."

"A look?"

"When Webster opened the door of the apartment. Just for a second, she had a look."

Eve shook her head. "Sticking with facts. She had means and opportunity, so I want us to dig deeper there. She's de-cades younger than all but one of this women's group. Does she have friends her own age? Tanaka said Ms. Greenleaf joked about Arnez looking after her. Checking in, did she need something from the market, that sort of thing."

"It's considerate."

"Maybe. It also adds to the information pile on the Greenleafs, gives Arnez more easy access. 'Got your quart of soy milk and your egg substitute.' Then you get the: 'Come on in, have a cookie.'"

"Well, I don't usually get a cookie, but I sometimes pick up a few things for Rhonda Grappler—do you remember her from when you lived there?"

"Yeah. Down the hall—from Mavis now. I hauled her trash to the building recycler if I was around. And she had to be cruising toward the century mark when I lived there."

"A hundred and two now."

"And Greenleaf's thirty years younger, healthy and active," Eve pointed out. "I get it may just land on considerate, friendly neighbor. Add she had a legit reason to be in the bedroom. But she's the only one who stands out in this group right now. The rest have known each other for years—and most of them decades."

"Okay, I'll play. Arnez and Robards move into the same building, and two floors up—same footprint—from the Greenleafs."

"Greenleaf and Tanaka met Arnez slightly before that when they went into the shop Arnez manages. I don't see that as coincidence, as Greenleaf has a lot of clothes, it's a neighborhood shop. High-end, but they have sales, and some people—it escapes me—just like to look around at stuff in shops."

"They call looking around at stuff in shops shopping. Or browsing," Peabody considered. "You browse around so you can see the stuff, then decide what to buy or not buy."

"If you decide what you want to buy before you go in, you

can just buy it and save time. If you're not going to buy anything, you can just stay home."

"Sometimes you don't know what you want to buy until you see it. Hence, browsing provides the opportunity to see what's available, and if you want it for your own."

"So if you didn't see it in the first place, you wouldn't want it? And if you didn't want it before you saw it, doesn't it follow you didn't need it?"

Peabody narrowed her eyes. "Those are snare-Peabody-in-a-trap questions. I take the Fifth and move on. Wait!" She shot up her index finger on both hands. "When people browse and shop and find what they want and buy it, it's good for the economy. It increases the tax revenue, and allows the merchant to meet their overhead and make a profit so they can stay in business."

"Uh-huh. I'm sure all the people hauling shopping bags are thinking: I've done my civic duty, contributed to the economy, and now the merchant I bought all this stuff I didn't actually need from can put food on the table tonight."

Eve glanced over. "Is that what you were thinking when you bought that pink jacket?"

"No, I was thinking: Pretty. But it still works that way. Anyway . . . So they meet while browsing at Très Belle, and then Arnez and Robards move in."

"Which automatically makes contact easier." The easy contact, Eve thought, was going to matter. "To move there, Robards has to commute to Queens for his work, to see his family."

"But she can walk to her work, and he's a defender. What's best for her."

"Maybe what's best for her is to kill the captain—but we're not there yet."

Eve told herself to run it through, but avoid getting stuck on it.

"They make friends," she added. "Enough she's invited into this group of longtime friends."

"McNab and I are about to move into a beyond-mag house with your oldest friend and her family. Because Mavis and family and McNab and I are friends—through you—and because we moved into the same building—where they took over your old apartment when you moved in with Roarke.

"Relationships are complicated," Peabody concluded, "and have a lot of intersections."

"Tell me." Eve said it fervently. "I'm keeping them on the list. They're low on it, but they stay on. If we don't find a connection, they're clear."

"You really think we will? Find that connection?"

"Can't shake it," Eve admitted. "Something about her, just something, from the minute she came in with Greenleaf."

"I wasn't there, so I don't have that. But we'll dig, and hard."

"That's the deal." Eve pulled up at the gate. It opened.

"Your vehicle's on the Open Sesame List. That's what Mavis calls it."

"Right. Sesame's a seed, right? I know it's from a story, but why pick a seed to open something?"

"It's a frosty word. Sesame! Doesn't it look abso-mag?"

It did. While she'd been in Europe, the grass had sprouted up into a blanketing green lawn, shaded here and there by young trees or flowering shrubs. Long gone were the dead and dying branches, the overgrown weeds and patches of dirt and scrub.

A wide, paved walkway led to a covered front porch where chairs painted a bright, happy blue, a bench in popping purple, stood ready for people to sit. Pots in every color of the rainbow and more held thriving flowers.

The front door—somewhere between that bright blue and

popping purple—of the big, sprawling brick house already stood open.

Saying nothing, Eve pulled into the paved parking area, got out of the car, then stood, hands in pockets, studying the house.

"If I'd imagined a house Mavis would make her home, it wouldn't have been this. And I'd have been completely wrong. It's her, it's so much her. And you," she added, glancing at Peabody.

"It's both of you, which shouldn't make sense. But it does. It's also a miracle of major proportions. This—the house, this yard business. A couple of months ago, it looked like some rich guy's neglected shithole. Now? Yeah, it's abso-mag."

"I love it so much. I feel like we sort of saved it, you know? It was sitting here, all sad and empty, waiting for the right people to bring it back, fill it up."

"You're the right people," Eve told her.

"You have to see inside. It's an even bigger miracle."

As they walked to the house, Mavis ran out to the porch.

"Jesus, she got bigger."

"Well, she's six months along."

And in tiny leaf-green shorts and a baby-belly-clinging pink-and-white-striped tee, she looked it. She had her hair—currently pink with some leaf-green tipping—scooped up so it bounced as she did.

A couple of bouncers, Eve thought. No wonder Mavis and Peabody fused a friendship.

"You're back! You're here! Check it!" She threw her arms out, then up.

"Jesus, she shouldn't bounce like that. I can see what's in there sloshing around, banging its head against her rib cage."

"Number Two's just fine," Peabody assured her.

Number One came barreling out the door and kept coming.

She wore cropped overalls in pink with big purple buttons to match the shirt under them. Her curly blond hair bounced, like her mom's, in ponytails on either side of her ridiculously pretty face.

"Das! Das! Das!"

She came at Eve like a heat-seeking missile, then leaped up, fully expecting to be caught. With little choice, Eve snagged her. She smelled like cherries. And since Eve tasted them when Bella smacked kisses over her face, Eve suspected a recently consumed cherry popsicle or sucker.

It wasn't bad.

She babbled, laughed heartily, then linked her arms around Eve's neck, hugged fiercely.

"Rub Das."

"She wants me to rub her?"

"La-la-la," Peabody said, and Bella laughed again.

"La-la-*love* Das."

"Oh, well, hell."

"Hell," Bella echoed with a smile.

"You'll get me in trouble. Anyway, love you back."

Who wouldn't? Eve thought.

"La-la-love, Peadobby."

"She's almost got it," Eve noted.

"We've been practicing. How about giving me some?" Peabody held out her arms. Bella dived into them to smack more kisses between babbles.

Peabody settled Bella on her hip as they walked to the house with Bella babbling.

"We'll see August next time," Peabody told her. "McNab's coming soon, and Roarke, too."

"How do you know what she said?"

"You get an ear for it."

"We missed you!" Mavis threw her arms around Eve as fiercely as Bella had. And what was inside the growing bump, bumped.

"God, it's moving in there."

"Number Two's happy to see you."

"It can't actually see me." Unsure, Eve eased back. "Can it?"

"Bellamina, baby's kicking."

"I want!" She scrambled down from Peabody, pressed her ear to Mavis's belly. "Boom, boom!" she said, and laughed like a maniac.

"How was Greece, how was Ireland? I want to hear. We'll open some wine. Not for me," she added, patting her belly.

"Not for me. I've still got work. But I want to check things out."

"So much is happening. It's beyond the beyond. The amazing maga-god crew knocked off about an hour ago, but they finished Leonardo's studio."

Now Peabody bounced. "Totally?"

"Totally and too totally tremendo. He's up there basking around and fussing. My studio's complete-o, too. They're moving the rest of the equipment and furniture in tomorrow."

Mavis did a hip wiggle that brought Eve more mental images of sloshing fetuses.

"And the— No, wait. Sheesh! You didn't get to see Peabody and McNab's place at all last time with Dorian acting like a you-know-what before she came around. How's she doing at the school?"

"Roarke checked in while we were away. All good. But you'd know that," Eve said. "You'd have checked with Sebastian, who'd have found a way to check."

Mavis just rested a hand on her belly and smiled. "How about we go around, go in through Peabody's side?"

"I run!" Bella announced, and did just that.

"You know what's absolutely ultra mag? She can. She can run wherever she wants. This one will, too."

They started around to the side of the house.

"It looks great out here, Mavis. Seriously."

Now Mavis added a shoulder wiggle to the hips. "Let me say, you ain't seen nothing yet."

As they rounded the house, Bella scrambled up the steps of a slide in the play area. That had been there weeks before, and the beginning of a vegetable garden, the young flowers and vines, the barest bones of Peabody's water feature.

As Bella slid down with a delighted *Whee*, Eve stopped in her tracks.

"Holy shit, Peabody."

Water spilled and tumbled down stones from a height of about four feet. The stones formed ledges and drops that invited more spills and tumbles that ran into a kind of rocky stream ending in a small, glittering pool, where a stone dragon kept guard.

Flowers, moss, other greenery pushed out of spaces in the rocks.

It looked as if nature had decided to set a waterfall in a backyard in downtown Manhattan.

"Isn't it the abso-poso ult?" Crossing her hands over her belly, Mavis just beamed.

"Holy shit," Eve repeated. "It's all I've got. You killed it, Peabody. Holy shit."

"It really worked. About halfway through I panicked, and thought it was going to look like somebody—me—just piled a bunch of rocks together. Leonardo talked me through it."

"My moonpie."

"How?" Eve wondered.

"He said the same thing happens to him sometimes with a design. And sometimes he's right, and it turns out wrong.

But he can fix it when that happens. He can see where he went wrong if he went wrong, and fix it."

"Well, it's freaking beautiful."

"It absolutely is," Roarke said from behind her. "Peabody, you're a wonder." He kissed her cheek. "A genuine wonder."

Bella spotted him, shouted, "Ork," and came running.

He scooped her up, kissed her. "I believe you've grown. And you as well," he said to Mavis.

"Bunches of progress. Here." A pat on the belly. "There." A smile for Bella. "In there and out here. We picked tomatoes and peppers—from our backyard—over the weekend. Lettuce, too. Peabody made a salad—put nasturtiums in it. And we all sat right out here and ate what we'd grown."

She swiped at a tear. "I know I'll get to the point, one day, that I don't get drippy whenever I stand out here, see all this, watch Bella play. But right now? Every single time."

"Mama cwy happy," Bella announced.

"Yeah, she does. Let's go inside, in Peabody's place, before I flood. How about we start in the kitchen, Peabody?"

"My happy place. On the side, we have doors straight into the living area, and one into a mudroom."

"I saw," Eve said. "You went with that not really purple, not really blue color."

"Plum Blue. We wanted to keep it coordinated. We've got the full accordion doors on the back."

"Peabody tried to balk," Mavis said, "but coordinated won. Do it, Peabody!"

Peabody took out her 'link, coded in. And Bella applauded when the glass doors slid open.

Not as wide an opening as Mavis had, Eve noted, but plenty wide enough.

She'd seen the images on Roarke's tablet, but . . .

"I'm saying what I said when I got a load of the waterfall. But silently, so Mavis doesn't give me the hard eye."

All the soft colors Peabody wanted—cabinets, some with glass fronts, counters, miles of them. Shelves already holding tools and dust catchers—nice-looking ones, Eve admitted—arranged with Peabody's artistic eye.

What Roarke had called a living wall served, Eve supposed, as a focal point. Pots of quiet blues held green plants that spilled or climbed or spread.

"My sister made the pots."

"I heard. When I heard, I figured it would look weird, which is fine. But it doesn't."

"McNab thought of it. And the baking counter—it's custom for my height."

"Yeah, he gets points. And pie. It's you, Peabody. The wall there, the whole thing. It's just completely you."

"I get drippy, too," she said as her eyes filled and she ran a hand over a counter. "I always had a home. Homes. Because that's how I grew up. My home, my grandparents', cousins'. I always had a home. McNab, too. And we made the apartment home, but we always knew that was temporary. This is . . ."

She drew a breath. "This is ours. I know we'll help. With security, with the kids, the garden, with just being here. But Mavis and Leonardo gave us ours. We'll never forget it."

"Don't make me cry again." Mavis wrapped around her, swayed. "You're ours, too, so think about that. I'm going to go get Leonardo. He won't want to miss. Let's get Daddy, Belle of mine."

"I run!"

"You bet. Show them around, Peabody. We'll find you."

"Okay." Peabody sniffed, swiped. "Okay. So the dining room—it's all open now. My mom's making the light—I think I told you. Blown glass."

"Yeah."

"She says it's almost done, but won't show me. But I have the basic measurements, so I was going to build a table."

"Of course you were," Eve murmured.

"But then, last weekend, McNab and I went to this place in Brooklyn. A giant thrift store, flea market, antiques, or just old stuff place. I found this great sofa for the living room, just need to reupholster it—but that's not the big find. I saw this table and it reminded me of the one my dad made, the one they still have. Live edge, this big, thick plank of oak, farmhouse-style legs. It'd seat twelve. We have the counter here when it's just us, or casual stuff. It was damaged—somebody's dog had chewed the hell out of a couple of the legs. But fixable, and affordable if we really, really squeezed.

"Then I checked because it just reminded me of my dad's work. And I found his name and the date on the underside. He always signs his work. I started bawling."

"And no wonder. The fates led you right to it."

Peabody nodded at Roarke. "I felt just that. The date? The year I was born. I mean, what are the odds—in Brooklyn?"

"Fate doesn't trouble with odds," Roarke told her.

"I guess not, because there it was. The guy selling in that area came running over because I'm sitting on the floor blubbering. Anyway, he knocked fifteen percent off, and McNab squeezed another five out of him. It's in the garage—since we don't have cars, at least right now, I'm using it as a workshop. I'm not telling my dad. We're hoping they come out for Thanksgiving. We'll be in by Thanksgiving."

At her hopeful look, Roarke rubbed her shoulder. "You will, with time to spare."

"I can see just how it'll look there. I'm going to start hunting for chairs. I don't want new, and I don't want them to match. Coordinate's different. So the dining room'll take awhile, the living room, too," she added as she led the way.

"I swear I'll decide about the feature wall—yes or no—by the end of the week. But I'm thinking we already have one with the fireplace and the bookshelves."

The bookshelves, still empty, flanked the fireplace Eve remembered as old and grimy.

It gleamed now in its frame of wood, as did all the wood trim Peabody had raved about at first sight.

"So I think just soft walls—the way it flows into the great room area—and street art. Classic old-timey for the sofa. I guess I'm going for urban farmhouse."

She hadn't gone soft in the powder room, but bold, artistic, eclectic.

"We were going to put our office downstairs, then we decided hey, let's use that for another living space, like a party space, or kick-back-and-watch-a-vid space. We're going to put a bar down there, a big-ass screen. So we went for the office here."

She opened double pocket doors, and left Eve blinking.

Peabody had said something about splattering paint on the walls, and they'd done just that.

Name the color, it splattered to create a ridiculous, wild, mad space that reminded Eve of EDD.

"We had the best time doing this. Just a free-for-all, paint everywhere. You should've seen Bella."

Eve glanced back as she heard Bella and her parents approaching.

Leonardo, looking dreamily happy, hugged Eve from behind, set his chin on the top of her head. "Now she wants her playroom walls done like this."

"And we'll do it, won't we, Bella?"

Racing into the room, Bella turned circles. "Paint!" And flicked her little hands everywhere. "Woo!"

"We're going to put the partner's desk my dad's making right in the center. They used this as sort of a formal parlor. And Jesus, the wallpaper. I mean, jeez," Peabody corrected. "We'll have screens, a sit-down-and-talk-it-through area, an

AutoChef station in the closet. McNab's building our comps systems. Roarke and Feeney are in on that."

"Fun for us."

"You people have strange ideas of fun. It's a good work space," Eve said, "even with the crazy walls."

McNab pranced in. "Am I late to the party?"

He sure as hell fit in with the crazy walls.

"We have to duck out of the party soon," Eve told him. "I've got work. And . . ." She pointed at Peabody. "Deal."

"What's the deal?" McNab wondered.

"We've got to push on the dead or disgraced cop list."

"Oh, that's smooth." He put his hands in the hip pockets of his many-pocketed, canary-yellow baggies. "I got another chunk done. Why I'm a little late. Sent to your home and office units, Dallas."

"Then I'd better get to it. Listen, we'll come back when we close this case. Get the full house tour, both sides. It looks great, very seriously great."

"Let's make another deal." Mavis snuggled into Leonardo. "The first Saturday night after you close the case, you come for dinner and a tour. We're getting a grill. Peabody actually knows how to use one, and she's going to teach Leonardo and McNab. Bella, Number Two, and I are opting out of that one."

Eve glanced at Roarke, already knowing she'd get a nod. "Okay. That's a deal."

Since he'd sent his car away, Roarke got behind the wheel of Eve's as the family—because damned if that's not just what they were—waved them off.

"It's coming right along, and ahead of schedule."

The gates opened.

"So in before Thanksgiving."

"I'd set October, but now I think the middle of September. They may still have some fussing to do—we need a this for that space. Or thinking like Peabody: I need to paint that table. But the work, I think yes, mid-September."

"I see a lot of you in there."

"Do you?"

"The if you take this wall out here, you'd have this. If you leave this wall here, you'd have that."

"It's given me a great deal of fun and satisfaction to be part of it. It's a happy place now, and will only get happier."

"I have to agree with you there. Bella and the next one, they're going to grow up in a home, with the kind of people we never knew existed at that age. Mavis and Leonardo, they're great at all this. Then you add Peabody and McNab. You've got the handy with the Free-Ager and the geek. It's a sweet deal for all of them."

She rested her head back, closed her eyes.

"I was going to suggest dinner out on the way home, but I can see that's not an option."

"Sorry. The investigation's not in a happy place. Do you know an organization called Open Doors?"

"Somewhat familiar. What's its purpose?"

"Former female inmates. Offering housing when needed, training to move into the workforce, that sort of thing."

"Ah, yes, I know of it. Are they connected to Greenleaf?"

"No—one of their staff was, but she's in the clear. How about Another Chance?"

"Very well, yes. Dochas often coordinates with them."

"Darlie Tanaka."

"Not familiar—wasn't that one of the names Elizabeth Greenleaf gave you? Her women's group?"

"Good memory, yeah. She runs it, and she's clear. How about Della McRoy, so I don't waste my time there."

"Yes, I know her a bit and, if my opinion counts, you would be wasting your time there. She founded Open Doors, as I recall now, and works tirelessly to fund and promote it, along with her other good deeds. I find her extraordinary, actually."

"Fits, and your opinion counts. I can't say I wasted time hitting those angles. They had to be hit, the people had to be questioned and cleared. I can wish I had the time back, but it wasn't wasted."

"We'll have a meal, and you'll tell me how I can help."

"I've got finances to dig into."

"And so you give me my evening's entertainment."

"I need to update Whitney, so I'd like to do holo."

"Easy enough."

For you, she thought. She really needed to get a handle on that. Soon.

"If I deal with the finances and have time left, I can take part of this list of dead and disgraced cops. It also sounds entertaining."

For you, she thought again.

"I'll take you up on it. It's a fucking long list. Jenkinson got his promotion."

"That's very good news, but you expected it."

"It was fun to see him squirm a little when I announced it in front of the bullpen. I meant to tag Yancy, just to tell him you really liked the painting."

"I spoke with him. So did Sinead."

"Really?"

"He told me she contacted him first thing this morning. It meant a great deal to him."

"I'll still tag him." She put her head back again. "Did we really only get back to New York about twenty-four hours ago?"

He laid a hand over hers. "Murder has no sense of timing, does it now?"

"Sure as hell doesn't. Can we have spaghetti and meatballs?"

"What a fine idea that is."

10

When they drove through the gates, Eve admitted—to herself—if she had the choice, she'd have dropped flat on the bed and slept for the next ten hours.

Since she didn't, why mention it?

As they walked to the door, Roarke took her hand, kissed her knuckles. "Food will perk you up."

So it showed, she thought. No need to mention it.

Summerset loomed, of course, and the cat padded over to ribbon through Eve's legs as if he hadn't been royally pissed at her the day before.

"And how was your tour?"

"You'll have to get down there soon," Roarke told him. "Peabody's waterfall is a study in artistic and mechanical talents."

"I saw it and more a few days ago. And I agree. I thought you might stay longer, have dinner with them."

"Work." Eve headed for the stairs.

"Ah. Of course."

Sensing the tone, she shot a look over her shoulder, and grabbed Roarke's line. "Murder has no sense of timing. So," she added, "you should watch your step."

In her office, she shrugged out of her jacket, tossed it aside.

"A meal first, Eve. You're flagging."

"I really need to update Whitney."

"And given the time, he's very likely at his own evening meal. We'll have ours, then you'll update him."

"Crap, you're probably right. I'm going to text him, ask if he'll be available for an update in . . . an hour. That gives me time to eat and get some things organized."

"Good plan. Go on then, take ten minutes to work on your book or your board, whichever, and I'll deal with the meal. You can update me while you eat. Practice."

She took the ten for the board, as the visual always worked for her. And the visual still put Arnez/Robards on her list. Since, at the moment, she had no one else on that list, they hit the top of it.

At least until she had a chance to dig deeper into the dead and disgraced list.

"All right, come eat, have a glass of wine."

He'd opened the doors to the little balcony, as they both enjoyed the air. And he'd added a side salad to the pasta—but she wasn't going to bitch about it.

"I thought I had a hot one," she said, and told him about Serene Brenner.

Roarke listened, nodded, sipped wine.

"And you're sure she's clear?"

"Her alibi's solid. I sent the security feed into EDD in case she messed with it, but that's not going to pan out. She has two people backing her up, and the vid she said they watched—that checks, and the time watched checks. Her parole officer considers her a success story, and her record since getting out is clean. Plus . . ."

"Plus?"

"She didn't ring. She just didn't."

"But there are others."

She stabbed into a meatball. "A hell of a lot of others."

"And I'm to look into the finances of that hell of a lot?"

"Maybe, eventually. Tonight, I want you to dig hard into Arnez and Robards."

Watching her, he wound pasta on his fork. "The neighbors."

"Because they do ring, and I don't know if that's just because, Jesus, the opportunity was right there. Get friendly, take the time, make the effort. And because you've done that, plan the rest out. Go into the bedroom—remember Greenleaf's always running late—unlock the window while she's not looking."

She ate, then waved her fork.

"All you have to do is walk out with her, signal your partner, who's two floors up. Down the fire escape right after dark, kill the captain, set up the suicide, get back upstairs. I'm thinking she planned to get back into the bedroom, lock the window again, but we were there, and that part fell off."

She ate, cursed, ate more. "Sometimes it's just that simple. Sometimes it's not, but sometimes it is."

"All right, I'll look, and deep."

"You don't see it."

"I trust your instincts," he qualified. "But you did say the list is long."

"Yeah, it is. And somebody else could've gotten friendly enough to get in there. Dropped in to see the captain when his wife wasn't there, for instance."

She could see how it played—and just that simple, too.

"Just a casual drop-by, 'How's it going, Martin' deal. Then you say you have to use the john, and zip into the bedroom. Ten seconds."

"And his widow wouldn't know to mention it to you when you asked."

"Yeah. Or they just watched the place long enough to get the routine."

He nodded. "People are often more predictable than they imagine."

"Yeah, they are. Somebody else could live in the building or have a connection there. They could've used your magnet trick, or just gotten in a few days before when the apartment was empty. Didn't worry about relocking the window because deed's done."

She picked up her wine. "Sometimes it's not simple."

"Agreed. Do you want my instincts?"

"You're not the expert consultant, civilian, for nothing."

"Well then. I don't see the magnet tool in this."

"Because?"

"You'd first have to know their habit—more of a rule, isn't it really?—of keeping everything locked."

"Yeah." Winding pasta, she nodded. "You've got that."

"If you know that, you've already likely found a way in. And if you've found a way in, why trouble yourself with the extra time and risk? Then add that the security feed's looped and overwritten every two days, wasn't it? So much simpler to just walk into the building—either mastering or buzzing in through that connection. A connection with the Greenleafs or another tenant. Unlock the window, then walk away."

"You're risking they'll notice, lock it again."

"You are. But your odds are good they won't in only a few days."

She pointed her loaded fork at him before she ate. "You'd have used the magnet."

"I would, again most likely. But my purpose in getting in would've been—in the long ago—to steal, not to kill. You're looking for someone who had one purpose—or two, as the suicide needed to be staged."

"That takes me straight back to Arnez and Robards."

"On one hand." With a shrug, he drank more wine. "On

the other, the lady of the house admits to unlocking them to clean in the spring. If the investigator accepted the suicide, it's an easy step to considering she simply neglected to lock that single window. Either way, Captain Greenleaf's dead, so the purpose is accomplished. Why worry about such a small detail, and one that can be explained away? More?"

He lifted a finger before she could debate. "The timing, Webster's unexpected arrival. If the killer heard Webster, any plans to finesse the lock would weigh against discovery. Escape takes precedence."

"I'll agree with that. Another problem. We can't know who else the captain might have told about his wife's plans. My issue with that is this wasn't an impulse kill, something put together on the day of or a couple of days prior. It took time."

"It certainly seems so," he agreed. "A cop in prison has a great deal of time, as would someone connected to him or her."

"And I've yet to find any connection to Arnez or Robards. Yet," she repeated.

"I'll start with the finances. We'll clear this up, then I'll set up your holo-meeting."

"I'll clear this up. You set that up. You were right," she added.

"Oh, about too many things to mention. But what specifically in this case?"

"The food helped. I've got a boost going, so I'm going to use it."

While she dealt with the dishes, she went over her report in her head. When she came out, Roarke stood at her command center.

"It's ready when you are. You can take it from here?"

"Yeah. I could've gotten it going. It would only take me four or five times as long as it takes you, but I could do it."

She paused to look over at her board. "You made good points. The killer had purpose. They also believed they had another couple of hours. Maybe planned to plant a few more suicide seeds. But then Webster's knocking on the door. The only thing to do is get out, and fast.

"Can't go out the apartment door—and maybe that was the plan. Lock the window after you come in, do the job, plant the seeds, go out the door. Could've had a hole to wait in, another apartment, a stairway, the basement storage/laundry areas. It's going to connect to a cop, and a cop's going to know one of the first things the investigator's going to do is check the security feed. You wait that out, walk out. And clear."

"It doesn't shorten your list."

"Not even a little."

"I'll see what I can find on your favorite suspects."

Once more Eve studied Arnez's photo. "She was right there. If she's in this, was that really smart or really stupid? I haven't decided."

When Roarke left her, she positioned herself, then called up the holo.

It always gave her a quick, internal jolt to see Whitney in casual clothes. He sat at a desk in a simple navy T-shirt. And still, the wardrobe didn't lessen the sense of command.

"Commander, thanks for opening your schedule this evening."

"You've had a full day. More than," he added. "What do you know?"

"There's a lot I don't. I can say, after background checks, interviews, and verifying movements and times, the captain's family is clear. We've begun the process of delving into anyone the captain investigated, with emphasis on those who were removed from the NYPSD, who faced criminal charges. Those who self-terminated after same or were killed or

died—and those connected to them. Family, spouses, partners."

She ran through the progress of the day, including the interview with Serene Brenner.

"I remember Detective Brenner. You're confident she's
clear?"

"Yes, sir, fully confident. Detectives Peabody and McNab
are continuing work on compiling the list, as I will be. We'll
start running through those individuals tomorrow."

"I spoke with Elizabeth Greenleaf shortly ago. They plan
to hold the memorial the day after tomorrow. I want as many
as we can manage, in full dress, to attend. You and your
investigative team will be excused from that duty if necessary."

"We'll attend, sir, if at all possible."

"That's good enough. We're after a cop killer, Lieutenant.
If you can pull more of your division in, do so."

"Understood."

"I also want you to watch your six."

"Sir?"

"Lansing lost his badge today, immediate termination for
cause. His own captain supported that decision. He didn't
take it well, and the record of his . . . reaction supports that
decision and the cause for it. Nor did he accept any personal
responsibility for his behavior in your bullpen."

"I didn't expect him to."

"Watch your six, Dallas," Whitney repeated. "Lansing
worries me."

"Yes, sir."

"And keep me updated on the investigation. It's going to
track back to a cop, one who might have been, at one time,
under my command."

He said nothing for a moment. He didn't have to, as she
could see the weight heavy on his shoulders.

"Good hunting," he said, and signed off.

She shut down the holo-program, then programmed coffee. She sat at her command center and started hunting.

About an hour in, she decided to make her first contact, working chronologically back from Greenleaf's retirement. The last internal investigation he'd headed involved an officer with more than eight years on the job, and a file with more than a couple of reprimands, and several complaints and accusations of excessive force.

Officer Drake Milrod's last night on the job involved a trans woman in her sixties, inebriated and walking home from a party. Milrod pulled his patrol car over, turned off his body recorder, and ordered his partner—a boot with under three months in—to do the same.

Officer Agnes Carte had enough sense to ignore the order, and her record clearly showed Milrod taunting the woman, who was drunk enough to initially be amused.

He then tossed her to the ground, and in the process of cuffing her—for no fucking reason, Eve noted—broke two of her fingers, punched her—face, body.

When Carte attempted to stop him, he assaulted her, drew his stunner, threatened her with it. Then used it on the civilian.

Carte called for assistance, and Milrod stunned her. As she went down, her recorder showed Milrod stunning the now unconscious woman again.

By the time other officers arrived, Milrod had a story about the woman attacking him, his partner getting in the way.

The woman died en route to the hospital—head trauma, neurological distress. Carte suffered a concussion. And her recording clearly documented the events.

The internal investigation, after Milrod's suspension, bore out Carte's documentation, her statement. Greenleaf recommended termination, and Milrod was charged with second-degree murder, assault, misuse of his service weapon, and a host of other charges.

Although he was currently doing twenty-five off-planet, he had a brother, both parents, and an ex-wife alive and well.

Not easy to plot revenge and murder from an off-planet cage, but he'd made public threats against Greenleaf, Officer Carte, and the prosecutor.

She started with Carte.

"Officer Carte, Lieutenant Dallas."

"Yes, sir. I know who you are."

"I'm primary on Captain Greenleaf's murder investigation."

Carte, a dark-skinned Black woman about Peabody's age, closed soulful brown eyes. "You want to talk to me about Milrod. Lieutenant, he's got another solid twenty off-planet."

"I'm aware. Has he attempted to contact you since his incarceration?"

"No, sir."

"Has anyone associated with him contacted you for any reason?"

"Not since his trial, no, sir. Lieutenant, I've tried to put that behind me. I had barely two months on the job, I was just trying to do the job, learn, be a good cop. I testified against him, and a lot of other cops didn't want to work with me after that, so—"

"Then they were wrong. Dead wrong. I've reviewed the incident, I've reviewed your recording and statements, the log that verifies you called for backup, stating your partner was out of control. You did everything right and absolutely nothing wrong."

"I appreciate that, sir, but it's taken me years to get to a place where I'm trusted and have trust. I just want to keep it in the rearview."

"Understood. There's been no contact?"

"No, sir, and I would have reported same. When he gets out in twenty, if he comes after me, he won't find me so easy to put down. Captain Greenleaf was supportive and professional—plenty weren't. Some still aren't. I was sincerely sorry to hear about his death and the circumstances."

"All right, Officer. Let me add this. If you continue to find a lack of support, I'd take you on. I value solid cops."

Those soulful eyes closed again. "That means a great deal, sir. More than I can say. I don't want Homicide. I still see her face. Mandy Levins, age sixty-three. But thank you."

"If you ever change your mind, the door's open. You did all you could do, Officer. You did the job. Remember that."

She moved on to the brother. Paul Milrod—age thirty-six, father of two, married seven years—lived in Albuquerque and worked as a therapist specializing in minors.

When he answered his 'link, his quietly handsome face held a carefully blank expression.

"NYPSD?"

"That's right. I'm heading a murder investigation here, and the victim was the Internal Affairs captain in charge of your brother's case five years ago."

"I see. I don't know how I can help you."

"How often do you speak with your brother?"

"I haven't been in contact with him since he contacted me when he was charged and demanded I not only come to New York as a character witness for his trial, but give him twenty thousand for a lawyer. I did neither. Prior to that, we hadn't communicated since I went to college, at eighteen. That would be about eighteen years ago."

He held up a hand.

"Let me save us both time. Drake was a bully, all his life. He bullied me all of mine until I got away. He bullied our parents, his ex-wife, and anyone else he could. He should never have been given a badge and a weapon."

"I've reviewed his file, Mr. Milrod, and don't disagree. Would he contact your parents?"

"No. They'd tell me. They live out here now. He broke their hearts countless times. He demanded they mortgage their home to pay for his lawyer, and threatened them—his own parents. He struck our mother, Lieutenant. And that was the final blow, literally. He's exactly where he belongs."

"Do you know of anyone who might assist him in exacting revenge?"

"I don't. He hasn't been in my life nor I in his—thank God—for eighteen years other than that single, ugly conversation. I honestly can't help you, and I would."

She believed him.

"I appreciate you taking the time to talk with me."

"No problem. If I could add something?"

"Please."

"He's a dangerous man, but only to those he sees as weaker. Because like so many bullies, he's also a coward. I was the younger brother, someone he saw as weaker—and he wasn't wrong for a number of years. My mother's a woman, so weaker. His ex, a woman, so weaker. It's unlikely he'd see this police captain as weaker and follow through. Even if he could find a way."

"Thank you for your input."

"Good luck."

She sat back, thinking it through as she wrote it up.

Milrod, unlikely. Not smart enough. No finances to buy even a cheap, sloppy hit.

She glanced over as Roarke stepped in. "Maybe you're having better luck than I am."

"I doubt you'll see it that way." Since it was there, he picked up her coffee, drank some. "Arnez and Robards. There's nothing in their finances that veers off the norm. She's worked, at least part-time, since she was fifteen. She, and her mother, as

I checked, cobbled enough together for college, which she did primarily by remote and added more working hours. She's solid enough financially."

He set her coffee back down, decided to switch to water for a bit.

"She's moved around in jobs, as you know, but strategically. No hidden accounts, no odd deposits or withdrawals. She pays her bills on time. Other than rent, her biggest expenditure is wardrobe, which given her career track makes sense.

"Her mother relocated to Georgia with her cohab about four years ago. I didn't find any travel there on her part, so assume they're not close."

"No family pictures I saw in her apartment. Not any."

"That would track, wouldn't it? She's lived in New York all her life. She had grandparents on both sides, but none live in the area and, again, there's no travel to indicate visits."

"Not all families are families."

"Truer words," he agreed. "Robards, however, continues to work as a mechanic in his old neighborhood, very near his family. And his finances show he supports them, generously when he's able. He makes a good living through his employment, adds to it by restoring and selling classic cars. He's enterprising and apparently skilled. He does quite well for himself.

"Again, there's nothing shady in his finances. I have to tell you that angle's a dead end."

"Okay, if there's nothing there, there's nothing. What about the grandparents? Arnez?"

"Her maternal grandparents—divorced. She lives in Reno, and he in Memphis. Paternal, still married, relocated to Wisconsin, where the grandmother had family, about twenty years ago. They've since retired to Tampa, Florida. Again, no travel connecting either way, no sign of financial gifts or assistance. I can't tell you if they're in contact with each other, but it seems doubtful given the rest."

"Okay. All right." Getting stuck after hitting a dead end equaled stubborn. Or stupid. "I've got to move on."

"Why don't I help you with that?"

"I can give you some names. You could stick with finances."

"My favorite thing." Because he could all but see the tension in her shoulders, he stepped behind her to rub them.

"But do you really think money's the angle?"

"It's going to be a cop, or someone connected to one. I still think the easiest way to gain access to the Greenleaf apartment and, to their routine, is from the building, or a neighboring one. I've run the tenants in the building, and nothing pops. But say there's something hinky in their finances? Income or outlay—payment for the kill, or payment out for some sort of blackmail. Or an addiction that could be exploited."

"All right then, I'll look. Send me the names. Two hours more. Two hours," he repeated, "then we call it. You're losing that post-dinner boost."

"Maybe. But there's coffee."

"Two hours more," he repeated as he started back to his office. "It's a fair deal."

Since it was, and his work would save her a lot of time, she didn't argue.

She dug in, continued the process of working back in time. The odds, she calculated, favored someone with a fresher grudge. Alternately, someone released from prison within the last three to five years.

She pushed on both, using a split screen. She managed a few more 'link conversations because she remembered the Earth rotated on its stupid axis.

By the time she'd used up her two hours, she felt she'd eliminated or shot several names to the bottom of the list.

"I know, I know," she said when Roarke came back in. "I'm just wrapping up. I've eliminated four, five with Brenner, and have three more very low probability. I only want to look through what you just sent me."

"I can run it down for you." He took her hand, tugged her to her feet. "My best calculations," he continued as he walked her out of the office, "take another three off your suspect list, and leave one more in that dead-low probability. You can look at the names and the data in the morning."

"Great. Only half a million to go. No, seriously, it's good, solid progress. And you adding another three or four to it helps. Peabody and McNab came through on the deal. So more names to check, but they started the elimination process, so it's almost a wash there."

The cat stretched over the bed. He slitted one eye open, then closed it again as Eve shrugged out of her weapon harness.

"And I've got two we're going to want to interview. Maybe we get lucky."

She sat on the side of the bed to take off her boots.

"Making good, solid progress gave me another boost."

"Did it now?"

"It did. And it occurs to me we haven't kicked the cat off the bed in over three weeks."

He sat beside her. "We wouldn't want to spoil him, would we?"

"No." She swung around, straddled him. "You know what I think?"

"I'm getting a glimmer of an idea."

"Bet it's more than a glimmer."

She took his mouth with hers, enjoying the moment.

Their house, their bed, their soon-to-be annoyed cat.

Work waited, but for morning. The night was theirs, too.

"Nice shirt," she commented as she worked open buttons. "So I'm resisting just ripping it open."

"I have more shirts."

"And still. It's good to be home." She peeled the shirt away, tugged the leather tie out of his hair. "Even with the last— what—twenty-six hours, give or take, it's good to be home."

He drew her shirt up and away. "The Grecian sun's given you a glow." He trailed a finger over her cheek, down the shallow dent in her chin, along her throat.

"New York will take care of that before too long."

"So I'll enjoy it while it lasts."

And he pressed his lips to her throat. Then shifted, flipped her so she lay back on the bed.

Galahad grunted, leaped down, stalked away.

It made her smile.

"He ought to be used to it by now. Then again . . ." She drew Roarke down with her. "I don't think I'll ever get all the way used to it, either."

Because it was always new, he thought when their lips met again. Gloriously familiar, and still brilliantly new. The taste of her, the feel of her skin, the shape of her—he'd find her in a world of dark. And still, the thrill of having her could strike fresh and sharp each time, every time.

They rolled over the bed, playful now even as pulses thickened. Her heart beat strong and fast under his lips; her hands moved quick and firm over his back, down his hips.

They took each other deeper—little nips, long strokes until he felt himself simply merge with her. Beat for beat, breath for breath.

When he slipped inside her, a slow joining, she cupped his face in her hands.

She saw everything in his eyes, that wild Irish blue. Everything she felt lived in them, everything she brought to him, all they gave and took from each other.

Need lived there, and desire. That would always be a thrill. But love, so steady, so endless, so real, dominated all. And that would always, always be a wonder.

For a moment, her body burned, simply burned with all of it. Then the burning became a drenching warmth that rolled her to peak, rocked her there, let her fall, then rise again.

And all, all of everything, shined inside her while their eyes held.

He said her name, only her name, before their lips met again.

The moment he let himself go, she wrapped tight and went with him.

11

Her body clock popped her awake before dawn, again.

Beside her, the sheets felt cool enough to tell her Roarke had been up, dressed, and in his office for some time.

Curled in the small of her back, Galahad slept on.

She called for lights at ten percent, rolled out, and hit the bedroom AutoChef for coffee.

Since she was up in what felt like the middle of the damn night, she might as well do something. She pulled on gym shorts, a tank and, with the coffee, took the elevator down to the gym.

She decided on a three-mile run and, drinking coffee, scrolled through the programs. She chose one set in New York called Flight or Fight.

Silence fell on Fifth Avenue under a blazing summer sun. Old flyers, takeaway cups, mangled shopping bags scuttled or fluttered along the empty streets. Display windows in the Midtown shopping mecca showed frozen-faced mannequins in sparkly dresses and sleek suits.

Or, behind shattered glass, they lay broken, naked, and some eerily splattered with blood.

She didn't mistake the dead body half-in, half-out of a

broken window as a mannequin. The blood looked fresh and plentiful and, as she jogged closer, she noted the right shoulder—or more accurately, the lack thereof.

A cop was a cop, even in a hologram workout program, so she ran over to investigate.

Urban War era? she wondered. But she saw no signs of bombing, heard no sound of street fighting, no military or paramilitary presence.

What she did see when she reached the body was what had once been a man greedily chomping on the DB's leg.

The dead woman's eyes snapped open. She growled. And what was snacking on her rose up from his hands and knees to shamble forward.

"Seriously?"

Eve reached for her weapon. Instead of a stunner, she held a handgun. Resisting the instinct to aim for body mass, she remembered the weirdly entertaining zombie vid she'd watched with Roarke and went for the head shot.

When he dropped, the dead, mostly devoured woman began to crawl out of the broken window. Mindless hunger glowed in her eyes.

Eve shot her between them.

And they came, shambling out of broken windows, climbing out of manholes, dragging themselves over the sidewalk.

She said, "Well, shit," and ran.

By the time she got back upstairs, Roarke sat, the cat across his lap, a pot of coffee on the table. Out of habit, she supposed, he had the screen on mute while the stock reports flashed on.

"Why were there zombies?"

He smiled at her. "Some say it comes from a virus."

"I figured on a three-mile run since I was up, pulled a program that fit the timing, and zombies are chowing down all over Midtown and up to the Upper West."

"Ah, Flight or Fight, was it? And which did you choose?" he asked as she hit the pot for more coffee.

"Both. Zombie doorman over on Fiftieth nearly had me, but I mostly decapitated him with the revolving doors. I just wanted a run."

"You could've ended the program, picked another."

"That's like quitting. Anyway, I worked up a sweat. I'm grabbing a shower."

As she went, Roarke scratched Galahad between the ears. "She had more fun than she'll admit."

When she came out, the cat sprawled across the bed and Roarke had breakfast under warming domes.

"So, what planet did you buy while I was fighting zombies?"

"Actually, this morning dealt with fine-tuning some projects in the South Pacific."

He removed the warmers to reveal golden omelets, flaky croissants, and some sort of little parfait topped with peaches.

"However, this afternoon, you might be interested to know, I'll be looking at some design options for the venue area of your building."

She knew she'd find spinach inside the omelet, but when she cut into it, she also discovered ham and cheese. "It's not my building just because you slapped my name on the deed."

He topped off both their coffees. "Darling Eve, your name on the deed is exactly what makes it your building. I can also tell you Stone, the justly reviled tenant, has decided to relocate both his club and his living quarters to Jersey City."

"Yeah? Well, bad luck to him. Asshole. Speaking of someone else, who wasn't an asshole but connected to a previous case, the guy who does the metal sculptures. Where Eliza Lane stole the cyanide."

"All right, yes."

"Peabody went goofy over this lamp he had. Since I got a

look at her part of the house, yeah, I can see it. Still, you're more up on what she's doing and where and all that. If I had him send you a picture of it, or one like it, maybe you could see if it'd work somewhere in her new place."

"I could, yes."

"Solid." She shoveled in eggs. "Then there's this garden sculpture deal Peabody said Mavis would go goofy over and, yeah, she would. Lane commissioned him to make it so she could steal the cyanide. He's probably finished it by now, or maybe he scrapped it considering. Anyway, we've got to get them stuff, right? When they finish the new place, you've got to give them stuff."

"Housewarming gifts, yes. And listen to you, thinking ahead to appropriate gifts."

"It's not thinking ahead so much as not having to think. And it's definitely not browsing," she added, thinking of her conversation with Peabody.

"Browsing?"

"You probably had to be there."

Steam poured out when she broke open her croissant. She slathered it with butter that melted on contact.

"All right then. Have him send me the images. I expect if Peabody thought they'd work, they will."

"Good, then it's done and no thinking or browsing. Better yet, no shopping. I've got to spend the day thinking about wrong cops and the people who love or loved them. Because that's what it's going to be. Maybe I'll hit Mira up for a consult, see if she leans there.

"Greenleaf's memorial's tomorrow."

"Will you attend?"

She shrugged, ate. "Depends on where we are. Paying respects matters, but—"

"Finding his killer matters more."

"It does. The suicide matters," she added as she ate. "Not

just killing him, but staging it as suicide. To cover, or to spread more pain? I think I'll talk to Mira, fit that in somewhere today."

"Isn't death enough pain?"

Shaking her head, she sampled the parfait and wondered if the peaches came from their own trees out in the back.

Either way, tasty.

"Your loved one's murdered, there's shock and grief. There are maybe ifs and whys. Suicide's a different kind of pain. He left me, he chose this. Why didn't I see he was in crisis? So is this a strike at the wife, the family, too? Maybe. Or it's a mirror."

He lifted a brow as he topped off their coffee. "Ah."

"Yeah. Payback for the loss of someone who committed suicide, someone Greenleaf—in the killer's mind—drove to it. Someone who left his or her family with that different kind of pain and grief. Any way you look at it, it's going to matter."

She pushed up. "I've got to get dressed. The zombies took me longer than the thirty."

"Zombies have no respect for schedules."

Who could argue? she thought as she moved into her closet. And she'd damn well get her own clothes together for the day.

She grabbed khaki trousers—sort of the opposite of black—then a navy jacket because summer, lightweight. A sleeveless white shirt seemed just fine.

She had navy boots sitting right there, so why not?

She waffled over the belt—brown or navy—then spotted a navy one with thin brown leather woven through.

She dressed quickly—don't give him a chance!—and came out carrying the jacket.

As she strapped on her weapon harness, she glanced over at him.

"Okay, what?"

"I was just thinking how fresh and professional you look."

She grabbed her badge, her 'link. "Is that a flick?"

"Not at all. In fact, looking at you, a bad guy might think: Ah well, she'll be easy to take down, won't she then? And won't he be surprised when he's splayed out at your feet bleeding from the ears?"

She had to grin, then swiped a finger down herself. "This says all that?"

"To me it does." He rose to draw her into his arms. "I've a packed one today, but you'll let me know if there's some finances that need looking into. A man wants his entertainment."

"I can do that." And kissed him. "The club venue design deal? Maybe something Mavis or Avenue A would play in."

He kissed her. "We'll keep that in mind. See you take care of my fresh and professional cop."

"Top of the list."

On the way into Central, she texted Feeney to request McNab for another day. Cutting down names of potentials also hit top of the list. She considered texting Mira directly about a consult, then decided not to rile the dragon admin. She'd go through channels.

Keep working backward chronologically, she told herself. But focus on the suicides. Maybe the wrong angle, maybe, but they had to be weighed and/or eliminated, so start there.

She'd take the suicides, divide the family connections who'd taken that route when their cop was dismissed or incarcerated.

Start filtering. The cop—if alive—had connections in New York. If incarcerated, someone connected managed to gain access to the Greenleafs. If previously incarcerated, the cop settled back in the city, or had those connections.

If dead, same deal.

But suicide played a part in the whole.

Probably.

She ran it, ran it, ran it, different angles, more theories as she fought morning traffic.

When she pulled into the garage, she'd worked out a general plan for the day.

She spotted him as she got out of the car. He'd obviously stood behind one of the pillars, waiting.

No cheap suit this time. Trousers, a black shirt. Add unshaven and unkempt, and a look in his eyes that said he'd found a bottle or two to spend the night with.

"Lansing, you're only making it worse."

"Worse for you without your bullpen of assholes around you."

"Do you really think going for me is helping the captain?"

"I put you down, somebody else takes over. You've got Webster fooled, you may have Whitney fooled. But I know what you are."

She gestured up. "Garage cams, Lansing. My own recorder, again. Don't be an idiot. Walk away."

"I'll take my chances. Somebody like you has a badge and I don't? That's bullshit."

She set as he started toward her. And they both heard the car pull in and squeal to an abrupt stop.

Baxter piled out of his ride. "What the fuck, Lansing?"

"Stay out of it, Baxter," Eve snapped out.

"Dallas."

"That's an order."

"He doesn't bother me. Fancy suit, fancy ride." Lansing's lip curled. "Just another one of your assholes. I can take you both."

When he got close enough, she smelled the boozy breath and figured he actually thought he could.

She let him take the first shot, and supposed he considered the solid backhand to the face an insult.

She tasted blood.

"Not just off the job," she said as she blocked the next blow. "That's going to put you in a cage."

"I don't fucking think so."

She didn't use the back of her hand, but her fist. He staggered back, then came in hard.

Even drunk and out of control, he landed a few. More than. When his fist connected with her left breast, the pain radiated straight through her.

Riding it, she spun into a back kick that knocked him back, followed with a cross jab that made her knuckles sting, then just swept his legs out from under him and put him on his ass.

"Stay down!"

As she reached back for her restraints, he pulled a clutch piece out of an ankle holster. The stream went wide, missed her, and hit the oncoming Baxter.

"Goddamn it!" She kicked the stunner out of his hand, yanked out her own. "You hit? Baxter, are you hit?"

"Yeah, but no." Baxter planted a foot on the loose stunner, then opened his suit jacket as Eve slapped the cuffs on Lansing. "Magic lining. Let's hear it for Thin Shield. Goddamn it, Dallas, he fucking used a weapon on a fellow officer."

"He's not an officer. He's a drunk, shit-for-brains asshole. And you're under arrest for assaulting an officer, for possession of a concealed weapon, for using same on an officer."

"Fuck you, fuck you both."

"Yeah, well, you're the one who's fucked. Baxter, do me a solid. Park that fancy ride of yours and take shit-for-brains up to Booking."

"Sure. Your lip's bleeding, LT, and you've got blood on your shirt."

"Shit. Shit. Shit!"

"I've got a stain stick in my field kit. I can get it for you."

"No, just take this *fuckhead* off my hands. And contact EDD, have them scoop up the security feed. Ask them to pick up my recorder. I need to talk to people."

"Okay. You took a solid hit, you know." He gestured to her breast.

"I'm aware. Park and deal. And you," she said as Baxter jogged to his car. "You have the right to remain silent."

After she read out the Revised Miranda, she left him to Baxter. Mira's office first, she thought, for multiple reasons now.

"Lip's bleeding," some helpful uniform told her in the elevator.

She might've snarled, but her mouth already stung like wasps had held a playdate on it.

The admin was just setting up for the day. Eve thought: Give me any shit right now, be sorry for it.

Before she could speak, the admin's eyes widened.

"Lieutenant! You're hurt. What happened? Let me get you an ice pack. Do you need medical assistance?"

"I need a consult with Dr. Mira, as soon as possible."

"She'll be in any moment. Please, sit down. You're bleeding."

"I'm fine. Just give me a time, and I'll make it work."

They both heard the quick click of heels. Mira swept in, wearing a pale pink dress and matching hip-swinging jacket.

"Good morning. I— Oh God, Eve! What happened?"

"Lansing, in the garage, I need to speak with you about that and about my current investigation."

"Come in, sit down. Hold my calls. Where is Lansing?" she demanded as she steered Eve into her office.

"Baxter's taking him to Booking. He's not right, just not right. He'd been drinking on top of it."

"Sit down. I mean it." As she spoke she strode to a cabinet, took out medical supplies. With a quick snap, she activated a cold pack. "Hold this on your jaw while I wand that lip."

"Here's better." Eve pressed the pack to her breast. "Bastard punched me in the tit. Damn!"

"I know," Mira murmured as she used the wand. "It's going to sting at first. Just breathe."

"Breathing. It's not about Greenleaf with him. It may have started there, but he's got some bug up his ass about me, particularly. Doesn't matter, he's going away for a while. He had a clutch piece and he shot a stream that hit Baxter. Had his piece on full. Son of a bitch wanted to do serious damage."

"Dear God. Is Detective Baxter injured?"

"No. He was wearing the thing—the magic lining."

"Ah, Thin Shield. Well, we all owe Roarke."

"Lansing's rep's going to do what he can—that's what reps are for. He would've appealed the termination, but that's off the table now. They'll call for a psych eval."

"Of course. I'll take that myself."

Relieved, Eve closed her eyes. "Good. Okay. That's enough with the wand, isn't it?"

"There. For now. It's going to be sore, and it's still a bit swollen, but the wound's closed. Bruising's coming up on your jaw, and the swelling there. Keep breathing."

"I never saw the fucker until yesterday. Anyway, I'll report all this to Whitney, but I need to consult with you on the Greenleaf investigation."

"Yes. I was so sorry to hear about his death."

"Did you know him?"

"I did. He was a dedicated public servant. He had a hard, firm line, and not all agree with how and where he drew it."

"Did you?"

"I respected his integrity and, when he felt it necessary to seek my advice, he respected mine. Use the pack on the jaw now, and let me see your breast."

"It's fine. Not the first time I've taken a hit there."

Mira's soft blue eyes could go very steely. "Have you forgotten I'm also a medical doctor? Let me see your other injuries and I won't have to call for MTs."

"Fine, fine." Eve started to unbutton the shirt, winced as her knuckles ached.

"We'll deal with your hands in a minute. I'm going to be very unprofessional and say I'm glad to see the state of your knuckles. It means you got plenty of hits in."

Struggling against embarrassment, Eve shut her eyes. "I think I dislocated his jaw. Spin kick. It was a good one. Definitely busted his nose."

"You've got considerable bruising here. I'm going to wand your breast. It's going to hurt a little, but then ease. You'll want to re-treat it every three to four hours."

"Okay. I'm going to talk about the case. I'll send you what I've got, but I'm hung up on the suicide ploy. Man! Jesus! Shit!"

It hurt. It fucking hurt.

"Keep breathing."

"Right. Let me explain."

She ran it through while Mira wanded, while the pain eased to a pulsing, rotted tooth kind of ache.

"I've run into him a handful of times in the last year or two," Mira said as she worked. "I certainly saw no signs of suicidal tendencies. Anyone who knew him would have known he wasn't a man to take that route."

"They thought they could pull it off. I think the window was a mistake, or they just couldn't get it locked before Webster came in. But killing him wasn't retribution enough."

"Smear his standing, further devastate his family. I want

to review everything, but— There now, that's enough for this round."

"Thanks. It's better."

Rising, Mira walked back to the cabinet. This time she came back with a stain stick. "Let's see what I can do about that shirt."

"It doesn't matter," Eve began.

"Don't be silly." Kneeling, she began to work out bloodstains while Eve stared at her, perplexed.

"But," Mira continued, "from your oral report, my first impression is the suicide ties in. I'll review, as I said, but at this point I'd suggest you look for someone who's connected— and emotionally connected—to a police officer Captain Greenleaf investigated. One who was relieved from duty, perhaps charged with a crime. But certainly one whose career in the NYPSD ended due to Greenleaf's findings."

"I'm getting most of it out," she muttered. "This former officer took his or her own life."

"I was leaning there. But wonder if the IAB conclusions and consequences led someone connected—a spouse, a child—to self-terminate."

"If so, I'd expect the killer to go after, or to have gone after, the spouse or a child. The captain would have come later, after he'd suffered that loss."

"Okay." She could see that. "Okay."

"It's a vendetta. Murdered with a service weapon, in his own home, leaving him—or planning to—for his spouse to find. Look for that in his case files."

"All right. I'll filter out the rest, for now, and focus there."

"Proper attention will get the rest of the bloodstains out. A few stubborn ones, but they're barely noticeable."

"Summerset'll notice. Trust me."

Looking up now, Mira smiled. "You've had a hard landing home."

"It's the job. I appreciate the help. All of it."

"You send me your data and I'll be sending you reminders to rewand, and wand anywhere you didn't tell me you're hurt."

Getting to her feet, Mira smoothed down the skirt of her pretty pink dress. "You could use a blocker."

"Yeah, probably. The neighbors. I've already run them. Nothing pops. And no family connection with anyone on the list—so far anyway."

With a smile, Mira laid a cool hand against Eve's swollen jaw. "Family's where you make it, isn't it? Take that blocker."

Family's where you make it, Eve thought as she headed up to Homicide. She knew that better than most. Maybe better than any.

So she'd push on the suicide mirror, then work the connections.

But first, she had to ask for a meeting with Whitney, and she needed to get a spare recorder so she could turn hers over to EDD.

When she walked into Homicide, Jenkinson and his tie du jour—a supernova scattering fiery space debris over electric-blue space—lurched to his feet.

"Jesus, Jenkinson, I've got a fat lip and an aching jaw, now you want to burn my retinas?"

"Baxter said that fucking fuckhead fuck punched you in the tit. That he fucking aimed for it."

"Christ." She muttered it as she instinctively crossed her arms over her chest. "He got worse."

"Fucking A. Tossed a fucking stream at Baxter."

"All good," Baxter said from his desk. "I got the magic. Lansing's in a cage, LT, and crying lawyer."

"Fucking coward" was Jenkinson's opinion.

"And Whitney's in your office."

"Great. Terrific. Peabody, come in when the commander's done."

"I will. Are you okay?"

"I haven't been in my office and I've been punched in the face, in the fucking tit. I've been wanded and cold-packed, and now I have to go over it all with the commander before I can do my damn job. I've been better."

In her office, Whitney stood at her skinny window, his hands clasped behind his back. He turned, took a long look.

"Sit."

"Sir, please take the desk chair."

"I said sit." And he jabbed a finger at the desk chair.

She sat.

He held up his PPC. "I've just reviewed the security footage from the garage."

"Yes, sir. I need to turn my lapel recorder over to EDD."

He simply held out a hand.

Eve removed the recorder, handed it to him.

"You tried to talk him down."

"Yes, sir."

"When Detective Baxter arrived, you ordered him to stand back."

"Yes, sir. I didn't see a weapon on Lansing, but I couldn't be sure he didn't have a clutch piece, which proved to be the case. I felt he wouldn't use a weapon on me, not at that time. He wanted to use his hands."

"Which you let him do. You let him take that first swing."

"Commander, I could have drawn my own weapon and re-strained him, but until he took that swing, it was talk. If I'd used aggressive tactics, I'd have no chance to de-escalate the situation. I pointed out that the garage security recorder, my own recorder was engaged. Baxter stood as a witness. And still he took the swing."

"I'm getting coffee, for both of us." He turned to her AC. "He'd been drinking."

"Yes, sir."

"And he laid in wait."

"It appears so, sir. Commander. Thank you," she said when he passed her coffee. "Commander, Lansing clearly has a personal issue with me. I don't know what it is or why it is. It could be it just started yesterday when he assumed I'd shut down the Greenleaf investigation as suicide. And now he blames me for the loss of his badge. Whatever his issue, he's lost all control. It didn't matter to him that he'd pay a price for assaulting me—that it would clearly be recorded and witnessed as same. What mattered was paying me back."

She sipped coffee, winced as the heat made her lip throb. But it was worth it.

"Dr. Mira intends to do his psych eval personally."

"You spoke with Mira about this?"

"I needed to consult with her on an aspect of the Greenleaf investigation. I'd obviously been in an altercation. And frankly, sir, I felt it best to inform her of the Lansing situation."

He took his coffee, stood at her skinny window again. "I can't disagree. I intended to go straight there after speaking with you. Saved me a trip."

He turned back again. "You did everything right, just as you did yesterday with Lansing. I think you should and could have dodged that backhand. That's a choice you made, one that will make it easier to get him the help, and the punishment, he very obviously needs.

"I intend to speak to IAB this morning. However, my information is no one else there has any issues with you or with your investigation. If I perceive otherwise, I'll deal with it."

"Yes, sir."

"I'm taking this mug with me. I'll get it back to you."

"No problem."

"When cops go wrong, it hurts all of us. Ice that jaw," he added, and went out.

Eve sat back, shut her eyes.

One minute, she thought. Just one minute of quiet—or as quiet as it got when her head still rang and everything throbbed.

Then she heard Peabody's clump, and sat up.

12

Peabody walked in with a cold pack in one hand.

"I already iced down," Eve began, but Peabody just put the pack on Eve's desk.

"You're going to ice again in a few minutes. Your jaw looks pretty bad. I can't see your left girl, but—"

Eve laid a hand over her breast. "And you're not going to."

"But I bet that hurts." She held out a blocker cupped in her other hand.

"I don't want—"

Peabody, eyes hard, shoved the blocker under Eve's face.

"Jesus, Peabody, I outrank you."

"Don't make me tag Roarke."

A fist in the throat would've been less of a jolt. "You wouldn't dare."

"Oh, oh, I dare. I double damn dare, so take it."

Eve snatched it, popped it, swallowed. "What are you so pissed off about?"

"What am I pissed off about? What am I pissed off about?"

Throwing her hands up, Peabody turned a circle. "He attacked you. He punched you in the face, in the *boob*, and for no reason. None. He was a cop, and he came after another cop. He freaking tried to stun you—missed and hit Baxter."

"Baxter's been busy," Eve muttered.

"What the hell do you expect?" Eyes on fire now, Peabody slapped her hands on her hips. "What the hell do you expect? You're the LT! He came after our LT, and he fired on one of us. If Baxter hadn't had the magic lining, he'd be hurt, too. I tell you, if Lansing hadn't already been in a cage, Jenkinson would've gone for him, and I'd've been right beside him. So would the whole bullpen."

"Which is exactly how it's not done. I handled it. It's handled. Maybe you need a soother before blood vessels start popping all over your face."

"I don't want a damn soother." Furious, frustrated, Peabody dropped into the visitor's chair. "Ow. Damn it!"

Eve sat back again. "Need an ass blocker?"

With a half laugh, Peabody scrubbed her hands over her face. "He attacked you, Dallas. He was waiting in the garage and he went for you, over bullshit. We're working the case. I know how late you worked because I got your final notes of the night. McNab and I worked as late as you did—I bet Roarke, too."

"He did."

"And this guy comes after you—twice now? What the hell?"

"He's not right. Whether he ever was, I can't say, but he's not right now. It's handled. And now the shrinks and lawyers and courts will sort the rest out. He'll do time—I won't back off there, because if it's not me, he'd find somebody else to pound on. He needs to pay the price as much as he needs the shrinks. And it's handled. So chill it down."

"Look, you're my LT, my partner, and you're my friend. I get a little cranky when someone punches you in the face."

"So noted, and appreciated." The red-hot fury—a little scary—had died out of Peabody's eyes. "Are we good now?"

"Maybe if I had coffee I'd be better."

"Then get it, because we've got work to do. I had a consult with Mira."

While Peabody got her coffee, Eve filled her in.

"You were already leaning there—to the suicide angle being key. This refines the angle more. I guess that's what Mira does. Refines and clarifies."

"Killing him wasn't enough," Eve said. "Plenty of ways to take him out if that's the only goal. It's still possible that part of the plan was just to end the investigation almost before it began. The captain took himself out, done. Or to leave the department and his family with the weight of believing he had regrets and guilt over the job he couldn't live with."

"But the mirror suicide rings loudest."

"So we're going with it. We cull suicides out of our respective lists, and focus there. Bump to the top any who used the same method. We'll include other means, but if we're right on the angle, it's going to mirror the method."

"Most common anyway, for a cop."

"It is. I've got a short list from Morris on suicide cops Greenleaf visited in the morgue over the last few years he was on the job, so there's that.

"I'm going to check with the lab, see if they've had any luck IDing the murder weapon. If not, and I think not or I'd have heard, we have to start going through records."

"What records?"

"It was police issue, not black or gray market. They'd removed the identifying number. But if a cop loses his weapon, it's reported, it's recorded."

"Supposed to be," Peabody pointed out.

"If it's not, he's not assigned another. If a cop retires, dies, is terminated, the weapon's turned in, recorded. If it's reassigned, that's recorded. If it's destroyed due to age or damage or malfunction, that's recorded."

"Right. I knew all that. So . . . we're looking for the category of stunner used on Greenleaf, one reported lost or turned in. Turned in, we track it to the new assignee and verify."

Peabody puffed out her cheeks. "That's going to be another slog."

"I'm going up to see Feeney and ask him if he can spare another e-geek to help with the slogs. Meanwhile, we cross-check. We're looking at cops who used a stunner to take themselves out. That weapon would also go into evidence. Could be kept there, could be destroyed after the case closed."

"Because maybe the killer used that same weapon to kill Greenleaf. That's a good one."

"Then get started. Coordinate with McNab on it, and I'll head up and tug someone else out of Feeney."

Eve took the glides to EDD. Good angles, she thought. Some solid lines to pull. It was almost worth getting punched in the tit to grab that early meet with Mira.

Almost, because even with the blocker that still ached some.

The circus of EDD distracted from that. Jenkinson's tie paled in comparison.

Wild colors, crazy patterns—and that was just the hair— dominated the space. Baggies, bibs, skin pants in crazed rainbows whirled around as those wearing them remained in near-constant motion.

She caught a glimpse of McNab, chair dancing in his cube as he worked. His usually sleek blond tail of hair now sported bright red streaks.

Probably in solidarity with Peabody's, Eve decided, and didn't bother to sigh.

She headed straight for the normality of Feeney's office.

He wore a dependably brown suit—this one summer weight and the color of dung baked in the strong sun. His tie, shades darker, hung just a little crooked, but was currently unstained.

His wiry hair exploded, ginger and gray, about his hang-dog face.

He leaned back against his desk, one foot tapping as he frowned at his wall screen.

He turned his gaze to Eve, and his basset hound eyes went hot. "That fucking shithead Lansing."

"Word travels."

"Homicide LT gets jumped in Central's garage by an ass-hole fired off the job for being an asshole, it travels fast and far. Then he fires on Baxter? You'd better tell me he looks a lot worse than you."

"His nose is busted, his jaw may be dislocated. His ribs have to hurt, and he won't be using his right arm easy for a while."

"Good. Shithead." He looked over her left shoulder. "How's the . . . ah, the, you know, the, ah, girl part?"

"God, is everybody talking about that? I'm good. Fine. Everything." Move on, she thought. And fast. "I could use more help on searches for the Greenleaf case."

He nodded, obviously relieved they'd tabled any discussion of Eve's girl part. "You've got McNab as long as you need him. What else?"

"I'm starting a secondary search, on the murder weapon."

As he listened to her rundown, Feeney picked up the wobbly bowl—a Sheila Feeney creation—from his desk, popped one of the candied almonds in his mouth.

"If your suicide cop got busted, they'd confiscate his weapon at the bust." He offered Eve the bowl.

"Right." She took an almond. "Might've had a drop piece—harder to trace—or he got somebody in Records or in Evidence to play along. Wrong cops know other wrong cops."

Feeney's face went tight and grim. "Yeah, they fucking do. The killer filed off the ID code because they didn't want it traced."

"Right, so it can be, and it's unlikely when it is, it'll connect to Greenleaf. We're already pushing on dead or incarcerated cops, but we're shifting focus to suicide cops. It's a lot to run, Feeney. We're eliminating, but it's slow going. Adding this is going to take it down to a crawl until we hit."

"I'll take it. Didn't much like Greenleaf, but he was a cop who worked and lived by a code. I'll take it," he repeated. "Send me what you've got. I'll pull McNab into the lab, and we'll work tandem on it."

"I appreciate it, a hell of a lot."

Feeney popped another almond. "He came after me once, Greenleaf."

"What? When?"

"Before your time, kid. Had to be nearly twenty years back. Bogus shit, and he cleared me, so that was that. Still didn't like him much," Feeney added, and popped one more almond. "But he had a code and he stuck to it. Whoever took him out's not just a cop killer, but a coward with it. So I've got this."

More than she'd expected, Eve thought as she made her way back to Homicide. With Feeney digging in, they'd push through faster and cleaner.

"Feeney's taking it," Eve said as she passed through the bullpen. She heard Peabody's *Oh yeah* as she veered toward her office.

With fresh coffee to keep her boosted, she copied all current data to Feeney. She took another minute to study the board, homed in on the crime scene, Greenleaf's slumped body, the angle of the stunner burns.

"Yeah, a coward," she muttered. "Taking an unarmed man from behind."

She swiveled back, brought up her portion of the list. She'd barely begun on the next name in line when she heard someone coming toward her office.

She only thought: What now? before Webster stepped into the doorway.

"Oh, Christ, Dallas. I just heard."

"It's done. It's handled."

"I knew he was . . . But coming at you this way, in front of another cop, in the damn garage."

"It's done," she said again. "You should know if he'd gotten through me, and Baxter, he'd have come after you."

After dragging his hand through his hair, Webster looked at Eve with exhausted eyes. "Yeah, I get that. Can I sit?"

"I'm going to update you. Give me a couple hours first. Feeney's agreed to work on the searches, so I expect progress today."

"Can't ask for better than Feeney. But it's more I want to update you. If I could have a few minutes."

She shrugged, gestured. "You know the risks of the chair."

"Yeah, I do." He sat, carefully, in her visitor's chair. "You know your budget would handle another visitor's chair."

"Why would I want that?"

He smiled at her, a tired, grieving man. "You know, I was crazy about you."

"Oh hell, Webster."

"No, no." He waved a hand. "I was, and stupid with it. And I crossed a serious line with the stupid, got just what I deserved. And getting exactly what I deserved straightened me out in more ways than one. It's hard to be grateful Roarke kicked the shit of out me, but I am. It set me straight, and in another direction.

"I talked to Martin about it—Beth, too. They mopped up the blood, listened, iced down my ribs and whatever. And let me know I'd crossed that line. No wiggle room on it. That's family—they'll mop you up, and tell you the truth. So."

He blew out a breath. "I went over to see Martin that night because I wanted to talk something over with him. I told you that in my statement. You never asked what I wanted to talk to him about."

"It wasn't and isn't relevant, and is your business."

"True enough, but I can't talk to him, and don't want to give Beth any more to worry about right now. In a strange way you're a part of why I wanted to talk to him, and I want you to hear about it from me."

"Fine. But since it's not relevant to the investigation, you're eating up those few minutes."

"It won't go into effect until you close the investigation, my captain agreed to that. But I've turned in my papers."

"What?" Genuinely stunned, she jerked up. "Why?"

"Because the woman I love and want to make a life with lives off-planet."

"But— You only met Angelo a few months ago."

He smiled again. "Didn't take you long to hook up with Roarke. When you know, you know. We've talked about it. Her coming here—resigning as chief of the Olympus police. Me going there, resigning from the NYPSD. I'm going there, because it feels right. I wanted to talk to Martin."

None of her business, she told herself. But . . . connections.

"You're talking a huge leap, Webster. What the hell would you do there?"

"I've thought about that, too. It's not impulse, Dallas. Can't be a cop, cohabbing with and eventually marrying my chief. I was leaning toward going private—"

He only smiled at her derisive snort.

"But with what happened to Martin . . . I want to teach, train. I want to help teach and train good cops. After this fuckup with Lansing, I want that more. It needs to be more than how to investigate, how to handle a suspect or de-escalate a situation, how to interview. It has to be about ethics, integrity, honoring the badge. I think I'd be good at it. I want to be good at it."

"You probably would be. It's just . . . a lot."

"A different direction, and I'll take it with Darcia. It's everything I want. I wanted to tell you. Now I'll get out of your way."

As he rose, Eve heard heels clicking down the hall.

Chief Darcia Angelo stepped into the doorway. Her dark hair fell in long waves to her shoulders. Though she must've recently traveled on a space shuttle, she looked runway fresh in a form-hugging cream-colored dress and sky-high heels.

"Darcia. I didn't expect . . . You came all this way."

"Of course I came. Don." Despite Eve's presence, Darcia opened her arms, took him in. "I'm so sorry about Martin."

Even as Darcia held him, Eve saw her eyes, her cop's eyes, focus on the board.

"I went to your place first." Turning her head, Darcia pressed her lips to Webster's cheek. "Dropped my bag. When I checked in IAB, your captain said you'd come to talk to Dallas."

Darcia drew away, held out a hand to Eve. "Lieutenant."

"Chief."

"I'll give you the room if you're speaking confidentially. But I want to say, I'll be in New York for a week, and am at your disposal if you can use my help in any way."

"That's appreciated. Webster can't be directly involved in the investigation."

"Of course."

"And neither can you, considering your relationship with him."

"Ah." Darcia nodded, but Eve saw some professional regret as Darcia looked at the board. "Understood."

"However, I can and will continue to keep Webster in the loop, and wouldn't object to him sharing information with you or any insight you might have."

"That's generous of you. I mean that. Don, your captain said you'd be needed to complete some work before leaving for the funeral home where they'll bring Martin later today. I'll come to you when you're done, then we'll go be with your family."

"It means everything you'd be here."

"Where else would I be at such a time? Let me know when you're ready, and we'll go."

He brought both her hands to his lips. "I won't be long. I appreciate the time," he said to Eve, then to Darcia: "I told her."

"Good. I'll wait for you. Not here," Darcia assured Eve when Webster left. "But if I could have a moment."

"Sure. What the hell."

"First, can I ask what happened?" She gestured to Eve's face.

"An asshole happened. He's sitting in a cage and looks worse."

"I'm glad to hear it. Next. You don't approve of our plans, of Don's decision."

"It's not for me to approve or otherwise."

"He holds you in high regard. So do I." Darcia smiled. "Which puts you on the spot."

"You want to know what I think. I'll tell you. I think when it mattered, you came. And when he saw you, I saw—for the first time since this happened—the stress and grief lift off him. That won't last, but that mattered."

"No, it won't last."

She looked back at the board, and Eve saw grief.

"Martin was his father, in every way that counts. I want, very much, to help you find who took his father from him, and I understand why you can't let me."

"I get why he's turning in his papers and coming to you. I don't get why either of you live on something spinning around in space."

"Earth's also something spinning around in space."

"Yeah, people keep telling me that. I think you're both going after what you want. And why not?"

"Why not?" Darcia agreed. "I'll leave you to your work." But first she stepped over, touched a hand gently to the crime scene photo of the body. "He didn't deserve this."

No, Eve thought when Darcia left. But no one did.

She'd barely gotten back to work when Peabody texted.

Ice down again.

"Who put you in charge?" Eve muttered. But she activated the cold pack and laid it on her sore jaw while she worked.

When she had three she felt warranted an interview, she walked out to the bullpen.

"Let's go talk to people."

"I've got one, I think, and McNab just sent me one," Peabody told her.

"So that makes five. Let's have some conversations. Run yours for me."

"Lieutenant Colton Jayne. He had a network of corruption going, and went down for it about sixteen years ago. Greenleaf headed the internal investigation. He got caught red-handed, Dallas, and the internal investigation was secondary, but he took himself out with a drop piece—he had two other cold weapons—before his trial. His wife stuck by him, claimed setup, filed suits against the department,

Greenleaf, the lead investigator. Didn't get anywhere, but she made a lot of noise. He took himself out sixteen years ago this month. And she works in IT for a company about six blocks from the crime scene."

"Worth a conversation."

"She was wife number two, about ten years younger. She had a kid about two when he self-terminated. She found him.

"Next, McNab gave me Marcia Lord, patrol officer. Disciplined twice for excessive force, then she broke a kid's arm—kid got pinched shoplifting. Instead of calling for medical aid, she cuffed him—broken arm, and she cuffed him. Eleven years old. Got caught on a bystander's cam—the kid screaming in pain, and her threatening to break his other arm if he didn't shut up."

"Okay," Eve muttered as her arm twinged in memory of the bone snapping under Richard Troy's brutal attack.

"Her father was on the job—detective in the one-four. She got his service weapon, took herself out. The father made some noise, got in Greenleaf's face, Whitney's face. He turned in his papers shortly after. He got a PI license, keeps an office in Alphabet City."

Eve nodded as they took the steps to her garage level.

"Former cop, PI, you could find a way to access Greenleaf. Plug the addresses in. We'll add mine and program for the most logical route to all five."

"What've you got?"

"Oglebee, Detective Justin, Organized Crime. Turns out he worked with them more than against them. Bought himself a fancy place in the Caymans with mob money, along with a fancy boat, fancy car. Lived the high life until Greenleaf dug down. Wife had already left him, but his son, eighteen at the time, stuck. He found his father. Death ruled suicide, but a lot of questions there. Oglebee knew where a lot of the bodies were buried, may have buried some of his own. His lawyers were pushing for immunity, witness protection."

"Mob hit?" Peabody asked as she started entering addresses.

"I'd give it fifty-fifty. The son applied to the Academy, denied. The son, Steven, is thirty-three now, works delivery for a food joint, and Greenleaf's building's in his area."

"Definitely a conversation."

Eve read off the addresses, rounded up the other two while Peabody programmed.

"Looks like we start with Lord, former Detective Eli."

Peabody studied Eve's profile as they streamed into traffic. "You should probably wand again."

"A little busy now, and I don't have a wand."

Helpfully, Peabody pulled one out of her pocket. "I brought one along."

"I'm driving. I'll get to it."

"I hear Lansing's claiming he pulled the stunner in self-defense. That you and Baxter were reaching for yours."

"Where did you hear that?"

"Jenkinson's got his ear to the ground on it."

"Well, it won't fly. We weren't, and the recordings will show that. And it's tough to claim self-defense when he carried an illegal concealed, and attacked first."

"You'd have been justified, stunning him."

"And that would've given him some wiggle room, so I didn't."

"His wife left him, and claimed physical and emotional abuse in the divorce filing."

Eve glanced over. "Do you think I didn't look him up?"

"Oh, well, sure. Maybe you don't know he's been keeping a file on you since Nadine's first book came out."

Eve's hands tightened on the wheel. "A file? How do you know that?"

"EDD's going through his e's. A little bird told me they'd found a file on you buried in them."

"Why is it a bird? A little bird? Birds don't tell anybody anything."

"Parrots do. They talk. And the little parrots—the parakeets—they can talk. My cousin Uma has an African gray, and it talks up a storm."

"That's just creepy."

"Oh, it's so cute!"

"Creepy," Eve insisted. "But it gives me a big clue why Lansing has it in for me. Now he can take his file and shove it."

It steamed her enough she pulled into a craphole, overpriced public lot rather than hunting up street parking.

She needed to walk.

"Refocus," she ordered. "Lord. His daughter—Did he have other kids?"

"No."

"Only child, one following in his footsteps, gets the boot, faces criminal—and no doubt civil—trials. She's disgraced, humiliated, and for doing her job. Any disciplinary in his file?"

"No."

"So either he worked clean, or he didn't get caught. But his daughter doesn't work clean, does get caught. And rather than accept the consequences, she ends it."

Walking helped—cleared her head, lowered the steam.

New York smelled hot and busy. The first lunch rush filled sidewalk tables, crowded glide-carts so the hot and busy added soy dogs, fries, pizza, burritos, and more.

She spotted a three-card-monte grift in progress half a block down.

The operator spotted her, folded it up in a heartbeat, and jogged away. She shrugged it off—not worth the pursuit.

Instead she paused outside of Lord's building.

Street level had a restaurant. It must've been decent, as people filled every sidewalk table and the servers hustled.

She mastered in the street door with a sign for Lori's School of Dance, Thompson Accounting, Creative Nail Artists, and Lord Investigations.

Inside, she didn't spare the single elevator a glance, and shoved open the door to the stairwell.

They climbed to three.

It seemed John Calhoun, Attorney at Law, and Murals by Tess hadn't rated an exterior sign.

Lord's office had a frosted-glass door bearing his name.

Eve opened it into a small reception area with two empty chairs, a compact coffee station, and a single desk.

An attractive brunette, around thirty, sat at the desk working on a comp.

She stopped work, sent Eve and Peabody a smile. "Good afternoon."

Eve held up her badge. "We'd like to speak with Mr. Lord."

"Do you mind if I scan your identification?"

"Go ahead."

With pretty, manicured hands, she took a scanner out of her desk drawer, verified Eve's, then Peabody's shields.

"I'm sorry, Lieutenant, Detective. We sometimes have people using false identification in an attempt to get information on one of Mr. Lord's clients. He's actually with a client now, but I don't think he'll be much longer if you'd like to wait. Or I can make an appointment for you."

"We can wait."

"Please help yourself to coffee or water."

Since she wasn't interested in either, Eve looked around. Small, she thought, but clean and organized. A single plant with shiny green leaves speared up from a pot under a light she supposed stood in for the sun.

It looked happy enough.

"How long have you worked for Mr. Lord?"

"Almost five years now. I love it," she said with another flash of smile. "It's not like screen shows or vids, and I thought it would be. That seemed exciting. But it's not like that, and it's still really interesting. We handle all sorts of investigations. Domestic, insurance, background checks, even missing persons, and sometimes do some work for Mr. Calhoun. He's a lawyer, on this floor."

"So you keep busy."

"Oh yes. Mr. Lord gets a lot of client referrals because he's very good at what he does."

The door behind her opened. The man who came out looked trapped between misery and fury.

"Do you need a follow-up appointment, Mr. Tibbits?"

"No. No. It's done. I'm finished."

Domestic, Eve concluded as he walked out. Cheating spouse or cohab.

The receptionist gave his back a sympathetic look as she rose. "Just one minute," she said to Eve, and walked into the boss's office.

She came out again. "You can go right in. I should tell you Mr. Lord has an appointment in about thirty minutes."

"We'll try to wrap it up before that."

The receptionist waited, then closed the door behind them.

Lord sat at his desk in an office easily twice the size of reception and just as clean and organized.

He had two windows at his back—street view—with privacy screens engaged.

He had a powerful build—broad shoulders, wide chest. He'd let his hair go more salt than pepper, cut short around a strong-boned, dark-skinned face.

He had big hands, and folded them on the desk as he took stock of Eve.

"You want to know if I killed Greenleaf. I didn't. But I'm not sorry he's dead."

13

That, Eve thought, was one way to do it.

Without waiting for an invitation, she sat in one of the fake leather chairs facing the desk.

"You blame Captain Greenleaf for your daughter's death?"

"He contributed. He could have recommended disciplinary action, retraining, psychiatric and mental health assistance. But he didn't, and he wouldn't. And Whitney, who'd barely sat his ass down in the commander's chair, wouldn't stand up for one of his own. Neither would her supervising officer. Nobody stood up for her."

"She broke a minor child's arm, failed to call for medical assistance, and threatened to do more physical harm. It wasn't her first use of excessive force on the job."

"And whose fault was it for not pulling her off the street the first time, or the second? They barely slapped her wrist for it when she should've been pulled back, retrained, and given counseling. Let me add that minor child had a history of shoplifting, truancy, and resisting."

Eve couldn't argue with the first part, not when she wholeheartedly agreed. But the second? "Do you think his history justified your daughter's use of excessive force?"

"No." The anger simply drained out of him. "And I told

her exactly that. In the end, I didn't stand for her, either, so she took my service weapon out of the lockbox and killed herself with it."

"It's a terrible loss, Mr. Lord," Peabody began. "But you did stand for her. You went to the commander, to the captain of IAB, to her supervising officer."

"A lot of good it did me, or her. Greenleaf held a hard line. And the media and cop bashers were all over it because of the vid."

"Because of the vid," Eve interrupted, "or because of your daughter's actions?"

"She was wrong. Jesus Christ, I was on the job for twenty-seven years, I know she was wrong. She needed a chance to get right, and no one gave it to her. Greenleaf, he had twelve years, four months, and ten days living after she died. I'm not complaining his time came up."

"Where were you on the night he was killed, between twenty and twenty-two hundred hours?"

"You saw the guy who just left? He hired me to check on his wife of not quite three years. She told him she'd signed up for some night classes, boost her chances of a promotion at work. Keeping it short, he got suspicious, hired me three days ago.

"It took me one night—supposedly her night-class night, Greenleaf's night. I staked out her apartment building, watched her come out and meet up with a male—Caucasian, brown and brown, about thirty. They got handsy right off."

Lord shook his head. "Not ten steps out of the building where she lives with her husband, and they're all over each other. They got into a cab. I tailed them a few blocks to what turned out to be his place. I got a clear enough shot of him to get an ID—I've got damn good equipment. Turns out they work together. So I sat on his building, and watched them come out on his balcony. Got plenty of money shots of them right there, all over each other again. They're all time-stamped. They went inside about eight, didn't bother with privacy screens, so I got plenty more money shots.

"She didn't come out, alone, until shortly after twenty-two hundred. Had a cab waiting, so they'd ordered one up. She blew kisses up to where he stood on the balcony in his boxers. I tailed her home. I surveilled, started at her apartment, at seventeen hundred, ended surveillance at twenty-two-thirty, after which I went home and wrote it all up. I don't have to copy you the file without a warrant, but I will if you keep my client out of it. He's got enough to deal with."

"Any proof you were the one doing the surveilling? Taking those money shots?"

"I'm a one-man operation. Always have been. Hell. No place to park with a good visual on the building of the guy the wife's screwing around with. I parked, walked up Spring Street, little bar/café right across from his building, outdoor tables. I grabbed one, ordered a blooming onion and iced tea. Got that receipt, time-stamped. The server's going to remember me. I told her I was a freelance photographer, taking street shots for an art book.

"She bought it. I'm good at what I do. Took a couple shots of her to sweeten the pot, and printed them out for her. She'll remember me."

"All right. We'd appreciate the file, and we'll keep your client out of it."

Lord swiveled to his comp. "I hope you find who did it."

"To congratulate them?"

He shot a look at Eve as he ordered a file copy. "No. I turned in my shield, but I believe in what it stands for. I still believe in law and order, Lieutenant. I'm not sorry he's dead, but whoever killed him belongs in a cage."

As they walked down to the street, Peabody shook her head. "He's a hard-ass, too, when it comes to his daughter. But I don't think he had anything to do with Greenleaf's murder."

"Three reasons why."

"Okay. He could've arranged for someone to do the kill while he was alibied, but it feels like he'd have been more 'I've moved on' instead of saying he's fine with Greenleaf being a dead man. Second reason. It seems like he'd have gone for Whitney—he was commander—or the supervising officer. And if he went for either, he'd have done it twelve years ago. Third, if the alibi pans out, and it's going to, it's just too neat and tidy and coincidental that he'd get someone to do the deed, that Mrs. Greenleaf's night out just happened to coordinate with the cheating wife's slut night."

"Solid reasons, and I agree. We'll check the file, the alibi, but it's not him."

"One down then. Maybe we could stop by that cart on the corner, grab something to eat on the way to the next."

No doubt the cart food smelled better than it would taste, but it smelled pretty damn good at the moment.

Eve considered a soy dog, then decided against as, if she loaded it up as it should be, too messy. She settled for cart fries while Peabody went for the dog, mustard only.

As they walked to the lot, Eve dug out a fry. One bite and her lip lit on fire.

"Shit!"

"It's the salt." Peabody winced in sympathy. "You need to wand again. It's just open enough for the salt burn."

"Fuck me," Eve muttered against the hand she pressed to the sting. Then she shoved the fries at Peabody.

"I really shouldn't, but . . ." She nibbled on fries, on the dog while they walked to the car. "We can get you something cold from the vehicle AC. Like an ice pop."

"Ice pops turn your tongue colors. How am I supposed to professionally interview a suspect with a purple or green tongue?"

In the car, she ordered a tube of Pepsi and held it to her stinging lip until it numbed.

They interviewed three more, all alibied tight, one who'd been in a birthing center with her husband for a full eight hours on the night in question. Since the little family was at home, Peabody got to coo over the new baby.

"She was so sweet!"

"She looked like a fish. Like a bald, human fish."

"Aw. But no way, Dallas. Yeah, she got a little teary over her father, but it rang true she'd made a life. And it's hard to arrange having a baby to cover conspiracy to murder."

"No, not her, and the guy before who eloped with his longtime cohab, and just got back from the honeymoon yesterday. Add he didn't seem to have any close ties with his older, dead cop brother, who ragged him about being gay. And then there was Colton, Jayne's widow."

"Who's next?"

"Another of yours. Oglebee."

"Oglebee, Steven," Eve said as she pushed through crosstown traffic. "Thirty-two, no marriages, no cohabs on record. One semester community college, booted for nonattendance. Application denied for the Academy. Bounced from job to job. Retail clerk, stock boy, online sales, currently delivery guy for Grab & Go."

"I have to be desperate to order from G&G," Peabody commented. "I've been desperate a few times. It's a mistake."

"He also blogs. Or more uses blogging to spew out his racist, homophobic, misogynistic, anti-trans, anti-government viewpoints wrapped in crazed conspiracy theories. He calls it *A Real Man*."

"He sounds nice."

"Yeah, a real prince. He lives over his employment. What's been his employment the last twenty-two months—that's a record. On the surface, he doesn't seem smart enough to have planned something like this. Mean enough? He ranks. But his father went down for corruption, stemming from mob connections."

"So the son may have inherited some of those connections, and brokered a hit on the captain."

"Possibly. Low-level connections, a favor for a favor."

She found a street-level spot between a couple of junkers. Then again, most of the vehicles on the block rated junk status.

The building housing the Grab & Go and the residential units over it earned the same rank. It stood grimy gray and laced with poorly executed graffiti.

Her favorite of the offerings demanded:

COX AND CUNTS UNITE

With a drawing of a giant penis rammed into a vagina created by someone with little to no understanding of the female anatomy.

"That doesn't look like a ginny—not a human one anyway," Peabody observed. "Plus, the scale of the weenie's way off."

"First I have to get beyond the fact a police detective uses words like *ginny* and *weenie*. No," Eve added after a moment. "Really can't get beyond it. I also believe the same artist painted those massive tits with smiley faces for nipples."

Peabody considered, nodded. "No mistaking the style. I sense the artist is depicting his hope—perhaps what he envisions as the hope of all males—to achieve a giant boner, and that the recipient of same will possess enormous, happy boobs."

"That's pretty good," Eve decided. "It almost makes up for ginny and weenie. Almost. Let's get this done."

They went inside where, as Peabody said, only the desperate go.

The counter displayed mystery meats slowly graying under warming lights. Soggy lettuce, tomatoes, lunch mystery meats, and onions that might have been chopped fresh sometime the week before gasped in coolers. Cardboard slices of pizza revolved, sad and shamed, in a countertop spinner.

The counter man—maybe seventeen and battling a vicious case of acne—sent Eve a hopeful look.

"What can I getcha?"

"Steven Oglebee."

"Oh." Disappointment smothered hope. "He's not on till like five. Five to midnight."

"Okay."

"Um, our heroes are on special."

"I bet they're special," Eve said as she aimed for the door. "We'll pass."

She mastered in the street door for the residential units.

"He's on five," Peabody said, and sighed. "Five floors, good cardio."

They hit the stairway, which smelled like the week-old onions with a hint of spoiled mystery meat. Noise boomeranged against the fire door on every floor, and the heat trapped inside was awesome.

"Good cardio," Peabody repeated. "And I can feel the water weight pouring off."

"Apparently real men live in dumps with no soundproofing and crap climate control."

"And that smell like a G&G dumpster."

When they came out on five, the heat dropped marginally, and the noise escalated. She heard the wild, fake laughter of a screen comedy, and some kid shrieking, *It's mine! It's mine!*

Behind Oglebee's door, silence.

Over it a security cam—a damn good one, she noted.

And on it, double police locks and a sign that read:

If You're Selling Something, Looking For A Handout,
Pushing God Crap Or Liberal Bullshit
Fuck Off!

"See, didn't I say he sounded nice?"

Eve tapped the sticker just above the locksets that proclaimed him a proud member of the Men for Freedom militia.

"And a nutcase."

She pressed the buzzer. Then leaned on it until she heard someone inside curse.

He shouted through the closed door, "Can't you bitches read?"

"Can you?" Eve held her badge up for the camera.

He opened the door enough for it to crack against a double security chain. "The fuck you want?"

"A few minutes of your time here, or considerably more of it at Central. You get to choose."

"I don't have to open this door unless you got a warrant. I know my rights."

"No, you don't have to. I can get a warrant, and if I have to take the time to do so, I'll probably be irritated. I tend to take more time to get things done when I'm irritated."

"I can see what my lawyer has to say about that."

"You can. If you want to contact him now, we'll wait. Since we wouldn't want to waste the taxpayers' time, we'll get that warrant while we do. Which will now include a search of the premises, since the distinctive smell of Zoner's emanating from your apartment. Or we can come in and have a conversation."

He snorted. "Shit. You think I'm worried about getting busted for Zoner? For my personal use?"

Cliché or not, she thought, he had beady eyes. She figured they suited him.

"Since you've been busted, twice, for possession with intent to distribute, yeah, you might want to be a little worried about a third bust. Up to you."

"Neither bust stuck."

She just smiled. "Bet I can make this one stick. Or, we have a simple, civilized conversation on another matter."

"What matter?"

Enough, Eve thought. "Open the door, Mr. Oglebee, or I get that warrant."

He slammed the door, but the security chain rattled.

When the door opened again, she got a good look at him.

Paunchy, getting doughy around the jowls—and trying to hide that with a full beard that needed grooming. He wore his medium brown hair in a military high and tight.

He wore a T-shirt of the Confederate battle flag, and apparently without irony, had the Don't Tread on Me symbol tattooed on his right bicep.

In his bare feet he stood about an inch shorter than Eve and, from the look in his cloudy blue eyes, didn't care for that. Or her.

He made that clear by snarling, "Females got no business being cops. Now, what the fuck you want? I'm working."

"Your shift starts at five."

"My real work." He jabbed a finger toward a workstation and the state-of-the-art system on it.

Damn good furniture, too, she noted, for a delivery guy in a low-end apartment in a crappy building.

"Your blogging?"

"Females aren't my audience. Unless they know their place."

"In the interest of time, we'll let that ride." He smirked; she ignored it. "Your father was on the job."

"That's right. He was a hero. Put his life on the line every freaking day. Took no shit from anyone."

"He also took bribes and kickbacks from the Lorenzo family, which included individuals he was sworn to investigate."

Flags of angry red streaked across Oglebee's face, a wildfire over the bushy beard. "That's a dirty lie, a lie made up by that IAB stooge because my father was better than him. Better than all of them."

"By IAB stooge I assume you mean Captain Martin Greenleaf."

"Lying bastard, no sense of loyalty. No respect for the blue line. My father had eighteen years on the force, he risked his life to make sure the people of this city were protected, and that son of a bitch hounded him into the grave. Sure, he took money—that's how he gained their trust so he could build a solid case and take them down."

"Is that what he told you?"

"That's what I know!"

"Do you also know that Captain Greenleaf was killed on Sunday night?"

His smile spread. "Yeah, I heard. About fucking time. Took himself out's what I heard, because he couldn't live anymore with the guilt of ruining so many real cops. Real men, like my old man."

"You heard incorrectly. Homicide, not suicide."

"Yeah, you'd say that. Covering it up. That's what your type does."

"Female cops?" Peabody wondered.

"Females who get badges and get rank because they put

out. How many blow jobs did it take for you to make lieutenant?" he asked Eve. "Somebody popped you a couple good ones there. Looks like you like it rough."

Peabody said, "Uh-oh," but Eve shook her head.

"Whereabouts, Sunday night, between eight and ten P.M."

Something flickered in his eyes, flickered before he glanced away. "Like you said, my shift starts at five. I'm five to midnight."

"And if we go back downstairs, your supervisor and the log will verify you were on Sunday night?"

"So it's my night off." He shifted his stance, spread his legs.

"Whereabouts," Eve repeated. "Eight to ten P.M."

"Working. Right over there."

"Did you see anyone or speak to anyone, did anyone drop by who can verify you were home during that time frame?"

"I said I was fucking working."

"That would be a no. Have you ever been to Captain Greenleaf's apartment?"

"Why the hell would I? We ain't pals."

"His building's in your delivery area."

"So what? That doesn't prove anything."

"When I calculate the odds of you delivering to that building within the twenty-two months of your employment, they strike me as pretty good. You've got motive, you had opportunity, and your line of work offers a means. That's what people like me call a hat trick."

"That's bullshit. You're trying to come for me like Greenleaf did my father. What, did Greenleaf bang some lame slut back then and she popped you out? Or maybe you just like banging old men."

"Jesus," Peabody snapped. "You're really completely vile."

"I speak the truth!" He slammed his fist into his open palm as if that proved it. "I speak for men everywhere who know how to be men, and not soy-latte-sipping, limp-dick pussies.

Real men who are damn well going to take back the power from the frigid bitches and the queers and—"

"I bet you haven't been laid without paying for it your whole pathetic, narrow-minded, whiny little life."

Those red flags turned dangerously toward purple as he snarled at Peabody. "You get out. Both you cunts get out. Get your fucking warrant, and I'll get my fucking lawyer. We'll see who comes out."

"I'd say that concludes this conversation." Eve took Peabody's arm. "You'd be smart to get that lawyer, because we're not done." She nudged Peabody to the door and through it before she turned. And gestured toward his shirt.

"You know, they lost. But it tracks a loser would wear a loser's shirt."

In the hallway she gestured for the stairs. "You know how sexy you look when you're angry, Peabody. Now he only wants you more."

"God!" Peabody made a sound between a laugh and a groan. "I'm sorry. You weren't finished, and I just snapped."

"No, I was finished. We weren't going to get any more out of him. Not there and then."

"He could've done it, Dallas. Motive, means, opportunity, like you said."

"Means is a little up in the air, but with a solid partner, yeah, he could've done it. Or he could just be as full of hot, nasty air as this stairwell."

"Something off with him—more than his general fuckery." Peabody sent a last snarl up the stairwell. "How does he afford a D and C system like that? And that couch? That's going to go for two grand—McNab and I've looked at a lot of furniture since the Great House Project. The entertainment screen? Top of the line. He's got champagne stuff in a rot-gut, home-brew apartment. How does he afford it on what he makes at the G&G?"

"That's what we're going to find out."

As they walked back onto the sidewalk, she took out her 'link. "By tagging Roarke and asking him to dig into Oglebee's finances."

"Ah, I wouldn't tag him."

"Why not? He volunteered—and it's fun for him. Plus, nobody goes deeper faster." She paused on that with the image of the weenie and ginny in mind. "That wasn't a sexual reference."

"Bet it could be, but I'll let it slide. That's why," Peabody said, and pointed to Eve's face. "He's going to see you got punched, then he'll think about that, worry until you're home. If he sees it at home, it cuts out the next couple hours. You should just text."

Eve got back in the car. "That's a good catch. That's a very good catch."

"That's what partners are for."

"Is that what they're for? And here I thought it was for getting pissed when their partner got accused of giving out BJs and/or banging superior officers with about four decades on them."

"That, too. You were pissed."

"Oh yeah. Everything about him pissed me off, and we're going to make him sorry for it."

She texted Roarke.

> When and if you have time, and want the
> entertainment, financials on Steven R. Oglebee.
> Got a strong feeling you won't have to dig very
> deep. May have more later, but he's a standout.

She added his data and address.

"Let's go write all this up." She pulled out into traffic. "And we'll see who Oglebee worked with during his last few years on the job. See if we can pull any more on the son. He's not clean, Peabody."

"No, he's not. If you take the on-the-job Oglebee, I can push on the list. We should be able to pull out at least a couple more. McNab and I could take one or two on the way home."

"That works. We eliminated more, and we've got one possible. Focusing on the suicide angle's still the best method."

When her 'link signaled a text, she called it up on her in-dash.

> Just coming out of a meeting and going into another. After that, I could use some entertainment. We'll see what I can find before you get home.

> Thanks. In the field, heading back to Central to tie some things up. See you later.

"It's nice being with someone who gets the job," Peabody commented.

"Yeah, I guess. No," Eve corrected. "I know it is."

As she pulled into the garage, she flashed back to that morning. "It's got to help if the cop side of it isn't a complete asshole."

"You're thinking of Lansing."

"Among others."

"You really want to wand that lip again, ice down one more time before you get home."

"Yeah, yeah, yeah." Then she frowned as they walked to the elevator. "He kept a file on me, starting about the time Nadine published the Icove book."

"Jealous, probably. And convinced himself Nadine bribed you or something. Like maybe you and Nadine had a hot affair."

"Oh please." But that stopped her. "I wonder."

"I was joking about that part."

"I just wonder," she repeated, and tagged Nadine.

"Dallas, why are you always getting smacked in the face?"

"Keeps me mean and ready. Detective Lansing, IAB. Do you know him?"

"Lansing? I don't . . ." She shook back her streaky hair, angled her head as her foxy green eyes narrowed. "Oh yeah. I remember him. John, Jack—no, Joe. Joe Lansing, IAB."

"How?"

"He hit on me, pretty hard. Right after I got the crime beat, and I was doing a follow-up on internal investigations at the NYPSD. So, what, like four years ago—something like that. He didn't want to take no. I don't date cops—conflict of interest. Seems to me he was like nobody has to know. On top of the no for the first reason, I didn't like him. I mean he's good to look at, but I just didn't like him. And on top of that, it came out he was married, so absolutely no."

"Did he keep at it?"

"For a while. Tagged me a couple times. Even came by my place once—and that's when, if I'm remembering right, I told him I'd report him if he didn't back off. He got pissed, but he backed off. Why?"

"He's the one who punched me in the face. Now I've got the reason why."

"He punched you because I turned him down four years ago?" Nadine fluffed at her hair. "I know my own devastating charm, but . . . that's a stretch."

Satisfied, Eve got on the elevator. "Because that, then you and I have a professional and personal relationship. You wrote a big-ass bestseller about one of my cases. He's been keeping a file on me."

Amusement turned to mild outrage. "Well, for God's sake.

I'm sorry he punched you. I still wouldn't have gotten naked with him, but sorry."

"No need. It just made me itchy not knowing exactly why he went off."

"Give me some details. Did you deal with him due to the Greenleaf investigation? I want to—"

"Tag IAB," Eve told her. And clicked off.

"You should tell Mira what Nadine just told you. Whitney, too."

Eve nodded as the door opened and more cops piled on. "Trust me."

14

Eve went straight to her office and wrote up the new information on the investigation, then did a separate report to Mira and Whitney on Lansing.

Satisfied, she got coffee, put her boots on the desk, and took some thinking time.

One way or the other, she decided, Oglebee had something to hide—and a lot of rage he didn't bother to hide. The suicide factor weighed against him. But she wondered if he was capable of holding that rage in for years before he acted on it.

Maybe, maybe, she considered. Especially if there was some trigger within the last year—either in Greenleaf's life or Oglebee's.

It's time he paid, she mused. Yeah, she could see that. Pushing there, she began to dig deeper into his background, his travel, the medicals she could access, employment.

The harder she looked at his employment, the more certain she became Roarke would find something on him.

But an illegal source of income, tax evasion, whatever he was into didn't equal murder.

She set him aside and went back to her list.

She'd culled two more possibles when Baxter rapped on her doorjamb.

"Trueheart and I are clear, boss. We could assist until otherwise with the suicide cops. I got a vested—get it?—interest."

"Ha. What went down with Lansing had less to do with Greenleaf than it did me."

"And still. Son of a bitch used a dead cop as an excuse to go after you, and he added me in."

"Have Peabody pass five to Trueheart. I'll send you five. If you catch one, pass them back."

"That'll work." He waved a finger toward her face. "You ought to ice down again."

"I keep hearing that."

She kept at it. When she found one more possible, she got up, rearranged her board. Then sat another moment studying it until she got an incoming from Mira.

> I've spoken with Nadine Furst, acquired more
> details re Lansing. I've arranged a psych eval.
> You should know the PA has charged him with
> felony assault and assault with a weapon,
> possession of an illegal weapon, and other
> related charges. He has retained counsel through
> his rep, and said counsel's petition for release
> on his own recognizance was denied. Bail also
> denied until a full psychiatric evaluation.

Okay then, Eve thought. The PA was pushing it all the way. They'd deal at some point, but Lansing would likely get five to ten—closer to the ten if the PA kept up the push.

Either way, he'd blown up his career, would lose his freedom.

And because a woman had turned him down.

Not that simple, she admitted. Not nearly that simple, but another kind of excuse.

Maybe he'd been a decent cop once, she thought. Maybe. But she didn't care enough to take the time to scroll back through his history.

Once again, she set him aside, and this time got up and walked to the bullpen. She had three, and she could try to interview them all before she called it for the day.

"I've got three. I'm going to try to round them up, then work from home."

"I got one and a half," Peabody told her. "Half because the second's a stretch. But I'd like to follow up just in case."

"Do that. Take McNab. Feeney sent another couple. Nothing yet on the weapon, but a couple more possible conversations. We'll start there tomorrow. I want to look them over. I'll send you the addresses where we'll start."

"I've been through three," Baxter told her, "but none of them sing."

"I think I might have one." From his desk, Trueheart sent Eve one of his earnest looks. "I don't know if it sings, Lieutenant, but it hums."

"Listen to you." Baxter grinned at him. "Good one."

"Hum the tune," Eve told him.

"Ah, Lucy Millan. Detective, SVU. It's twenty years back, LT, but it feels like a fit. She killed her husband—second husband. Found out he was sexually abusing her daughter. The girl was fourteen. She stunned him, beat him, trussed him up, weighed him down, and dumped him in the Hudson River."

"Thorough," Baxter commented.

"She self-terminated awaiting trial—she was going to do some time and knew it. The minor child, Jessie, was given into the guardianship of her aunt, Millan's sister. Jessie ran away multiple times, ended up in the system.

She's been busted for illegals, for solicitation without a license. She had plenty to say about her mother's arresting officers, her aunt, Greenleaf, and others. She's working in a strip club, Lower Manhattan."

"All right."

"There's a little more."

"Keep humming."

"She shares a residence—not official cohabs—with a Curt Barrow. He's done time for possession of illegal weapons, trading in same, wholesale theft and sale of prescription meds, for assault with intent."

"That sounds like singing to me, Detective. You found her. Why don't you and Baxter take the first pass? Let me know what you get."

It's moving, she thought as she headed out. She didn't hold any real hope they'd tie it up before the memorial. But it was moving.

It took her close to two hours to interview all three on her short list. None of them sang, or hummed, but movement still, if only crossing names off.

When she drove through the gates, she decided she'd take a closer look at Feeney's results, sort them by highest to lowest probability.

And one way or the other, she'd take another closer look at Trueheart's find. Kid goes to the aunt—not her bio father. Why? Runs away multiple times. Why?

Obviously poor choices thereafter, all the way to hooking up with a bad character. Who could likely access a police issue.

Her mind on that trail, she walked into where Summerset and Galahad waited.

Summerset's brows lifted. "Well, I suppose it couldn't last."

"What?"

"You managing to come home without injuries."

She'd mostly forgotten, and now lifted a hand to her jaw. "Shit."

"Leave the shirt out when you change. I'll deal with the bloodstains."

Now she looked down. What was left was barely noticeable. But. "Shit."

And striding up the stairs, repeated, "Shit, shit, shit!"

Best to hit the bedroom first, she decided. Ditch the shirt, do a quick icing, wanding, whatever, before Roarke showed up.

Even if Summerset blabbed—and he fucking-A would—she'd be in better shape.

The cat leaped onto the bed, sat, studied her with steady, bicolored eyes.

"It wasn't my fault. And it happens. It just happens."

She peeled off the jacket, unhooked her weapon harness. She pulled off the shirt, stood holding it, wondering what Summerset meant by leave it out.

And Roarke walked in.

Like the cat, he gave her face a long, steady stare.

"From the looks of it, that happened considerably earlier in the day from when we spoke."

She shrugged, tossed the shirt on the bed beside the cat, who sniffed it and snarled. As she stood in her trousers and support tank, Roarke moved in to gently, very gently, cup her face.

"You're supposed to take care of my cop."

"I did. Believe me, he got the worst of it."

"And who is he?"

"Former Detective Joe Lansing. He's in a cage, and he'll stay there," she added quickly. She knew the icy flare that shot through those blue eyes. "He was in the garage, waiting, when I got to Central this morning. I couldn't take him down—Baxter drove in, and that didn't mean a damn to him. I had to let him take the first swing."

"Of course you did. You did," he repeated when she huffed out a breath. "I understand that. But you might've blocked it, at least a bit."

"I kicked his ass. Yeah, he got some hits in, but I put him down. He had a clutch piece, Roarke, and he pulled it. He was down and dazed, so he missed me, hit Baxter. His piece was on full."

Now she cupped Roarke's face. "Baxter had my anniversary present. If he hadn't had the Thin Shield under his fancy jacket, he'd have gone down hard."

"Christ Jesus, the man's lost whatever senses he might have once had."

"Not my fault. If you want to point fingers, point at Nadine."

"Nadine, is it?" Roarke angled his head, then brushed his lips over the bruising. "I want to hear what part she's played, but hold it while I get a cold pack and a wand. Am I seeing all your injuries?"

"He got through on the ribs a couple times. And he punched me, fucking hard, in the left tit. But otherwise—"

She broke off when those eyes went burning hot, and a vicious string of incomprehensible Irish seethed into the air.

"I'm not sure I've heard any of that before."

"Let's just leave it as it's lucky for him he's in a cage. Let me see."

Now she sighed. "I had to show it to Mira already. Mortifying." But she tugged down the tank. And he hit the Irish curses again.

When she looked down, she saw why.

"It's pretty bruised up." Then annoyance spiked into fear. "You are not pulling Summerset in here for this."

"No, but you'll sit, let me tend to you."

"He's cost me time," Eve said as she sat on the side of the bed. "Lansing's cost me time on the Greenleaf case. So stupid," she added, and closed her eyes. "So stupid."

"Here now, just try to relax. I'm going to wand that lovely breast first. Tell me what this has to do with our Nadine."

As she did, he wanded, iced, wanded until the aches and twinges barely registered.

"It's not about Nadine, either," Roarke commented, "but about him, all of it about him, and his need to feel and be superior to women, without having any real affection and certainly no respect for them."

"It's that, and it's more, and I honestly don't give a rat's ass. He cost me time. He pulled my focus away from Greenleaf. And the son of a bitch had my tit making the rounds at Central."

Now Roarke laughed before kissing her swollen lip, tenderly. "What an extraordinary visual—and even more outrageous crime. Take a blocker."

"I took one already."

"When?"

"Okay, awhile ago." She popped the little blue pill he held out. "I have to get back to work."

"And so you will. But you'll have a meal first, and a glass of wine. It can be pizza."

"It can?" Gingerly, she touched a finger to her lip. "Is it going to sting?"

"It shouldn't, no, and while you have the pizza and wine, I'll tell you what I've dug up—so far—on Steven Oglebee."

"Already?"

"I was home before you, as it happens, and well into it. Wine, food, and I'll tell you."

Another deal, she thought as they walked to her office. And a good one from her standpoint, since it involved pizza and information.

"Why don't you take ten to update your board so that's off your mind before we eat?"

She stopped, studied the board, studied him. "You know, every now and again it's irritating you get me pretty much all the way through. But most times, like now? It's pretty great."

She took the ten and felt more relaxed when her board reflected her current thinking and the data as she knew it.

Then she sat with him at the table by the open balcony doors and lifted a glass of red.

"First," she began, "I know you were packed today, so thanks, big-time, for squeezing Oglebee in."

"I'll take the thanks, big-time, but the fact is, poking there gave a packed and occasionally difficult day a nice lift."

"I get the packed because you're you—and I get you, too. Why difficult?"

The big-time thanks, he thought, for her to ask when he knew how much she wanted to hear what he found. "Some gaps needed filling on some wheels and deals, as you'd call it, set in motion before we left for Greece."

"You didn't work much there, or in Ireland."

"We didn't work," he corrected. "It was our time. Now we're back." He lifted his wine as well. "And what we do is what we are. And that suits us."

He slid a slice of pizza on her plate. "And so. Steven Oglebee."

"If he were clean, you'd have said so straight off."

"True enough, and he's far from clean. I'll also say he's not particularly bright. I can't tell you if anything I found helps in your investigation, but I can tell you he enjoys considerable unreported income. He hides it, but not being particularly bright, he doesn't hide it particularly well. He has an account buried under a shell—a thin one, purported to be a security company—Protect and Serve."

"He's got a cop obsession. A male-cop-only obsession."

"He uses the name Steve Justice as owner. He funnels cash in from a short list of clients. I've the names for you, but I can already tell you they're fake. He deals in cash, and cash only, and pulls in between eight and fifteen thousand a month—all deposits under the minimum for reporting, as are all withdrawals. He has a beach property in the Caymans, titled under the shell company, and travels there via shuttle, using the name Justice, every four to six weeks."

Roarke sipped some wine. "It's clear to me he's washing money for clients not named under the shell."

"I can get a warrant on this much."

"And when you do, you'll find what I did that you can't use until you get that warrant." He shrugged. "I was curious. I suspect some of his deliveries on his legitimate job aren't just fast food, but that's for you to find out. What he has— and I only had to brush some dust off the surface—is connections to low-level mobsters, very likely the offspring of those his father had connections with.

"It's a simple setup," Roarke continued, "and very low-level. A shipment of electronics or fashion or mechanical parts, whatever, is diverted. Oglebee sells the products for a commission. Cash. Simple, as I said, slightly sloppy, but he's had some success with this system over the last ten years."

"He keeps a crap apartment, a crap job. Buys expensive furniture for cash—or takes a part of a shipment for himself. Gets himself a place at the beach, and uses that as a way to wash money. And I bet your very fine ass and mine with it, he feels entitled. His father did a lot of the same. The son likely sees that as a payment for being on the job. Fucker."

"I wouldn't disagree. But as I said, I don't know how any of it ties into Greenleaf's murder."

"Maybe a low-level mob hit. Maybe. Another payment for services rendered. A delayed payback for his father."

She considered as she took another slice. "He'd have wanted to do the kill himself. The suicide setup plays in, brings it to a nice closed circle, as he'd see it."

"You're working on a but."

"Yeah. But why not work out a solid alibi? He's connected enough to at least have something in place. Not very smart, fine, but that's dead stupid. This murder was planned; why leave out an essential part of the plan?"

"Possibly he never considered he'd be questioned. Suicide, Eve. He could have seen that as cover enough."

"Yeah, yeah, and I'll work that angle. Still stupid though. You only need to have a couple of the bad characters you're hooked up with swear you were playing poker or getting trashed somewhere."

"You'd pull that straight apart," Roarke commented. "It could be those he's connected with weren't willing to risk it for someone at his level. He's only a tool. A well-paid one, but there are plenty like him who could serve the same purpose."

"I'll get the warrant, and we'll bust him on what you found, what we'll find. Trip him up when I've got him in the box.

"It's good information, and it's a good lever to pry out more. Right now, I see him as fifty-fifty, at best, on Greenleaf. I need more than that."

"You have other names."

"Peabody and I are going to hit another chunk of the list—thanks to Feeney—tomorrow. And we'll keep digging on the rest."

"I can help with that."

"Guess you could. The more we eliminate, the tighter we can focus on who's left. Baxter and Trueheart took one.

I should hear from them soon. Peabody and McNab have a couple, and I took three on the way home. I want to carve out time for the memorial tomorrow. Not just to pay respects, but to see who shows."

"And anyone on the list who does."

"Means they're worth a second look. It's moving," she added. "It's slow as hell, but it's moving. We're looking in the right place," she murmured, shifting to look at the board. "It wasn't random or impulsive. It was cold, calculated revenge with a faked suicide chaser."

"You still like the neighbors."

Oh yeah, she thought, and absently sipped wine, he got her, all the way through.

"I can't let go of it—and it doesn't make sense because I know we're looking in the right place. And nothing I look at, twist, turn connects either of them to Greenleaf, to a dead or disgraced cop he investigated. But they were on the spot—perfect alibi for her. No motive for either. They look like two people living solid if ordinary lives."

"And yet."

"Yet."

"Would you like me to look at them again?"

"You looked, and there's nothing there. I'm keeping them on the board, but I know we're looking in the right place. And neither of them are in that place."

"I'll take some of your names. Maybe we'll find the one who is in that place before the memorial."

"Okay." Even as she rose, her 'link signaled. "Going to be Baxter or Peabody. Maybe they already found the one."

She saw Baxter's name on the ID screen, answered. "What've you got?"

"We're booking Jessie Millan and Curt Barrow. Not on Greenleaf, Dallas. They were both busy on the night in question running a shipment of stolen meds down to East

Washington. We busted them with part of the shipment—they skimmed—and what was left of the payment. They jacked a car—and we've got the owner IDing them both. Used it to transport the drugs. Jacked the car about nine Sunday night. Still had it parked outside their apartment, for fuck's sake.

"Trueheart reviewed the toll cams, and we've got them heading south about the time of the murder. We got them, but not on murder."

Elimination mattered, she reminded herself. Plus. "It's still a good bust. Write it up for me."

"You got it."

"Another off the list," Eve said when she clicked off. "We'll see if Peabody gets luckier."

She didn't, so Eve crossed off two more even as she bumped other names into the possible category.

She had to remind herself the list might be long, but it wasn't endless. Eventually they'd zero in on one.

"I have two for you," Roarke said as he came back. "And the reasons why another two don't work."

"Looks like we hit the same ratio." She leaned back in her chair. "Feeney sent me one, and three to cross off. We're coming to the end of the list. The connection's there, Roarke. I've second- and third-guessed myself on it, and I know it's there. Maybe just buried deeper than we can see."

"Time to give it a rest for the night. You need another treatment."

"I feel okay."

"And you'll feel better, sleep better, with another treatment. Come now, Lieutenant, it's closing in on midnight."

She knew the equation.

Arguing equaled time wasted.

Added to it, aches and sneaky pains had crept in, and they equaled a distraction.

The cat beat them to the bedroom. He had a sense of these things.

"Sit," Roarke told her. "We'll start with that face of yours."

She sat while he took out a healing wand. And watched his eyes focus as he worked.

"Do you ever get tired of playing nurse?"

"More, it annoys me to see bruises on you."

"It annoys me, too. If Baxter hadn't gotten Lansing in lockup fast, Jenkinson might've found a way to put some on him. Then Peabody. Jesus, she actually threatened me."

"Our Peabody?"

"Shoves a blocker in my face and says if I don't take it, she's telling you. Like we're twelve and she's going to tattle on me if—" Her eyes narrowed when he smiled. "Oh, you like that one."

"Quite a bit, actually."

"Try this one then. I'm going to tag you about Oglebee's finances when we're in the field, and she says I should text so you don't see I got punched in the face and worry about it."

"Looking after both of us, wasn't she?"

She had to sigh. "Maybe."

He touched his lips lightly to hers. "Jenkinson, Peabody, and all the rest aren't just cops, aren't just a team. You've made yourself a family. Now then, let's see the rest. Off with the shirt."

She let him lift off the loose T-shirt she'd changed into, then looked down when she saw the cold light in his eyes.

"It's better. Right? It looks better. Not that I spend a lot of time looking at my tits, but—"

"I do whenever possible. It's better, yes. Bleeding poxy bastard. I wouldn't have put bruises on him over this. I'd have twisted off his cock at the fecking root."

Out came the Irish, she noted, and found herself oddly touched.

"He got worse." She laid a hand on his cheek. "And he'll pay for it a lot longer. He went after Peabody yesterday. Not physically," she said when Roarke's gaze shot up. "That got lost in the chaos, but he started on her before Jenkinson got in his face. She didn't want to write it up. Probably felt like piling on to her. But she did, and it's not. He's not fit to have a badge."

She let out a sigh as he ran the wand gently up and down her ribs.

"Angelo's on-planet. You knew," she realized.

"I did. Webster contacted her when I took him out to walk. And she contacted me shortly after to let me know she was taking time. She came to see you?"

"Not me, really. Webster. Forgot." She let out another sigh when he put the wand away. Thank God that was over for now. "He came in, wanted to talk to me about what he wanted to talk to Greenleaf about." She dragged the shirt back on. "He's turned in his papers."

She stared at him when he walked to the AutoChef. "You knew?"

"I didn't, no. But I'm not at all surprised. He'll be relocating to Olympus then?"

"That's the plan."

"You don't agree?"

"It's not for me to . . . Okay, no, I didn't. Jesus, he's got, what, sixteen, seventeen years on the job? He's got rank, and he's that close to making his twenty? He's leaving the job, New York, and freaking planet Earth? But— What's that?"

"A soother. It'll ease the last aches, and you'll sleep better."

"I don't want—"

"It'll top off the wanding. And it's double chocolate."

"Hand it over, Nurse Nancy," she muttered.

He drew it just out of her reach. "I'm thinking I'll switch it for the carrot and spinach blend."

"I got punched in the tit."

He handed it to her. "All right then. Webster. 'But,' you said."

"Right. But. When I listened to why, to what he wanted, I got it. Or started to. Then Angelo walked in, and I got it all the way. I know what it's like to have someone who means everything, someone who can lift the hard and heavy off you just by being there."

"They love each other."

She gulped down the soother, and the rich chocolate made her system smile.

"Not always enough, is it? But it's a hell of a strong start. So he'll move to Olympus and train cops to be cops, not bullies with badges."

"Is that his plan?"

"It is now, and he'll be good at it. I love you."

"And I you."

"So we need to make a pact."

"Do we?" He smiled at her as he undressed. "And what sort of pact is that?"

"Neither of us, ever, says to the other: 'Hey, we have to leave planet Earth and go live on some space colony or outpost or station.'"

He slipped into bed, drew her to him. "I can agree to that, with one qualification."

"What's the qualification?"

"I'd only say that, and you'd only agree to that, if planet Earth is in immediate danger of exploding, imploding, or becoming uninhabitable to life forms."

"That sounds fair. Okay, we have a pact."

"We do indeed. Lights out."

He'd been right, of course. Between the wanding and the soother, she dropped almost immediately into sleep.

Where dreams found her.

In the room where he'd died, Greenleaf sat at his desk. But in place of the wall screen, the shelves, the window, photos of cops papered the walls around him.

Dead ones, disgraced ones, cops in cages.

"I did the job," Greenleaf told her. "A badge doesn't put you above the law, Lieutenant. A badge means you toe the line of the law. Serve and protect."

"I know what the badge means, Captain."

"Did they?" He gestured to the faces surrounding him.

"Not everyone you looked into crossed the line. Those who did? That same law stripped the badge from them."

"Do you think I got them all?"

"We never get them all. You knew that when you headed IAB, when you decided to take on other cops."

"I knew what it meant. I stand by what it meant." He gestured to the walls. "How many of these have you looked at?"

She scanned the faces. "Too many."

"What did you find?"

"So far? That you did the job, as you saw it, your duty, as you saw it. Too many here exploited the job. Too many dishonored their badge, used it for gain, for violence, for power."

"You came from violence and cruelty. I know because you know," he said when she didn't respond. "You worked to become a cop, one who took the oath to protect and serve to heart rather than continue the cycle of violence and cruelty as some do. You could've chosen otherwise."

"No, I couldn't have."

He picked up the glass—the iced tea—watching her as he drank. "You chose a man who crossed the line of the law, many, many times."

Even in the dream, even knowing it for a dream, she felt her blood heat.

Hard-ass, she thought. In life and in death.

"The man I chose—if *chose* is the word—gives his time and skill to help find justice for the dead. And he's bled for it. He came from violence and cruelty while badges looked the other way. And still he honors the badge as much as I do."

With a slight shrug, Greenleaf set the glass down again.

"You're a violent woman."

"Maybe. Yeah."

"But not once have you exploited your badge for personal gain, to cause harm, for power."

Now she shrugged. "I've been known to lean on it some."

"A different matter. But a dirty badge left unpunished taints us all. If I pushed hard, some would say too hard, I believed that absolutely."

"The ones I'm looking at now needed to be pushed, and hard. But there were others, Captain, in your long career who fell into the gray."

His eyes held hers, unwavering. "In my job no gray could or did exist. Black or white, Lieutenant. Right or wrong. An absolute. I believed in the oath taken. In the end, I died for it."

With a long sigh, he looked at the walls, all the faces.

They stared back, she saw, with rage, with a kind of terrible thirst.

She put a hand on her weapon.

"They haunt me. Not because I was wrong, but because they were. They haunt me," he repeated. "And now they'll haunt you."

The walls became men and women, ghosts that took form, and forms that fell on Greenleaf like wolves.

And she couldn't stop them.

She woke with a jolt in the dim light of predawn. The cat bumped his head against her side as Roarke stroked her face.

"There now, a dream. I'm here."

He drew her into his arms, held her close. "It's all right now."

"I'm okay. Hard dream. Not a nightmare. Well, at the end, I guess, but . . ." Closing her eyes, she laid her head on his shoulder. "I'm okay."

"You'll tell me."

"Greenleaf at his desk, all the cops I've been looking at—like he looked at—photos plastered on the walls."

She told him the rest.

"He knew they were coming, and he didn't fight back. He just watched me while they covered him. Watched me try to stop them. They'd come for me next, and I would have stopped them. I'd have taken out as many as I could."

She breathed out. "But I woke up."

"He was a different kind of cop, wasn't he then? One who did his job at a desk—just as you saw him. And you, Lieutenant, do a great deal of yours on your feet. I wonder if you think while one of those photos may be responsible, in some way, for his death, many of the others would stand and watch it happen without remorse."

He kissed her. "But not you. You wouldn't and couldn't stand and watch."

"He said they'd haunt me now."

"And was this one there?" Roarke asked, tracing a finger over her jaw.

"No. But he wasn't Greenleaf's. He's mine. And I'm okay. It gave me something to think about. And now I'm thinking about coffee, and that it's nice to wake up and find you here. I'd rather it be with you sitting over there with the cat, but it's close enough."

"You'll have your coffee and another round with the wand. Then we'll both sit over there."

15

Because she needed to shake it off, she grabbed a shower. And with the water beating hot, the steam rising thick, she pressed her forehead to the tiles.

All those faces on the walls. All those faces filled with rage becoming men and women.

Cops, who'd sworn to protect and serve.

They'd torn Greenleaf to pieces, and he hadn't fought back. He'd just accepted, as if he considered that, too, a part of the job.

No gray, she thought. He'd seen the job, his world, in black-and-white. Was that her perception of him, she wondered, or the reality of him?

Did it matter?

She'd fought, as she'd fought Lansing and countless others since she'd taken the badge, taken the oath.

Because she was a violent woman, or because she considered it a part of the job? Some of both?

Did it matter?

Either way, she decided, she'd fight till the bitter, bloody end.

So she let it go until the dregs of the dream drained away with the water.

And because she couldn't see a way out of it, she sat while Roarke tended her bruises.

"Better," he said after another wanding, and traced a finger along her jaw. "Considerably better."

"Bruises heal; death doesn't."

"Now, that's a statement."

"You fight back, deal with the bruises, and you keep doing the job. That's the deal you make. But he didn't fight back—in the dream, I mean." Which, she realized, hadn't drained away after all. "He just sat there and took it. Is that how I see him, or is that who he was?"

"He didn't have a chance to fight back, did he? In the reality of it. Taken from behind as he was."

"Didn't have a chance," she repeated slowly. "Taken from behind. Looks like you get my subconscious more than I do. He didn't have a chance to fight, not at the end. But he spent his entire career fighting—his way, in absolutes. From a desk mostly," she considered. "And he died at a desk. Was that irony or planning?"

She pushed up, stalking around the room in a raspberry-colored robe. "Irony's sort of like coincidence—unless it's deliberate. This was planning. Wife's night out, he sits at his desk, back to the door. Ball game on the wall screen while he's checking headlines, reading articles, playing comp games, having a cold drink.

"Waiting for Webster, but the killer doesn't know that."

"You're back to the neighbor who could put him just there, at his desk, when they left."

"Yeah, that's handy. But it's a habit, so Arnez wouldn't be the only one who knew or counted on him being just there. At a desk where—if that's how you needed to see it—he passed judgment."

"All right."

He poured more coffee, then patted the seat beside him. "Come sit now. Eat. Food fuels the brain as well."

"Does it matter he died at the desk?" she wondered as she walked back to sit. "And that's a bullshit question. Everything matters."

Under the warming lids Roarke lifted were pancakes. She barely registered them before globbing on butter, swamping them in syrup.

"It's a precise plan—I knew that—but if the desk played in, it adds another weight to the planning, the motive. It'll matter. Maybe not right now, but eventually.

"I didn't like him."

"You're not required to, Eve. Haven't I seen you go to the wall for a victim you actively disliked?"

"I didn't like him," she said again. "But I didn't really see him beyond the IAB head who sat in judgment at his desk. I knew better. Christ, I know the damage dirty cops can do, but I didn't like him, didn't like his hard-line absolutes. Even though . . ."

"You're often a hard-line-absolute sort yourself."

"I'm sitting here eating pancakes with a former criminal, so how absolute could I be?"

"Suspected only—and certainly reformed."

She shifted to him, smiled. "If I had a massive brain fart and asked you to steal . . . What's a good one? Has to be a— the *Mona Lisa*, because everyone knows that one. I needed you to give me the *Mona Lisa* to hang in my closet, you'd break into the—Where is it?"

"The Louvre, darling."

"Yeah, there. And I'd have it in my closet."

"What a man might do for love," he murmured, and ate pancakes. "Sadly, you'd never ask."

"No, but I'm eating breakfast with someone who could

and would if I did. What is it with that painting anyway? Just some woman with a smirk."

"Ah, but she's glorious." The Irish in his voice warmed with admiration. "You have to see her in person, have her eyes meet yours to fully appreciate the sheer magnificence of her. Not a smirk, no, not at all, but a smile both benevolent and knowing."

"So you've seen her in person, and had her eyes meet yours."

"I have."

"When the place—the Louvre place—was open or closed?"

Now he smiled—not so benevolent, but very knowing. "Why not both?"

"And again, eating pancakes with you, so my absolutes are pretty well shot to shit. But Greenleaf's stayed firmly in place. I didn't like him much, but since I've looked into him, his work, his . . . code, Feeney called it, I've sure as hell come to respect him."

She considered as she drank coffee. "He'd have had a file on me. That's SOP when a cop uses maximum force, and I have. IAB investigates, and the cop goes through Testing. But he never came after me."

"Perhaps the respect was mutual."

"Maybe." She polished off the last bite of syrup-soaked pancake before she stood. "I'm wearing black in case I can squeeze time to make his memorial, and can't squeeze it to change into uniform."

"Make it lightweight," Roarke advised her. "We're in for a steam bath today."

"I like it hot."

"As well I know," he said as she walked into her closet.

She came out moments later—black trousers, black tank,

black boots and belt, black jacket in hand—and thought how quick and easy mornings could be if she could grab black daily.

She strapped on her weapon harness.

"He said, in the dream, they'd haunt you. The dead and disgraced cops."

Eve nodded. "Yeah, he said that."

"Will they?"

She picked up her badge, studied it. "No. Dreams are weird, and I think that he'd think they would. But no. One thing the captain and I can agree on, in the absolute? Wrong cops taint us all. If he made a mistake, if he pushed too hard on any of the cops on those dream walls, that's on him."

She pocketed her badge and the rest.

"The ones he took down who earned it? They'd come after me, same as him, but they don't haunt me."

"Only put bruises on you."

"Before I kicked their asses."

"Before," he said, and walked to her, rubbed his hands on her shoulders. "Do me a favor then and take better care of my cop today."

"If you'd seen the other guy, you'd know I took pretty good care of her yesterday."

He'd worry, she thought as she walked downstairs. Wishing he wouldn't couldn't stop it. So she'd take the best care of his cop she could manage.

She'd meet Peabody at the apartment of Taylor Noy, age twenty-four, the daughter of former Captain Louis Noy, Anti-crime.

Noy had taken his own life—with his service weapon—at the age of fifty while under investigation for what turned out to be a twenty-six-year career span of corruption.

Over two decades of bad acts, Eve thought as she drove

through the gates, polished over with citations for bravery, shiny medals, promotions. He'd run a small, tight syndicate of cops on the take. Witness tampering, political bribery, protection rackets.

A syndicate Greenleaf had exposed with the help of a rookie Noy had begun to groom. Officer Kent Boxer's body had been found in a meat locker, hanging from a hook. He'd been tortured and beaten before his throat was slit.

Two days later, with the walls closing in, Noy opted out rather than face charges.

His family lost their home and everything else Noy had accumulated through his corruption.

Just shy of five months later, his nineteen-year-old son, Brice—criminal justice major, NYU—hanged himself.

Noy's wife, Ella, now living on Long Island, had remarried the previous year.

The daughter, Taylor, Eve's first stop, had an apartment, Lower West, so convenient to Greenleaf's—and worked as an on-air reporter for *Inside Sports*, New York Bureau.

Pretty sweet gig for a twenty-four-year-old, Eve mused as she drove downtown. But how did it feel to have your father go from hero cop—one with bars—to disgraced and dead? To lose everything, including your older brother?

Instead of living your nice upper-middle-class life, you have to struggle. No more lovely brownstone, no more private school.

Now your own mother shakes all of that off, marries someone else, moves to a fancy neighborhood on Long Island.

Could trigger something, could demand payback for all those years, all those losses.

Worth a conversation.

She hunted for parking, lucked into a spot only a block and a half away from her destination.

Roarke hit it on the steam bath, she thought as she started

to walk. It might've been shy of eight A.M., but the temperature was already on the rise, and the air lay still and thick over the city.

She passed a glide-cart already doing brisk business on iced coffee. It smelled like someone had tried to freeze bricks of mud.

She considered the circumstances where she might actually drink iced cart coffee, and found none.

She paused outside of Taylor Noy's building. An old pre-Urban brick, well maintained, good security.

Maybe a brisk ten-minute walk from Greenleaf's building. Very possible their paths could cross.

She glanced at the time, then spotted Peabody hustling down the sidewalk.

She wore her red-streaked dark hair up in a high, bouncy little tail.

Jesus.

The pink boots, black pants (that was something, at least), and a shirt and thin, flowy jacket in pale, pale green.

"What, are you going to a garden party?"

"What? The jacket? Come on, it's mag-plus. Leonardo was helping me organize some of my fabrics, and he saw this, sketched out this jacket design in like two minutes. Then he made it, right there and then."

To Eve's sorrow, Peabody executed a stylish turn.

"I'm wearing a Leonardo!"

"Now that we've got that settled, the hair. What's your excuse there?"

"It's really hot?"

Since she couldn't dispute that point, Eve headed toward the main doors. "Did you read the file?"

"Affirmative. Captain Louis Noy. Seriously bad cop. We're here to talk to Taylor Noy, his only surviving offspring, since her older brother followed his father's lead and self-terminated. Nothing popped on him—the son. Still shy of twenty. Sad."

"He had an application in for the Academy, and had already been accepted, deferred until he graduated from NYU."

"Yeah, I saw that," Peabody said as Eve mastered in.

"Noy was grooming the rookie who rolled on him—and Boxer died for it. Hard to swallow he hadn't started grooming the son. Either way, Taylor Noy lost her father, her brother, her home, her school—and now her mother's remarried.

"She's first floor," Eve added.

"Happy day. No stairs."

Eve walked to the apartment door. Door cam, intercom, solid locks.

Knocked.

A female voice came throatily through the intercom. "Yes? Can I help you?"

"Lieutenant Dallas, Detective Peabody, NYPSD." Eve held her badge up to the camera. "We'd like to speak with you, Ms. Noy."

Suspicion tinted the voice now. "About what?"

"Captain Martin Greenleaf."

"I'm going to verify your identification."

"Go right ahead."

A couple minutes later the locks thunked. The woman who opened the door wore a short, body-skimming red dress and had bare feet. Her honey-brown hair fell in perfect twists nearly to her shoulders and framed a stunning face.

She'd won the DNA lottery with diamond-edged cheekbones, a full, shapely mouth currently dyed the same color as the dress. Perfect skin, polished bronze, only made deep green eyes greener.

"I'm a reporter," she said, "so I know how reporters work. I needed to make sure you weren't. Come in."

She stepped back into a living area full of color and clutter. "I don't apologize for the mess because I like it. I've got about twenty minutes before I have to leave for work, so I'll start by saying I heard about Captain Greenleaf. I'm sorry about it. I'm sorry for his family. I know what it's like to lose a father."

"He headed the investigation into yours."

"Yes, he did. Crap. Sit down. That was nine years ago," she added as she plopped down on a sofa. "What does that have to do with what happened to Captain Greenleaf?"

Since it faced the canary-yellow sofa Taylor chose, Eve sat in a chair of shockingly bright blue with yellow swirls. It made her think of Jenkinson's ties.

"Why don't you tell us where you were on Sunday night, between eight and ten P.M.?"

"I'm a suspect?" What came off as genuine shock widened those green eyes. "A *murder* suspect? Because of my dad? Whoa. Wow. You're really reaching back."

"We'd appreciate knowing your whereabouts."

"That's easy, and easy for you to verify. I was covering the Mets—home game. They took the field at eight-ten. Skimmed the Pirates, two to one."

Sitting back, Taylor crossed her legs.

"Highlights. The Pirates scored their only run with a two-out, solo homer top of the fifth. Kato drove it out on a one-one pitch. Fastball," she added. "Right over the plate, and Kato got the fat of the bat on it, and bam!

"Bottom of the eighth," she continued, "Macron took first with a base on balls, then took second on a wild pitch. Blanski's on deck. The Pirates brought in Willes as relief, but it didn't help. Blanski's double made it two to one, Mets. In the ninth, Parks put the Pirates down, one, two, three. Strikeout, fly ball, a chopper—Blanski at short to Rodrigo at first—for the final out at about nine-forty-five. I spent the next twenty minutes—give or take—interviewing players. On air. Live."

She smiled a little. "Damn good game."

The same game, Eve thought, playing on Greenleaf's wall screen.

"Why the hell would I kill Captain Greenleaf? My father," Taylor said before Eve spoke. "Let me tell you about my father, Lieutenant, Detective. He was a good dad. Hell, a great dad. Attentive, loving, fair—firm, but fair. If he had to miss one of my games—I played baseball spring and summer, basketball fall and winter—he got the recording and watched it.

"I had a damn good childhood—until. Happy, secure. I adored my dad. He was a hero to me. Then I learned that outside our house, our family—where he's always going to be a hero to me—he was anything but. It was all a lie. He cheated, he stole, he manipulated."

She closed her eyes. "And worse. He didn't tell us about the investigation, about the trouble, not at first. Looking back, I think he assumed he'd shake it off. I didn't really notice anything was wrong—I was fifteen, sports mad, starting to think seriously about boys, and thrilled I got permission to do this very part-time job at a fashion boutique. Because I liked clothes.

"Then . . ."

She breathed deep, shifted her gaze toward the window and the street beyond.

"There was something different in the house. He told my mother—I didn't know that until later. I sort of noticed, but Brice, he noticed. My dad favored him. I can say that without rancor," she added as she looked back at Eve.

"Brice was the golden child. He was going to be a cop, like our dad. It's all he ever wanted—to be like our dad. But there was something different between them, right before it happened. Brice wouldn't talk about it, not to me. I didn't really ask because my life was rolling. I had this little job, school, friends, and this boy who liked me.

"Maybe I noticed Dad was distracted. He didn't ask about practice or the game he'd missed. But I noticed the night two of his cops came to talk to him. Detective Riley and Detective Krotter—they'd come around plenty. Barbecues, holidays, whatever. But this was different, and even I could tell."

"Different how?"

"No joking around, no chitchat. They just went into my father's office, closed the door. Brice was out on a date. My mom was up in their room. Crying. I didn't know about the crying then, but she knew terrible things were coming. I went up to my room, listened to music, talked to this boy who liked me. He asked me out. I was so excited."

It brought a slow, sweet smile to her face.

"My first date—slow starter there because baseball, basketball. It was just pizza and a vid, but I had to ask my dad. I went downstairs—his door was still closed. I knocked. I opened the door because this boy wanted to take me out. And I found him."

"That must've been horrible for you," Peabody said.

"It was horrible, in every possible way. There he was, my hero, sitting at his desk, his weapon, which he always, always secured when he got home, on the floor. I told myself he was asleep, even though I knew he wasn't. I kept telling myself he was asleep as I screamed."

"When did you find out about the investigation, about Greenleaf and IAB?"

"I honestly don't know exactly. A lot of it's blurry. Brice was angry, inconsolable. My mother struggled to be strong. Everything came down around us, all he'd done. Brice said it was lies, all lies. I believed that. I had to."

She paused, shook her head. "But it wasn't. It was truth.

"We lost the house, I had to switch schools—which at fifteen was just another tragedy to me. I gave my mother such grief over that, put the blame on her. I'm ashamed of that. Then, just as I was beginning to see and feel clear again, Brice.

"My mother found him—another gift to the family."

Taylor curled her legs up under her in a move Eve saw not as much casual as looking for comfort.

"He lived at home. He had a partial scholarship, and I know Mom scraped together enough to fill the gap, to keep him in college. We found out later he'd stopped going to classes, and he'd been struggling to bring his grades back up. We had this little apartment—me sharing a room with Mom. Brice had a small bedroom of his own. She found him in the morning. He'd been gone for hours when she went in."

"You lost your father, your brother in under six months."

"That's right." Taylor nodded at Eve. "If you think I blame Greenleaf for any of it, you couldn't be more wrong. It's on my father. All of it. Every bit of it. I loved and love my father, but the man, the cop, he was? He left us in disgrace, in grief, in despair. I don't forgive him for that."

She closed her eyes again; when they opened, the green shined clear and hard. "I'll never forgive him for that. I know he didn't kill that young officer—one barely older than his own son. But he was responsible. I think that's what he couldn't live with. But I'll never know, will I?"

"And your mother?" Eve asked.

"Unlike Brice, and because of Brice, me for a while, Mom never blamed Greenleaf. She hadn't known, Lieutenant. My father was very skilled. He handled all our finances, and he had complete control. That's how he did things.

"It shattered her when she found out. She'd have stood by him if he'd faced the consequences. She loved him and, even shattered, she'd have stood by him. You must know she was investigated, too, and found blameless. She's happy now—all the way happy. She got married—almost a year ago. They're happy. Cal's a great guy, an honest guy. Please don't drag her into this. She's never hurt anyone in her life."

"Did your brother know?" Eve wondered.

"I'll never know that, either. I can only tell you he worshipped our dad, and he refused to accept what happened and why. He was nineteen, Lieutenant. Nineteen, and he couldn't live with the sins of the father. My mother and I have, for nine years. It's enough."

"We appreciate your time and cooperation," Eve said as she rose. "I'm sorry for your losses."

16

Out on the street, a fender bender tied traffic into a Gordian knot. Since a couple of beat droids were handling it, Eve walked on.

"I bought it," Peabody said. "All of it. She still has daddy issues, probably always will, but more because she knows and accepts what he was and did."

"We still check the alibi. Pull up *Inside Sports* and Sunday night's Mets game."

The same game, Eve thought again, if irony played a part, Greenleaf had on-screen when he died.

"Make sure she was there, and live. Roarke's already checked her financials and didn't flag any withdrawals that indicate she or her mother bought a hit. But let's take a look at the stepfather. Just check all the boxes."

"Can do. But you bought it, too."

"Yeah, I did. But he died at his desk."

"Noy?"

"Noy, just like Greenleaf. At his desk, service weapon on the floor. In his home. It's a mirror. Maybe. The two detectives who came to talk to him that night are still in cages. No evidence they reached out of those cages for a hit after nine years. Two other cops in Noy's division are lifers, off-planet, for the torture and murder of Officer Boxer."

Eve got into the car, sat a moment.

"Three others are out now, but relocated. I couldn't find any travel, anything in their financials, any evidence they're in this. And one killed herself, so her father's on today's list—her only family."

"Is he next?"

"No. Two more programmed in before him. One after." Since the traffic remained at a standstill, horns blasting, curses streaming, Eve hit vertical, streaked over the spreading knot, zipped around the corner, then slid down into the stop-and-go on the avenue.

Peabody white-knuckled the chicken stick with both hands.

"Coffee," she choked out. "Is there time for coffee?"

"When isn't there? After we hit the first five, I want to go back to the house, write those up. We'll look over the next group—not many more now. We'll see how many we can work in before Greenleaf's memorial."

"Yeah, sure, okay." Color came back into her cheeks as Peabody gulped coffee.

No buzz on the next two—the first a widow and her thirteen-year-old son, the next the surviving brother.

"He didn't have to move on, like the widow," Peabody commented. "He never liked his brother in the first place. Add he's got a family of his own—two kids. I don't see him risking that for revenge after seven years."

"And the brother took himself out in his ride, not at his desk at home. It's a small detail, but it's sticking for me."

The second-to-last on the morning list took them to the Lower East Side and the market owned and run by Onkar Jain, father of Officer Divya Jain, deceased.

She'd hit the morgue's list, too. Greenleaf had logged in to see her body.

Eve grabbed a loading zone nearly in front of the market, flipped up her On Duty light.

The outdoor display showcased flowers and fruit, colorful and fragrant. Inside, the floors sparkled, the shelves held stock neatly organized. The counter, snowy white, held point-of-purchase items to tempt the impulses along with two checkout stations, both manned.

A girl of about sixteen worked one side, her glossy black hair braided down her back and ending in a bright pink tip.

She recognized the man at the second station as Onkar Jain from his ID shot. The hooded eyes, the deep facial creases, the carefully trimmed dark hair.

He stood hardly taller than the girl, with a scarecrow build under his stiff white shirt and pressed black pants.

Eve waited until he'd finished with a customer before she stepped forward. He greeted her with a smile.

"How can I help you?" he asked, his voice deep and lightly accented.

"Mr. Jain, Lieutenant Dallas, Detective Peabody." She palmed her badge discreetly. "NYPSD. We'd like to speak with you."

The smile vanished; his face went blank. Carefully blank. "Is there trouble?"

Before Eve could answer, the girl murmured to him in their native tongue. His gaze swept up over Eve as he nodded. Then he patted the girl's cheek. "I'll be a few minutes."

He gestured to the back of the store, then led the way. He used a swipe card to deactivate the alarm on the rear door before stepping into a short alley where the recycler not only worked but appeared to have been scrubbed recently.

"My niece recognized you. She saw the vid. I did not.

You've come to question me about the murder of Captain Martin Greenleaf."

"We're investigating his death and making inquiries. Captain Greenleaf was in charge of Internal Affairs when your daughter was implicated, in 2052, in the corruption inside Anti-crime."

"He never gave her a chance. She was twenty-three years old. She took her own life rather than live with the shame."

"You resented Captain Greenleaf?"

"Resent? A small word for what I felt. I came to this country at eighteen, to build a life. I worked, and hard, to make my place. I would say I chose poorly for my wife, but I had Divya. I had Divya when her mother left us. A good, sweet, loving girl, my child who wanted to be police to protect people, to keep our city safe. I curse the day she put on the uniform.

"I curse the devil Louis Noy, who pressured her, intimidated her, corrupted her."

"Captain Greenleaf named your daughter as part of Noy's syndicate."

"She told me all, in her despair, when she learned they had killed another police. A young police. She told me she'd believed Noy—her superior—when he told her they were doing good. But she broke rules and laws to follow him. She was disgraced, grieved. She knew the young man they killed, and his death weighed so heavy on her heart. I told her we would go to this Captain Greenleaf, tell him all she knew. We'd beg for mercy."

"Did you?"

"That night, while I prayed, she took her life. She wrote me asking my forgiveness. She said she deserved no mercy. And in my grief, I went to this captain and asked him to take her name away from the others, to give her this last respect. But he would not."

"He couldn't, Mr. Jain." Sympathy saturated Peabody voice. "He couldn't doctor the files."

"She was my only child. The others went to prison, but they live. Noy did not, but I wished him to live. I wished to know he suffered day by day, year by year."

"And Greenleaf?"

"He didn't give her a chance. In life or in death."

"Can you tell us where you were Sunday night, between eight and ten P.M.?"

He sighed, looked into Eve's eyes with his sorrowful ones. "I don't take life. Life is precious. The most precious gift. My daughter took hers in grief, somehow believing it would atone for the taking of another. She was young."

He sighed again.

"We stay open until eight on Sunday. At closing I, with Jamid—a boy who works for me—cleaned. On Sunday we do deep cleaning and full restocking. I let Jamid listen to music while we work. It isn't music to me, but he works well with it. We were done at nine or near to nine."

"You have surveillance cameras."

"Yes, people will take not always what they need, which is forgivable, but what they want, which is not. But this is a loop. Seventy-two hours, so not for Sunday now."

"After nine, when you left the market?"

"I live upstairs, but I took a walk. My neighbor, Ms. Lu, walked her little dog, Cyril. I'm fond of Cyril. I work too many hours to keep a little dog, but I walked with her and the little dog, Cyril, then went home."

"If you could give us Jamid's contact, and your neighbor's contact, it would be helpful."

"It's procedure. Divya would say, 'Papa, it's procedure.'"

"Yes," Eve said, and felt only pity. "It's procedure."

In the car, Peabody snapped her safety belt in place with

a hard click. "Noy took the easy way. He should be locked away. Mr. Jain didn't kill Greenleaf."

"Why—other than the alibi that's going to check out?"

"He's too kind, and murder would disgrace the daughter he loved."

"That, plus he's a rule follower. One more." Eve hesitated, then pulled out of the loading zone. "I knew this one."

"The dead cop?"

"Ansel Hobbs. We were at the Academy together. I slept with him once."

"Oh. Okay. Oh."

"Nothing major, either side. When we graduated. Sort of a 'lots of drinks, bang it out, move on' thing. I didn't see much of him after that, and less once Feeney took me on in Homicide. I ran into him at the Blue Line right after I made detective. I got this itch."

Peabody's eyes widened. "You had sex with him again?"

"No! Not that kind of itch. Something off about him. I didn't think much about it at the time, but now . . . According to the files, he'd have already been dirty. A few years later, when he got caught doctoring evidence for a fee, I wasn't surprised."

She made a turn, settled on another loading zone.

"In under twenty-four hours, he'd taken himself out. He was engaged to the woman we're going to talk to."

"Cela Spaceck," Peabody remembered from the file. "Thirty-four, single. Licensed therapist."

"Right. Considering the graduate, lots of drinks, bang it out, you take the lead on this one."

"Sure, but that doesn't seem like a conflict."

"Maybe not. But we keep well inside the lines. This is her place, she works out of it."

The pretty townhome had a pot of white flowers on the stoop and privacy shades on the windows.

Top-of-the-line security—cams, palm plate, security swipe.

Eve pressed the buzzer.

A human voice answered. "Ms. Spaceck's offices. May I help you?"

"NYPSD, Lieutenant Dallas, Detective Peabody."

"Are you serious?"

In answer, Eve held up her badge. The door buzzed, locks thumped free.

Inside, a short hallway with gleaming floors opened into a tasteful, on-the-plush-side living area. Or they'd designed it to resemble one. A woman in a cream-colored suit and a head full of black braids pushed up from a curved-leg desk to hurry across the room.

"Excuse me! I just couldn't believe—I read both of Nadine Furst's books." She shot out a hand to Peabody. "I loved your character's smart mouth! It's a pleasure to meet you both." She pumped Eve's hand in turn. "How can we help you today?"

"We'd like to speak with Ms. Spaceck."

"She's with a patient, but should be finishing up very shortly. Can I offer you anything?"

"We're good. Have you worked here long?"

"Since Cela—Ms. Spaceck—opened her practice. Three years now. Please, sit down."

They settled on opposite ends of a peacock-blue sofa. Quiet, soothing watercolors decorated the pearl-gray walls. The air smelled like lemon blossoms twined with lavender.

"I did see the vid, too, and it was excellent. Well, obviously, Oscar winner and all that. But I seriously loved the book. And the follow-up! I was terrified all over again. I mean to say, it brought it all back. Rumor is, Ms. Furst is already writing a third."

"That's the rumor," Eve said, and hoped to leave it at that.

Her hopes would've been dashed, but the door across the hall opened.

The man who came out looked about fifty with pale blue eyes that showed signs of recent weeping. He hesitated, looked nervously at Eve and Peabody, then cleared his throat.

"Ms. Spaceck said next week, as usual."

"We'll see you then. Have a good rest of your day."

"I'm going to try."

He hurried out.

"Give me one minute."

The receptionist walked to the door, poked her head in. A minute later, she walked back.

"You can go right in. I should tell you Ms. Spaceck only has fifteen minutes before her next appointment."

"We'll keep it as brief as possible."

Eve stepped in to what she'd have called a good-sized parlor. No desk, but two good leather chairs the color of honey and a deep-cushioned copper-toned sofa.

Tables, lamps, a glass-fronted friggie holding water. A mini-AC, plants—thriving. And a woman with mocha-colored skin, hair the color of her chairs cut sharp and blunt to her chin. She stood tall and curvy in a sleeveless black dress and appraised Eve and Peabody with iceberg-blue eyes.

"Lynn's starstruck."

"We're police, Ms. Spaceck," Peabody said somberly. "Not stars. Thank you for seeing us so quickly."

"Of course. But if this is about a patient, you're going to need a warrant. And if you have a warrant, I need to contact my attorney."

"It's about Captain Martin Greenleaf."

The eyes went from haughty to puzzled. "I'm not sure who that is."

"Captain Greenleaf headed Internal Affairs when Ansel Hobbs self-terminated."

"Oh." After a long breath. "Oh. I'm not sure I knew that."

"Captain Greenleaf was murdered Sunday night."

"I see. No, actually, I don't. Sit down, please. I can give you coffee, tea, water, and about fifteen minutes. Why do you want to talk to me about the murder of a man I didn't know who investigated a man who's been dead for nearly eight years?"

"We'll take the seat and the fifteen." Peabody spoke briskly as Cela went to the friggie, got water for herself. "You and Officer Hobbs were engaged."

"I was engaged to the man I believed Ansel to be." Cela took one of the chairs, cracked the tube of water. "Then I learned he'd lied to me, repeatedly, that he'd broken the law he'd sworn to uphold, and made a mockery of my faith in him."

"Did he speak to you about the investigation, about Captain Greenleaf?"

"He told me he was in trouble, and why. He wanted me to pack up, just pack up everything, my life included, and run with him. We'd dated for nearly a year, had been engaged a few weeks, had just moved in together."

She sipped the water.

"I can't tell you if he mentioned that name—I don't remember. I was stunned, angry, I couldn't believe what he was telling me. He'd taken bribes, planted evidence, doctored it, altered reports—all for money. He tried to claim the money was to give me the life I wanted, and that was— frankly—bullshit. He said we had to leave the city or he'd be arrested. He'd lose his job, probably go to prison, but he had enough put away to get away, start a new life.

"On lies," she said. "I refused. I was so angry. I saw everything I'd envisioned my life—our life together—becoming shatter. I said horrible things to him."

She pressed her lips together, then took a long drink.

"Horrible things, and I regret them. In my shock and anger, I offered no support to him. No promises to stand by him, the man I'd said I loved, whatever came. He pleaded, he cried, but I wouldn't budge. And then I walked out on him. I spent the night with a friend.

"I found him the next morning when I came back for my things, still riding stiff-backed on my high, high horse. I said horrible things, I walked out. And he didn't run. He took his own life."

She set the water aside. "It wrecked me. For months I sleepwalked through the day, lay awake at night. Then I decided if I'd known more about myself, about Ansel, if I'd understood more, I might have helped him. So I went back to school, and studied, and got my license. Three years ago, I began seeing people who needed someone to listen, someone to help."

She breathed deep. "And I actually do understand now why you're here. You want to know where I was and what I was doing—Sunday night, you said?"

"Between eight and ten P.M."

"That's inconvenient," she murmured. "Sunday I went sailing with a friend, and was home—alone—before seven. Generally, habitually, Sunday evenings are for reviews on my patients, plans for the upcoming week."

"Did you see or speak to anyone?"

"My parents, but that was directly after I got home, so well before eight. I made some pasta, had a glass of wine, then I worked until about ten. I did some yoga and was in bed by eleven. I would have the security footage of me coming in that night, and it would show I didn't go out again. That and my word? That's it."

"If you'd provide a copy of that, it would be helpful."

"Of course." She rose. "Lynn will get it for you now. I

want to say, Ansel was responsible for his own choices. There would be underlying reasons for them, but they were his choices. The man who was murdered? He wasn't responsible for them."

"Hobbs had family," Eve said.

"Yes. His parents—divorced—a stepsister. They weren't close. We'd dated, as I said, for a year, had started planning our wedding, and I hadn't met them. I still haven't. Possibly an underlying reason."

Possibly, Eve thought, but regardless, she didn't see Cela Spaceck plotting murder.

They accessed the copy. Eve knew it would support Spaceck's statement, but every detail mattered.

"Do another check on the parents and stepsister," Eve told Peabody as they stepped back into the steam bath of summer. "We'll be thorough."

"I think he loved her. So does she."

"Not enough" was Eve's opinion. "We'll go in, write these up. We should be able to put together another batch before Greenleaf's memorial."

"Right. Since I took the lead, maybe I should drive."

Eve didn't bother with the no. "You have two speeds," she said as she got behind the wheel. "The hundred-and-ten-year-old lady in a sedan approaching the same age, or the sixteen-year-old kid who just jacked a sports car."

"That's so not . . . untrue. Maybe it's because I don't get enough practice."

"Find a reason to requisition a ride sometime, then let me know so I can stay off the roads while you practice. Meanwhile, check the alibis, then write up the last two."

"I'm scanning Spaceck's security for Sunday now. I've got her leaving at about ten hundred hours. She looks really nice, all casual chic."

"Really? Gee, what's she wearing?"

"Okay, okay, just saying. No activity, no in or out throughout the day. I've got her returning, going in at eighteen-fifty, and . . . Wait, she's coming out again at—Oh. Watering the flowers on the stoop, going back in. No activity, front or rear cams well beyond Greenleaf's TOD."

"Write it up," Eve said, and pulled into the garage.

"Speaking of write-ups, are we going to bag Oglebee on the fraud, theft, and so on?"

"Satisfying, especially since we have no lead suspects or suspects on the murder. But time-consuming. I'm turning it over. Let somebody else have the trouble and satisfaction."

"It'd be a nice bust," Peabody considered as they walked to the elevator. "But I get it."

The elevator, while currently empty, smelled like fresh urine and old sweat from the puddle that likely contained both.

"Somebody pulled in a pisser." So saying, Eve turned right around and opted for the stairs. "What are you doing?" she asked when Peabody worked her 'link.

"Reporting it to Maintenance."

"Aw. That's really sweet. They may get around to dealing with it sometime this decade."

"I made a contact there."

"Since when?" Eve switched to glides.

"When you were on vacation. One of the vending machines malfunctioned—"

"Big surprise."

"And sort of vomited coffee everywhere. I got in a conversation with Hazel—that's her name—while she was cleaning it up. She's a big Mavis fan. I got her a disc of a practice session Mavis did in her new studio."

Peabody looked over with a smug smile. "And Hazel says she's on it."

"You bribed her. Kudos."

"I think of it more as a quid pro quo."

When they reached Homicide, Eve saw Webster—in dress blues—sitting on a bench. He rose.

"Your wolves wouldn't let me into your den."

"Go ahead and get started, Peabody. You can come in now," she said to Webster. "I told you I'd keep you in the loop."

"I know, but I haven't heard from you since . . . Face looks better."

She exchanged a look and nod with Jenkinson and his atomic tie as she passed through the bullpen. "Peabody and I just came in from the field, where we conducted five interviews this morning. We conducted interviews yesterday, and we're eliminating possible suspects."

When they reached her office, she turned to him. "You know how it works, Webster. We're working on it. We're working the angles. We just don't have anything solid at this point. Where's Angelo?"

"She's with the family. They're having a private thing before the official memorial. A family thing."

"You should be there."

"I'm going. I was hoping I could give them something."

"You can. The investigation is ongoing and active. It's fucking active, Webster. Feeney's working it, and he's got McNab on it. Baxter and Trueheart did an interview and subsequent report on same, after shift yesterday. Roarke's doing financial checks on his own time, one of which will lead to an arrest on unrelated charges.

"We eliminated five more this morning. Peabody's checking alibis, but that's just to keep it clean."

He dropped down in her ass-biting chair without complaint. "I'm not questioning your work, Dallas. I just want to give his wife and kids something to hang on to. Especially today."

"I just gave you something they can hang on to. Give them that, and don't give them what I'm telling you cop to cop. Understood?"

"You've got something."

"I've got what my gut and my experience tell me is a solid theory. But it's a theory. The faked suicide, taking him down at his desk. I think it's a mirror, so I'm working on that reflection. I'm theorizing that whoever planned this out wanted that mirror, and is therefore connected to someone Greenleaf took down, or was in the process of taking down, who sat at their desk, took their service weapon, and used it. It narrows the suspect field, but it's still a wide field."

"That's good," Webster said quietly. "That's a good, solid theory."

"And telling his wife and children that theory does nothing but twist them up, especially today."

"You're right, and I won't." But his face had cleared of grief. "I appreciate you sharing it with me." He got to his feet. "I'd like to share it with Darcia. Cop to cop."

"No problem."

"Nobody sticks out?"

"Not yet."

"All right." He scrubbed his hands over his face. "Okay. Are you going to make it to the memorial?"

"I plan to."

"Good. They're having a kind of wake for him at his daughter's house after the memorial. You'd be welcome."

"I think they'd rather I work the case."

"Yeah, they would. Thanks."

When he left, she pressed her fingers to her eyes, tried to push away the grief he'd left behind.

She updated her board first, then sat to write up the morning's work.

She added a note for Mira.

> The mirror theory sticks for me. So the Noy case stands out. Suicide, at desk, service weapon on the floor beside the chair—not in the same position or distance, but on the floor beside the chair. The body found by a family member—in this case, the teenage (at the time) daughter. She's clear. While we'll take a deeper look at the wife and her current husband, that's shaky at best. But if there's one case that reflects, there's bound to be another in Greenleaf's long career.
>
> Does this read as viable to you?

As she sent it, Peabody's clomp came down the hall.

"Just wanted to tell you the alibis check. As for Noy? The widow and her new husband, they attended a dinner party in Oyster Bay Sunday night—arrival about seven, departure about ten-thirty. Plenty of wits there. Also, the new guy comes off clean. No criminal. One previous marriage, ending in divorce almost twelve years ago. One offspring, female. He's a financial adviser—runs his own firm. Nothing hinky shows. Maybe Roarke could look deeper, but I didn't find anything on him."

"Okay. I might pass it to Roarke just to wrap it tight."

Peabody glanced over as Eve heard more footsteps.

"Hey, Feeney."

"Hey." He paused at Eve's doorway. "Got a minute?"

"Sure."

He looked more hangdog than usual. Peabody must have seen it, too, as she simply stepped back and left them alone.

17

"Got two more for you."

He stood, hands in the pockets of his baggy brown suit.

To Eve's eye, it didn't look like he'd slept in it because he didn't look like he'd slept much at all.

"Thanks. We went through five this morning."

He nodded, wandered to her skinny window. "Anything?"

"Did you know Louis Noy? Captain, Anti-crime."

"That one still leaves a stain. Anti-crime, my ass. Spent his whole fucking career taking payoffs, planting evidence or ditching it depending on the payload. Connected?"

"Nothing I can find, but it's the only one that stands out."

She laid out her theory while he nodded, stared out the window.

"We'll add that in, add a filter, see what we dig out."

"Okay." She got up, programmed coffee for both of them. Something here, she thought. He'd get to it in his own time.

"The two I brought you? I knew one of them. Rookied with him. Sanctimonious bastard, or that's how he played it. Turns out, as he worked his way up to lieutenant, he was hustling street LCs, banging plenty of them, but taking a cut, hustling dealers, taking a cut there. Anyway, he got busted, took himself out. Had two ex-wives by then, a couple kids.

"I want to take that one, do those interviews. I knew the son of a bitch."

"Okay."

"Doesn't fit the new filter, but—"

"We've still got to cover it."

"Yeah, gotta cover it." As Eve often did, Feeney paced the small space, one eye on the murder board.

He stuck his hands in the pockets of his rumpled suit. "I didn't much like Greenleaf. Always had a stick up his ass."

"I didn't, either, same reason."

Feeney just nodded, hands in his pockets, eyes on the board.

"Plenty of times, you look at IAB as the enemy," he said. "Cops got a job to do, right? Who needs that second-guessing, microscoping-what-it-takes-to-do-it bullshit? They're not on the streets, not going through the door. They're not living it."

"No, they're not."

"And some who go into IAB, they put a target on a cop's back because they want that power, like holding it over you. But . . . Hell, the truth of it is, you gotta have the watchdogs because some fuck up. Maybe make a mistake—and that's human and, for fuck's sake, cops are human. But maybe it's not a mistake, maybe it's some son of a bitch using the badge as an excuse to do what we're supposed to use it to stop.

"An excuse to pound on somebody, an excuse to get their palm greased."

He turned to her then.

"You know what it's like when you go after another cop, a wrong cop. You went after Oberman, dirty as they come, and you nailed her ass. And still some are going to look sideways at you for it."

"She'll spend the rest of her life in prison, and I'm sitting here. I can live with the sideways looks."

"Yeah, there's that. I was proud of you, what you did, how you did it, why you did it."

"You were part of it," she reminded him. "You, EDD, my partner, my bullpen."

"It was your op, right down the line. Anyway," he said, and looked away again. "You start looking at these poor fucking excuses for cops, too many of them. You start thinking one's too many, but, kid, they just keep coming. Makes you sick. Pisses you off, and makes you sick on top of it.

"And you think how Greenleaf did this every goddamn day. Not one bad cop, not a handful, but dozens and dozens. Yeah, maybe he drew a hard line, and maybe I look at some and think too hard, but that was his job. He did it every goddamn day, and he lived with it. What makes me sick and pisses me off, he did every day for years. He took out the trash, Dallas, and somebody had to."

She got up, closed her door.

"I had a dream about him last night."

"Greenleaf?"

"And all the cops we're looking at now, all the cops he looked at. At the end of it, he said they haunted him, and now they'd haunt me. I thought, I really thought, that's bullshit. They don't and won't haunt me. But he was right. Or the dream was. I think they did haunt him, and now me. Not the way I figured he meant. What they did, cops like Oberman, and these?"

She tossed a hand toward her board. "The dozens and dozens, what they did using a badge like it was a free pass to do whatever the hell they wanted, the ones who smeared the badge, twisted the law trying to justify what they did? That's what haunts me. Pisses me off. Makes me sick.

"So when I go to his memorial today, it won't be just to pay my respects, not even to do my job and see if anything or anyone pops out for me. It'll be to acknowledge that. He honored the badge, and paid the price for it every day. You taught me to do the same."

"Hell, I didn't have to teach you that. If I hadn't seen that in you, I wouldn't have taken you on."

"Worked out for both of us. Have you had anything to eat today?" she asked, then realized, with a jolt, she sounded like Roarke.

"Nah. Couldn't work up to it."

She crossed to the AC. "How about a burger?"

"Don't think I have the stomach for it, kid."

"We'll split one. Take a seat. I knew one of the cops on the wall," she said to distract him as she programmed the burger—and fries with it.

"Yeah? Who?"

"Hobbs, Ansel. From the Academy."

Baggy eyes narrowed, he sat. "Yeah, yeah. I ran him through. Didn't hit me then you'd have been in the same time."

"Doesn't look like he connects on this."

She rounded it up as she set the burger on the desk. She didn't think she had the stomach for it, either, but the smell was glorious.

She considered the penknife in her pocket, then opened a drawer, took out a combat knife. And made Feeney smile.

"You keep that sticker in your desk?"

"You never know, do you?"

She sliced the burger neatly in half. Because she knew Feeney, she went back, ordered a tube of cream soda for him, a Pepsi for herself.

She sat on the corner of the desk, picked up her half.

"There are more good cops than bad, Feeney."

"Fucking A. We've both got a division of them. Word is Webster turned in his papers."

"He did." She sampled a fry, felt genuinely joyous when

her lip didn't sting. "He's starry-eyed over Angelo. He's moving to Olympus, figures to work at the Academy there, training new cops."

Feeney grunted over a mouthful of burger. "Ain't enough money in the fricking universe—and that includes all Roarke's—could get me to live on some rock spinning out there."

"I hear that. Plus, New York needs good, solid cops on the job."

He picked up his cream soda. "To the job."

"To the job," she agreed, and tapped tubes.

He looked better when he left and, when she weighed that against lost work time, it won by a few hundred miles.

More, she understood what had dragged her down all day. Same damn thing, she thought.

Same damn, dirty thing.

Peabody popped into the doorway. "We should—" She sniffed the air like a hound. "Burgers!"

"Burger, singular. Feeney needed to eat."

"Oh. Well."

And oh hell, she thought.

"Get one if you want."

"No, but if I'd known the option, I wouldn't have choked down what claimed to be a Cobb salad from Vending. I was going to say, if you wanted to do dress blues, we should change."

"Right."

More time lost, she thought, changing, then changing again. But . . .

They haunt me, he'd said.

"We'll do that. I've got a couple more from Feeney. We'll pay our respects, come back, change again, hit those."

Peabody waited until they reached the locker room before

she asked, "Is he okay? Feeney? He looked off when he showed up."

"He's fine now."

"Burgers'll do that."

"Yeah, they will."

Eve pulled on uniform pants. They took her back, she realized. Way back.

"He knew somebody on the list. It can hit hard when you've got any kind of a history."

"And even when you don't." Peabody buttoned up her uniform jacket. "McNab and I talked about it last night. How you know there are bad eggs or apples or whatever the hell you call them, but when you really look, look at the spread of what Greenleaf covered over the course of a career? It hits hard."

She sat to put on the hard, shiny uniform shoes. "I thought about how I stood there in that shower stall, naked and terrified, when Oberman came into the locker room down at the old gym. Talking about killing like it was just business. I guess it was, to her."

"She'd still be using her badge to do what was just business to her if you hadn't stood up. What the hell are you doing with that silly hair tail?"

Peabody finished flipping it up, pinning it down. "Fixing it so my cover sits straight."

And when she'd done just that, she looked, to Eve, pretty much like the old Peabody.

"Let's go."

They'd chosen to hold the memorial outdoors, in a green space near the daughter's home. A good thing, Eve decided, as by her gauge about two hundred attended.

Plenty of cops, she noted, including Whitney and a lot of

other brass. She spotted Chief Tibble and his wife, Whitney and his, Morris, Callendar, Mira.

Webster and Darcia sat with the family. Various photos of Greenleaf stood among generous flower displays. The largest stood on an easel and showed Greenleaf in his own dress blues and shining captain's bars.

Appropriate, Eve thought, since he'd been a cop most of his life.

People spoke, and she listened to eulogies with half an ear as she scanned the crowd.

She picked out Elva Arnez and Denzel Robards easily. She wore a slim black dress and black sunshades against the beat of the sun. He wore a black suit and tie. Not used to that, she decided, as he periodically tugged at the tie or rolled his shoulders against the restriction of the suit jacket.

The widow's friends sat just behind the family, with the addition of the one who'd come from Maine, along with their spouses if they had them.

She saw no one else she'd interviewed. No one else she'd put on her board.

The widow sat, shoulders straight, even as tears slid down her cheeks.

She saw cops whose faces read they'd come under orders. But they hadn't walked his path, she thought. She had now.

She made note of faces she didn't recognize, in case. In case, in case, those faces showed up later.

But for now, there were only words and weeping. And watching.

At the end, people moved up to give the family condolences. She saw Tibble take both of the widow's hands in his, bend down to speak quietly.

She saw Arnez dab at her eyes under the dark glasses, and Robards put an arm around her in comfort.

"A lot of cops came," Peabody commented.

"A good chunk of them came under orders."

"Oh. You think?"

"Yeah, I think," Eve said, still watching.

"Santiago and Trueheart stayed back because neither of them were on the job when he was, and somebody had to stay back in case something hit. Jenkinson asked Baxter to stay back, too, and some of the uniforms. But you didn't order anyone to come, and everyone else in the bullpen did."

"That's right. Is there anyone in our squad you wouldn't go through the door with, Peabody? Anyone you wouldn't trust to back you up, a hundred percent?"

"No," Peabody said immediately.

"There you have it. Let's get to work."

At Central, she changed out of uniform, then pulled two more possibles, using the new filter, out of the list to make four with Feeney's two.

In the bullpen, she went to Baxter's desk.

"Are you clear?"

"My man and I are looking into a cold one, since it seems to be a day when murder's taking a little break. We're clear enough."

"I've got four more to interview. You and Trueheart take these two." She handed him the data. "Peabody and I have the others."

"Hey, partner," he called back to Trueheart. "We're gonna ride."

"Peabody," Eve said.

"Ready to ride. Where to?"

"Tribeca, the West Village."

"West Village. Street art!"

"We're not shopping."

Peabody hustled to catch up. "I've got eyes, and they'll know what I want when they see it. They know what McNab wants because we talked it over. Just two interviews?"

"For now." When the elevator opened nearly empty, Eve risked it. "There aren't many more on the list that fit the parameters now. If we don't hit, we'll have to widen that."

"I know it sort of feels stalled, but eliminating narrows the field."

So why did it feel like she was spinning her wheels? Eve thought. "We'll have a handful left in this direction tomorrow. If we bottom out, we need to change direction."

And when they returned to Central, Eve felt those wheels still spinning.

"Maybe Baxter and Trueheart got something." Peabody had a Village street scene canvas tucked under her arm.

"The only one who got anything was you."

"And I appreciate it. It only took five minutes."

Because it had, Eve decided not to bitch about it.

When she walked into the bullpen, Roarke sat on the corner of Jenkinson's desk, apparently unaffected by tiny rainbow-hued dinosaurs roaming over electric green.

"And here's the boss," Jenkinson announced.

"Hit the list again," Eve told Peabody, and gestured toward her office. "Am I getting another gift?" she asked Roarke.

"Sadly, no. Just a few loose ends to tie on the old one. And since it's late in the day, I thought I'd see how long it might be before my cop wrapped things up."

"I'm wrapping nothing up, and getting fucking nowhere." After dragging her hands through her hair, she dropped down at her desk.

"Ah. Coffee."

"Yeah, yeah, coffee. Had a talk with Feeney, and I ended up being you."

"You bought Zimbabwe?"

"No. Did you?"

"Not today, but it seems like something you'd consider, being me."

She just shook her head. "I pushed him to eat a burger. Half," she corrected. "I had to eat the other half to get him to eat. He looked so damn tired, so off. All these dirty cops. Looking at them day after day. It hits hard."

He skimmed a hand over her hair before he set coffee on her desk. "I know it does."

"That's all you knew once, back in Dublin. Dirty cops."

"And now I know their opposite. You're frustrated it's not falling into place for you yet."

"Because it should be. If I'm pushing in the right direction, it should. The payback, and the specifics of it. At home, at his desk, service weapon on the floor, suicide. I turn it this way, that way, but every way I look at it, if someone just wanted him dead, easier, simpler, more direct ways, so the specifics matter. But—"

"No one fits. Yet."

"Not that many more to go through using those filters. If I widen the field back to just dead, disgraced, terminated for cause . . ." She shook her head again, drank coffee. "It doesn't sit right. But then I have to ask am I going at it so narrow because I can't shake off the hunch."

"Is it a hunch, or is it deduction?"

She hissed out a breath. "Sometimes they're not so much different."

"In my experience, your hunches have a solid base in deduction."

"Well, my hunch deduces this is the right direction, and I've missed something." She shoved up. "Where did the killer get the service weapon? Feeney's working that, and coming up with nothing there so far. We nail that, we're a step closer."

"What are the options?"

"You'd know that as well as I do, but okay. Steal it—which should be reported and logged. Another cop or someone with access lifts it out of inventory or Evidence and manages to cover that up. Black market, a street deal. We've got the weapon, so the model, the years that model was issued and used, and that model's been out of service for fifteen years."

"What happens when it's put out of service?"

"Destroyed, melted down, and that's logged, too. Obviously this one wasn't. But the ID number's gone. The lab can't pull it out."

"What else do you know about it?"

"It was fired multiple times before Sunday night. It was wiped clean. Greenleaf's prints are on it, but too clear and positioned incorrectly to substantiate he used it on himself, at that angle."

She held up a finger. "Wait. Another possible filter there. Shit, I missed that. Shit. Who was on the job on the list during the period that model was issued? I've accounted for the model—and the logs checked. But logs can be doctored, and not a stretch if you're dirty anyway. Take care of the ID number, and you've got a drop piece.

"I missed it."

"Seems as though you've caught it," Roarke corrected.

"Not fast enough. I don't know what the hell good it's going to do me, but it's another detail."

She paused, studied her board. "You've got the piece. It's not the one—not the one used by the person you're avenging—but it's theirs. A weapon they used, then tucked away. Didn't turn it in—or did, then lifted it again once it was logged. Should've been marked down as destroyed after. A bribe could take care of that, or a distraction. A threat."

A new scent, he thought. He'd ride it with her.

"Would it go back to a family member then, or close friend, lover? Someone not only bent on revenge, but who'd have access to the personal belongings of the one they're avenging."

"That's what I so deduce. It fits right in. We're not looking in the wrong direction, damn it. It fits. All the pieces fit this way, this profile.

"Hold on."

She snatched up her 'link. "Feeney, add another filter."

Roarke sipped his coffee while she ran it through for Feeney, quick, precise. And thought it was always a pleasure to watch her work.

Yes, she'd caught a new scent now, he decided, and the fatigue and frustration that had vibrated from her had turned to energy and focus.

"That's a damn good angle," Feeney told her. "We should've seen that."

"We see it now."

"Yeah, we do. We're going to run the whole batch through with all the filters. Make damn sure nothing slipped through. Good catch, kid."

When she clicked off, she stood another moment, eyes on the board. "Alibis, plenty of them, and they hold. And the ones without a solid alibi don't give off any major buzz. None."

She shoved her hands in her pockets. "Need to look there again anyway. Finances, nothing pops. But you wouldn't need to pay for a hit if you called in a favor. If you had somebody invested in the payback same as you. Someone not connected, at least it doesn't show."

Yes, indeed, Roarke thought, she'd caught a fresh scent.

"I need to—" She broke off, turned as she heard someone coming. Baxter stepped in.

"Roarke, looking sharp."

"As you do, Detective."

"Do my best. Serious thanks for this." He opened the jacket of his sharp suit to show the Thin Shield. "Saved me a solid jolt."

"I'm glad to hear it."

"So, LT, nothing on the two we talked to. One was front row center at her kid's school play—and that checks. The other was on a big date at Calypso. He used the fancy restaurant to propose right about Greenleaf's TOD in front of wits. Also checks out. And he said yes."

"New angle, new filter." She ran it through, as clear and precise as she had for Feeney.

"That's a good one."

"Tell Peabody and, if you stay clear, work it with her."

"You got it."

"I've got to write up the last interviews, then start digging on this again."

"I'll get out of your way," Roarke added.

"Getting in my way pushed out this new angle, so thanks."

"Happy to be of service. I could be of more if you want to do your write-up, then leave near to end of shift and do the digging at home. I could amuse myself, then go home with you, help with that."

"What about Zimbabwe?"

"It'll still be there."

"Actually, there's a set of financials. Peabody ran them, but—"

"And there you've provided my amusement. Send them to me and I'll find a spot, entertain myself until you're done."

"Sounds like a deal. Seriously, thanks. Bitching to you stopped the wheels from spinning."

"Wouldn't you want them to?"

"Not when they're stuck in the mud." She revolved her index fingers to demonstrate.

"Ah. Well then." He took her shoulders. And though she eyed the open door, she didn't hear anyone coming. She kissed him.

"Give me about an hour to clear things up here. I'll send you the data, then I'll tag you when I'm done."

She got fresh coffee when he left, then sat. She took one last long look at her board.

"I think you're on there. In my gut I think you're on there. But if you're not, you will be."

Because she needed to focus on the report, the details of the interviews, she set the new angle aside. Its time would come, and soon.

Halfway through the first interview, her communicator signaled.

Dispatch, Dallas, Lieutenant Eve. Report to 210 Beach Street.

"That's Carlie Greenleaf's address."

Affirmative. Male victim, Greenleaf, Benjamin, found hanging by the neck on premises, currently unconscious, transported to Saint Anne's Hospital. Called in by Webster, Detective Donald, with request for your immediate dispatch.

"Acknowledged. On the way. Son of a bitch!" She leaped up, rushed out. "Son of a fucking bitch. Peabody, with me, now!"

She spotted Roarke at Santiago's desk. Since Carmichael's was empty, she decided murder hadn't taken much of a break after all.

Roarke reached her as she strode to the elevators.

"We got another goddamn filter," she told them both. "Unless we buy Ben Greenleaf just tried to hang himself at his sister's house right after his father's memorial, somebody did it for him."

"Is he dead?" Peabody asked as they pushed on the elevator.

"Not yet. At the hospital, unconscious. Noy, this fits Noy. Son hanged himself. It fits. Work it, Peabody, add this in. We'll see how many others, if any, it fits. Because it sure as hell fits that.

"Damn it." As the elevator stopped again, more cops got on, she shoved off for the glides.

"Somebody like Noy, and with his rank? He could've made off with his decommissioned service weapon. He'd have found a way, and easy enough. At his desk, weapon on the floor. Son hangs himself a few months later. They didn't wait that long, but they're mirroring."

"If he makes it," Peabody said as she worked her PPC, "he could ID the killer."

"If," Eve repeated, and jumped on the next glide.

18

Peabody got into the back of the car before Roarke could.

"I can use the room," she told him. "I'm getting a couple offspring suicides."

"Hanging only. Mirror details."

"Okay, that changes that."

"It's a connection." Eve hit the lights, the siren and streaked out of the garage. "To Noy, or someone like him, and Greenleaf. Someone who came to the memorial, and went to the house after. Someone who's inserted themselves into the Greenleaf family. Had to know them, had to have been in the apartment before, in the daughter's house before. Had to know the layout to make this work."

She sped through a red light, and swung hard around an all-terrain that didn't take the siren seriously.

"Why don't I let Feeney know this last development," Roarke suggested. "He can add it to his search."

"Do that. Cops right on scene," she muttered. "Webster and Angelo for sure, and likely others. It's fucking ballsy."

"Add cruel with it, trying to kill, and perhaps succeeding, the son on the day his father's memorialized."

Eve spared Roarke a look. "The cruelty's part of the point."

She braked in front of the townhome, double-parked beside a cruiser. A beat droid stood at the door.

She engaged her recorder.

"Lieutenant. Sir, Detective Webster is inside, and the scene is secure. I have the door. My counterpart has the rear. Two uniform officers are assisting the detective."

"Stay on the door."

She'd expected to find more people inside. About a dozen sat or wandered the living area—including a couple of cops she'd seen at the memorial service.

The uniform on watch turned to her. "Sir."

"Webster."

"In the back, Lieutenant. My partner is upstairs, holding the crime scene secure."

Roarke handed Eve a field kit.

"Peabody, start taking statements. I'll start on the scene. Roarke, do me a solid and tell Webster we're here."

She went upstairs and found a uniform standing at a doorway.

"Report."

"Sir. The nine-one-one came in at sixteen-forty-eight, for the MTs and a police response. My partner and I arrived along with the MTs at sixteen-forty-two. The beat droids responded. They were just down the block. Detective Webster ordered them to take the front and rear doors. The victim, ID'd as Benjamin Greenleaf, the brother of the owner of the residence, was unconscious on the floor inside this room. Detective Webster told the MTs he'd performed CPR, successfully, as the victim wasn't breathing when he found him, and with the assistance of a Chief Angelo, cut him down. The MTs transported him to Saint Anne's. He was still out, LT."

He gestured behind him. "The noose is there, the overturned chair."

She glanced back when Webster came up the stairs, Darcia and Roarke behind him.

"I've got this, Officer. We'll keep the droids on the doors. You and your partner head to Saint Anne's and keep the victim secure."

"Yes, sir."

"Shit. Roarke, I've got these officers blocked in."

"I'll take care of it." He laid a hand on Webster's shoulder before he started back down.

"Don't say I have to stay out of it. I know it. I found him. Beth saw him go upstairs, said he looked upset. She asked me to go up, maybe talk to him. It took me a few minutes."

He dragged his hands over his face. "Goddamn few minutes, just like with Martin."

"Don." Darcia took his hand. "You know better."

"I came up. I didn't know exactly where he'd gone. I called him. He didn't answer. I almost went back downstairs. Jesus, I almost went back down. Let him have a few minutes to himself, I thought, some privacy. But all the doors were open up here, except this one. So I opened it, and saw him."

"What did you see?"

"Okay." He breathed in, breathed out. "I saw Ben hanging from a rope—that rope. I saw the overturned chair. I shouted, rushed in, grabbed his legs, shoved him up. Darcia came in."

"I was at the base of the stairs," she said. "I'd just come in from the small parlor where I'd gathered up some dishes. I heard Don shout, set them down, and ran up."

"She cut the rope. I had a penknife in my pocket. She got it out. The rope was secured to the hook near the window— you can see the swing chair they took down from it. She got up on a chair, cut the rope."

"The overturned chair?"

"No." Darcia shook her head. "The one by the little desk. I didn't want to disturb the scene more than necessary."

"I got the rope from around his neck, started CPR because he wasn't breathing. Darcia."

"Some of the family started up, I held them off, then took over CPR so Don could call it in."

"We got him breathing," Webster continued. "The MTs, the uniforms and droids got here fast. The MTs stabilized Ben, got him transported. I ordered the beat droids to take the exterior doors and the uniforms to stand on the scene here, and on the wits downstairs. I let the family go, Dallas. Luke and Shawn took the younger kids to their place. And the rest are at the hospital."

"All right."

"Ben would never do this. Never. And here? Look around. This is the kids' playroom, their game room. Their room. He'd never—"

"I know it, Webster. Not attempted suicide, attempted murder. Where are all the people who came to the wake?"

"Most everybody had left. Darcia and I were cleaning up the debris, hoping the rest would take the hint. Beth was exhausted. Carlie was in the kitchen, ah, Mina, too. I took dishes in before I went up to check on Ben."

"Whose blood?" Eve gestured to drops on the floor, smears on the rug.

"His. Blow to the back of the head."

"I need you to put together a list of who you know was here."

"Okay."

"Go be with your family. There's nothing else you can do here."

"Someone hit him from behind. Blood on the back of his head. They hit him from behind, then lifted him up high enough to put that noose around his neck. There had to be two of them. He's not a heavyweight, but it would take two. Haul him up, hold him up, secure the noose. That's more than one person."

He scrubbed at his face again. "And I'm not telling you anything you don't know."

"Try this. Why would he come in here?"

"I don't know." Webster dropped his hands. "I just don't know. Beth said he looked upset. She thought maybe he got a text or call that upset him because he was putting his 'link back in his pocket as he went upstairs."

"I've got the scene, Webster. We'll come in, take statements at the hospital when we're done."

"Come now." Darcia took Webster's hand. "The family needs you there. We go where we're needed."

As Darcia led him away, Eve pulled Seal-It from her field kit. When Roarke started back up the stairs, she tossed it to him. "Might as well seal up, too. He came upstairs, to this room. Kids' playroom. Potentially got a call or text, and that's what lured him here. Had to have it set up, because Webster was only a few minutes behind him."

From where she stood, she scanned the scene again.

"Victim is identified as Greenleaf, Benjamin, older brother of the owner of this residence, and currently being treated at Saint Anne's Hospital."

She stepped into the room, gestured again to the blood trail. "The victim entered the room. Blood spatter indicates he was struck. Blow from behind. Hit him as soon as he came into the room."

"That makes it hard to fake a suicide," Roarke pointed out.

"They weren't worried about that this time. The suicide didn't stick with the captain, so that's blown. The point here? Kill the son, murder by hanging, and that mirrors Noy. Maybe others, we'll see, but Noy."

She took samples of the blood for her kit, marked it before she crossed over to the window.

"According to Detective Webster's statement, corroborated by Chief Angelo, he discovered the victim hanging no more than ten minutes after the victim came upstairs and entered."

She crouched to examine the rope, and where Darcia had cut it.

Pulling over another chair, she examined the short length of rope still secured to the hook. "Strong knot. Two fresh cuts. One cut from Webster's penknife to get the victim down. It looks like the other end was cut from a longer length of rope. The lab will confirm, if so. It's a sloppy noose—effective, but sloppy. Strong cord, and the length used? You could easily hide this in one of those elephant-sized handbags, a good-sized briefcase, messenger bag. Hook's handy," she continued. "But you had to know it was here."

"A room set up for kids to enjoy." Roarke scanned it. "Gaming station, the chairs, sofa that would take a beating. Colorful walls, a crafts table and supplies, so on."

He looked down at Eve. "Of all the rooms up here, they chose this. A destruction of innocence, another emotional blow to the family. How could the children ever play in here again?"

"Exactly. A deliberate choice. And one they'd cased before today. Webster's right. It's all but impossible for one person to do this. The rope, secured only to that hook—strong hook, designed to hold some solid weight. But the slack wasn't long enough so someone could put the noose around his neck while he's prone, then use the length to pull him up, secure the slack elsewhere."

She rose. "Angelo kept her head, didn't move that chair. I'm going to bet we find a mirror in the files—how it's placed, even the type of rope used. Maybe down to the sloppy noose."

She walked over to a pair of shelves, took down a Little League trophy. "Kid got MVP last season—good for her."

"Christ Jesus, they'd use a child's trophy for this?"

"And didn't bother to wipe the blood off it." She bagged it, sealed it, labeled it. "Didn't have time, or didn't care. Probably both. Had to move fast—so much risk. Do they get off on the risk? But you've got to get out and away before anyone wanders upstairs."

She moved back to the door, studied it. "No inside lock. Couldn't lock the door from in here. Gotta get back downstairs, or . . ."

She took out her communicator as she walked out, contacted the sweepers. And went room by room. Found it.

"Here's the way." She walked to the French doors in the main bedroom. "The smart way if you know the house. "Small terrace, steps going down to the not-much-bigger patio area. Go out, down."

She did just that.

"There's a gate—locks and security on it, but a way out."

"The security feed might tell the tale if they were sloppy there as well."

"I'm not counting on that, but we need to check. How about you find the security hub? I want another pass upstairs."

She went up, timing how long it took at a fast walk to reach the door of the crime scene. Eighty-six seconds. Even at a cautious slink, under two minutes. At a jog or run, a lot less.

Say your goodbyes, she thought. If you're close enough to the family to know the house, you'd have to say your goodbyes, make it look like you're leaving.

You'd want people to notice you're leaving.

Then slip upstairs.

Or . . .

You've already unlocked the gate, the French doors—if they were locked. Double back that way, go up, into the playroom and shut the door.

Pull out the rope, secure it to the hook.

Text the target. Text is smarter than a call—no conversation. Wait.

One of you behind the door with the trophy. He comes in, strike.

You need him unconscious—no struggle, no noise, no wasted time.

Shut the door, drag him over. One holds him up, the other gets on the chair, secures the noose. Turn the chair over— that mirror—slip out, down to the master bedroom.

Out, gone while the victim strangles to death.

Somebody'll come up eventually, she thought, as she started downstairs. But how long does it take for a man to strangle?

Sloppy noose gave him half a chance, but even with that, ten minutes? A lot less for brain cells to start dying.

You have to feel pretty confident the job's done.

But a grieving woman worries about her son, and a friend goes to check on him.

You lose.

"I just finished getting statements," Peabody told her. "Most of the ones still here were Mrs. Greenleaf's friends, the ones we've already talked to—except for Arnez—and the one who came down from Maine. Their spouses, a couple of the daughter's friends and theirs who helped with the food, and a couple of IAB cops."

"Upshot?"

"Some were in the kitchen area, dealing with dishes, putting food away, the rest were in the living area. I have all the names and locations. The two cops were on the point of leaving when they ran upstairs, heard the commotion and ran up. Ah, Darlie Tanaka noticed the victim go upstairs, but didn't think anything about it. Just that he needed some quiet time.

"No one noticed anyone going up before he did," Peabody continued. "Anja Abbott was sitting next to Mrs. Greenleaf, and heard her ask Webster to check on her son. She did see Webster go up, and thinks it was maybe five minutes later. She can't be sure, but about five minutes. Everyone still here's accounted for, Dallas. No one was alone during the time frame."

Roarke walked in. "The security system, cameras, alarms, were shut down."

"Shut down?"

"Manually, at fifteen-forty-five."

"I want to see the feed, what we have before shutdown."

"I thought you might. I sent a copy to your PPC. Or we can look on the monitor in the security room."

"Let's take the room."

"The hub's in the basement."

"Peabody, the sweepers should be here any minute. Get them started. Where's the basement?"

Roarke led the way. "It's nicely finished," he commented. "A sort of media room. It looks to me as if the younger ones gathered down there. Another family area. Dishes still scattered about."

A casual family area, Eve noted, and yeah, dishes scattered, empty tubes that hadn't made it into the recycler. Half-empty ones, a nearly empty bowl of chips.

They'd set up the security hub in a storage room where tubs, clearly labeled, held holiday decorations, off-season clothing, beach gear.

"It was up and running." Roarke cued up the feed to seven hundred hours, set it on fast-forward, slowing when the victim and his family arrived that morning, then again when the younger brother and his arrived. Again with Webster and Angelo.

She watched Webster leave—it matched the time he'd come to Central to speak with her. Watched him return, go inside.

Then the family left together.

No one entered until the family returned.

Then others, in couples, in groups.

The first of those left about fourteen-thirty. Departures started out as a trickle, then a steadier stream until the feed cut off an hour later.

"That's it," Roarke said. "The whole system was shut down."

"Smart," Eve mumbled. "You can say you're leaving— hug, hug, wipe a tear away, then either not or double back and no cam to catch the lie. We'll have the sweepers down here, too. They wouldn't be that sloppy, but we'll go over everything.

"I need to talk to the sweepers, then get to the hospital. I need to take statements from the family, and hopefully the victim."

"I'll stick with you."

As they walked upstairs, she glanced over at him. "Is it off that Arnez is the only one of the 'let's go out and drink wine and gab' group who wasn't there?"

"Well, when I was a member of a 'we'll have a pint or two and shoot the shite' group, it wasn't unusual for one of us to call it earlier than the others."

"But that's criminals, not upstanding citizens."

He gave her a quick pat on the butt. "Either way, someone has to be the first to leave."

"Sweepers are upstairs," Peabody said. "Do you want to leave the droids on the doors?"

"Let's leave them in place until the family gets back."

She went up, spoke with the sweepers. When they went out, she gestured Roarke toward the wheel. "You take it. Do you have to know a code to shut down the security system?"

"Not that one. It's a simple switch—and clearly marked so you wouldn't shut it down by accident."

"Which makes it handy to do on purpose." She shifted around, asked Peabody the same question about Arnez leaving as she'd asked Roarke.

"I don't really think so. She's younger than most of them, and doesn't have the long history. They left around sixteen hundred—that's about," she added.

"You asked?"

"I knew you'd want to know. It's about then, according to Cassidy Bryer. I made it a casual question, like: I guess Ms. Arnez and Mr. Robards couldn't make it to the wake. And she said, no, they were here. They left about four, maybe quarter after four—she guesses."

"Fifteen to thirty after the system's shut down. And somewhere in the neighborhood of thirty to forty minutes after that, Ben Greenleaf's bashed in the head and hanging from a rope. It's just so fucking handy."

Annoyed, she contacted Feeney. "Any matches?"

"Not down the line, no. Got some attempted suicides— none by hanging. Got a couple who managed it, but not by hanging."

"It's going to be Noy."

"Is Greenleaf's kid still alive?"

"We're heading to the hospital to find out."

"Let me know either way. My oar's stuck deep in this one."

"I'll tag you. Thanks. It's going to be Noy," Eve said again when she pocketed her 'link. "It's too good a fit not to be."

"I'll drop the two of you off, park, and find you."

Nodding absently at Roarke, Eve got out at the hospital entrance.

"We go through Noy's file again, every inch of it. Plenty of others went down when he did; maybe the connection's there. We talk to his daughter again, and his wife, the new husband. Their friends, their neighbors, their friend's neighbors. The son—his friends, people he went to school with, people he banged, people he didn't bang."

She stopped at the main desk, flashed her badge. "Benjamin Greenleaf, admitted shortly after five, head wound, strangulation."

"One moment."

Eve turned back to Peabody. "The son went to private school, then NYU. We dig there."

"Patient Greenleaf is in critical care, eighth floor, east. Family only."

Eve held up her badge again.

"And yes, of course. I do need to scan your identifications."

Once scanned, Eve headed for the elevator bank.

"If you're really looking at Arnez—"

"Public school." Eve rolled heel-to-toe, toe-to-heel as she waited. "Most of her college by remote—but NYU's business school. Worked through it. But they both grew up Lower West. Not the same neighborhood, but the general area."

"They'd have been about the same age."

"That's right." Eve held back as people filed off the elevator. She got on, called for eight east. Texted Roarke so he could skip the desk.

"Maybe they knew each other," Peabody conceded. "But wouldn't she, if they did, blame Noy for what the son did? If she's going to blame somebody, and blame them enough to wait nine years to cash in?"

"Logically, sure. Murderers don't always follow logic, do they? We find the connection. Whoever, whatever it is, we find it."

She got off the elevator, assumed she'd go through the same routine at the desk there. But Webster paced in front of it.

She thought the shadows under his eyes had shadows.

"Dallas. He's going to make it."

"That's good news."

"It's great news, Webster." Peabody laid a hand on his arm. "Really great news."

"He's been in and out a couple of times, but . . . They're worried he could have brain damage . . . lack of oxygen. They're doing some tests. He's concussed, and his throat— He's going to make it," Webster repeated. "We just have to wait to see what he's up against."

"Has he said anything?"

"No. No, but he squeezed Mina's hand. She said when he came around for a minute, he squeezed her hand when she spoke to him. She let him know she—we—everybody was here."

He paused, pressed his fingers to his eyes. "Did you find anything?"

"The security system was shut down at fifteen-forty-five, manually, at the source."

"Nobody in the family would've done that."

"It looks like some of the younger people hung out down there."

"Sure. I was going to do a round down there, hauling up dishes and trash. None of them would touch the security, Dallas. It had to be whoever went after Ben. Jesus, look at the timing!"

"I am. I have."

"Sorry." He held up a hand. "Sorry. A little wound up."

"Am I going to be able to talk to him?"

"I don't know, honestly. They booted us while they run

the tests." He glanced back. "The family's in the waiting room. Luke and Shawn, too. Their nanny has the kids—the younger ones. Ben's kids are here, and Carlie's two oldest."

"We'll start with them."

Eve could think of little more depressing than a hospital waiting room—unless it was a hospital room.

Most huddled together. The brother-in-law paced, but stopped when Webster led Eve and Peabody inside.

Ben's wife, Mina, gripped the hands of the kids who flanked her.

"I'm sorry to intrude at such a difficult time," Eve began.

"Somebody tried to kill my dad." The girl next to Mina snapped it out while her eyes welled. "They already killed my grandpa. What are you doing about it?"

"Baby." Mina pulled her close. "No. Don't now."

"I'm scared." She pressed her face to her mother's shoulder. "I'm scared."

"I'd be scared, too." Peabody stepped forward, crouched down. "But Webster told us the doctors said your dad's going to be okay."

"They don't know for sure."

"And it's scary. We're trying really hard to find out who did these awful things. Maybe you can help."

"How?"

"We need to find out everything we can. I think maybe you were downstairs, in the family room, the basement?"

"Yeah." The girl sniffed, laid her head on her mother's shoulder. "So? A bunch of us were."

"Maybe some people came down to talk to you, or to say goodbye if they were leaving."

"I guess, yeah. Don did, and Darcia did—they brought more chips down. Aunt Carlie, Uncle Luke—they were mostly checking on us so we didn't trash the place."

She rolled her red-rimmed eyes. "As if."

"Right."

"Cassidy came down for a few minutes." This from the teenage boy sitting beside his grandmother. "And Win—he's the old guy who takes Grandpa sailing sometimes. We went with them a couple times."

"Detective Dickinson—he worked with Grandpa." One of the other kids piped up. "And another one like that, but he was really old."

"My Little League coach," Carlie's daughter remembered.

That would be Olive Metcalf, Eve thought. The MVP.

"Coach Mike. He came down awhile." She knuckled a tear away. "He really liked Grandpa. And the neighbor guy—ah—"

"Denzel," her brother said. "He fixed Dad's car once."

Though they reeled off a few more, Eve made a note of Denzel, mentally circled it.

"Ms. Greenleaf," she began, and stepped toward Beth.

Then everyone stood at once as a doctor came to the room.

"He's awake and responsive." He said it with a smile, and Eve felt the tension in the room drop out of the red zone.

But he held up both hands as everyone started forward. "Hold on now. I can't let you all go piling in. We're still waiting for test results, but he knew his name, his wife and kids' names, the date, his date of birth. He's disoriented and has a whale of a headache, his throat's raw.

"But he's a tough guy." He winked at Ben's kids. "I'm going to let your mom go in and see him."

"Please." Ben's daughter sent the doctor a pleading look. "I'll be quiet. I won't even talk to him. I just want to see him. I just—"

"It would help," Mina said. "It would help him to see his children. I promise you. His heart and spirit. It would help."

"Five minutes." The doctor wagged a finger at the kids. "And no partying in there."

"Thank you." Mina looked back at her mother-in-law. "I—"

"No." Beth shook her head. "You go. You go now. We can all wait."

"The nurse will take you in. Five minutes," he repeated, then turned to the rest.

"We'll give them the five. Then we'll open the privacy screens. You can all see him through the glass. We'll see how he does. If he's not too tired, you can go in for a few minutes, Mom."

"Thank you."

"Doctor. Lieutenant Dallas, NYPSD. It's important we speak to Mr. Greenleaf as soon as possible."

He gestured her out to where Roarke stood waiting off to the side.

"I understand, Lieutenant. Trust me. You have your job to do, and whoever did this to my patient needs to be stopped. But he's weak, still disoriented. And he's damn lucky. Another few minutes, two, three, maybe four at most? Maybe we could've brought him back, but he'd have suffered severe brain damage. The shape he's in—the lucky shape—it still exhausted him answering a few standard questions."

"I understand, Doctor . . ."

"Ricardi."

"Dr. Ricardi. I understand, trust me on that. But I do have a job to do. Whoever did this to him killed his father only days ago."

"Give her my turn." Beth stood, then leaned against her daughter. "Any of our turns. It's more important. He knows we're here. He knows we'll be here."

"They did this while we were gathered in my home to mourn our father." Carlie's voice snapped like ice. "Let her talk to Ben. Then you do your job, Lieutenant. You find the bastard."

"That's exactly what I intend to do."

"Let's see how he does," Ricardi cautioned. "He may need to rest after this quick visit with his wife and kids."

"We'll wait," Eve said. "As long as it takes. While we wait, Ms. Greenleaf, you need to answer some questions."

"Come sit. She's doing her job," Beth said to her daughter before Carlie could object.

"You're right. Come sit."

19

"Peabody, talk to the family." Eve nodded toward the waiting room. "You're better with the tone they need right now. Maybe one of them saw or heard something they didn't realize at the time."

"I've got that." As Peabody went back into the waiting room, Eve stepped over to Roarke.

"I don't know how long we'll have to wait until we interview him. When we do, we're only going to have about five minutes before the medicals boot us."

"You'll make the most of the five."

"Intend to. Meanwhile . . ." She glanced back toward the waiting room. "If you're sticking, can you do what you do?"

"I do so many things."

"Then do the find-a-place-to-work thing you do. Maybe coordinate with Feeney. It's going to be a connection to Noy—just too specific not to be. But if there turns out to be another, we need it fast."

"I can do that."

"I'm going to stay out here, leave the family to Peabody for now, and go over the data on Noy and the cops who went down with him again. I'll tag you after I talk to the victim."

Eve simply leaned back against the wall and got started.

She'd barely skimmed the surface when Mina led her two children back. All of them wept.

Mina paused near Eve, pressed a kiss to her daughter's head, then her son's. "Go back in, be with Grandma. I'll be right there."

She nudged them both into the waiting area, then turned to Eve.

"He knew me, knew his children. Don and Darcia saved his life, and more, I think, saved him from serious brain damage. Not all the test results are back, but I know my husband. He'll recover from this, mind and body."

"I'm glad to hear that. Very glad."

"I think you are, and maybe not only because he may help you with your work." She looked down the hall, swiped the drying tears off her face. "The doctor said he needs to rest a bit, and talking is very difficult because . . ."

Her lips quivered as she touched a hand to her throat.

"It helped him to see us. I felt that. I believe that. He needs to see his mother, his brother and sister."

"Understood."

"But I agree with Beth. You'll talk to him first, when the doctor says he can see someone else. Twice now, they came into our homes. They took a good man's life, and tried to take another. If not for Don, my children would grieve their father now instead of shedding tears of relief that he said their names and smiled at them.

"You talk to him first. Then you go find the bastard who tried to kill my husband."

"Ms. Greenleaf, can you tell me where you were when your husband was attacked?"

"In the kitchen, I think. Just coming out of the kitchen. I heard shouting, ran out, and saw Luke and Jed running upstairs. Others ran that way, too. I didn't see Ben go up. I don't know if I'd have thought anything of it if I had."

"Did you see anyone leave, shortly before or after you heard the shouting?"

"No." She closed her eyes, took another moment to think. "No," she repeated, and slowly shook her head. "Most had already left before that. I took a kind of head count before I went to the kitchen because we were going to put some of the food away. Leave enough out for those remaining, to be polite."

Again, she closed her eyes. "I saw . . . the kids downstairs—mine, Carlie's, Luke's, some of the other cousins, a few school- and teammates. Fourteen downstairs. About twenty upstairs—including the family."

Nodding, she opened her eyes again. "Yes, about that many."

"Okay. That's helpful. If someone had threatened your husband—"

"He would have told me," Mina said immediately. "What threatens him, threatens me and our children. He would have told me."

"All right. If anything comes to mind, no matter how irrelevant it may seem, please contact me."

"Believe me, I will."

Mina went into the waiting area; Eve went back to work.

It took another twenty minutes before the doctor walked down the corridor. "I'm going to give you five minutes with Ben."

"All right."

"I need to speak with the family first."

"You're going to give them good news. It shows," she added when Ricardi's eyebrows lifted.

"Good. I'm glad to know it does. I expect in both of our professions it's easy to harden off. I never want to harden off."

He moved past her. "Greenleaf family, the tests are back. And it's all good news."

Eve listened to the sounds of joy, the sobs of it.

"Now, he's still a bit confused, and he's very tired, but he's cogent, and he's asked for all of you. Once the police talk to him, I'll let you go in, small groups, a few minutes only. Then I'm going to suggest you all go home, get some rest—because that's what Ben needs. Rest."

"I want to stay with him tonight," Mina said, and looked toward Carlie.

"We've got the kids, don't worry."

"I can arrange for that," Ricardi began. "But—"

"A couple of us are going to camp out right here." Carlie joined hands with Luke. "We'll rotate shifts, but a couple of us will be here. That's how the family works."

"Why am I not surprised? Lieutenant, Detective? After them, groups of two or three at the most. Five minutes each. Work that out.

"He's a lucky man," Ricardi told Eve as he walked her and Peabody down the corridor. "The strong family support will go a long way toward his recovery—physical and mental. It doesn't hurt he's in prime physical shape, but even that wouldn't have helped him avoid serious complications if he'd hanged there another minute or two."

He paused outside wide glass doors. Through them Eve saw Ben, very pale so the raw bruising on his throat stood out in violent contrast. He lay still on the white sheets in the narrow bed, eyes closed.

Various cords connected him to the monitors that beeped, the screen that flashed, and all the trappings that made a hospital room even worse to her mind than a hospital waiting area.

"He has some expected confusion and memory gaps," Ricardi told her. "His larynx is severely bruised, so he needs to rest his voice as much as possible. I don't want him overly stressed or pushed."

"It's not our first time interviewing a trauma victim."

"I don't suppose it is. Five minutes. You're on the clock."

Eve stepped in, gestured Peabody to one side of the bed while she took the other.

"Ben." She waited until his eyes, also bruised, opened. "Lieutenant Dallas, Detective Peabody."

"I remember you." His voice came out raw, as if the words squeezed through a rasp.

"If you can answer with a yes or no, nod your head or shake it. Did you see who did this to you?"

He shook his head.

"Has anyone threatened you?"

Another shake.

"Did you have a reason to go upstairs, to that specific room, at that specific time?"

Those bruised eyes lost their focus, blurred as she saw him fight to think through the fog.

"Do you remember going upstairs?"

He lifted a hand, wagged it back and forth.

Sort of, she concluded.

"And into the kids' room—the playroom, game room?"

Same response.

"Did you see anyone in there or near there?"

No.

"Sorry, I'm going to need more than a yes or no on this one. Why did you go upstairs? A call, a text? Your mother said you had your 'link out, put it away as you went up. And looked upset."

"I—" He closed his eyes. "Sorry. Hard to think."

"Before you went upstairs, what were you doing?"

"I . . . I was going to get a drink. I needed a drink. Long, hard day, almost over. And . . . Dory texted me. Yeah, that's right. I remember."

"Your daughter texted you?"

He nodded. "Can't quite remember . . . She called me Daddy—only does that these days when upset or wants something. *Please, Daddy, don't say anything. Come up to the Kid Zone*—we call it Kid Zone. Can't remember . . . *Too many people. Sad. Please. Don't tell Mom.*"

He opened his eyes again. "I thought she was downstairs in the family room with the other kids. She and my dad . . . Close."

He lifted a hand, pressed his thumb tight to his finger. "She's only twelve, never lost . . . never lost anybody."

"You didn't tell anyone, and went upstairs?"

He nodded. "I think. It gets—not blurry, more jumpy after that. I went up. Door's closed. Privacy. Not like her, so sad, upset. Needs Daddy. Went in. Is it dark? I think . . . sun blocks engaged. Got them installed to cut glare on the gaming screens. And . . . I woke up here. They won't tell me what happened. Nobody will tell me."

He grabbed Eve's hand. "What happened?"

She felt the urgency in his grip, heard it in the rapid beeps on the machines.

Ricardi came in.

"That's all for now. Ben—"

"He needs to know what happened," Peabody said. "He woke up in the hospital and doesn't know why. How would you feel?"

The doctor walked around to Eve's side of the bed. "Ben. I need you to stay calm. Your family needs to see you, and you need to see them. So you need to stay calm."

He looked at Eve, nodded.

"It wasn't your daughter who texted you, but whoever killed your father. They set you up, lured you upstairs, knocked you out, and tried to hang you."

He reached for his throat. "Hang me."

"Your mother saw you go up, saw you were upset, worried. Asked Don Webster to check on you. He did, found you. He and Darcia Angelo got you down, did CPR, called the medics. So you're not only alive, but the doctor here—who doesn't seem to bullshit—says you're going to be fine."

"You are and, if you behave yourself, I'm sending you to a step-down unit, then booting you out altogether within forty-eight hours. So behave yourself."

Ben's eyes filled, but there was rage burning through the tears.

"In my sister's house, in the Kid Zone, at my father's wake. They used my little girl."

Eve leaned down close so he could look into her eyes. "They won't get away with it." She straightened. "I need Ben's 'link."

"His wife will have his personal property. He really needs to rest now."

Nodding, she stepped back. "They won't get away with it," she repeated, then walked out.

"What are the chances we recover his 'link or the kid's?" Peabody wondered.

"Zero, but we follow through. Tag Roarke, will you? Let him know we're wrapping it up here. Ms. Greenleaf—Mina," Eve qualified in the waiting area. "Could I see the items your husband had on him when he was admitted?"

"Yes, they gave them to me when we got to the ER." She opened her purse, took out a plastic bag.

Eve saw a wallet, a silver cash clip, a handkerchief, key swipes.

"Where's his 'link?"

"Ah . . . not here. He must not have had it on him."

But he had, Eve thought, and turned to his daughter. "Could I see your 'link?"

The kid's eyes filled as she hunched her shoulders. "I wasn't careless. I swear, Mom, I *swear*!"

Eve crouched down before Mina could speak. "When did you notice you didn't have it?"

"I don't know. I guess when we got here, and I was going to tag my friend and tell her my dad's hurt. And it wasn't in the stupid purse. I had to carry a stupid purse because Mom said I had to wear this lame dress for respect, and there's no pockets. Mom—"

"It's all right, Dory," Mina told her, watching Eve. "Just answer the questions. It's all right."

"When did you last use it?"

Dory blew out a breath. "I dunno. I, yeah, I tagged Olive. My cousin Olive to tell her we were all going downstairs to hang."

"Did you take it downstairs with you?"

"Well yeah, in the purse because no stupid pockets."

"Did you keep the purse on you?"

"Jeez, no."

"Dory."

"No, ma'am," Dory corrected.

"Where did you put the purse with the 'link when you got downstairs?"

"On the bar. I *know* it was in the dumb purse, and then it wasn't. I didn't just lose it, Mom. I *swear* I didn't!"

"It's all right." To prove it, Mina wrapped an arm around her.

"Can I look inside the purse?"

Dory rolled her eyes, but got up to get the little bag from a table, handed it to Eve.

Inside Eve found tissues, a key swipe, a bright red wallet, gum, and no 'link.

"What does it look like, your 'link?"

"Like a 'link," she said, then shrank from her mother's

long, hard stare. "Sorry. It's the Zipcom from two years ago. It was my brother's, and I can't get the new one until I prove I'm not careless. But I wasn't, and—"

"We bought a safety case, because she can be," Mina interrupted. "Mets colors, Mets logo."

Eve nodded. "You a Mets fan?"

"Check it!"

"Me, too. She wasn't careless," Eve said as she straightened.

"Yes, I understand that. It's not your fault, baby."

"I need the numbers for both 'links," Eve said.

"But why . . ." Dory trailed off, glanced at her older brother, who sat, eyes grim, mouth set. Then around the room. "Somebody took my 'link, and used it to hurt my dad. I'm not stupid! Why's she going to care about my 'link unless . . ."

After wiggling out from her mother's arm, she stood, fire in her eyes as she looked at Eve. "I hope when you find them, you hurt them."

"Dory." Then Mina sighed. "So do I."

Hard to blame them, Eve thought as she left them. Roarke joined them at the elevators.

"I've got a couple 'link codes," she told him. "You could try to track. If they're smart, they ditched or destroyed them. Even if they kept them—trophies, resale—they probably shut them down, took the thing out of them."

"Yes, of course, the thing. And why am I tracking these 'links?"

"One's the vic's, the other's his kid's. They used that, sent a bogus text from her to get him upstairs. Anything from Feeney?"

"As you already suspected, nothing fits, not as neatly as Noy."

"Had to be. Peabody, contact the daughter, the widow. I want them in formal interview, asap. They know something. They may not know they know it, but they do."

She took her first truly clear breath when she stepped outside. She preferred the summer steam bath to hospital air.

"I'll remote the car. It's a bit of a hike."

Eve shook her head at Roarke. "Walking's good. Need to think."

"Straight to v-mail on the daughter," Peabody announced. "Left a message. Trying her mother's now. Same thing."

"Try the new husband. Knew how to get to the kid's 'link, knew just the tone to use to get the father upstairs. Knew the kid was in the basement. Still risky. Damn stupid risky."

"V-mail, Dallas."

"None of them answering their 'links. Son of a bitch." She yanked out her own. "Webster, I'm sending you three ID shots. I want to know if you saw any of them at the memorial, at the house."

She scowled as Roarke steered her to the left. "A couple hours after Ben Greenleaf gets strung up, none of them answer their 'links?"

"I can track those 'links as well," Roarke told her.

"That's a negative, Dallas. Same from Darcia," Webster responded. "And I showed them to Carlie, Jed, Shawn. Luke's with Ben, with his mom, but if none of us saw them—"

"Okay. Dallas, out. Track 'em," she said to Roarke.

He unlocked her DLE. "Take the wheel. First code?"

When she'd given it, plugged in Taylor Noy's address, Roarke settled back.

"Well now, that was absurdly simple. People really should shield their devices better than they often do. She's in Vegas."

"What the hell is she doing in Vegas? There's no indication of gambling in her data."

She reeled off her mother's code.

"And so is her mother—same precise location, which is . . . Ah, the Get Hitched wedding venue."

"For fuck's sake." She gave him the last number.

"And the stepfather is also in attendance. Or his 'link is."

"Maybe Taylor Noy decided to elope to Vegas," Peabody suggested. Or . . . he's got a daughter. I remember he's got a daughter."

"Check it."

"I—Oh, you mean check it out, not like check it. Give me a second. Here she is, Sasha, age thirty-three, cohab Milli Yarsborough, age thirty-six—together five years. I'll get their contacts."

"No need," Roarke said as he worked. "According to the Get Hitched registry, Sasha and Milli should be getting hitched right about now. That's romance."

"Fuck, fuck, fuck! Peabody, leave another message, add the stepfather and the frigging newlyweds into it. Contact Dallas, asap. Just to round it off, Roarke, check on their travel. Let's find out when they left for Vegas."

"Already on that, Lieutenant. They left, all five of them, on a private shuttle, from Long Island direct to Vegas. Wheels up at noon. Ah, I see they checked into one of my hotels, and the father put the honeymoon suite for the happy couple on his card. Another suite—two bedrooms—also on his card. Since it's my place, it's simple for me to verify."

"No need. They're connected—somehow—but not suspects. I need to talk to them. Need to dig into it. Peabody, I'm dropping you at home. Go over the Noy data—every inch. I'm going to do the same. Two pair of eyes on it."

"Make it Central. I can pick up my painting, grab McNab. We'll have three pairs of eyes on it."

Roarke shifted to look back at Peabody. "You bought some art?"

"The first of the street art for our collection. Remember how we talked about doing a sort of gallery?"

To save her sanity, Eve tuned them out.

When she dropped off Peabody, she sat a moment longer. "I want to go by, hit Arnez and Robards with Ben Greenleaf, gauge their reaction. But if I'm right, they'd be prepared for that."

"Prepared to hear he's dead, not alive and on the way to recovery."

"Yeah, so why not let them believe what they're prepared for? Let them think they won, let them lie low. If they're part of it."

"Do you think they—or alternately someone else—would try again?"

"I'm not taking chances." She stifled the need to get in Arnez's face, and headed for home. "I've got guards on Ben, a unit on the sister's house, the brother's place, and will add one on the mother's apartment when she goes home if I haven't closed this."

"You think you will—I can see that. You think you'll close it before she goes back to her apartment."

"I'm going to shake loose whatever Noy's daughter and widow know that they don't know they know."

She slapped a hand on the wheel.

"Because they fucking do. The connection's there. Something's there, you keep looking until you find it."

"Until that happy event, why don't I look over the Noy file as well? Four pairs of eyes on it."

She thought it over as she pushed and shoved her way through the snarling traffic that signaled the end of a standard day shift.

"Let's try this. You take the widow, Peabody takes the daughter. If McNab's in it, he takes the stepfather. I'll take the dead son. That's in addition to pushing on Noy. When we've dug down as far as it goes, we shift to the cops who went down with him, split them up."

"Efficient time management."

"Maybe. More efficient would be to talk to the widow and the daughter. Now."

She used her wrist unit to update Peabody on the strategy.

At yet another snarl, Eve tapped her fingers on the wheel. Tried to will away the tension at the back of her neck.

No luck there.

"Why haven't you come up with something that just poofs us from here to there?"

"Poofs?"

"You know, like we're here. We want to be there. We push a button or something, and we're there."

Intrigued, Roarke shifted toward her. "Just us, or the entire car along with us?"

"You can't just leave a vehicle in the middle of the street. Come on."

"What was I thinking? So we, humans, animate—flesh, blood, water, bone, chemicals, organs—transport through time and space from one location to another, along with a vehicle, inanimate, and which consists of entirely different materials."

"Yeah, that."

He tapped a finger on her shoulder. "You, Lieutenant, would never push the button."

Since she wasn't going anywhere, she gave him a long look. "Why wouldn't I? I could be home right now, at my command center."

"In your car?"

"No. You poof the car into the garage."

"I see. Bloody clever of me. You still wouldn't push the button."

She sneered at the traffic. "Right now I would."

"You wouldn't, darling Eve, because you'd start thinking of the what-ifs. What if, along this strange, poofing journey, your organs, bones, what have you, mixed with mine? You could end up with three arms, or my rib cage."

"Or your dick."

"I'd certainly miss it. Or this malfunction—they do happen—caused your molecules to merge with the car's. Now you've got tires for legs, perhaps a steering wheel for an ass. Or the program missed your feet. Now you're sitting at the command center footless, and your feet are stuck on Sixth Avenue."

"Now I'm going to have nightmares."

"You did ask."

"Yeah, I asked. They do it on those vids you like. The space vids. They're always poofing from the starship to the planet, wherever. And the wherever up out there most always has breathable air, and temps that don't fry your eyes in their sockets. Which makes no sense. Still, they poof."

"Beam," he corrected, "not poof, beam. It's why it's called science fiction, darling. But since you're interested, I'll look into it."

"Really?"

He smiled at her. "The concept is something science has toyed with for generations. But those what-ifs are profound."

She spotted a gap in the snarl and zipped into it, through it.

"I've got one. What if you're poofing and somebody else is poofing in the same direction at the same time, and you collide?"

She slapped her hands together.

"Now you're stuck together with a complete stranger.

"I wouldn't push the button," she decided. "But that doesn't mean traffic's not a bitch from hell."

"Yet it's given us time to have this fascinating conversation."

"Always an upside." She glanced at him again. "Would you push the button?"

"I rarely find myself in that much of a hurry, and find myself fond of my molecules just as and where they are."

"And because you could lose your dick."

"That would top the list of my concerns."

She finally reached the gates.

"Since the human body's made up of blood, bone, and all that, how come when they poof—beam—their clothes, which aren't, poof with them? Why aren't they naked when they get there?"

"It's a mystery," Roarke concluded. "But now, the next time we watch one of the *Star Trek* oeuvre, I'm going to imagine them all naked."

"Bet there's a porn vid that already does that."

Now he laughed. "I'll look into that as well."

20

When they went inside, Summerset waited.

"Together and unbloodied. A good day."

"Not for everybody," Eve said as the cat padded over to ribbon between her legs. "I want to check in with the sweepers," she added and headed for the stairs.

"Attempted murder of Captain Greenleaf's son at his father's wake." Roarke watched his wife and the cat trot up the stairs. "It weighs on her."

"Yes, I can see that. Bruising's fading nicely, but the jaw's still a bit swollen. She could use another pass with the wand."

Roarke nodded. "At least no one punched her in the face, so as you said, a good day. Aren't you and Ivanna off to the ballet then?"

"We are. In about an hour."

"Enjoy."

"We will. There's some very nice sea bass, crusted with caramelized honey. You'd enjoy it."

"Then we will."

Upstairs, he found Eve not at her command center, but her board. She spoke on her 'link as she updated it.

The sweepers, he thought, and crossed over to choose a wine. Thinking of the sea bass, he uncorked a Vermentino.

"I'm going with coffee," Eve told him. "Not ready for wine."

"I am. I'll take this to my office. I'm on the widow. Why don't we say we'll have dinner in an hour?"

"Sure, whatever."

He walked to her, tapped the shallow dent on her chin. Another wanding, yes, he thought, but didn't mention it. "The son's been dead for near a decade. You'll find what you'll find in an hour."

"If Noy's daughter or widow get back to me—"

"We'll adjust, won't we? An hour for now."

At her command center, she programmed coffee.

Brice Noy, she thought. He'd have been twenty-eight if he'd lived. Same age as Elva Arnez. Coincidence?

Bollocks.

Something there.

He'd been a good student, she concluded as she began to dig. Acing his way through his private school right from the start. The private school his father paid for through graft and extortion.

Did the son know? Maybe. Maybe. But the daughter claimed she hadn't—and she'd come off believable.

Not the athlete his sister had been, but a joiner.

Honor society, debate club, student council, class president.

She flipped through school photos.

Good-looking kid, even through the awkward years when to her eye kids seemed to be all teeth.

She found no disciplinary actions in his school files. He'd been valedictorian at his high school graduation. And the photo of him in cap and gown looked like Hollywood casting.

All-American boy, going places.

A short employment history. Mostly volunteer work, summer work. Homeless shelters, soup kitchens.

Paid intern at his father's precinct, civilian liaison, the summer after graduation.

No criminal—not surprising, considering his father would've taken care of that, if necessary. No indication of problems or treatments for illegals or alcohol abuse.

The perfect son?

She set that aside, began on Elva Arnez through the same period.

Public school. Decent student. No athletics, no clubs. A couple flags for truancy. Signed up for the school/work program as soon as she was eligible, and maintained those decent grades.

Even improved them some.

No more truancy flags—a disqualifier for the program.

And nothing that showed how or where her path would have crossed with Brice Noy—or his sister, mother, father.

Not yet.

Graduated about dead middle of her class, and got into NYU's business school. Remote option. So some classes at NYU while Brice Noy attended, but no other common area.

And the fact remained the size of the campus, their fields of study put them in different worlds. Gould Plaza for her, Washington Square South for him.

He, the joiner, joined. A fraternity, another debate club, the university's honor society, a student mentoring program— and completed his freshman year in the top five percent of his class.

Yeah, she thought. By the data, a young man with a bright future ahead.

Arnez joined nothing, stuck primarily with remote classes and worked close to full-time. And excelled in her business classes.

Both lived at home. She couldn't have afforded dorm

life. He could have, but why? Nice house, happy family—according to the sister. Easy trip to classes, college activities, and a nice home-cooked dinner every night.

She saw their lives now, as they'd been.

He, the good, shining son of what looked like, on the surface, a good, shining family. Smart, social, working toward following in his father's footsteps. Already with a place reserved for him at the Academy. And no doubt, in Eve's mind, a place waiting in his father's division.

And she, the hardworking, ambitious daughter of a single parent who'd wanted more. No clubs, no joining, not when she wanted that more.

Eve flipped through her school photos as well.

A beauty, and one who'd learned how to make the most of it as she hit her teens.

On impulse, she brought both their high school senior year photos on split screen.

"A remarkably attractive young couple," Roarke commented as he walked in.

"Yeah. Too bad I haven't found much of anything that links them. Lived about a fifteen-minute walk from each other, but in different social and economic strata. Different schools, different interests. NYU brings them together, but doesn't. She's mostly remote and, if and when she attended in person, her building's nowhere near his."

"A concert," Roarke suggested, "a sports event, a club."

"Yeah, possible. Trouble is she's working, and in retail, and in retail, your high school or college student—"

"Gets the weekends, and often the evenings," Roarke finished.

"Yeah. He's a serious student, one who makes a point of making connections, contacts. She's looking to boost her status—career-wise, at least. Likes nice clothes, looks good in nice clothes, works to get them. He's straight line, she's lateral moves. They both have a goal. His is to be a cop like his father—either like him," she qualified, "or the kind of cop he perceives his father to be. Which is a lie.

"She's advancement in her chosen area. Wants to manage, and wants to manage a fancy shop. Maybe wants her own shop, but I don't think so."

"No?"

"You own, you're on the hook. Something goes wrong, you're on the hook. You manage? You're in charge, but not on the hook. Do your job well, and I bet she does, you have some power, but then you go home with a paycheck. And you look at Robards, he's the same there. Do the job, get your pay."

"As billions do."

"Yeah, as billions do. Anything on the widow?"

"My take is she's a lovely woman who after dealing with a very hard blow—two very hard blows—did everything she could to raise her daughter and build a life. Have some wine now, and I'll tell you why over dinner."

"Maybe Peabody or McNab hit something."

"And if and when, you'd be the first contact, wouldn't you?"

He set the wine beside her, walked into the kitchen.

She swiveled around, stared at the cat, who stared back at her from his sprawl on her sleep chair.

"Why the hell hasn't Taylor Noy checked her damn v-mail?"

"It may be because she's in Vegas, celebrating her sister's wedding."

"I was asking the cat," Eve muttered.

"As he's a bright cat, no doubt he'd give you the same answer."

She picked up her wine, circled her board once, then walked over to stand in the open terrace doors.

The air felt good, she decided. Heavy, but good.

"I don't see a connect, not a strong one—and it has to be strong—between Arnez and the daughter, either. That age gap is big when you're kids, teens. And the daughter focused on sports. No common ground."

When she turned back, he'd put two plates on the table, a basket of bread, the wine.

"Sea bass," he told her, "honey crusted on a salad of grilled pineapple, habanero, and some sliced avocado. A nice summer meal—Summerset recommended."

"Okay."

It looked . . . colorful, she thought. And didn't include spinach, so who was she to complain?

"So the widow," Roarke began when he sat across from her. "Ella Noy, solid upper-middle-class upbringing, native New Yorker. Brooklyn. Parents are still married—to each other. First and only for both. One sibling, older brother, golf pro, in South Carolina, where the parents winter."

He lifted his wine. "Do you want to know about her childhood, early school years, and so on?"

"Not unless it applies."

"I don't see why it would. *Normal* is the word I'd use. She majored in sociology, went on to social work, moved to Manhattan. Lower West. In her mid-twenties she was engaged to a law student, about to take the bar. Before he could, he was killed, stabbed multiple times in a robbery at a liquor store where he'd stopped to buy a bottle of wine to take to her parents' for dinner."

"Noy responded."

"Detective Noy took primary," Roarke confirmed. "He apprehended the fiancé's killer, who's still inside—he was eighteen at the time he put those multiple holes in another human being. And a couple in the clerk as well, who survived.

"Three years later, she and Noy married. She became a

professional parent on the birth of their son, and remained so until Noy's death."

Eve ate some fish, surprised it wasn't good. It was damn good.

"So she gave up her career."

"Chose another career," Roarke said. "She focused on motherhood and volunteer work. Homeless shelters, child advocacy, fund-raising for the school her children attended once they did. She increased the volunteer work when both children hit school age. From all appearances, Eve, all data, she's led a fairly blameless life, a productive one, and one where she attempted to give back."

"All right. Who came up with grilling pineapple and putting honey on fish?"

"I couldn't say. Brilliant, isn't it?"

"It's pretty damn good."

"There's nothing to indicate," he continued, "that either she or Noy strayed re their marriage vows. Then again, he was a liar, a cheat, and may have covered his tracks well there. There's also nothing to indicate she participated in Noy's corruption and, in fact, a rather thorough investigation after his suicide found nothing. He kept a separate account, laundering the money he took in. And still, she lost her home and, months later, her son."

"I get she took some hard hits. I'm looking for connections."

"I couldn't find one. The obvious connection to Greenleaf, of course, but in fact, he stood up for her. The woman picked herself up, went back to work—after twenty years out of the workforce."

"Couldn't have been easy," Eve admitted.

"It couldn't have, no. Her parents helped her financially until she got on her feet. In her lifetime, she lost three people she loved to violence—two self-inflicted.

"She volunteers with a suicide hotline," Roarke added. "It appears she met her current husband at a fund-raiser—she a raiser, he a donor. She's now able to focus on her volunteer work again, which she does."

"Okay, who loved her, Noy, the son, the daughter enough to plot to kill Greenleaf to mirror Noy's suicide, and attempt to do the same with Ben Greenleaf?"

"Is it love then?"

"Love, obsession, loyalty, obligation." She gestured with her wine. "We start with love. Maybe Noy did have a side piece, maybe long-term. Or somebody who pined for the wife. Then she gets married to somebody else—could be the trigger. I'll show you who loves you. I'll kill for you."

She set down the wine, ate more fish.

"Or someone in love or obsessed with the son. Brice Noy, perfect in pretty much every way."

"Was he?"

"Ace student, valedictorian, class president. Also volunteered at homeless shelters, and real good to look at. I'm going to try for some of his old teachers, classmates tomorrow. Maybe somebody worshipped him the way he did his father.

"I didn't push the sister there, not the first round. Now I will. Whenever she answers her goddamn 'link."

She shoved away from the table. "I'm going to try her again."

"Do that. Then why don't we deal with these dishes before the cat disgraces himself? We'll take a walk."

"A walk?"

"It's cooled a bit. We'll have a walk, then refocus."

"Still v-mail. Ms. Noy, Lieutenant Dallas. Please contact me as soon as you receive this message. I have some important follow-up questions."

"Dishes," Roarke said when she stuffed the 'link back in her pocket. "And a summer evening walk."

"Then refocus. Okay. All right."

A walk never hurt—it was kind of like pacing, but in a direction.

"I doubt you'll need your weapon on a walk to the pond," Roarke pointed out once they'd dealt with the dishes.

"Right."

She'd already ditched her jacket—as he had—so now unhooked her weapon harness.

"Come now." He reached for her hand. "We'll clear the minds, at least a bit. Then see what comes into them after. You've got your 'link with you if Taylor Noy gets back to you."

"The wedding's got to be over by now," she said as they started down. "Even if they hired a marching band, it's got to be over."

"A marching band, is it now?"

"Or opera singers, or those people who do backflips."

"Acrobats?"

"Those."

"And I expect, after the drums and trumpets, the backflips and the fat lady singing, they'd have a celebration. Dinner, toasts, and, as it's Vegas, some gambling, maybe a show. You'd prefer to talk to them face-to-face, wouldn't you?"

"I'd prefer to talk to them, but yeah, face-to-face is first choice."

"And that's unlikely to happen until tomorrow—at least. I can get you to Vegas easily enough if need be."

"Well, crap."

She stepped outside, breathed in the air.

"Yeah, maybe. Then Peabody would be all: 'Oooh, Vegas!' Then find a way to get around me and lose some of her hard-earned pay in one of those stupid machines that gobbles up hard-earned pay like Galahad does those cat treats. And that's after she spots half a dozen things in shops that'll somehow be just perfect for her craft room or home office."

Roarke slung an arm around her shoulders. "You're beautiful when you're cranky."

"Kids are cranky. I'm pissed." But she tipped her head toward his shoulder. "It's the mud."

"The mud?"

"The mud my wheels keep getting stuck in. And I *know*, I fucking know most of it's because I'm hung up on Arnez and Robards. And nothing connects. Whoever did this had an investment, a strong, personal investment, in Noy, either him or the whole family. Possibly to one of the cops who went down with him, but then why mirror Noy's death, his son's? It is possible. But so far, nothing there, either."

He guided her through the garden with its drifting summer scents.

"All right then. Why are you hung up on Arnez and Robards? Specifically?"

"Specifically? The unlocked bedroom window. She was there, opportunity in her lap. They not only live in the building, but developed a relationship, so they knew the Greenleafs' routines, habits, basic timetables. The window's a big sticking point."

"Stuck-in-the-mud point. It's a strong one," Roarke allowed.

"But," she said, "it might have been unlocked days before, weeks before. Might have been opened that night from outside. All but the last risks one of them noticing and relocking it. Much lower risk of that if you unlock it an hour or so before TOD."

"And? I can hear it. You're not saying it, but I know my cop and can hear it."

"And." She hissed out a breath. "I know how it sounds, but there was a look. When Arnez and Elizabeth Greenleaf got back to the apartment on the night of the murder. When Webster opened the door, Arnez had a look."

"What sort of look?"

"Excitement. Just for an instant when the door opened. Just a . . ." Eve snapped her fingers. "But it was there, in her eyes. I saw it. Then came confusion, then calculation. Boom, boom, boom," she said, snapping her fingers again. "I saw it, and I thought: She's in this."

"I didn't see it, but I was looking more at the wife. Why weren't you?"

"She wasn't going to be in it. Webster. He's not stupid, not naive. Everything he said about her, about their marriage, the family. She wasn't going to be in it. But she's got somebody with her. Who the hell is this? And why is she excited?"

"If you saw it, it was there."

"Excitement, confusion, calculation. All there and gone in the time it takes to breathe in and out again. And."

They reached the pond with its white floating lilies, its young weeping tree, its skirting flowers. But she didn't sit on the bench. She paced.

"And, and, and. When we talked to them the next morning, everything was so damn pat. He's all about how she had a terrible night, was so upset. He's a little nervous, but covers it well."

He knew his cop, so played to that.

"People are often nervous after the murder of someone they knew, and with cops at the door. It's more than that."

"Yeah, more. She comes out, and her eyes are wet, but they're not red, not swollen. She doesn't strike me as somebody who's in emotional upheaval—but she plays it that way. He's protective, solicitous. It's all about her for him.

"All about her for him," Eve repeated. "No family photos. None. People are always putting pictures around—family, friends. Okay, her father's gone, she's not close with her mother. But he's close to his. And he has sisters. He helped pay for their education, for the married sister's wedding. He helps support his mother financially. He's stuck with the same job since he started working. There's innate loyalty there. But no photos. Because she doesn't want them."

"And why is that?"

"Because it's all about her. Not even them as a couple, but her. I'm your family now. I'm number one. And he's the type who goes along. Raised by a single mother, two sisters. It's his job to protect the women in his life. She's the planner; he's the shield. He killed Greenleaf for her."

She jammed fisted hands in her pockets. "I fucking know it. He came through the window she'd unlocked. Killed Greenleaf, dropped the weapon, and wrote the note just the way she told him to. Then he went out again, probably texted her—something innocuous, but an all clear. Then she sat with the woman whose husband she'd just had killed, whose life she'd just shattered, and drank wine, laughed. She's got it in her, Roarke. I can see it."

"That's a great deal of mud."

"It could've worked, but for a couple of glitches. Webster. That's a big glitch. Cops already on scene means she can't get into the bedroom, relock that window. Without Webster, she comes in with the wife, maybe steers her toward the kitchen. Maybe the wife calls out to Greenleaf, but he's in his office, no worries. How about some coffee? Love some, just gotta pee first. Or anything along those lines. Zip into the bedroom, use a cloth if you're smart, relock the window, and done."

"You said a couple glitches."

"Sweepers, Morris, me. Greenleaf's prints on the weapon

don't jibe with suicide. The stunner wounds don't jibe. Now you. The note doesn't jibe. It leaves out love, leaves out family. Just like she does."

"Hardly a wonder you're hung up on them."

"They did this. Murder and attempted murder. I know it."

"No doubt you've the right of it." When she frowned at him, he took her hands.

"I won't say your instincts are infallible, but bloody close. You've fairly terrifying observational skills. You saw what you saw, felt what you felt. Even so, you've pursued every angle, covered all the ground possible. Now you've concluded what you've concluded. So no doubt you've the right of it."

And just that dissolved the rock pile of tension in her shoulders.

"I know they did this. But I don't know why. I can't find the why. Where's the deeply personal connection? Because it has to be there."

"You'll find it. We'll find it. You've bloody well convinced me."

"I've dug down to the whatever it is where you've hit bottom."

"Bedrock?"

"That's good enough. I need to talk to the Noys. Maybe another consult with Mira."

"Which never hurts. Tomorrow," he said, anticipating her. "Do you think they'll try to kill again, someone else?"

"No reason to think they will, every reason to believe they won't. It's specific payback, a mirror. Plus, they missed with Ben Greenleaf. They may not know that yet, but somebody will tell them. If anything, they'd try for him again. Not now," she qualified. "Later."

"Will they run?"

"Why? As far as they're concerned, they got away with it. She's covered, her alibi for Greenleaf's as tight as a skin suit. Robards isn't the connection, Arnez is. It's all about her. And the connection's either down deep or it's tenuous—to everyone but her. Or both," she murmured. "Tenuous, barely there, right? To everyone but her.

"I need to get her in the box."

"Ah, there now. The walk did you good. You're figuring a way to drill down into the bedrock."

"Maybe. The walk did work—and talking it all the way through didn't hurt. You've got to follow the evidence, not just a . . ." Another snap of her fingers. "Look in somebody's eyes. But put it all together? I've got to get myself a drill."

She smiled at him. "Tomorrow. It got dark," she added.

"It will do that at night."

"Yeah, yeah. The lights look nice. They set the trees and the flowers off—and the house. All of it. Summer ought to last longer."

"We should take advantage of it while it's here." He drew her in.

She answered the kiss, let her body relax into it, into the warmth, the quiet. Then his nimble hands unhooked her belt.

"Come on!" With a laugh, she nudged him. "Here?"

"I like it here." He skimmed his hands up, over her. "A lovely summer evening, even a bit of a moon. The scent of roses and lilies, and you. Put my cop away for now, my darling Eve."

"Your darling Eve doesn't usually roll around naked on the grass with you."

"She doesn't, no. But then again, it wouldn't be the first time, would it?"

She judged the distance from the house, and calculated that unless Summerset had field glasses, they were private enough.

She reached for his belt. "You wouldn't want grass stains on your suit pants."

"Let's risk it."

He took her to the ground.

The grass, soft, springy, cushioned her, and felt somehow erotic against her skin when he tugged off her shirt.

And another long, hard day melted away under him, under his body, his hands, his mouth. So she wrapped around him, wanting to give him that same gift.

A summer night, dark sprinkled with light, the scent of flowers and green. And him.

Lightly, he pressed a kiss to her bruised breast.

"It's better," she told him. "Enough I mostly forgot about it."

"I didn't." A wanding to come, he thought. But for now, gently. Gently, every part of her so precious to him, and he could show her.

Soft kisses along her jawline with lazy strokes of his hands designed to relax more than arouse. A slow, deep meeting of lips and tongues, then drawing it out and out so the pleasure whispered between them.

Sweet. There were times his strong warrior needed the sweet. As did he.

With a sigh, she slipped his shirt away, ran her hands over the muscles of his back, his shoulders. In the pretty sparkle of lights, their eyes met. She was with him, he thought, as he needed her to be.

Her heartbeat, matching his; her breath merging with his. And in her eyes, a reflection of all he felt. A love both quiet and fierce.

He touched his lips to her brow, her cheeks, his hands slow and sure as he undressed her.

Tending her, she thought. No one had ever tended her before him. It swelled inside her, the knowledge she could love like this, be loved like this.

She took him in, wanted that union as much as her next

breath. More. The belonging, the merging, the quick slice of glory as he brought her to peak. And the soothing balm of release.

"Once more," he murmured. "Once more, under the moon."

Once more, they took the slice, the soothing, and the sweet together.

She lay, naked, on the grass, under the moon—and under him—by a pond with air thick with flowers and late summer heat.

It amazed her. She supposed it always would.

"You suggested I take off my weapon so it wouldn't end up on the ground."

"I may have anticipated."

"Now we're all sweaty, and it's a sure bet I've got grass stains on my ass." She pressed her lips to his shoulder. "Worth it."

"More than. Let's have a swim."

"I am not swimming in that pond."

"Isn't it convenient we have a pool? Let's have a swim there, then we can see about drilling that bedrock for an hour or two."

"We could do that." A couple of laps to wake her back up, then the drilling.

When he rolled away, she found her shirt, started to put it on.

"What're you doing?"

"Getting dressed."

"You'll just have to undress again to swim." He plucked the shirt away, began to gather up scattered clothes.

"I'm not walking naked to the house and down to the pool."

"Whyever not? It's perfectly private."

"Summerset."

"Is at the ballet with Ivanna."

"He's not in the house?"

"He's not. He and Ivanna are enjoying *The Firebird*. They'll have a late supper after."

"The house is Summerset-free? Why didn't you say so?" With a hoot of delight, she scrambled up and ran naked toward the house.

21

They swam and, before she dragged on a T-shirt, he managed to wand her again. They drilled, with him at the auxiliary of her command center, until midnight, when he persuaded her to shut it down until morning.

And just after four A.M., her 'link signaled and woke her.

"Lights at ten percent," Roarke said. He stood, nearly dressed, beside the bed. "You sleep through a wicked storm, but that wakes you."

Lightning flashed and, in the following boom of thunder, she saw—at last—Taylor Noy on the display.

"Block video. Dallas."

"Hey!" Taylor hadn't blocked hers. She had some sort of big white flower over one ear, a thin pink strap falling off one shoulder, and was clearly very drunk.

"Ms. Noy—"

"Just turned on my 'link. We all turned 'em off, 'cause my sister got married. In Vegas, baby! I had lots of lots of champagne."

"Okay. Ms. Noy—"

"So I'm pretty much drunk, and I won sixteen hundred dollars shooting craps. I don't know how to shoot craps, but I won sixteen hundred dollars doing it."

"Congratulations."

"I kissed this man—he had to be ninety—right on the mouth. There might've been tongues, can't be sure about that. He was my good luck charm, so what the hell, right? How are you?"

"It's important I speak with you and your mother as soon as possible."

"My mom?" Taylor dropped down on a bed. Eve caught sight of a headboard that rivaled EDD with its gold and red swags. "She had a lot of champagne, too. Everybody did! We had such fun! Sasha got married."

"I can come to you. Are you staying in Las Vegas?"

"Aw. Want to. Can't. We gotta come home tomorrow. Except for Sasha and Milli. They're on their honeymoon. In Vegas, baby!"

"What time will you be back in New York tomorrow?"

"Um . . . um. Two o'clock? Yeah, that's right. Why?"

"It's very important I speak to you and your mother." Eve remembered the damn rotation of the Earth. "Is that two New York time?"

"Yep. Two o'clock, West Islip shuttle station. My step-dad's got a car picking us up. It'll drop them off, then take me home. He's sweet that way. Cal's such a sweetheart. He booked Sasha and Milli the honeymoon suite. It's got its own little heart-shaped pool and—"

"Ms. Noy . . . Are you sober enough to understand and remember what I'm saying?"

"Sure. I'm drunk, but not stupid drunk. Maybe a little bit," she confessed. "Like a hundred percent drunk and, say, ten—maybe fifteen—percent stupid drunk."

"I'd like you to write this down. Can you write this down?"

"I've got an app for that." The second sparkly pink strap slipped down when she shifted. "Hey, there it is!"

"When you land—write this down—when you land, contact me."

"When we land, tag—the fifteen percent can't spell *lieutenant* right now. So tag Dallas. 'K, got it."

"And take the car to your mother's house, stay there."

"Stay at Mom's." Now she frowned. "Stay there . . . How come?"

"I want to talk to you and your mother. I can come to you. It'll be simpler that way. Will you do that?"

"Sure, why not? Contact you, go to Mom's. I got it! I think I need to puke now, so see you tomorrow!"

Eve sat, staring at the blank screen on her 'link.

"You can always contact her in the morning—don't forget it's three hours earlier there," Roarke reminded her. "Have some pity for the hangover, and be civilized. Wait till noon our time."

On another roll of thunder, Eve buried her face in her hands. "How can you look like that after four hours' sleep? Less?"

"Clean living."

"Since when?"

He came around the bed to kiss her. "Go back to sleep. You can easily grab another two hours."

He kissed her again, then left her and the cat beside her.

"Go back to sleep," she muttered, and lay back to go over the conversation with Taylor as thunder boomed. "Who can sleep after all that, and with all this noise?"

Apparently she could, as the next thing she knew it was six-fifteen, and Roarke sat drinking coffee with his stock reports and tablet.

"Feel better?" he asked her.

"I will after coffee."

She grabbed some, then a shower before she went straight to her closet.

"It's still August," Roarke told her, "but the storm's dropped the temps some, and it'll be fresher for it."

"Great."

Knowing she'd never get away with full black two days running, she grabbed khakis, a tan jacket with some navy running through it, which made it easy to snag a navy tank.

She came out to whatever Roarke had chosen for breakfast.

"Nice choice," he told her as she sat and poured more coffee.

"Nice choice," she echoed when he took the domes off bacon, fluffy scrambled eggs, golden hash browns. "I want to do more drilling before this afternoon, and try to get that consult with Mira."

"Well focused, aren't you now, Lieutenant?"

"It's them. I'm out of the damn mud because it's Arnez and Robards. I just have to find the why, and prove it. Get them into the box."

She ate while Roarke pointed a warning finger at the everhopeful Galahad.

"He won't roll on her. He'd go down for it solo if he had to. But he could let enough slip. He's not a killer."

"And yet he killed."

"I bet those shiny-armor knights didn't think they were killers when they sliced somebody's head off to protect the damsel. I can play it that way if that's how it runs. But I need the why."

"And hope that Noy's widow and daughter can give it to you."

"It's there. Maybe she had a thing for Noy, went for older men."

"That would be quite an age gap."

"Yeah, but it happens. He was powerful, and that can be seductive. More likely a thing for the son. Taylor said no special girlfriend back then, but maybe they kept it quiet. Or he didn't see her as special, but she did."

She shrugged, ate some more. "I'll find it."

"I'd appreciate if you let me know when you do. I find myself invested."

"You put in plenty of time, right from the start, so yeah, I'll let you know."

She pushed up, strapped on her weapon harness. "I want to get started. I've dug up—or maybe it's drilled down to—some of Brice Noy's old teachers, classmates. I'm going to try to make contact with a couple on my way in."

"Arnez and Robards have no idea what they've started, or how hard they'll fall. I'd wish you luck, but luck has nothing to do with it." He rose to kiss her. "Tag me—and meanwhile, take care of my cop."

"I'm hoping to talk to a college professor and a former member of a high school debate club. I doubt they'll take a swing at me, but if they do, I'll block it."

He watched her go, toying with the button in his pocket. And hoped she came home unbruised and unbloodied.

Eve went out, got in her car, calculating she'd started early enough to catch both potential interviewees at home.

Professor Elaine Gleason lived on the Upper West Side in an old rosy brick building with generous windows. A dog walker ambled by with a pointy-eared, square-jawed brown dog. The dog strutted as if he owned the city. A spotted dog the size of a small tank galloped toward him, his walker jogging to keep up.

Eve expected an ugly battle.

Tank Dog stopped, lavished Pointy-Ears with sloppy tongue kisses. Pointy-Ears accepted them as his due while the respective walkers smiled and cooed.

Dogs, Eve thought as she walked to the building's entrance, remained a mystery to her.

Inside, she took the stairs to the third floor. A man answered the buzzer on the Gleason apartment. Mid-fifties,
trim in a blue shirt and worn jeans, he had a head full of
shaggy, gray-streaked brown hair and hooded brown eyes.

"Good morning." His voice made Eve think of someone
spotlighted on a stage, reciting poetry. "Can I help you?"

"Lieutenant Dallas, NYPSD." She offered her badge. "I'd
like to speak with Professor Gleason."

He smiled at her. "Which one?"

"Professor Elaine Gleason."

"Ah, you want my partner in crime. I probably shouldn't
joke about crime to the police. Elaine!" He raised that made-
for-poetry voice. "Cop's at the door. Come in, Lieutenant. Is
there a problem?"

"No, sir. I'd like to speak to Professor Gleason about someone she taught a few years ago."

"Have a seat. She's probably got headphones on. I'll go
get her."

Both walls flanking the doorway he went through were
shelves. The shelves were filled with books—dozens and
dozens of real books.

Roarke would have loved it.

The furniture—with plenty of seating—looked old. Not
antique old, simply well established in the space and well
used.

Conversations happened here, she thought, studying the
arrangement. Lots of conversations.

And among the books, the casually comfortable furniture,
were framed photos. A lot of them.

Elaine Gleason walked out with her husband. She wore
loose cotton pants with a baggy T-shirt and had her mass of
brown hair tugged back in a messy tail.

"I'm sorry, I was— Oh for Pete's sake, Henry! You didn't
tell me it was Eve Dallas." She strode forward on bare feet,

hand extended. "I'm absolutely thrilled to meet you. Henry, Lieutenant Dallas. *The Icove Agenda*."

He looked blank, then blinked. "Oh, yes, of course. I didn't put it together."

"I teach criminal justice at NYU, so naturally I've followed some of your cases. I also run a student book club—Crime and Punishment. We read Nadine Furst's book last year. I've scheduled her new one for our first read in the fall semester. I would love to bring you in as a guest lecturer."

"Ah—"

"I'll nag you about it later. Please, sit down."

"Should I make coffee?"

"I'm fine," Eve told Henry. "I won't keep you long. Professor Gleason."

"Make it Elaine—the *professor* can be confusing considering."

"Elaine—"

"Henry and I just got back from two weeks at the beach—North Carolina—with our children. I was just catching up on things, and read about Captain Martin Greenleaf's murder. You're primary on that, correct?"

"Yes."

"I'm assuming this pertains, and you want to ask me about Brice Noy."

"I do." And that sped things up, Eve thought. "You remember him."

"I do. An excellent student. Bright, questing. I may not have remembered him for that alone, not after close to a decade. But his father's fall, and suicide, then Brice's. Yes, I remember him very well. Do you remember me speaking of him, Henry?"

"I do now."

"He was never the same after his father's death. Angry, brooding. He began missing classes."

"I spoke to him once about getting counseling. He said he'd think about it, in a way that told me he wasn't ready. He blamed everyone but his father."

"Captain Greenleaf?"

"It's why I recognized the name when I read it. Brice brought him up when I spoke to him about counseling. But he bounced back, a little, for a short time. His attendance and grades improved. It seemed like a mission—not just to keep his scholarship, but to prove something."

She lifted her hands. "Then he took his own life. Nineteen, wasn't he? Or twenty."

"Nineteen. Do you know if he had any close friends, most particularly, a specific girlfriend?"

"Friends, yes. Before the tragedy I'd say he had a number of friends. He was a sociable sort, very personable. Fraternity brothers, the book club, other interests. As for a specific girl, none I remember. My sense is that he didn't tie himself to one girl."

Eve took out her 'link, brought up Arnez's photo. "Do you remember her?"

Elaine took a long, careful look. "She's striking, not a face easily forgotten. No, I'm sorry, I don't remember her."

She shifted to Robards.

"No. He's not familiar to me."

"You said he'd bounced back. Do you remember any event, anything that happened or changed before his suicide?"

"I'm afraid I don't. He seemed determined to pull his grades back up, but he wasn't the same sociable, engaged student he'd been. Distant, I'd say. Focused, but distant."

"All right. Thank you for your time."

"I wish I could be of more help."

"You gave me a clearer picture of him. That's always helpful."

She moved onto the next.

The debate club friend remembered him, but like the professor, no specific girl. And no recognition of Arnez or Robards.

She checked the time, found herself irritated she had hours to wait before Taylor and her mother landed.

She took a chance and, when she reached Central, went to Mira's office rather than her own.

The dragon stood at the gate.

She pursed her lips. "You look well healed, Lieutenant."

"Yeah, I'm good. I need ten minutes."

"You seem consistently unaware that Dr. Mira has a schedule."

"You seem consistently unaware that murder and mayhem happen all around us."

"Not at all," the admin said equably. "As for mayhem, the doctor is speaking with former detective Lansing at this very moment re his court-ordered psychiatric evaluation."

"I'll take the ten whenever she has it."

"Is this regarding Lansing and his attack on you and Detective Baxter?"

She could lie, Eve thought, but had a feeling dragons saw through lies. "No, not directly. It's regarding the Greenleaf investigation. Look, I've got the captain in the ground, and his son who's lucky to be in the hospital rather than the morgue. I'll take five minutes."

"I'll let Dr. Mira know."

Stuck with that, Eve took the glides to Homicide.

At least she didn't get blasted by Jenkinson's tie.

"They caught one," Baxter told her. "About a half hour ago. Trueheart and I are still clear if you want a hand."

"My office," she said. "Peabody."

"Will we all fit in there?"

Ignoring Baxter's question, she kept going.

Coffee came first.

She pointed to the AC when the three trooped in.

"Make it fast. Prime suspects." She tapped Arnez and Robards's pictures on her board. And while they got coffee, laid it out.

"Different schools." Baxter shrugged that off. "I dated plenty of sweet young things who went to a different school. How about you?"

Trueheart more hunched his shoulders than shrugged. "Not really. I didn't date all that much in high school."

"Late bloomers still bloom. Plenty of other ways to meet girls."

"Such as?" Eve asked.

"Community centers, at the vids, game parlors, pizza joints. I could go on."

"Please don't. They didn't just meet. She became invested in him, in the family, in his father. Either one or all three. So far, we haven't connected them. But it's there, the connection's there."

"It'd have to be pretty strong for her to kill Captain Greenleaf and try for his son," Trueheart commented.

"That's right. And she managed to make a strong connection to the Greenleafs in about a year. I'm going to say she knows how to insert herself. Peabody and I are reinterviewing Noy's daughter this afternoon, and interviewing her mother. Meanwhile, I have the names and contacts of several of Brice Greenleaf's teachers and fellow students."

"We can take some," Baxter told her.

"I crossed two off this morning on the way in. Both described him as sociable, smart, engaging, and engaged. No specific girl, no serious relationships. And neither recognized Arnez or Robards."

She looked back at the board. "Someone will. We keep filling in the picture on him, find out if anyone knows what triggered his suicide. And show them Arnez and Robards.

"You catch one," she added, "pass what's left back to us. I'll send you the names."

"We got it. FYI, Loo," Baxter added, "Mira's doing the psych eval on Lansing this morning."

"I heard. How did you?"

"Jenkinson."

Of course, Eve thought. "Let's stay way away from there."

"Happy to." Baxter thumped Trueheart on the shoulder. "Let's ride, brother."

"Are there any female students on the list?" Peabody asked when they'd left.

"Yeah, some."

"We should start there. A girl's more likely to notice another girl if she's cozying up to a guy she's cozied up with, or wants to."

"That's a point. Give me five, then we'll ride, too."

She split the list, went heavy on the females on hers and Peabody's. Checked the time. Still too early, according to Roarke, to send a reminder to Taylor Noy.

She spent the morning eliminating, and got one maybe from a woman with a baby on her hip who sucked its thumb like it was coated with opium.

"A maybe's better than a no."

Back in the car, Eve shook her head. "A maybe means bupkis in court. A maybe doesn't give us probable cause. We'll go back in, write these up. I can send that reminder to Taylor Noy now."

"I wouldn't want to get married in Vegas," Peabody commented. "I mean, it could be fun, but I want the big whoop. Like you had."

"I guess that was a big whoop."

"And so, so beautiful. When we decide to go for it, I want a killer dress, a zillion flowers, and everybody there. Maybe get Carmichael to sing."

"She does have pipes." Eve looked over. "You're not—"

"No. No, not there yet. I mean, we've got the Great House Project, settling in after, Mavis's Number Two. Anyway, I like where we are now. We both do. So we can stick there until.

"And anyway, anyway—I'm taking a boost from the maybe. She really seemed to think she recognized Arnez. Just couldn't pin it exactly."

"And when Arnez's lawyer points out our wit might have recognized her from shopping in one of the stores she's worked at, we're back to zero."

In her office, she sent the reminder to Taylor Noy, got a thumbs-up emoji in response. She started writing up interviews and heard the familiar click of heels.

She rose to her feet before Mira got to the door.

"I didn't expect you to come to me."

Mira shut the door. "I wanted a moment. I can't tell you anything specific about my discussion with Lansing. I simply want to say I'm very glad you weren't more seriously injured."

"All right."

Mira looked at her dead on. "Very glad, Eve."

"I got it. You want some of that tea?"

"Thanks, but I really only have a few minutes. You wanted to talk to me about the investigation."

"These two." She tapped the board. "They killed Greenleaf and tried for the son. I can't tell you why they did, at this point. But I can tell you why I know it. When I do, you can shoot holes in that, or tell me if my conclusions are valid."

"Maybe I will have that tea. No, I'll get it. Tell me."

Eve laid it out, carefully, point by point.

"It's a mirror of the Noy suicides. A service weapon for the father's, a rope—and the same type of rope—for the son's."

She pointed to the side-by-side crime scene shots on all four incidents.

"Someone had to know those details. Had to have access to both Noy scenes or knowledge from someone who did."

Mira nodded. "I agree."

"They had to know about the window in the captain's place, and where and how to disengage the security in his daughter's house. Had to be inside the house to lift the kid's 'link. Used the playroom. Ben didn't have a bedroom there—not his place—but he'd have spent time with his kids and his siblings' in that room."

She tapped her board again. "These two fit. Access to both residences, knowledge of both residences and the family routines. They built up trust. They knew the kid was downstairs and the father would go up in response to the text. They knew the way out without going back down."

Eve hissed out a breath. "And I saw it on her face. I saw it when she got to the captain's place."

"You build a good case."

"That's missing an essential piece. I'm going to find it."

Mira walked to the board. "She's stunning."

"Everybody says so."

"No father in the picture, a single mother working outside the home—and going back to school to advance in that work. Long hours. No siblings, a limited family life."

"No family photos. None."

"Mmm. So you said. Then, the handsome boy with, by appearances, a happy, loving family. It would be attractive. She's an ambitious woman, willing to work to reach her goals. It's possible the handsome boy, the family, were another ambition. It would be interesting to know, if you're right, how much work she put into reaching that goal, only to have it taken away."

Mira put down the teacup. "It's a valid theory and, though there are gaps and untied ends, I won't shoot holes in it. But you need that essential piece."

"I'll get it."

She turned to Eve. "From the looks of your face, I assume Roarke saw to it you had proper treatment."

"Yeah." Instinctively, Eve put a hand over her breast. "Everywhere. It's all good."

"Let's keep it that way. I have to get back. Let me know what you have after interviewing Noy's widow and daughter. They'd certainly know the details needed to mirror Louis and Brice Noy's suicides."

In under two hours now, Eve thought when Mira left. Time enough to write up the interviews, then drive out to Long Island.

When she walked out to the bullpen, Baxter sat at his desk.

"No hits, LT—one sort of maybe not sure."

"Jenkinson and Reineke?"

"Pulled somebody into Interview A."

"All right. We're in the field. With me, Peabody."

"I was kind of thinking you might get a copter." Hope lived. "Save the drive time."

"We've got time to drive it."

One hope died; another was born.

"Maybe since it'll take awhile, I could have five minutes to tell you about progress on the Great House Project."

"I was just there."

"Things are really moving."

Since it would take awhile, Eve decided to let her blather. She could listen with half an ear and get the gist. And while getting the gist, she could work out what to do if they struck out in West Islip.

Head to Queens, get Robards alone. Pull on his protective instincts until he tripped over them. She needed enough, just enough for a search warrant. She'd find something in that apartment that tied Arnez to Noy. Deep personal connection, you kept mementos.

"What do you think?" Peabody asked her.

The GHP, Eve reminded herself. "I think if you keep finding stuff in flea markets, you're going to have to open one of your own."

"There's so much space." Peabody sighed on the thought.

A handful of times Eve reconsidered her objection to the copter, but considering all, they made decent time.

Fancy homes, she noted, many with nice views of the water. A lot of country club types enjoying those views, she imagined. Private shuttle types.

A lot different from being married to a cop, even one who pulled in plenty with graft and extortion.

The former widow's current home hit the fancy, she thought when she pulled into the long paved drive. Dignified fancy, all white, black shutters on the windows, double black doors. It rested on a smooth green lawn with tall, leafy trees.

And backed, as far as she could tell, on more smooth lawn that led to the water.

"I like ours better."

"What?"

"I was just thinking, this is a really nice house, traditional, all manicured. But I like ours better. More personality. I wonder what the kitchen's like."

"Peabody."

"I'm not going to ask."

Even as they got out of the car, a slick black limo pulled in. Taylor popped out of the back. "You beat us here."

"Got lucky with traffic."

"First, I'm sorry about the drunken babbling last night. We celebrated pretty hard."

"Understandably."

"I've never been to Vegas—what a trip! Never gambled. I won that sixteen hundred at craps—God knows how. Then before we left today, I thought, hell, I'm putting a hundred of it in that slot machine. And I won five thousand dollars!"

She threw back her head and laughed at the sky.

"Can you believe it? I think I used up all my luck, so I'm never gambling again.

"Mom, this is Lieutenant Dallas, and Detective—sorry, forgot."

"Peabody."

"My mother, Ella Rosen, her husband, Cal."

Tall, he had an athletically lean build, a handsome, raw-boned face. His dark shock of hair had touches of gray at the temples.

"I hope we didn't keep you waiting long." Cal offered a hand.

"Just got here."

"Let's go inside." Cal put a hand on Ella's arm, rubbed as if in comfort.

"I don't know what I can possibly tell you," Ella began. "I haven't seen or spoken with Captain Greenleaf in years, and even then . . ."

"We'll try not to take up much of your time."

Eve stepped inside the large, airy entranceway that flowed into a large, airy living space with soaring ceilings.

The fireplace of dark gray stucco rose up two stories.

The furniture was in dreamy blues and greens—maybe, Eve thought, to reflect the trees and the water. Tasteful, down to the marble floors.

"Please have a seat. Can I get you something to drink?" Cal offered.

"We're fine, thanks."

"Is it all right if I stay? Ella's a little nervous."

"That's no problem. There's no need to be nervous, Ms. Rosen."

"It's not an interrogation, Mom." Taylor took her hand as the three of them sat on a couch. "We're just talking."

"It's difficult to bring up the past," Peabody put in. "I'm sorry we have to."

"I understand. I'm so sorry about Captain Greenleaf, sorry for his family. I never blamed him. How could I?"

"Ms. Rosen, we don't believe you were involved in the captain's murder. You're going to hear soon enough. Someone tried to kill his son late yesterday afternoon. His older son."

"Oh my God. That's horrible. It's incomprehensible."

"By hanging."

She went dead pale, and her hand trembled as it groped for her husband's. "Like Brice."

"Yes. We believe someone mimicked Captain Noy's suicide, then attempted to mimic your son's."

"But who would do that? It's insane. Who—one of the people under Lou's command? I haven't had any contact with any of them. What Lou did . . . maybe I was stupid."

"Stop that," Cal told her.

"I never had a single clue, not until . . . The night he told me what he'd done, been doing, and what could happen. He tried to justify it. He'd done it for me, for our children. For the family."

Sorrows, old sorrows, shadowed her eyes. "Lou was devoted to our family, so maybe that was partially true. But it was also partially a lie. I fell apart. I couldn't even look at him. And a few nights later . . . God, Taylor found him. My little girl. I'll never forget the sound of her screaming."

She inhaled, sharply. "And I'll never forgive him for exposing her to that shock. For using our home for his final choice."

"We got through it, Mom." Gently, Taylor pressed a kiss to her mother's cheek. "We got through it, and we're okay."

"Ms. Rosen, according to the file, they found three more

weapons locked away in the house. Do you know if he had more elsewhere?"

Ella shook her head, sighed. "I didn't know he had those. I didn't know about the separate accounts, the cash in the safe. I didn't know so many things about Lou."

"And Brice?"

"I knew my son. He was as ignorant of what his father did as I was. But . . . he couldn't accept that what Lou had done was wrong. He adored his father. He couldn't accept what he'd done, so others were to blame. But he's gone, Lieutenant. He's been gone for nine years."

22

"Who was he close to, besides his father, besides you and his sister?"

"Oh, Brice had so many friends. He made them so easily. After, he cut himself off from them, or most of them. He was so angry."

"A girlfriend?"

She smiled a little. "He had lots of them, too. His father told him: Don't get serious about a girl. You need to enjoy them—respect but enjoy. You've got your education, your career ahead of you. Establish yourself, then think about getting serious with the right girl.

"He always listened to his father."

"He liked dating," Taylor said. "Having a looker—and he could get the lookers—to go out with, but never more than a couple times or so with any one of them. I want to say he took things seriously. His grades, his direction."

"He did." Ella looked across the room and, as Eve had already noticed, among a grouping of photos was her lost son.

"Lou and I were so proud of him."

"Maybe someone who wanted to get serious when he didn't."

"Brice knew how to play it. Even I could see that." Taylor

shrugged. "He kept it light because that's how he wanted it. He was careful not to let a girl get stuck on him."

"Well . . . Ellie." When Taylor laughed, Ella shook her head. "She had a major crush on him."

"I guess, maybe. But he didn't encourage it."

"Ellie?" Eve heard the ping.

"One of his strays—or it started out that way. He met her when he was buying me a Christmas present. They struck up a conversation. Ella, Ellie. Lou called me Ellie once in a while, and apparently that was a conversation starter. Brice ended up bringing her home to dinner."

"A lot," Taylor added.

"Yes, but in a friendly way. She and your father really hit it off. Sweet girl, and lonely, I think. An only child, as I recall, with no father at home and her mother worked long hours. I guess she was sort of an honorary member of the family for a while."

"She did hook me up with my first summer job. I appreciated that. But she and Brice were never a thing. I really can't think of anyone who—"

She broke off when Eve held up her 'link. "Do you recognize this woman?"

"I—yeah. That's her. That's Ellie. Right, Mom?"

"Yes. Yes, but I don't understand. I . . ."

"Do you know her full name?"

"Ah . . ."

"Arnez," Taylor supplied, and her eyes went cold. "I think it was Elsa or Elva, but Arnez was her last name. I worked part-time that summer with her." She tapped above her breast where a name tag would be. "Ellie Arnez. Did she do this?"

"She's a person of interest. When's the last time you saw or spoke with her?"

"Cal."

"I'm going to get you some water. Okay, honey. You sit here with Taylor."

"I could use some, too, Cal. Thanks. She kept in touch for a while," Taylor continued. "We appreciated that, as most of Brice's friends stepped back—or he'd broken things off with most of them. It was so ugly."

"She stuck by Brice over those months. I thought it was a good thing. He had someone to talk to. When he died, she was devastated. It actually helped me to comfort her. Even as time passed, she kept in touch. Came by, or got me on the 'link. We'd talk about Brice, and what she was doing. School, work. She always sent me flowers on Mother's Day. Except, now that I think about it, this past year."

"You'd remarried, and you've moved out here."

"Yes. Yes. I haven't heard from her for months. Almost a year, I think."

"Did she come to your wedding?" Peabody wondered.

"Oh, no. It was the second time around for both Cal and me. We had a small ceremony here, at the house, just family and a few of our closest friends. I didn't invite her. I wouldn't have thought to, honestly."

Eve showed them the photo of Robards.

"No, I don't recognize him. Taylor, do you?"

"No. Ellie and I didn't click the way she and Brice did, or the way she did with our father. She was older, and she wasn't interested in sports. I thought it was weird the way she'd come over, sit and talk with my dad like she did even if Brice wasn't home. I told Brice that, and he said to lay off her. How she had it rough at home. But she always had really nice clothes. She asked Brice to her senior prom."

"I remember," Ella murmured. "He took her, of course."

"And when I said that was weird, he told me she didn't have any friends, not really. Poor friendless, fatherless girl. I didn't see it then."

Her face hard, set, Taylor looked at Eve. "I didn't see her then. I see her now.

"Dad slipped her money sometimes."

Ella turned to her. "He did?"

"I saw it once, and when I asked him why, Dad said sometimes you just need a little extra. And not to say anything about it to you or Brice. So I didn't."

"How did she react when the investigation on Captain Noy came out?"

"Outrage," Ella said immediately. "God, I'd really forgotten all of this. Thanks, Cal." Still pale, but steadier, Ella took the water he offered, sipped slowly. "Outrage at whoever turned evidence—we didn't know—outrage against IAB, and Captain Greenleaf in particular."

"Did she specifically mention the captain?"

"Yes. Yes. Incessantly. I didn't want to discuss it with her. I was trying so hard to keep us all afloat and, my God, it was so painful. I didn't want to discuss it with anyone."

Ella laid a hand on her husband's cheek. "I realize now I've never really talked to you about all of it. I wanted it behind me, so I put it behind me."

"It is behind you."

"I thought it was. But Ellie . . . She huddled with Brice in those weeks after Lou's death, and they were outraged together. I should've stopped that. I should have. But I was—"

"Shattered, Mom," Taylor finished. "You were shattered. So was I."

"So were you," she murmured, then looked at Eve.

"Her reaction after your son's death?"

"Grief, so much grief to share. She was so young, so crushed."

"She didn't blame Dad," Taylor said.

"No, she didn't blame Lou. It was the people who hadn't

stood by him who were to blame. It was IAB and Captain Greenleaf, and everyone else. She was shattered, too, Lieutenant. Lou was a hero to her, and Brice . . . You don't actually believe she could—and after all this time."

"We'll talk to her. In the meantime, if she contacts you, please don't tell her what we discussed here. And contact me."

"She adored Lou," Ella said. "So many did."

Outside, Eve strode straight to the car. "We've got to move."

"You were right. I knew you had to be right after the last briefing, but . . . You were right."

"Terrific. Tag Baxter. If they're still clear, I want them to head to Queens."

"We could—"

"I know where Queens is, Peabody. We're going after Arnez. Tell him to shadow Robards until we get the warrants."

She contacted APA Reo on the dash 'link.

"I need warrants."

Reo blinked her blue eyes and answered in her mild Southern drawl. "I know I've got my surprised face around here somewhere. Just let me find it."

"Fast, Reo."

"I've also got a shocked face in my collection. Is this the Greenleaf case?"

"Elva Arnez, Denzel Robards—upstairs neighbors."

Eve went through it while Peabody briefed Baxter.

"I see where you're going," Reo interrupted. "But—"

"I'm not done. We just interviewed Noy's widow and daughter. They identified Arnez—a tight family friend, a close relationship with Noy and his son in particular. She knew about Greenleaf's connection, had it in for him specifically at the time Noy and his son went down. But she got really friendly with Greenleaf and his family over this past year. Never mentioned she knew Noy. Never mentioned it to us during interview."

Reo held up a hand. "Nine years later, correct? You could say Arnez wanted to move on. Didn't mention it because oops, neighbors, and finds she likes them. Didn't mention it to you for obvious reasons."

"I don't say that. Do you?"

Reo dragged the hand through her fluffy blond hair. "No. Not when you look at the whole picture."

"Get me warrants. Murder One, attempted murder, conspiracy to murder. I need search warrants for their apartment, any storage unit in that building or others, her place of employment and his. Toss in his mother's place. They may have a hidey-hole there."

Reo's lips vibrated as she blew out a breath. "And here I thought I might actually leave work on time today. I'll talk to the boss, talk to a judge. And I'll see you at Central."

"Fast," Eve repeated, and clicked off.

"Baxter and Trueheart are en route to Queens," Peabody told her.

"Good. Now tag Mira, fill her in." And she tagged Roarke.

His admin, Caro, came on-screen. Her perfect white hair crowned a calm, pleasant face. "Lieutenant. Roarke's in a meeting and asked me to intercept if you contacted him."

"Okay. Just let him know I'm bringing them in. He'll know."

"Of course. Do you want him to contact you?"

"No. I'll be busy. Thanks."

Eve considered, then thought: Fuck Lansing. And tagged Nadine.

Camera ready, of course, in a collarless red jacket. "I'm about to break the Greenleaf case. No details, Nadine, so don't ask. Just be ready."

"I'm never not."

"Consider this a gift, because of Lansing."

She clicked off before Nadine could respond.

"Are you worried about him? Lansing?" Peabody asked her.

"Worried, no; pissed, yes. And I'm going to stay there awhile."

She hit lights and sirens, hit vertical, and soared over a line of traffic.

Due to praying and holding her breath at the same time, Peabody didn't speak again until they reached Manhattan.

"I'm not sure a copter would've been much faster. Baxter and Trueheart are on the garage. Robards is there."

"They hold for the warrant." She cut the lights and siren. "And that better be it," she added as her in-dash signaled incoming.

"It is. Reo comes through."

"Send the Robards arrest warrant to Baxter, tell them to pick him up. I need search teams on the garage, on his mother's place. Have Uniform Carmichael set that up."

"Their apartment?"

"Have uniforms meet us at her dress shop. They can take her in after we bust her. We'll take the apartment. That'll give her some time to sit in holding, stew over it."

"She'll lawyer up."

"Yeah. That doesn't worry me." Because she had that essential piece now. She had the why.

She didn't bother to hunt up parking, just doubled it in front of the shop.

Fancy shop, Eve thought, pure white stone, sparkling glass. Behind the glass the fake people posed in fall clothes, deep, burnished colors, tall, glossy boots, thigh-length swing jackets.

Why did people want to buy sweaters in August?

The door gave a light, musical trill when she opened it.

Inside, the air was cool and smelled like freshly peeled oranges.

Artistically arranged displays showcased the burnished, the glossy, the sparkling, and the smooth.

A stick-thin redhead in sleek black stood beside a woman in a floral summer dress. They discussed a tiny, shiny purse shaped like a heart.

"Just the perfect size to hold the essentials," the redhead said. "A stunning accent with a cocktail dress or a formal gown. And, of course, the classic Delago safety clasp and signature red silk lining."

She glanced over at Eve and Peabody, sized them up. Her greeting smile pumped up a few degrees. "Ladies. I'll be right with you."

"Put this behind the counter for me." The customer passed the purse to the clerk. "I want to browse a bit more."

"Take your time. Good afternoon," she said to Eve. "I adore your boots. Carlotta's, aren't they?"

"No, they're my boots." Because she didn't want to alert Arnez, she didn't pull out her badge. "We need to speak with the manager. Ms. Arnez."

"Oh, is there a problem?"

"Yeah, there is. Arnez."

"Yes, of course, she's in the dressing area with a client. I'll get her." She turned, saw her customer—ears obviously pricked—holding up a midnight-blue dress, its three-inch gap between bodice and skirt connected by slim, vertical silver bars.

"Should I start a dressing room for you, Ms. Adolfo?"

"Yes, do that." She handed over the dress. "I'll browse a bit more first."

To see what's going on, Eve thought as the clerk walked to the dressing area. Well, hang on, sister, you're about to get a show.

"Ms. Arnez will be right with you," the redhead informed Eve. "I have dressing room two for you, Ms. Adolfo. Should I put that in for you?"

"Mmm." Adolfo passed over a burnt orange velvet tunic, then wandered to a display of shoes.

Arnez strode out on sky-high silver sandals paired with a white, body-skimming dress. "Oh, Lieutenant Dallas. I'm terribly sorry, but I'm with a client. If you wouldn't mind waiting a few more minutes—"

"Actually, I do. Elva Arnez, you're under arrest—"

The shoes the browser held thumped to the floor.

"What! That's crazy!"

"Charges include murder in the first degree, attempted murder, felony assault, conspiracy to murder. Peabody?"

"You have the right to remain silent," Peabody began as Eve walked over, pulled Arnez's hands behind her back and, after the quick, expected struggle, cuffed her.

"Do you understand your rights and obligations?" Peabody asked her.

"I don't understand any of this! Murder! I haven't killed anyone."

"My partner can read off the Revised Miranda again, very slowly, until you understand."

The look she shot Eve was pure venom. "I understand my rights. I understand this is ludicrous. I want my lawyer."

"You can contact him or her once you get to Central. Good timing," she added as two female uniforms came in.

"Peabody, collect any personal items Ms. Arnez has on premises, bag them for these officers to transport. Put her in the patrol car and wait," she told the officers. "Then escort this individual and her personal items to Central. Book her on all warranted charges. Allow her to contact her attorney or legal representative."

Mortification flushed Arnez's face. Fury burned through her eyes as the uniforms perp-walked her to the door.

"You're going to pay for this." She hurled the words at Eve. "Believe me."

"If I had a dollar for every time I heard that one, I could probably buy that silly heart purse."

"A Delago evening bag can go for twenty large," Peabody told her.

"Get out." Eve just shook her head as the uniforms took Arnez out. "I could buy it with my you're-going-to-pay-for-this dollars, but why would I? It would barely hold my badge."

Which she held up now to make things clear to the clerk, whose mouth still hung open, and the customer, who watched with avid eyes.

"Does she have a purse, a handbag, a briefcase?"

The redhead blinked. "A—a handbag, in the back."

"Let's go get that," Peabody said.

The customer studied Eve. "That was fascinating. My first arrest. Obviously not yours."

"No. Are you seriously going to drop twenty K on a bag you can't even fit your 'link in?"

"I have a mini for that. And a weakness for Delago bags."

Peabody came out with a handbag that could swallow a couple hundred of the Delagos.

"What should I do?" the clerk asked Eve. "What do I do now?"

"I'd find another manager."

On the sidewalk, Eve watched the cruiser drive away.

"That was satisfying. See if McNab can bounce over and take the e's. Unless Feeney wants to do it himself. Let's go toss the apartment."

She ignored the blast of horns, the fists shaken in her direction, the creative curses that followed.

"Feeney wants it."

"Thought he might."

She took a loading zone near the apartment building.

"I can't believe they'd keep the 'links—Ben Greenleaf's and his daughter's."

Eve shrugged as she mastered in. "Maybe. Maybe not. But she never figured we'd connect her with Noy and, without that, no motive. The length of rope they used came from a longer length. You could see it had been cut to size. We find that, lab matches it, there's the attempted. We don't need the 'links."

They walked up the stairs, mastered in. Sealed up.

"Dallas, Lieutenant Eve, Peabody, Detective Delia," she said for the record, "entering the residence of Arnez, Elva, and Robards, Denzel, for a warranted search and seize."

Different flowers, Eve noted. Fresh and different than the ones days before.

"See if there's a utility closet in the kitchen area. That's the most likely place to keep rope. I'll start in the bedroom."

Eve walked back.

Big bed, padded headboard in deep blue, light spread in a pale tone. And the requisite mountain of pillows.

She took the closet first.

Her clothes. All hers. Where did he keep his? Eve wondered.

Hers filled every inch of it, with a section designated for shoes and bags. Plenty of them.

A couple of tiny shinies among the big-ass bags, Eve noted. She wondered if Arnez had scored herself a Delago at her employee (former now) discount.

But her attention focused on a large box that sat on the shelf above the long rod. A fabric-covered box, with a pattern of tiny pink and red hearts.

Reaching up, she lifted it down—had some weight to it. She carted it out of the closet and set it on the bed. No lock, she noted, but then again, her closet. Her space.

She opened it, sighed.

"Too easy," she murmured. "Almost not satisfying. Almost."

"Got the rope!" Peabody came in with a neatly coiled length of rope in her sealed hands. "It's the same rope, Dallas. A fresh cut on one end. It was just there in the closet."

"So were these. In her closet. Just her closet. He must have another space for his." Eve lifted out some photos. "Somebody hasn't moved on."

"That's Arnez with Brice Noy. Holy crap, lots of pictures. Her with the Noy family, with Noy, senior prom with Brice. Mag dress!"

"Yeah, that's important. Everything's in sections. Brice or her and Brice in this one, family in this one, Greenleaf—you can see some were taken from the window. Fucking shots of the fire escape, the window lock."

"It's all right here. A section for mementos. That looks like a wrist corsage—like the one she's wearing in the prom photo. She preserved it. An old 'link."

"What do you bet there are old texts and tags on it—from Brice, to Brice?"

"I'd bet a Delago evening bag if I had one. Jesus, Dallas, we've got her cold."

"Not quite cold, but close. That should be Feeney."

While Peabody went to answer, Eve tried the 'link. Passcoded, but it had batt life. So charged up recently.

She turned when Feeney walked in. "How old is this model?"

"Let's see." He frowned over it. "Ten, maybe twelve years."

"Just right. I need to get what's on it. Her 'link'll be in Evidence, so will Robards's. There's a small room off the living space. Office setup. Comp. I'll let you know if we find any more e's."

Feeney looked down at the photos. "She was pretty tight with Noy and his family."

"Yeah, she was."

"They took Greenleaf out for doing his job. He died in the line, Dallas."

"Yes, he did. And they're going to pay for it. Peabody, find Robards's stuff. He probably uses the closet in the office. I'll finish in here."

Eve fisted her hands on her hips, looked around.

"You're not half as smart as you think you are, Elva. Let's see what else you have tucked away."

While Eve searched, Peabody hustled back. "Look at this!"

She held two evidence bags, each with a 'link. One matched the description of Ben's daughter's.

The stupidity of killers rarely surprised. This made the cut. "Jesus Christ, they kept them."

"He did, anyway. Disabled them, so no way to track. He's not an e-guy really, but handy. I bet he figured he could use them for parts, or wipe them and enable. Dallas, he's got framed pictures on a shelf in his closet. It's kind of sad, really, he had to keep them there. Photos of his family, of him at work with coworkers, of him and Arnez."

Peabody stepped to the bed. "Hey, that's her prom dress."

"Tell me if she'd keep a dress like this for ten years."

"It's a great dress—but for a teenager. Everything she wears and has is now. She'd never wear this anywhere."

"She also kept the jewelry she's wearing in the photo. Have a look. Is she going to wear these earrings, this necklace now?"

"They're sweet and, no, she doesn't wear the sweet. Where were they?"

"Dresser's got a jewelry drawer. These had their own compartment. Bag it up, will you? We've got Robards cold enough, but I'm pretty sure he'd take the fall for her, and she'd let him. To get her? We use Brice Noy. Let's go get her."

She took two tablets in to Feeney. "Anything?" she asked him.

"You wanted old texts and tags, I got 'em. Plenty of them, ranging from nine to eleven years. Haven't read them all— like I said, plenty. But I did a quick search using *Greenleaf*. I got a couple winners."

He handed her the 'link.

From Brice to Arnez:

> The sonofabitch Greenleaf might as well have
> put that stunner to my dad's throat. He killed
> him, Ellie. He fucking killed him.

Arnez to Brice:

> He'll pay for it. We'll make him pay, I swear. No
> matter what, no matter how long it takes. Then
> his family will know how it feels.

"There's more, but you should see this one before you get her in the box. I checked the dates—this is the night the kid hanged himself.

> I went to see that bastard Greenleaf. They took
> my spot at the Academy away. I went to beg him
> to fix it. Begged him. All I ever wanted was to be
> a cop like my dad. I need to be a cop, need to
> clear his name. I've done everything right, and
> he said he couldn't do anything about it. How

it wasn't up to him. How I should finish school,
reapply. How he'd put in a good word for me
when I did. Fucking liar. Everything's ruined,
everything. I've got nothing now.

You've got me. Always, always. He won't
get away with it. And we'll clear your dad's
name, Brice. We will! That bastard Greenleaf ruined everything, and we'll ruin him.
We'll make him sorry. Make them all sorry.
I love you.

I have to go. I'm tired. I'm just so goddamn tired.

I'm here for you. I'll always be here for you.

But Brice didn't respond.

She looked from the 'link screen to Feeney.

"Take her down," he said.

They hauled what they'd found to the car.

"Check in with the search teams, Peabody. If either of them
are done, pull them here to cover what we didn't. We've got
enough. Anything else is icing."

"This festered in her all this time," Peabody said as she
texted. "Festered so she found someone she knew she could
dominate and manipulate like Robards. Until she could get
a place in the same building as her target. Festered while she
planned this all out, made friends with them.

"The team on the dress shop's finished. They'll move to
the apartment."

"Didn't they used to—when a wound festered, didn't they
cauterize it? We're going to burn her ass, Peabody."

"That poor kid," Peabody murmured. "Brice Noy. He
needed help. She made it worse. She didn't mean to, but she

did. The spot at the Academy? Greenleaf couldn't have done anything about that, either way."

"No."

"She didn't even address that, no real comfort or sympathy for him over losing his spot. All she could talk about was payback."

"Because that's all that mattered to her," Eve said as she pulled into the garage. "It's what mattered then, it's what mattered now."

On the glides at Central she texted Reo.

My office, asap.

On the way. She's lawyered; he hasn't.

She's going to need a damn good one.

"We take him first, Peabody. Get him into Interview, and I'll brief Reo. And let Mira know. And Whitney. Captain Greenleaf died in the line. He'll want to be there."

She went straight into her office because the anger was too huge, and needed to be tamped down and rechanneled.

She got coffee more from habit than need, drank it while pacing off the rage.

Reo, in her bold red suit, walked in.

"Sit," Eve told her.

"I want your coffee."

"Sit," Eve repeated. "I'll get the coffee." She nodded at the boxes on her desk. "I'm going to unseal those so you can have a look, and I'm going to run it for you."

Reo sat, drank her coffee, listened, looked.

"In possession of the rope."

"It's on its way to the lab, but it's going to match."

"And the two 'links. From his closet, you said."

"That's right."

"He's done. I can make a deal with him—life on-planet—if he rolls on her."

"He won't. What he's going to do is claim it's all him."

"And expect us to buy that with all you have?"

"He won't flip on her. I can and will trip him up on details, but he won't flip. No point in a deal, Reo, for either of them."

"I wasn't intending to offer her one," Reo said. "Nail her down, Dallas. Nail her down, and we'll put them both away. The PA's office has a very dim view of cop killers."

"He's in Interview B," Peabody said when she came to the door. "He's been crying. It shows."

"Good. Two minutes."

23

After she'd gathered what she needed, Eve met Peabody outside Interview B.

"You take him," Eve said, and handed Peabody the evidence box and files.

"What? Me? Oh, you want me to soften him up, play good, caring cop so you can come in hard."

"No. I want you to take him, hard, soft, however you need to take him."

Eve opened the door. From the table, Robards looked up with red-rimmed eyes.

"Record on. Dallas, Lieutenant Eve, and Peabody, Detective Delia, entering Interview with Robards, Denzel, on the matter of case files H-6759, FA-12829, CM-4921, and related charges."

Eve took a seat.

"Have you been read your rights, Mr. Robards?" Peabody asked.

"I don't know what's going on. I—"

"Please answer the question." She snapped it out, whip sharp.

"Yeah, they did that, but—"

"Do you understand your rights and obligations in these matters?"

"I understand that, but I don't understand anything else. I need to talk to Elva. Nobody will let me talk to her."

"We might be able to arrange that later." Peabody chose the brisk, all-business cop. "Right now, you need to talk to us."

Peabody opened a file. "How long have you known Elva Arnez?"

"Nineteen months. And two weeks," he added.

"And how, in that amount of time, did she convince you to kill Captain Greenleaf and his son, Benjamin Greenleaf?"

"She—how—" He pressed his lips together. Hugged his elbows. "That's crazy! That's just batshit. She'd never, never do that. Elva's a beautiful soul, a—a tender heart."

Peabody folded her hands over the file. "Are you claiming you convinced her to murder these people?"

"We didn't kill anybody! I don't know how—why," he corrected, "you'd say something like that. We were friends with Martin and Ben."

"Makes it worse, doesn't it, Lieutenant? Even worse that these two shit stains would use friendship, a family that opened their homes to them, in order to kill."

"It does. What do you figure, Detective? Two consecutive life terms, off-planet? They could actually end up with three."

"I figure the three. Either way, neither of them will ever get out of a cage. An off-planet cage."

"We didn't do anything! It's whacked, totally whacked you think we did."

Obviously shaken, he leaned forward as if desperate to explain.

"Jesus, Elva wasn't even there when Martin died. You *know* that. And you're trying to say murder when it was suicide. Because he was a cop, like you. And Beth won't get the insurance money if you say he killed himself. We're sorry it happened, but—"

He broke off, jolted when Peabody shoved to her feet. "Bullshit!" She tossed crime scene printouts on the table. He winced, looked away.

"What? You're shy about looking at your handiwork? Can't look at the dead body of a man you called friend? You think we don't know what we're doing? You really think we're so stupid we'd buy your half-assed setup?"

"I don't know what you're talking about." A line of sweat dribbled down his left temple, and his gaze jumped everywhere except for the photos of the dead.

"Really? Then I'll walk your lying ass through it. Your Elva unlocked the bedroom window in your *friend's* apartment. And when she gave you the all clear—we've got your 'links, asshole—you went down the fire escape, went through the window. You walked through the apartment where you'd been welcomed, put a stunner on high against your *friend's* throat, and murdered him in cold blood."

"That's crazy." And while sweat continued to roll, he began to shudder as if he sat in a brisk winter wind. "You'll never prove that because it's crazy. Martin killed himself. It's sad, but it's—"

"You put his fingers on the weapon, dropped it, just like Elva told you. But you're idiots who know squat about basic science and forensics. Look how clear these two prints are on the weapon."

Peabody jabbed her finger on the crime scene shot.

"No prints to show he'd handled the weapon, no prints to show he'd checked or set the weapon on high. What, you think we'd buy he'd wiped the stunner clean before he used it?"

"He—he must have. He—"

"Bullshit. Just two prints, so clear and pristine on the weapon? Couldn't be clear and pristine, physically impossible, with a self-termination."

"I don't understand what—"

"Damn right you don't, even though you stood there and watched him convulse, you don't understand. That's why you fucked it up.

"How did it feel?" she demanded. "How did it feel to jam that stunner against his throat, jam it hard, hold it there while his body convulsed? While you watched him die. How did it feel?"

Tears streamed to plop like rain on the table. "No. I didn't."

"Yes, you did. You jammed that stunner so hard, held it there so the probes lacerated the skin. Did it seem quick to you, those few seconds it took?"

Squeezing his eyes shut, Robards shook his head.

"And when his body stopped convulsing, you pressed his fingers to the weapon for those two clear, perfect prints, just like Elva told you. You wrote what she'd told you to write. Then you went back upstairs, signaled her it was done, just like she told you. You didn't know Detective Webster was coming, didn't know we'd discover his body so quickly. You barely missed each other."

She circled the table, stood behind him. "Even that wouldn't have mattered because you're *stupid.*"

"And cruel," Eve murmured.

"Oh yeah, can't forget the cruel. You left him there for the woman who'd loved him for decades and decades to find. The woman who'd cooked for you, invited you to family dinners, holidays. You wanted to hurt her."

Tears ran down his face, mixed with the sweat. "I never wanted to hurt Beth!"

"But you had to, didn't you? You had to hurt Beth to give Elva what she wanted. I mean, hell, what choice did you have? But even that wasn't enough. You stood at the captain's memorial, pretending to feel grief—you don't have feelings. And in his daughter's home, you used a child—a *child*—to try to kill his son."

"No. No. You don't know that. You're just making things up. That's what cops do."

Peabody tossed a photo of the rope taken from the kitchen closet. "We found this in your apartment."

"I—it's just some rope."

"It's cut from the rope used when you tried to hang Ben Greenleaf."

"It's not."

"It is. Our lab verified." Not yet, Peabody thought, but they would. "Oh, and how about these? You had these in your closet."

She set the two 'links on the table.

"I . . ."

"Where did you get them?"

"I just found them. I found them."

"Really, you found this one in Dory Greenleaf's little purse, on the bar in the family room of her aunt's house? And this one? You just happened to find that in her father's pocket before you put a noose around his neck?"

"No, no, I . . . found them on the street."

"When?"

"Yesterday, I think."

"You think?" she snapped out. "You think?"

"Yesterday!" Terror in his eyes, he shouted it. "I found them yesterday."

"When yesterday? Where exactly on the street?"

"I . . ."

"Quick! Two disabled 'links that just happen to belong to the man you tried to murder and his daughter. Where, when, how?"

"I don't know! I want to talk to Elva!"

"You're not going to talk to Elva. Maybe, just maybe, when she's in the women's lockup off-planet and you're in the men's, they'll let you write love letters to each other."

"She's not going to prison. You can't do that to her. You won't!"

"Oh, yes. Yes, she is. Yes, we can and, yes, we will. She planned it all out, she told you just what to do, and you obeyed like a lovesick puppy. You did this for a woman who doesn't love you. She still loves the boy who died nearly ten years ago."

"That's a lie!" Fury burned through the tears, and the hands he'd clutched together pounded on the table. "You're a liar, like all cops are liars. We're going to get married. We're going to make a family."

"No conjugal visits between inmates off-planet. Tell us how it went down, Denzel. Maybe we can work it so you do the time on-planet, so your mother, your sisters can visit. She's going down, no way to change that."

"She's not! She didn't do anything. I—I did it all. I killed Martin—you're covering it up. You're covering up everything he did to ruin her life. I hung Ben. I did it all. She had nothing to do with it. She didn't even know."

"Is that right? How'd you get the window open? How'd you manage to lift a hundred-and-eighty-five-pound unconscious man up to hang him? Where'd you get the service weapon?"

Tears still ran, but he folded his lips. "I did what I did. I'm not saying anything else. I killed Martin and I tried to kill Ben. Elva wasn't part of it."

"You're going to take the fall for a woman who doesn't love you. Who used you to do her dirty work."

"She loves me. I saved her. That's all I'm going to say."

"Your white charger looks really tired, Denzel. Interview end."

As he laid his head on the table and wept, they stepped out.

"Good work, mean-ass Peabody."

Peabody rubbed at the back of her neck. "I started feeling sorry for him—but I didn't let it stop me. It's what you expected him to do."

"Yeah. We can trip him up on the details later, because none of it's going to hold. Have him taken back down; have her brought up. Seriously, good work."

"Thanks."

Reo stepped out of Observation with Mira.

"A fool for love," she said.

"And a killer with it."

"He didn't plan any of it." Mira walked with Eve as she stared holes through a vending machine. "He's a follower. And he feels remorse."

"She won't. I don't trust this machine. Or any of them. I'm getting a cold drink from my AC."

"Allow me. You're handing me a solid case on two cop killers. What'll it be?" Reo asked.

"Pepsi."

"Remorse or not"—Reo plugged in coins—"he's going off-planet, and he'll never get out." She handed the tube to Eve.

"Thanks."

"Peabody kicked butt in there."

"She's got it in her. Somebody like him though? It costs her some."

She cracked the tube, drank deep.

"You, too," Mira said.

"No, doesn't cost me. I'm just tired of the whole fucking mess. It's so senseless. A lot of them are, but this? She's spent nearly ten years of her life plotting and planning and calculating how to murder, to revenge a dirty cop and a boy who didn't love her. Any more than she loves the stupid fuck who killed for her.

"I need to set up for Arnez."

As she walked to her office, she pulled out her 'link.

"We have them," she said to Webster without preamble.

"You made an arrest?"

"Two. Have one confession—half bullshit. We're about to bring the second into Interview. If you want to observe, get here."

"Who?"

"The Greenleafs' friends and upstairs neighbors. I don't have time to brief you, Webster. Interview B, Observation. Hear it for yourself."

She cut him off, and cooled her throat with Pepsi.

She'd take a few minutes to collect herself, she thought. Just level off. Maybe, as usual, Mira had it right. Maybe the interview with Robards had cost her—a little.

But mostly it infuriated her.

She could go into the box with Arnez pissed off. As long as the anger held well under the surface. The job wasn't about her feelings, but about law, about justice.

So she'd take a few minutes to collect herself, to drink the damn Pepsi, to stand at her window and look out at New York.

Street traffic snarled, and the airtrams glided by. Drivers, passengers heading home after the workday. Her work wasn't done, but when it was, she'd go home. And she'd shake it all off.

One more time.

She didn't hear him come, not when he moved, always, like the cat burglar he'd been. But she sensed him as he stepped into her office.

He angled his head, those wild blue eyes on her face. "You don't look like a woman who was right all along and made two arrests."

"I am a woman who was right and made two arrests. I've got Arnez and her lawyer coming up to Interview. I'm finished with Robards."

"I'm sorry I missed it."

"Don't be. He's pathetic, pitiful. He's an idiot." She set the tube down before she hurled it.

"I had Peabody take him. She did good. She broke him."

"All right."

"It was all there. All of it." She walked to her comp when it signaled. "Including this. Lab report on the rope we found in the goddamn kitchen closet of their apartment. Rope cut from the length they used to try to hang Ben Greenleaf. He had their 'links—Ben's and his kid's—in his closet. Not the bedroom, because that closet's all hers. The home office closet where he keeps his clothes, and pictures of his family because she doesn't want to see them.

"And what does he do when Peabody breaks him? When tears are running down his face? He claims Arnez had nothing to do with it, no knowledge of it. He did it all on his own. Just him, in his shiny, blood-streaked armor."

"You won't let that stand."

"Fucking A. It's all her, just like that apartment's all her. They live where she wanted, how she wanted. He can have his things, as long as she doesn't have to see them. She has a man who loves her enough to kill for her, and she uses that. You better believe she recognized that and exploited it. And she uses him to kill, to exact revenge for a dirty, corrupt cop who couldn't face the consequences, and a boy who decided he'd rather blame everyone else and die."

She shut her eyes. "The boy didn't have to die. Shouldn't have died. But nobody saw he was on the edge, not even the mother who loved him and was trying so hard to hold her family together."

She opened eyes full of rage and pity. "And Arnez, because she couldn't see past it, kept him on the edge with her drumbeat of payback. Her need to be the one the boy turned to, held on to.

"The boy didn't love her; the man she used to kill did. It didn't matter. Doesn't matter. She'd let the man who loves her take the fall for her. I won't."

Saying nothing, Roarke stepped to her, put his arms around her.

"I'm fine. I'm okay."

"You will be."

"Robards loves her. Instead of saying, 'Sorry, don't feel the same,' so he could move on, or building a real life with him, she uses him to get what she wants. What she's wanted for almost ten years. Now he'll spend the rest of his life in a cage."

"You'll see she does as well. I've no doubt you're right and she used and exploited his feelings for and about her. But he chose, Eve."

"He chose." Nodding, she drew back. "His life, as he knew it, is over. Now it's her turn."

"Go take her down, Lieutenant."

She walked back to Interview B. "Ready, Peabody?"

"Ready. Her lawyer's Marcelle Congera. I did a quick search and she's low-rent. She's handled some misdemeanors—public intoxication, disturbing the peace, and a bunch of civil suits. Nothing heavy."

"Let's make sure Arnez gets what she paid for."

"You don't want me to take her."

"Not this time. She's mine."

Eve opened the door. "Record on," she began, and read the details for the record before she sat.

If she felt a smug little thrill seeing Arnez in the orange jumpsuit, well . . . she could be petty.

The lawyer wore a pale blue suit. About forty, Eve judged, with a long, thin neck, her shoulder-length black hair swept back from a sharp-featured, disapproving face.

"You humiliated my client at her place of employment, an act that could cost her her position, and did so in your aggressive attempt to find a scapegoat over a retired police officer's death. We intend to pursue a civil suit."

"Oh, well, in that case . . . Bring it. Your client will be pursuing her bullshit civil suit from a cage on Omega."

"Don't be ridiculous." Congera pursed her thin lips. "I intend to file a motion of dismissal, all charges, and another for false arrest."

"File all the motions you want—but I'd get a solid retainer before I did any work. I've got this feeling, Peabody—do you have this feeling?—that Ms. Congera's client hasn't been fully truthful and forthcoming with her legal representative."

"I share that feeling."

"For instance," Eve said, "I wonder if Ms. Congera's client disclosed that she had a close connection to Louis Noy and his family—including his son, Brice. She sure as hell didn't disclose same when questioned after Captain Greenleaf's murder."

"I fail to see—"

"Then get your eyes fixed," Eve suggested. "Captain Greenleaf investigated Louis Noy—formerly Captain Louis Noy of the NYPSD—for corruption, extortion, witness and evidence tampering, among other things."

"That's hardly—"

"Not quite finished. Louis Noy killed himself, at his desk, in his home office, with his service weapon. Brice Noy, at nineteen, hanged himself. They remembered you—Ellie—Ella and Taylor Noy remembered you very well. Funny you didn't mention this connection."

"Why would I? It was years ago. They were acquaintances. How would I possibly know Martin investigated Captain Noy? Why would I care?"

"Acquaintances?" She took out the prom photo, the pre-served corsage.

"They've been through my things, my personal things." Fury rose red and hot over Arnez's cheeks. Her eyes blazed with it.

"A duly executed search." Eve set the warrant on the table. "And look here. You even kept the prom dress." Eve plopped the bagged dress on the table. "And oh, here's another thing." She took out the sealed 'link. "Tags and texts on this old model you kept in your treasure box."

"Those are my personal property. You have no right to my personal property." She rounded on Congera. "Fix this!"

"A duly executed search," Eve repeated. "Tags and texts between you and Brice Noy. Intense tags and texts after his father's disgrace, after the suicide. You knew who Martin Greenleaf was when you moved into the building."

Congera looked a bit off-balance, but she rallied. "Souvenirs from nearly a decade ago are hardly evidence of a crime. Any more than my client's acquaintance with someone Martin Greenleaf once investigated is evidence of a crime. You've overreached, Lieutenant."

"They went through my things." Arnez pounded a hand on the table. "Do something! Do your job."

"Ms. Arnez." Congera patted her arm as if to soothe. "They had a warrant, but this? This means nothing. Mementos from your teenage years. They're reaching."

"Yeah, we reached into that treasure box and found all these photos. Lots of them—all of the Noy family. Nobody else but you and the Noy family. No other friends, no other families, teachers, pets, whatever. Just you and your . . . acquaintances."

"If this is all you have, Lieutenant, I'll go file my motion to dismiss."

"I wouldn't be too hasty," Eve warned as Congera started to rise. "You want something more current? Let's see what we have in our NYPSD treasure box. What do you think, Peabody?"

"Oh yeah." Peabody nodded when Eve took out the photos. "Those are gold."

"I can't show you the actual ropes, as they're on their way into Evidence from the lab. Got the lab report right here though. See this length of rope? That's the one used to hang Ben Greenleaf in his sister's home at their father's memorial. And this one?"

Eve nudged them both over. "That's the rope we found in your client's kitchen closet during our duly authorized search. As you see in the lab report, same rope, and the cuts on the end of each? Perfect match."

"I've never seen that rope before. I wasn't even there when Ben was attacked."

"Sure you were, because you attacked him. How about these?" Eve took out the two 'links. "This one you took out of Ben's pocket after you bashed him in the head with his niece's baseball trophy. And this one? His daughter's, the one you took from her purse and used to text him, as if from her, to lure him upstairs so you could kill him."

"These are outrageous accusations." But Congera no longer looked convinced.

"I've never seen those 'links. Obviously they planted them. Fix this! You fix this or you're fired!"

"We're not Louis Noy," Eve snapped. "The dirty cop you made into a hero, a daddy substitute. And you were there. You shut down the security, stole the kid's 'link, said your goodbyes before you slipped upstairs. Texted Ben, knocked him unconscious from behind, and, while he was out, put the noose around his neck, left him hanging. You went out through the master bedroom, the terrace doors, and out through the side gate.

"The trouble?" Eve continued. "Webster, again. He went up to check on Ben, found him, saved his life."

"I was nowhere near Carlie's house when Ben was attacked. Denzel will swear to that."

"Well . . ." Eve shrugged. "He had his chance, didn't. We already interviewed him."

"Then he's *lying*! Lying to protect himself. If he's done these horrible things, it's not my fault."

"Huh. If he's lying and he tried to kill Ben, how could he have done it alone if you were together?"

Arnez's eyes flicked once before she dug in. "After we left the memorial, Denzel told me to go on home, that he had to run a few errands. I had a terrible headache, so I went home, took a sleeping pill."

She'd bury him without a second's hesitation, Eve thought. Because it's all about her.

"I wonder why the security cams at your apartment building don't show you coming home alone. I wonder why they show both you and Robards entering the building, together, less than thirty minutes after Ben was attacked."

"I—I meant I took a walk to try to clear my head." Casting her eyes down, she rubbed her temple. "It's been a terrible few days. I took a walk, and Denzel caught up with me. Then I went in, took the pill."

"So, somehow he doubled back—on his own—went back into the house, set Ben up, bashed him, then managed—on his own—to haul a hundred-and-eighty-five-pound unconscious man a foot off the ground. Then he left, and miraculously ran into you in time for the two of you to enter the apartment building together."

"I'm not saying he did any of that. I'm saying I didn't. I certainly didn't kill Martin. I was with Beth and the others."

"It's interesting, I think, that ninety-eight seconds after security shows you leaving the building on the night of Martin Greenleaf's murder, you texted Robards. *All clear*, you texted. We have your 'links, too."

"So what? Just letting him know we were on our way to the bar."

"Right. And also interesting, some seven minutes after time of death, Robards texted you. *It's done*. You answered with a heart emoji."

"I . . . I'd asked him to tidy up. He'd left a mess, and I was annoyed. He just wanted me to know he'd done that."

"Obviously, my client has already proven she was elsewhere when Captain Greenleaf was killed. Therefore—"

"You unlocked the window. You know Beth's habits— you've made a point to. Into the bedroom, and she's fussing with shoes. Unlock the window with access to the fire escape. You text the all clear. Robards texts you it's done."

"You can't prove any of that. It's absurd."

"You used one of Noy's drop weapons. Did he give it to you—for protection maybe—the way he slipped you money now and again? Men like him like to buy loyalty. He sure bought yours."

"Say nothing, Ms. Arnez. Lieutenant, I want to consult with my client."

"He never loved you. Brice never loved you."

Eve said it quietly, and saw it hit home.

"He didn't keep a box with photos of you, of mementos to take out and look at, and think of you. He brought you home because he felt sorry for you—"

"Liar. Liar."

"He liked people, liked being with them, helping them. He liked girls. He didn't like you the way he liked other girls—so many of them. You must've hated them, the girls he spent time with instead of spending it with you."

"You don't know anything about it."

"I think I do. He took you to the prom." Eve laid a hand on the dress. "And told his sister he was taking you because you didn't have any friends. A pity date."

"That's a lie." She hissed it out. "You didn't know Brice. You don't know anything about him."

"I've been getting to know the boy he was, so handsome, so bright. Kind. A boy from a happy family with a father at the head of it. You wanted him, wanted that family, that father. So you stuck, you had a goal. Brice was the goal."

"Lieutenant," Congera interrupted. "This is pure speculation."

"Conclusions based on evidence. You inserted yourself into his family to achieve that goal—and maybe found something in Noy you didn't have. That daddy figure. You inserted yourself into the Greenleaf family because you had a goal. Kill Captain Greenleaf, make it look like suicide, mirror your hero. Pay Greenleaf back. Not finished yet. Kill the son, mirror the boy you loved, pay them all back.

"Kill a good man, try to kill his son, all in memory of a boy who never loved you. He just felt sorry for you."

"He *did* love me! You know *nothing*. Brice loved me. We were soul mates. We were going to get married, have a family. He was *everything* to me."

Sitting back, Eve smiled. "That sounds like a lot more than an acquaintance."

"Ms. Arnez—Elva—please don't say anything else. Let me—"

Arnez smacked Congera's hand away.

"She's not going to get away with saying those lies. Martin Greenleaf destroyed the best man I ever knew. He destroyed my *family*! He killed the only one I'll ever love. And for what? For what? For his rules, his regulations, his righteous line of right and wrong? Why should he have a life? Why should he have a happy family? Where is mine?"

"You used one of Noy's drop weapons. Did he give it to you or did you take it?"

"I took it. Why shouldn't I have something? His wife, his daughter, all they could do was cry. They were *ashamed* of Louis. Ashamed. I stood up for him. Brice and I stood up for him. I was more a daughter to him than that sniveling little brat. And his wife? Saint fucking Ella? She just forgets him, forgets him and her own son? Marries someone else. They can go to hell, just like Greenleaf."

"You planned it all out, the timing, the method. Did Denzel help with that?"

"Denzel can't plan his way out of a grease-soaked job in someone else's garage. I gave my father and the man I love justice."

It was all there, Eve thought, all there in that striking face. The fury, the hate, all the bitter years of them.

"Step one, get an apartment in the building. Step two, become friends. That leads to step three, get to know the family, earn their affection and trust, learn their routines. It really pissed you off when Ella Noy married Cal Rosen. She didn't even invite you to the wedding."

"As if I'd have gone. Love is forever. She disgraced herself and the memory of her husband, her son. I thought better of her. I was wrong. She tossed them aside. Well, I didn't."

"How did you talk Denzel into going along with murder?"

"Not murder. Justice. He understands what Martin did, how he destroyed my family. He'll do anything for me."

"I'm withdrawing as counsel for Ms. Arnez. Ms. Arnez, I advise you to remain silent and consult another attorney immediately."

"Oh, fuck you. You had one job and couldn't do it."

"Former counsel for Ms. Arnez exiting Interview," Eve said. "You're entitled to legal representation."

"And I'll do better next time. Much better. I did what needed to be done, and I'll find a lawyer who'll make that clear. Louis and Brice would be proud of me."

We'll play that tune, Eve thought.

"I'm sure Louis Noy would be proud, proud of how well you planned it out. You chose a night you'd have an unassailable alibi," Eve began. "You unlocked the bedroom window to give Robards, your partner, access to Captain Greenleaf's apartment."

"Yes, yes, yes."

"When you sent the all clear, Robards entered by that unlocked window via the fire escape. He used the weapon you'd taken from Noy after Noy's death, and killed Martin Greenleaf. He left the drop piece, after putting the captain's prints on it, wrote the suicide note, and exited by the same window."

"This is boring," Arnez decided.

"Won't take much longer. The glitch in the plan. Detective Webster, who arrived shortly after, and brought me into it. And we're there when you return with the widow. You can't get back into the bedroom and lock the window."

"It was perfect. It should've been perfect. It didn't matter about the damn lock. I wasn't there."

"Since the suicide plan didn't work, you felt you needed to move on Ben quickly. Is that right?"

"Why wait? Let's not waste time now, either. Denzel shut down the security. I got the little brat's 'link, sent the whiny text after we got upstairs. Daddy came right along. Bang on the head—that was my pleasure. String the asshole up, go out—you figured out how. That should've worked, too. He should be dead, like my Brice."

"The rope, the 'links?"

"Oversights. We weren't suspects, should never have been looked at twice. How did you connect me to Louis and Brice?"

"We're cops. We do our job."

"Captain Louis Noy was a cop, and would've crushed you like a bug."

Now Eve smiled. "You're welcome to think so. Maybe it'll get you through the first few decades in an off-planet cage."

"I levied justice for two good men. My father and my lover. No one who's ever loved would convict me."

"Here's a media bulletin," Eve said as she rose. "Noy was neither a good man nor your father. The subject has confessed on record, all charges. Have her taken down, Peabody. She's entitled to other legal representation if she chooses. Interview End."

As she walked to the door, Eve glanced back.

Yeah, she thought. She could be petty.

"I bet Brice Noy never banged you. Not even a pity bang."

Arnez looked at her with dead eyes. "I'll kill you one day."

"You go right ahead and believe that. Maybe it'll get you through the decades after the first few."

Epilogue

After stepping out, Eve walked down to Observation. Whitney came out first.

"Good work, Lieutenant."

"Thank you, sir."

"Damn good work," he said as he walked away.

Reo just shook her head. "You sure made it easy for me."

"She made it easy for both of us. She's got some ego."

"Malignant narcissists usually do," Mira commented. "'He didn't love you.' You turned the key in that lock, and she couldn't let those words stand."

Darcia stepped up, offered a hand. "Thank you."

"It's the job. You know that as well as I do."

"I do, and thank you anyway."

"Can I have a minute?" Webster asked Eve, then looked at Roarke. "Can I have a minute, private, in her office?"

"That would be up to the lieutenant."

"Sure."

"I don't know how Martin missed it," he began as they walked. "How he missed what was inside Arnez. Except—I didn't see it when I met her. I didn't see it in Observation, not until you were well into it. But you did."

"Her guard was down when you opened the door that night. I saw something. I'm getting coffee. You want?"

"No, I'm not going to keep you. I'd like to tell the family, if that's good for you."

"No problem. Webster, if you hadn't been there, I wouldn't have been there. I wouldn't have seen. If you hadn't been there, Ben would be dead. Remember that."

"Yeah. Well. I'm going to go tell the family. And I wanted to . . . I wanted to tell you goodbye. With this done, I'm going to go back to Olympus with Darcia next week. Start my life with her."

"I'm going to say good luck. And not in a snotty way. I mean it."

"I know it. Don't kick my ass for this," he said, and hugged her. "Thanks," he murmured, then pulled away. "And I mean that. New York's in good hands, Lieutenant."

When he walked out, she went to her window, took a long breath. And turned when Roarke came in.

"Webster and Angelo are going to go for it on Olympus, starting next week."

"Darcia told me. I think they'll be very happy together."

"Looks that way."

He brushed a hand over her hair. "And you?"

"I went into Interview pissed, had a headache starting to bang from the pissed. But in there? I could see how to . . . turn the key in the lock, like Mira said. And I stopped being pissed, and just did the job."

She glanced back at the board. "Almost done now. Just have to deal with the paperwork. That's the job, too."

"I'll wait while you write this up. Then we'll go home, have some wine. Shake this week off."

Shake it off, she thought. That'd been her plan.

"You know what I think?"

"I'm always interested."

"I'm thinking, and I'm wondering about that pub you've got—the one with the snug thing we all went to during the Dawber case, with the burgers. Feeney's all about their fish and chips."

"I remember, yes."

"I'm wondering if we could do that, go there, in the snug part like we did. Whoever's up for it in the bullpen, Feeney, McNab, Reo maybe—I think I still owe her some drinks. The Miras if they wanted. Maybe tag up Morris. I think I'd like a couple hours and a couple beers with good cops and the people who work with them. I think I could really use that."

"It's a wonder to me that I find I'd enjoy a couple hours with good cops as well. I'll arrange it."

"Thanks." She slid her arms around him, rested her head on his shoulder. "I know what love is," she murmured, then drew back to cup his face. "And it's not what drove her to kill. This is love," she said, and kissed him.

"It is. Yesterday, today, tomorrow. It is."

"I'm going to write this up, close it down, put it away. Maybe you could round up whoever wants in on burgers, beer, and whatever."

"I'll do that. And echo your commander. Good work, Lieutenant."

"I didn't do it alone," she said as he left. She'd had good cops and the people who work with them.

Now she sat to finish the job, and put it away.

Author's Note

Suicide rates in the United States continue to rise. It's a tragedy that not only cuts a life short, but leaves behind grieving loved ones, friends, and neighbors.

The 988 Suicide & Crisis Lifeline offers free, confidential help all day, every day. If you or someone you know is at risk, please call or text 988 and reach out to someone who wants to help.

Read on for an excerpt from

RANDOM IN DEATH

by J. D. Robb

Available soon in hardcover from
St. Martin's Press

Prologue

Gimme Avenue A 'cause they slay.

Pleased with the rhythm in her head, Jenna Harbough rocked her hips to the beat.

They may be old, but they rock and they roll.

Probably they wouldn't like the "old" bit, but from her sixteen-year-old perspective, anyone heading toward, like, forty or whatever hit *old*.

I mean, jeez, even her parents liked their music. Which was why they'd agreed to let Jenna come, with her two besties, to the club to hear them live and in freaking person.

Avenue A played twice a year at Club Rock It, and for one night in the summer Rock It locked up the alcohol and opened the club to the under-twenty-one crowd.

Anyone who knew their music history was up on how back in the long-gone day, like in the 2040s (talk about old!), Avenue A had their first real gig at Club Rock It. So they paid that back twice a year, even though they were totally rock gods *EXTREME* who played for sold-out crowds in stadiums and huge concert halls.

Though she'd campaigned to go on this once-a-year night for three years, she'd gotten the absolute, no-way no. Until this time!

Now she danced with Leelee and Chelsea while Avenue A *slayed* with "Baby, Do Me Right."

And she danced close enough to the stage that she could see the sweat on Jake Kincade's face. For an old guy, he was still looking frosty extreme. Maybe because he was really tall. She liked the way the lights hit the blue streaks in his black hair—and how they sort of matched his eyes.

Dr-ream-y!

But more, she loved how his fingers just freaking flew over the guitar strings.

One day hers would do that. She knew she'd improved. She practiced every day, and knew, just *knew*, one day she'd stand onstage and slay the crowd with her music.

She had a demo disc in her purse. Her biggest dream of the night involved finding a way to get it into Jake Kincade's hands. She'd only put one song on it, the best she'd written, and she'd worked really hard on the demo.

Maybe it wasn't all studio slick and professional, but you had to start somewhere. And the guys of Avenue A had been about her age when they really got going, so, maybe.

They segued into "It's Always Now," a classic crowd-pleaser, and more people swarmed the dance floor.

Jenna didn't mind—the more the better. And she was so caught up in the music.

Then, just for a second, for one tiny second, Jake's eyes met hers. He smiled; she died.

On a squeal, she grabbed Leelee's hand.

"He looked at me!"

"What?"

Then she grabbed Chelsea's hand as Jenna's face flushed so deep she felt the heat in her toes. "Jake Kincade looked right at me. He smiled at me!"

"On the real?" Chelsea demanded.

"So on it! Holy shitfire!"

She bounced and bopped with her friends to the last song of the set.

"Me and a rock god locked eyes. We had a moment."

"You've gotta find a way to get him your demo, Jenna. You totally smashed it," Leelee assured her.

"Maybe I could—Ow!" When something stung her arm, she closed a hand over it. Some guy shot her a hard grin and the middle finger before he melted into the crowd.

"Asshole jabbed me!" Then forgot him and just danced.

"I've got to sit a minute," she said when the song ended. "Make a plan, and—Whoa, I'm sort of floaty. That look!"

"I'm dying." Chelsea put a hand on her throat, stuck out her tongue. "Need sweet, fizzy hydration."

"Go, grab our seats, Jenna, and we'll get drinks. We'll help with the plan."

"Solid."

She felt a little woozy as she tried to get through to their tiny table. Floaty, she thought.

Then the heat came back, but like a million degrees. As she tried to breathe it away, she rubbed at her arm where it felt like a big, pissed-off hornet had taken a bite.

Need that sweet, fizzy hydration, she thought. But then her stomach cramped, and terrified she'd puke and humiliate herself, she tried to bolt to the bathroom.

Jake swiped at sweat as the band's drummer, Mac, grinned at him. "We still got it, boss."

"Ain't never gonna lose it. I'm going out to catch some air. Jesus, you'd think Harve and Glo could get a decent temp control in here."

"And lose this ambiance?" Renn, keyboard, tossed Jake a tube of water.

"Thanks. Back in five."

He glanced out at the crowd as he had during the last song in the set, but still didn't see Nadine. Probably headed for the john—and good luck with that, he thought.

She earned big points for coming with him tonight. Rock It wasn't a dive or a dump, but as clubs went, it clung to its Alphabet City roots.

Never going to be fancy, never going upscale. And proud of it.

But his ace reporter, bestselling writer, fucking Oscar-winning lady had come on a night that remained important to him and his friends, his bandmates.

It reminded them of their roots, their beginnings. And just how far they'd come.

He made his way through the back of the house—such as it was—and slipped out the alley door.

And breathed.

Even in the sweltering summer of 2061, the air outside blew cooler than in.

He cracked the tube, drank deep.

He smelled the overstuffed recycler, but that didn't bother him. It, too, reminded him of his roots, the skinny, gangly kid from Avenue A who'd worked after school and weekends to save enough for his first guitar.

He'd written music when he should've been studying because the music had been first and last for him. Always.

He remembered busking in subway tunnels with Leon, then Leon and Renn, before they'd hit fifteen. And watching Mac play the drums at their high school's band concert. Then Art slid right in, and they became Avenue A.

Practicing in the storage room of the apartment building, then in Mac's uncle's garage.

Then fast-talking Harve into letting them play, just one gig, before they were old enough to buy a beer.

That one gig turned into two weeks that summer, and ended with a recording contract.

So yeah, an important night to him. Avenue A had a lot of beginnings—that first guitar, Mac's uncle letting his nephew bang away on an old drum set. His mom telling him to grab a dream and ride it.

A lot of beginnings, and Club Rock It ranked high.

He started to turn to the door, but it flew open. A girl stumbled out.

The kid had a mass of pink-tipped brown hair and wore a tiny black skirt with a midriff-baring red top. Her face was white as chalk, her big brown eyes glassy.

She said, "I got sick."

"That's okay, honey. It happens."

Glo might have been vigilant about keeping the club alcohol and drug free on the underage nights, but kids found a way.

He sure as hell had.

"Let's get you back inside. There's a place you can sit down in the quiet, have some Sober-Up."

"Not drunk. Can't breathe right. He jabbed me! He jabbed me!"

Jake reached for her arm. Then her eyes rolled up white.

He caught her before she hit the pavement.

"Who jabbed you?" As he spoke, he noted her face wasn't white but slightly blue. She shook with cold.

A needle mark, red and raw, stood out on her left biceps.

"Goddamn it. Jesus." He yanked out his 'link as he lowered to the ground with her. Hit emergency. "I need an ambulance." He rattled off the address while he checked the girl's pulse.

Weak, he thought as he struggled not to panic. And getting weaker.

"You stay with me now. Look at me, okay? Look at me."

For a moment her eyes fixed on him. But blindly.

"Come on now, hold on. Help's coming. What's your name, baby? Tell me your name."

But he felt her go as he sat on the alley floor and cradled her in his arms.

Laying her down, he started CPR.

The alley door opened again. "Hey, Guitar Hero, Mac said—Oh my God, what happened?"

Nadine dropped down beside him.

"She's not breathing. I can't get her back. Her arm, look at her arm. She said someone jabbed her."

"I'll get an ambulance."

"On the way. Her arm. Needle mark. Only junkies who can't score a pressure syringe use needles. She's not a junkie. Come on, kid, come back. Fucking come back."

Beside him, Nadine looked at the needle mark, looked at the staring brown eyes of the girl on the ground.

She didn't tell him to stop the CPR, but laid one hand on his back as she took out her 'link.

"Jake, I'm tagging Dallas."

When he looked at Nadine, the despair simply covered him. "She's just a kid."

One, Nadine thought, who wouldn't get any older.

1

When Lieutenant Eve Dallas wasn't working a case, Saturday evenings often meant a vid, popcorn, and sex. With a Summerset-free house, as Roarke's major domo and the hitch in her stride had the night out with friends—whoever *they* were—the sex portion of the evening arrived early in the game room.

She'd bet Roarke she could beat him two out of three in pinball. She lost.

Or did she?

In any case, after dinner on the patio, a walk through the gardens, sex in the game room, they settled down on the sofa, with the cat curled at their feet.

She had Roarke, popcorn, wine, and an action vid with plenty of bangs and booms to cap off a Saturday at home.

Knowing Roarke, she expected a second round of sex as an encore.

And that suited her just fine.

He talked now and then of adding a media room to the castle he'd built in the heart of New York City. But she liked this routine, stretched out or curled up together on the sofa in their bedroom sitting area with the cat purring in his sleep and her husband's excellent body warm against hers.

Her life had taken a radical turn when he'd walked into it, she thought. She'd never get all the way used to it. Before Roarke, her life had been the job, and the job had been her life.

Now she had two things she'd never expected, never looked for.

Love and a home.

And those two things, she'd come to realize, made her better at the job, better at running her division, better at standing for the dead.

At a pause in the action, he reached over for the bottle, topped off both their glasses.

"We're going through a lot of wine, pal."

"Safe and snug at home." The mists of Ireland wove through his voice. "Something I intend to take advantage of in a bit of time."

"Is that so? Freeze screen," she ordered, and rolled on top of him.

So ridiculously gorgeous, she thought, with the carved-by-benevolent-gods face, the sculpted mouth, the wildly blue eyes. "No time like the right now."

She took that sculpted mouth, slid her free hand into the mane of black that framed his face.

Roarke set his glass beside the bottle, then nipped hers out of her hand to do the same.

She laughed as he flipped her over, and with a grumble, Galahad slid off the couch.

Then his hands were on her, slipping under her baggy Saturday-at-home T-shirt. And as the kiss turned greedy, she felt her need, the wine, the moment tie together in a single perfect thrill.

Nipping at his jaw, she worked her hands between them to flip open the button of his jeans.

Her 'link signaled.

"Oh, come on!"

Roarke angled his head to read the display on her 'link. "It's Nadine."

"Fine. I'll get back to her. Eventually."

But when she started to pull him down again, he shook his head.

"Eve, how often does Nadine tag you on a Saturday night near to eleven?"

"Never. Shit. Damn it."

When he eased away, she sat up, grabbed the 'link.

"Unless somebody's dead, I—"

"She is. I'm sorry, Dallas, we need you. We're at Club Rock It, the alley behind the club. Ah, it's on Avenue A, but I don't know the address."

"Who is she?"

"I don't know. A girl, teenage girl. Jake—they're play-ing a special under-twenty-one thing. I came out—alley at the back—and he was doing CPR. He'd called an am-bulance. The MTs just got here. He said she said someone jabbed her."

Eve's brown eyes went from mildly annoyed to cop flat. "She's stabbed?"

"No, no, a needle mark, on her arm. Or maybe a really thin blade. It wasn't really bleeding, but it looked raw."

"Tell the MTs not to move the body. I'm calling it in, and uniforms will respond, secure the scene. I'm on my way."

"Thanks," Nadine began, but Eve cut her off.

She noted Roarke had brought out brown khakis and a jacket, a navy tank, boots, belt.

She didn't complain about him picking out her clothes as she grabbed her communicator and called it in.

"You didn't tell them to notify Peabody."

Eve tugged the baggy summer Saturday shorts off long legs, pulled on the khakis. "No point screwing up her night until I know what it is." She dragged on the tank, then shoved at her choppy brown hair. "Sorry it screwed up ours."

"Lieutenant, it's what we do. She sounded frazzled," he added as he changed his shirt. "She rarely does."

"Yeah, I caught that."

She moved quickly, efficiently, a long, lean woman with an angular face, a shallow dent in the chin, and her mind on murder.

She pocketed her badge, then hooked on her weapon harness. "I'm not drunk, but—"

"A lot of wine, so Sober-Up all around." He detoured into the bathroom, came out with a pill for each. "I'll drive. I know the club."

She sent him a look as she shrugged on her jacket. "Is it yours?"

"It's not, no. But the building is. Ready?"

"Yeah."

They went downstairs and out to the car he'd already remoted. Her DLE, she thought, in case she had to stay on the job.

In the passenger seat, she put the window down. The fresh air, especially at the speed he'd drive, would give the Sober-Up a solid kick start.

"It's a club for teenagers?"

Roarke streaked down the driveway, through the gates.

"No. But every year, in the summer, Avenue A plays there one night for the teenage crowd. He told me about it just the other day. He gave a workshop at the school. Apparently, they had their first paying gig there when they were still of that age.

"They lock up all the alcohol," he added before she could comment.

"Maybe. Who runs the club? I want to run them."

"I don't have those names in my head at the moment."

"I'll find them."

Taking out her PPC, she got to work.

"Harvard Greenbaum and Glo Reiser. Harvard's not a name, it's a school. And what kind of name is Glo? Not seeing any criminal on Greenbaum, age sixty-three, New York native, married to Reiser for about twenty years, no offspring. She's got a fifteen-year-old assault ding, charges dropped. Age sixty-one, also a native New Yorker.

"The club's got a scatter of health department violations over the twenty-odd years they've had it. All addressed. No citations for serving the underage. Not one."

"Jake said they're fierce about that issue."

Maybe, she thought again.

The Sober-Up and the air whipping through the open windows cleared her head and gave her a nagging yen for coffee. She used the in-dash AutoChef to program some for both of them.

"You wouldn't know the max capacity for this club, would you?"

"I wouldn't, but recalling the size of it, I wouldn't say over two hundred."

"Two hundred teenage suspects, great."

"Some of those would be staff, maybe some parents."

"We're going to need Child Services," she said, and pulled out her 'link. "Even if it looks like an accidental OD, we'll need someone. Two's better."

"Someone else is about to have their Saturday night screwed."

She spotted the cruiser and the ambulance in front of the club. Easy to recognize the club, she thought, as it had a rainbow sign lit up with the name, and music notes jumping around it.

"Just double it beside the cruiser."

"Loading zone just there," he said, and pulled into it. "I'll get your field kit."

She flipped on the On Duty light, got out to take a look at the club.

The graffiti on the old brick seemed purposeful. Guitars, drums, a bunch of figures crowded together. Dancing, she decided, and walked to the uniform stationed at the front door.

"Lieutenant," she said.

"Officer."

"No one's attempted to go in or come out since we arrived. The owner, apprised of the situation, is keeping things calm inside by having patrons join the band onstage, like an open mic. Mr. Kincade and Ms. Furst are still in the alley with the victim and the medicals. My partner is there."

"That works. I've notified Child Services to assist with any interviews involving minors. You can direct them to the alley."

"Yes, sir."

"Stand by, Officer."

Taking the field kit from Roarke, Eve walked around the building to the alley.

Halfway down, the medicals stood with the uniform. Nadine stood with Jake, hands linked, a few feet away.

When Nadine spotted her, Eve held up a hand to keep her back.

"Stand by, Officer. What do we have?" Eve asked the MTs.

"Victim's fifteen to seventeen years old. We didn't go into her purse for her ID, Lieutenant, to keep the scene as clean as possible."

"Appreciated."

"Can't give you a definite COD, but it looks like an OD. Got a blue tinge to her skin, and the needle mark's fresh.

But I suspect a used needle due to the redness around it. She doesn't have any other visible marks. Looks to be a healthy weight, decent muscle tone. The ME'll be able to give you a better picture.

"We responded at twenty-three-oh-four, and she was already gone. Jake, ah, Mr. Kincade was attempting CPR when we arrived. But she was gone."

"All right. Again, I appreciate you preserving the scene as much as possible. I'll take it from here."

The second MT looked over at Jake. "You did everything you could."

Eve looked down at the body. Five-three maybe, weighing a buck and some small change. Dressed for fun with a tiny, shiny bag worn cross-body.

Eve opened her kit to seal up. "Roarke, why don't you take a walk with Jake and Nadine? Get them some coffee." She looked at Jake—pale, his eyes full of grief and a hint of shock. "I'll need to talk to you, both of you, but right now, I need to take care of her."

"She just . . . she just stumbled out the door, and—"

"I'm sorry this happened, Jake, but you need to leave her with me now."

"Come on, Jake." Nadine slid an arm around his waist. "We have to let Dallas do what she needs to do."

When Roarke led them away, she crouched and carefully opened the little bag.

A mini 'link, lip stuff, her ID, a key card, a little cash, and a disc marked DEMO FOR JAKE KINCADE.

She thought: Well, shit.

"ID in the purse on the victim is for Jenna Harbough, age sixteen, mixed race. Brown and brown, five feet, three inches, a hundred and six pounds. Photo matches."

Minus the pink tips in the brown hair, and the life in the big brown eyes.

After bagging the contents of the purse for Evidence, she took out her Identi-pad to make it official.

"Prints match." She read the address into the record, and realized it had to be next door to their friends Charles and Louise. "Parents, Shane and Julia Harbough, younger sibling, male, Reed, age twelve."

She took out her gauges. "Time of death, twenty-two-fifty-eight."

After putting on microgoggles, she leaned down to get a good look at the wound on the arm.

"Somebody jabbed me, she said, and yeah, that sounds accurate. The wound on the arm's fresh. It's also puffy, inflamed. Potentially, she could have self-inflicted, but there are no works on her person and no signs of illegals abuse. ME to confirm."

A boyfriend or girlfriend, maybe, who pressured her into trying something new? A rebellious, youthful impulse that went terribly wrong?

He jabbed me.

Or something else.

Gently, she turned the body, found no visible wounds.

Sitting back on her heels, she took out her 'link, tagged Peabody. Then straightening up, contacted the morgue, the sweepers.

"Have you been inside, Officer?"

"Yes, Lieutenant, briefly."

"An estimate of how many are in there?"

"Well, sir, it's packed. Gotta be a couple hundred."

"Okay. I need you to stand by here until the dead wagon comes to transport the victim. And the sweepers arrive to process this scene. After that, I'm likely to need you and your partner inside to help with crowd control."

"Yes, sir. It's a damn shame, Lieutenant. I've got a grandkid about her age. You hate to see a kid. I'll look out for her until they come to take her."

Since she wanted to interview Jake next, Eve walked back down the alley. She saw him with Nadine and Roarke standing by her vehicle. She stopped to give the second uniform instructions, then walked down.

"Nadine, how about you walk around the block with Roarke?"

"I don't want to—"

"I need to talk to Jake. Just Jake. Then I need to talk to you. Just you."

Nadine opened her mouth, then on a nod closed it again. She turned to Jake, lifted onto her toes, and kissed him.

As Roarke led Nadine away, Jake turned to Eve. "She thinks I'm going to fall apart, and she's not far wrong. I couldn't get her back, the girl."

"Did you know her?"

"No. I saw her. I realized I'd seen her out on the floor, dancing. Right before the end of the set. She looked so happy."

"You'd never seen her before tonight?"

"No."

"Her name's Jenna Harbough. Is that familiar?"

"No. Jenna." He repeated it, softly, then pressed his fingers to his eyes.

If you took away the misery, he looked like the rock star he was. Faded jeans and black high-tops, black tee that showed off a damn good build, the careless mop of dark, blue-tipped hair.

But his misery hung in the air around him like a haze.

"I went out for some air. It's frigging hot in the club. We were taking a fifteen-minute break between sets, so I went out, chugged down some water, got some air. And she stumbled out the alley door."

"Stumbled?"

"Yeah."

Eve heard him breathe in—the sound of a man steadying himself.

"She just sort of tripped out, you know? She said she'd been sick, and I figured she'd found a way to get some booze in. Glo's got a hawk eye there, but you have to figure some will find a way if they want to bad enough. I guess she looked a little drunk because I figured she was. I was going to take her back inside, into the office, get Harve or Glo. They'd be pissed at her, but they'd take care of her, call her parents, whatever."

He closed his eyes, and Eve let him have the silence. He was telling her what she needed to know without her asking.

"I didn't notice the needle mark right away. I guess because I was looking at her face. She was so pale—but then she said, 'He jabbed me. He jabbed me.' Twice, like that. And I saw the mark, I saw she wasn't white so much as that faint blue?"

"Yeah."

"Yeah." Now he passed a hand over his face. "I'd seen that before. On tour, one of the roadies. They brought him back, they got him in time and brought him back. But she just started to go down. I caught her before she hit. Her pulse was barely there, and she just . . . I called for an ambulance, but . . .

"I've never seen anyone die before, just . . . leave. I was holding her, talking to her, trying to get her to talk to me, tell me her name. Anything to keep her here. And she died. I could see it, but I thought, CPR. She's young, she'll come back, and the MTs are coming. Nadine came out looking for me, and when she said we needed Dallas, I knew the girl—Jenna—wasn't going to come back. Maybe if I'd—"

"Jake, what you just ran through for me couldn't have taken more than two or three minutes."

"Yeah, it was only a couple minutes. Felt longer," he murmured. "But yeah, it was so damn fast."

"I'm going to repeat what the MT told you, and you should listen because we deal with this every day. You did all you could do."

His eyes met hers. Not the wild blue of Roarke's, but a deeper blue now drenched in sorrow. "It doesn't feel like it."

"Do people—fans, groupies, like that—ever send or give you demo discs?"

He smiled a little. "Oh yeah. Why?"

"Something I need to look into. Can you tell me when you went outside, about what time?"

"I can tell you because I checked to make sure I got back before the fifteen was up. It was ten-fifty-five. We had one more short set before we closed out at midnight. We could go over a little, but when we're doing these, we try to hit last number at midnight. Kids have curfews."

"Right." She saw Roarke and Nadine coming around the corner. "I need you to come into Central tomorrow, to follow up. Let's make it ten."

"Okay, sure. Listen, does she have family? I know you can't tell me specifics, but—"

"Yes. I'll notify them tonight."

He closed his eyes again. "If they want to talk to me—I was with her when . . ."

"I'll let them know. It's your turn to take that walk."

"All right. Dallas, what she said? If somebody did this to her—"

"It's my job to find out. One more time around," she said to Roarke, then turned to Nadine.

"I've never seen him like this. He's always in control. I need to get him away from here, Dallas."

"Then let's make this quick. What time did the band break?"

"Oh, I don't know, just before eleven, I think. I knew the break was coming, so I made a dash to the ladies' before a hundred teenage girls had the same idea. When I came out, I looked for Jake, and Renn said he'd gone out to the alley. So I went out. I saw Jake doing CPR on the girl. I was going to call for the MTs, but he said he had. And, Dallas, I could see it was too late. He was trying so hard to save her, but she was gone. And I said I was going to tag you.

"And he looked at me when I did." Taking a breath, Nadine dashed a tear away. "And he looked at me as if I'd broken his heart.

"You can't suspect him of doing something to that girl. You know—"

"I don't, but at the same time, there's a procedure that has to be followed to clear him of any suspicion. You know that."

Nadine swiped at another tear, this time impatiently. "It's different when it's your person. You know that. And I know you," she added. "So I know you'll find out who did this to that poor girl."

"At this time, I can't conclusively say anyone did it to her."

Nadine pushed a hand at her streaky blond hair, gave Eve one long look with those shrewd green eyes. "You can't say it, but you know it."

"And you know the fact that Jake Kincade and Nadine Furst were in an alley with a dead minor female is going to explode all over the media."

Nadine set a hand on the hip of a pair of tight black jeans. "I'm a freaking reporter on the crime beat, so I know that very well. Only another reason I want to get him the hell away from here. We'll handle it."

"No interviews unless I clear it."

It took only that for Nadine to look and sound more like

herself. "You have heard of a little constitutional amendment we call the first?"

"If someone did this to her, wouldn't it just bring on a happy dance if they found their ugly little deed all over the celebrity gossip channels? Her name was Jenna. Let's keep her and your person away from that until we can't."

"You're right, and I wasn't going to do interviews. I just don't like being told I can't. Here they come. Roarke's a god-damn rock, Dallas."

"I know that, too. Take Jake home. He's coming in tomorrow morning for a follow-up. With some luck and Morris, I'll have a COD by then."

She glanced back at the club. "And with a shitload of luck, maybe a suspect tonight."

"What about the rest of the band? He'll want to know. They're family."

"I need to talk to them, then they can go. It's a process, Nadine. And there's Peabody with McNab. Take Jake home," she repeated, and headed in the opposite direction to meet her partner and her partner's person.

In his striped baggies and neon-pink tee, Detective McNab, one of the Electronic Detectives Division's stars, looked like he should be riding a unicycle and juggling.

His earlobe glittered with studs and tiny hoops; the tail of his long blond hair swung as he pranced her way.

Peabody clumped in her pink boots. She may have worn more sedate black trousers and quietly pink shirt, but she still sported those red streaks through her dark, and currently all flippy, hair.

"We've got a dead teenage girl in the alley waiting for the dead wagon. Inside," Eve continued, "we've probably got a hundred or more teenagers currently being stalled by the rest of Avenue A. There may be closer to two hundred with staff, any parents or guardians."

"How's Jake?" Peabody asked.

"He's holding up. We've got to start carving through the people inside, releasing them—and Child Services hasn't shown up yet. The victim's parents need to be notified. I have to take that now. Peabody, tag CS again, and tell them to get somebody's ass over here or I will fry any number of asses. Until that ass or asses are here to represent the rights of the minors, stick with adults, or with minors in the company of a parent or guardian.

"McNab, talk to the band, get times, locations. They took a break about twenty-two-fifty-five. Get the security feeds, front and back."

She described the victim and what she wore. "See if anyone saw her, saw anything. I'll be back as soon as I can."

She walked back to Roarke. "Appreciate you circling the block like that."

"It's a lovely night for a walk, if an ugly reason to need one."

"It's going to be a really ugly night for the victim's parents. I'm going to go do the notification."

"Without Peabody?"

"I can't spare her for this when we have all those potential wits and suspects in that club. Look, I don't know how long we'll be at this so—"

"You're about to go tell a mother and father their child's dead." He took her field kit to put it in the trunk. "I'm with you, Lieutenant."

He closed the trunk. "Have you run them?"

"Not yet."

"Why don't I drive while you do that?"

She paused to breathe, to let the night air blow away some hard.

"That works. They live next door to Charles and Louise."

"Do they now?" he murmured. "Whenever you marvel how big the world is, it reminds you how small it can be. Odds are they know each other."

"Yeah." She slid in the car. "Odds are. The victim had a disc in her purse. It was labeled. Demo disc for Jake Kincade."

"Ah well. Did you tell him?"

"No, it's need to know right now until I check it. I ran him through did you know her, have contact, recognize her name. All no. He said he saw her on the floor during the last song before they broke, dancing. I believed him. I'd have believed him even if I didn't know him. Plus, the timing's going to check out, which means he couldn't have stuck a needle in her arm, if he'd somehow hidden the fact from someone like Nadine, from me, from you that he's a vicious teenage girl killer."

"But it concerns you."

"It's a complication, a possible connection between Jake and the victim. His story rings true, and again it would even if I didn't know him. Add the timing. But it's a complication."

One she needed to unravel.

But first she had to forever change the world and the lives of three people.

They drove into the quiet Lower West Side neighborhood with its dignified brownstones and summer-green trees. She noted a couple of lights on in the house Charles and Louise shared. At least twice as many glowed in the Harbough residence.

Waiting up for their daughter, she thought. Probably checking the time, anticipating. She knew parents worried—she'd met enough of them—and some imagined the worst.

But none believed the worst until it came knocking on their door.

"She's a doctor," Eve told Roarke, "so that ups the odds she knows Louise. He's an exec at a Wall Street firm, heads his own division. They're twenty years into the marriage. She has an assault charge—she'd have been about her daughter's age. Unsealed at her request."

As she spoke, Eve got out of the car to stand on the sidewalk and study the house.

"She punched a guy picketing a woman's health clinic when he tried to bar her and her mother from going in."

They walked to the door flanked by carriage lights that gleamed.

Solid security, Eve noted as a matter of habit, and thought of the key card she'd bagged that Jenna Harbough would never use again.

She rang the bell, and felt Roarke's hand press briefly against her back in support.

The man who answered had a thatch of brown hair threaded with gray. Over his thin build, he wore gray sweat shorts and a T-shirt that read:

BECAUSE

His narrow face had what Eve took to be a weekend stubble. Though he offered a pleasant smile, curiosity filled his hazel eyes.

"Can I help you?"

"Mr. Harbough, I'm Lieutenant Dallas with the NYPSD." She held up her badge.

Before she could say more, he winced. "Oh Jesus, is she in trouble? Teenagers at a rock club, what could go wrong? Jule! Looks like we've got to post bail. Sorry, come in. She's missed curfew," he went on, "so the hammer's going to come down there."

"Mr. Harbough," Eve began again as they entered a foyer

with a living area through a wide case opening on the right, a smaller den on the left with a set of stairs leading up.

"She's not answering her 'link." A woman walked down the hall, frowning at her own 'link. Mixed race, a lot of wavy brown hair with shimmering highlights, and the big brown eyes she'd passed to her daughter.

"That girl is—"

She broke off as she looked up, saw Eve and Roarke.

Her eyes went blank, and her face took on a shade of gray.

"I know who you are. What happened to Jenna? Where's Jenna?"

"Dr. Harbough—"

"Say it." Julia reached out to grip her husband's arm.

"I regret to inform you your daughter is dead."

"What?" Shane's voice punched out, breathless and angry. "That's ridiculous. You need to leave, right now."

"Shane." Julia turned, wrapped around him. "Our baby. Our baby."

"It's not true. Stop this. Jenna's fine. She'll be home any minute. I'm going to go get her. I'm going to go get her right now."

"Shane." With tears streaming down her cheeks, Julia pulled back enough to look at his face.

And what he saw in hers had the anger in his draining into shock, denial, and terrible grief.

"No," he said. "No, no, no."

As he slid to the floor, Julia went with him, stayed wrapped around him.

"It's a mistake." Shaking, he sobbed it out. "It's a horrible mistake. She'll be home any minute."

"Shane. Shane, you have to help me. You have to hang on and help me. We have to know what happened."

"I don't believe it. I won't believe it. Julia, it's Jenna."

"I know. I know." Framing his face now, she kissed his

cheeks. "Come on now. Stand up. We have to know. It's Jenna. We have to know."

She helped her husband to his feet, then faced Eve. "We have to know what happened."

"If we could sit down, I'll tell you everything I can."

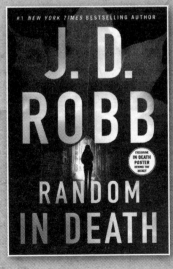